Praise for Irene Hannon
and her novels

"*Never Say Goodbye* by Irene Hannon
is sure to elicit a tear or two."
—*Romantic Times BOOKreviews*

"In *Crossroads*, Irene Hannon does a wonderful
job knitting together a tender romance with
issues single mothers face."
—*Romantic Times BOOKreviews*

"*The Best Gift* is a well-plotted tale by
Irene Hannon. The touching faith message
is beautifully integrated with an engaging
love story."
—*Romantic Times BOOKreviews*

"*The Unexpected Gift*, the final book in Irene
Hannon's Sisters and Brides series, is absolutely
stellar. Unique characters exude warmth, and
the ending will leave readers with tears of joy."
—*Romantic Times BOOKreviews*

IRENE HANNON
Never Say Goodbye

Crossroads

Steeple
Hill®

Published by Steeple Hill Books™

STEEPLE HILL BOOKS

Steeple
Hill®

ISBN-13: 978-0-373-65117-7
ISBN-10:   0-373-65117-1

NEVER SAY GOODBYE AND CROSSROADS

NEVER SAY GOODBYE
Copyright © 2002 by Irene Hannon Gottlieb

CROSSROADS
Copyright © 2003 by Irene Hannon

CONTENTS

Books by Irene Hannon

Love Inspired

*Home for the Holidays #6
*A Groom of Her Own #16
*A Family To Call
    Her Own #25
It Had To Be You #58
One Special Christmas #77
The Way Home #112
Never Say Goodbye #175
Crossroads #224

†The Best Gift #292
†Gift from the Heart #307
†The Unexpected Gift #319
All Our Tomorrows #357
The Family Man #366
Rainbow's End #379
**From This
    Day Forward #419

*Vows
†Sisters & Brides
**Heartland Homecomings

IRENE HANNON

An author of more than twenty-five novels, Irene Hannon is a prolific writer whose books have been honored with both a coveted RITA® Award from Romance Writers of America and a Reviewer's Choice Award from *Romantic Times BOOKreviews*.

A former corporate communications executive with a Fortune 500 company, she now devotes herself full-time to writing. Her emotionally gripping books feature hope-filled endings that highlight the tremendous power of love and faith to transform lives.

In her spare time, Irene performs in community musical theater productions and is a church soloist. Cooking, gardening, reading and spending time with family are among her favorite activities. She and her husband make their home in Missouri—a favorite setting for many of her novels!

Irene invites you to visit her Web site at www.irenehannon.com.

NEVER SAY GOODBYE

Hope deferred makes the heart sick,
but a wish fulfilled is a tree of life.

—*Proverbs* 13:12

To my mom and dad, who fill my life with love
and add joy and grace to my days.

Chapter One

Three years.

Three long, lonely years.

Three years without freedom.

Three years without the woman he loved.

Three years of hell.

And now they were over.

Scott Mitchell turned and took one last look at the bleak gray walls of the high-security prison where he'd spent the past three years of his life.

Where he'd reached such depths of despair that he'd seriously considered suicide. Where he'd spent agonizing hours reliving the tragic accident that had taken the lives of two innocent people.

Where he'd lain awake night after night yearning for the tender touch and sheltering arms of the woman he loved…tormented by the knowledge that she never wanted to see him again.

Where he'd finally found something to cling to in a long-neglected interest in horticulture, a hobby that became a passion and offered a temporary escape from the drab walls to a world of color and beauty and new life.

Where he'd acknowledged his mistakes and straightened out his priorities.

And most important, where he'd slowly, one tentative step at a time, rebuilt his faith and reconnected with his God.

Scott drew a deep, cleansing breath as he stared at the hellish place that, ironically enough, had put him back on the road to heaven. But it had been a harsh, brutal journey. The abrupt transition from power lunches to prisoner, from a world where individual rights reigned supreme to a world where no rights existed had been harrowing. He'd been stripped of his dignity, reduced to a number, looked upon with contempt. He'd lost everything he ever cared about—and that didn't mean the designer suits or sports cars or country-club membership he'd once valued so highly. No, the loss was much more basic than that—the people he loved and his freedom. Dear God, how he'd missed those two things, which he'd always taken so much for granted!

But never again, he vowed. He was a different man now, with solid priorities and two very clear goals.

First, he intended to make his faith the guiding force in his life.

Second, he intended to win back the heart of the only woman he'd ever loved.

The first would be easy.

The second would take a miracle.

But Scott believed in miracles. He couldn't have survived these past three years without one.

Yet winning back Jess's love would take a miracle greater even than survival. He knew that. But with the Lord's guidance and grace, he believed it was possible. It had to be. Because on a spiritual level, he needed her forgiveness and love to complete his re-demption. And on a very basic human level, he simply needed her.

And so he closed his eyes for a moment and prayed silently. *Dear Lord, show me the way to prove that I've changed, that my remorse is real and that I'm worthy of her love. Please give me the courage to persevere and steady me when I stumble. Don't let me lose heart if success is elusive. Help me remember that You are with me always, even on my darkest days, and that with You by my side, anything is possible.*

And then, with one last look at the forbidding walls, he stepped out of prison and into a new life.

Today was the day.

The man who had killed her daughter was free.

Jess Mitchell drew a long, unsteady breath and in-voluntarily tightened her grip on the coffee mug. Scott…her husband…the man she had once loved with all her heart…was free. And she hated him, with every fiber of her being. He'd destroyed their marriage and robbed her of the child of her heart, cutting short a life that had barely begun—as well as the life of a respected judge who'd died behind the wheel of the other car. That, too, had been a tragic loss, for he had been a man of principle and honor, a crusader for justice who had earned a reputation for integrity and courage.

As far as Jess was concerned, Scott deserved to rot in prison for the rest of his life.

Her hands suddenly began to shake and she carefully set the mug down, the taste of bitterness sharp on her tongue as she struggled to control a surge of anger—the same anger that had been her constant companion in the months following Elizabeth's death. Gradually a dull numbness had taken its place, insulating her from pain and allowing her to better cope with the world around her. But now the anger was back, and with it the raw pain.

Reaching out an unsteady hand toward the small glass-topped table in her breakfast nook, Jess shakily lowered herself into a chair. The February day was cold but bright, and a shaft of early-morning sun beamed through the skylight, illuminating the single daffodil in the bud vase in front of her. Gently she reached over and touched the delicate petals, so lovely but so fragile. There was something inspiring about daffodils, she thought with a bittersweet pang. The first harbingers of spring, they bloomed gloriously despite the risk of frost, announcing to those grown weary of the long, dark days of winter that the world would soon be warm and bright again. Perhaps that was why she had chosen this blossom for her table, she reflected. To give her courage to get through this difficult day.

Jess forced herself to take a deep, calming breath, thankful that at least she could once again find pleasure in the beauty of nature. She'd always loved flowers, and she was grateful that her work as public relations manager at the botanical garden gave her a ready supply.

But today, even the exquisite beauty of this favorite flower couldn't dispel her gloom or the inexplicable sense of apprehension that filled her with a restless anxiety.

Jess forced herself to think through her emotions logically, a technique she'd picked up through six months of counseling following the accident. First of all, it was only natural for her feelings of anger and bitterness to bubble to the surface on the day her husband was being released from prison, she reasoned. Knowing that he was now a free man, once more a part of the real world—*her* world—made it impossible *not* to think about the trauma and the tragedy he had caused. It was a normal reaction.

But there was no reason to feel apprehensive, she reassured herself. Though they'd had no direct contact since Elizabeth's funeral, she'd made her feelings very clear to Scott shortly thereafter via a letter from her attorney. As far as she was concerned, no matter the outcome of the legal trial, he was a murderer. And she never wanted to see him again. Period. Those two points had been clearly communicated.

Nevertheless, Scott had written to her. Countless times. She'd returned every letter unopened and unanswered, so he had to know that the strength of her feelings hadn't diminished. She fervently hoped that he would honor her wishes and stay away.

For a moment Jess considered praying for that outcome, but she quickly dismissed the idea. She'd given up talking to the Lord a long time ago. Why bother? He didn't listen anyway. In her darkest days her

once-solid faith had offered no explanations, no solace
for the senseless tragedy that had taken the life of her
daughter and turned her world upside down. She was
just as bitter toward God as she was toward her
husband. Jess had always known that bad things sometimes happened to good people. Had somehow been
able to reconcile that with her faith—until it happened
to her. Then all the words of comfort she'd once offered
to those caught in tragic situations seemed hollow and
trite. All she knew was that the loving God she'd always
believed in had let her down. Just as her husband had.

Jess pulled herself tiredly to her feet and drained her
coffee cup, hoping the caffeine would energize her.
She'd slept little last night—but what else was new?
Her sleep pattern had been erratic for years. Sometimes, when she was very tired and if she stayed up late
enough, she made it through a whole night. Other times
she was plagued with nightmares. But worst of all were
the times she'd awaken in the middle of the night,
overcome with memories of the love she and Scott had
shared early in their marriage, when their faith and
their devotion to each other were the foundation of
their life. On those nights, the loneliness and sense of
loss would overwhelm her, filling her with such a
hopeless yearning to recapture those early days of
intimacy and unity that she'd suddenly discover tears
running down her cheeks. And then she'd get up and
prowl through the condo, looking for anything to
distract her until the first light of day banished the
memories of the night to the far corners of her mind.

Jess rinsed her cup, glanced at the bagel she'd

planned to eat, and turned away, her stomach churning. Food rarely held much appeal anymore, especially today. Another sign of lingering depression. She knew that from counseling. She also knew there was a reason for her mood this morning. A trigger event. But she'd be okay. She'd get through today, and then she'd go on with the gradual process of rebuilding her life. And in time it would get easier. In time she would even feel normal again. Everyone told her that.

Jess clung to that hope. She had to. Because it was the only thing that helped her get through the endless stream of empty days—and the lonely, memory-filled nights.

"Jess?"

It was one word. Only one word, spoken through a poor connection. But she knew that voice as well as her own. You couldn't live with a man for eight years without learning the nuances of his every inflection.

Jess's heart stopped, then slammed into triple time. Her lungs seemed paralyzed, and she struggled to take a breath, fighting a wave of light-headedness. In the two days since Scott's release, she'd gradually calmed down, convinced herself that he was going to leave her alone.

But she'd been wrong.

Her first impulse was to simply hang up. But if he was still as single-minded and determined as he'd once been, he'd just call again, she realized in panic. Should she talk to him, reiterate that she wanted nothing to do with him? Or should she simply call her lawyer and let him handle the situation?

"Jess? Are you there?"

Softer now, sounding as unsteady as she felt, his voice still had that intimate, husky cadence that had always set her pulse racing. And she didn't want to hear it. Not now. Not ever. Without uttering a word—*unable* to utter a word—she simply followed her instinct. She hung up.

Scott heard the soft but very definitive click and slowly let out his breath. It had taken him an hour to work up the courage to call Jess—once he'd found her number. He knew she'd sold the house, because during the past year his letters had been returned marked "no forwarding address." But he was reasonably certain she'd still be in St. Louis. She'd always been close to her parents, and he was sure she'd relied on them heavily during the traumatic months following the accident and trial. So he'd let his fingers do the walking, and on the third try he had connected with her. But the connection had been purely electronic, he acknowledged with a sigh. And broken very quickly.

Slowly Scott replaced the receiver of the pay phone, then leaned back against the concrete wall of the filling station and allowed his gaze to rise above the run-down buildings around him. His breath billowed in frosty clouds toward the cobalt-blue sky, but even in his inadequate jacket he didn't feel the cold. His heart was pounding so hard, the blood rushing so quickly through his veins, that he was actually too warm.

Scott had hoped to accomplish several things with his phone call. Test the waters, for one. And Jess's silent hang-up had given him a definite reading on that: very cold. He'd also wanted to verify her address. That goal, too, had been accomplished. Though she hadn't said a word, he knew with absolute certainty that he'd reached the right number. He could sense her presence, her energy, coming through the line.

But more than anything, he'd simply wanted to hear the expressive, slightly husky voice that had filled his dreams for three long years. He'd clung to the memory of her bell-like laughter and the sometimes teasing, sometimes tender, sometimes curious and *always* enthusiastic tone that so clearly reflected her dynamic personality. Today he'd hoped to turn memory into reality. Even one word would have been enough to sustain him temporarily. On that score, however, he'd been less successful.

But he would try again.

And next time it would be in person.

"You seem quiet today, Jess. Everything okay?"

Jess looked at her father, then transferred her gaze to her mother. Though the question had been asked calmly and conversationally, she felt their undertone of worry. They'd seen her through some rough times over the past few years, had stood by her through her deepest despair, almost forcibly taking her to counseling sessions when all she'd wanted to do was huddle in bed under the covers in a dark room. As a result, they had come to learn every nuance of her moods.

While she was deeply grateful for their steadfast caring, it was a bit disconcerting to know that there was little she could hide from them. Certainly nothing as traumatic as Scott's phone call. She

realized now that she should have told them about
Scott's upcoming release two weeks ago, when her
attorney had called to alert her. But she had hoped
there would be no need to worry them. Had hoped
Scott would stay away and not disrupt the delicate
balance of her fragile existence. But that hope had
been in vain, and now she was faced with the difficult task of telling her parents about Scott's release—
and his call.

Carefully Jess set her fork down and reached for her
glass of water, willing her hand not to shake as she took
a sip. "I'm fine," she replied, struggling with limited
success to keep her voice steady, "but I was a little
upset yesterday. S-Scott called."

Her mother's fork clattered to her plate, and her eyes
grew wide. Her father looked equally shaken, though
his shock quickly gave way to anger as his face grew
hard and his mouth settled into a thin, unforgiving line.

"What do you mean, Scott called?" he said, his voice
taut with tension.

Jess drew a shaky breath and met his disturbed gaze.
"He's out, Dad. John Kane called a few days ago to tell
me that he was being released early for good behavior."

Jess couldn't quite make out her father's muttered
comment, but she knew from his tone that it wasn't
pretty. He threw his napkin onto the table and rose to
pace agitatedly.

"Good behavior? From a murderer? That's ridiculous. He deserved every second of his five-year
sentence—if not more."

"Frank, please try not to get upset," Jess's mother

pleaded, her own face pinched and drawn. "You know this isn't good for your blood pressure."

He paused and glared at his wife. "How can you be so calm about this, Clare? This is the man who killed your granddaughter and almost ruined your daughter's life."

Clare's eyes filled with tears and she groped in the pocket of her skirt for a tissue. "I know, Frank. I'm not happy about it, either. But what can we do?"

He began to pace again, and Jess could feel his seething frustration. "We can stop him from calling Jess, for one thing. If he's bothering her, that's harassment. We can get a restraining order."

"Please Dad…Mom…it's okay. That's not necessary," Jess assured them with more calm than she felt. "He only called once. And I didn't even talk to him. I just hung up."

That seemed to placate Frank, and after a moment he took his seat again. "Well, that's good. You did the right thing, sweetie. He ought to get the message. And if he doesn't, I'll call John and he'll take care of it. Okay?"

"Okay, Dad."

Clare reached over and took Jess's hand, twin lines of worry furrowing her brow. "Are you sure, honey? Because if you're scared, we can call John right now."

Jess stared at her mother. Scared? Of Scott? That thought had never even entered her mind. In fact, it was almost ludicrous. She might hate her husband for what he had done to her daughter and for ruining her life, but he wasn't a violent man.

"Why would I be scared, Mom?"

Clare's frown deepened. "Well, it's been three years, Jess," she said carefully. "And prison is a hard place, from what I've read. It can…do things to a person. Change them. Did he sound angry, or threatening?"

Jess thought back to the few words Scott had spoken on the phone. There had been absolutely no hint of anger or threat in his voice. On the contrary. He'd sounded anxious. And shaky. And…hungry.

Now it was Jess's turn to frown. *Hungry.* What an odd word to pop into her mind. And yet it was accurate, she realized. There had been a raw need in his voice when he'd spoken her name. As if he *had* to hear her voice, to connect with her in some tangible way. It was an oddly disconcerting realization.

"Jess?"

Her mother's anxious voice brought her back to the present, and she summoned up a reassuring smile. "No, Mom. He didn't sound angry. He sounded…the same."

"I can't believe he called you," Frank said, a thread of anger still running through his voice. "Why would he do that, when you made it clear you never wanted to see him again?"

"I don't know, Dad." Her own voice was suddenly weary.

"Well, let's forget about it as best we can and enjoy our dinner," Clare suggested, forcibly lightening her tone as she sent a "let-it-drop-for-now" look to her husband. "Your dad's right, honey. Hanging up on him was the best thing you could have done. He's a smart man. He'll get the message. You'll probably never hear from him again. Now, how about another biscuit?"

As Jess took the proffered breadbasket, she hoped her mother was right about Scott. But she wasn't optimistic. She'd heard his voice. And she didn't think he was going to give up until she talked with him. Which was something she did *not* want to do.

Maybe a restraining order was in her future after all.

A gust of frigid air whipped past, and Scott turned up the collar of his denim jacket before jamming his hands into the pockets of his jeans. He was chilled to the bone after waiting at the bus stop for thirty minutes, and the inadequate heater on the public conveyance had done little to dispel the numbing cold. The greenhouse looming in front of him promised a haven from the freezing temperatures, and he quickened his pace, breathing a sigh of relief as he stepped into the balmy oasis.

For a moment Scott just stood there, letting the welcome warmth seep through his pores as he scanned the interior. The facility was well maintained, with half of the space devoted to row after row of tagged trays containing tiny seedlings, while larger pots of healthy-looking perennials occupied the other half. Large rubber hoses lay neatly coiled at periodic intervals, and hanging pots were spaced methodically above the seedlings. The operation appeared to be orderly and well run, Scott noted with approval.

"You must be Scott."

At the sound of the gravelly voice, Scott turned. An older man had entered the greenhouse by a side door and now stood observing him from several yards away.

Make that "assessing him," Scott thought wryly, as the man's shrewd, slightly narrowed eyes studied him. Scott took the opportunity to look him over, as well. An unlit cigar was clamped between his teeth, and his fists were planted on his hips. His white hair was closely cropped in a no-nonsense style, and his attire—worn jeans that molded comfortably to his lean frame, and an open fleece-lined jacket that revealed a T-shirt containing the words Lawson Landscaping—spoke more to practicality than style. His stance and tone were definitely intimidating enough to scare off most potential job applicants.

But Scott wanted this job. Reverend Young, one of the local clergy who volunteered as a prison chaplain, had warned him when he set up the interview that Seth Lawson was a fair but hard taskmaster. That he expected a lot and cut no slack. But that was okay with Scott. He wasn't looking for any favors. He just wanted a chance to start over. And as an ex-con himself who had served time for armed robbery many years before, Seth was sometimes willing to give newly released prisoners that chance. Which was more than could be said for a lot of employers. Or people in general. Even though ex-cons had served their time and paid their debt, society was often unwilling to take them back. So the odds were stacked against them.

But Scott didn't intend to become another statistic. With the help of people like Reverend Young and Seth Lawson, he would make it. He straightened his shoulders and gazed steadily into the older man's razor-sharp, intensely blue eyes. "That's right. I'm Scott Mitchell."

Seth studied Scott for another moment, then nodded toward the rear of the greenhouse. "Office is back there. Let's talk."

He led the way to a compact but well-equipped office furnished with three unoccupied desks, several filing cabinets, a fax machine and a copier. Instead of sitting behind one of the desks, however, he continued toward a small conference room at the back, pausing as he passed the coffeemaker.

"Want a cup?"

Scott nodded, trying not to appear too eager. He was still trying to shake the February chill, and coffee would help. "Thanks."

"Cream?"

"Black."

Seth poured two cups, then moved into the conference room, shrugged out of his jacket and sat down at the round table. Scott followed suit—but he left his coat on.

"So tell me why you want this job," Seth said without preamble, chewing on his cigar.

Scott wrapped his hands around the coffee cup, letting the warmth seep into his numb fingers. "I need a job," he said honestly. "More than that, I need a chance to start over. I know something about horticulture, and I don't want a job with walls. This sounded perfect."

"It's far from perfect," Seth replied bluntly. "Most guys don't last more than a few weeks. It's hard work. Dirty work. And the pay's not great."

"I'm not afraid of hard work. Or dirt. And I don't need much money."

Seth considered that answer for a moment. "You have any family?"

A spasm of pain ricocheted through Scott's eyes. "I have a sister and brother-in-law in Chicago. And three nephews."

Seth glanced pointedly at the wedding ring on Scott's left hand. "That it?"

Scott drew an unsteady breath. "I also have a wife. In name, at least. She doesn't believe in divorce. But she never wants to see me again."

"Too bad. It helps to have family and friends around when you get out. But a lot of people can't handle the stigma of being associated with an ex-con."

"Jess isn't like that."

Seth's eyebrows rose. "But she never wants to see you again."

Scott swallowed past the lump in his throat. "For good reason. I made some bad mistakes."

"You also paid for them."

"In the eyes of society, maybe. I'm not sure about in the eyes of God."

Seth considered that for a moment. "How long were you in?"

"Three years."

"What did you do before?"

"I was in marketing."

When he named the company, Seth's eyebrows rose. "Were you in for one of those white-collar crimes?"

Scott frowned. "Didn't Reverend Young tell you?"

Seth shrugged. "Didn't ask. Doesn't matter. I judge people by who they are now, not what they did years ago. I was just curious. Don't get too many guys in here with your polish."

Scott took a sip of the scalding liquid, which suddenly tasted bitter on his tongue. "I'm surprised there's any polish left," he said quietly.

Seth looked at him shrewdly. "It's rough in there, all right. Takes a lot out of a man."

"Yeah."

"You have any money?"

Scott frowned again. The conversation was all over the place and he was having a hard time keeping up. "No."

"You're still married. Anything still in your name?"

"No. I signed it all over to Jess when I was convicted."

"Think she might give you a loan to get you started?"

"I don't plan to ask."

Seth folded his arms across his chest. "Be pretty hard to live on the salary I'm offering."

"I'll manage. I don't need much. Just a chance."

Seth nodded shortly. "That I can give you." He reached into his pocket, withdrew a wallet and laid several fifty-dollar bills on the table. "Consider this an advance on your salary. Get yourself a warm coat and some sturdy shoes. Be here tomorrow at seven."

Scott looked at the money. There was a time when he would drop twice that amount on a business dinner with several colleagues. In those days, money had meant prestige and power. Now it just meant survival. Funny how dramatically things had changed, he reflected. Slowly he reached for the bills and carefully folded them over. "Thank you," he said. "For the loan. And for taking me on."

Seth shrugged and stood up. "Don't thank me yet. It's hard, dirty work. You might not last a week."

"I'll last." The statement was made quietly—but with absolute conviction.

Seth looked at him speculatively, but made no comment. Instead he turned and led the way to the door. "Tomorrow morning. Seven sharp."

"I'll be here." Scott extended his hand, and Seth took it in a firm grip. The older man's probing gaze seemed to go right to Scott's heart.

"I was in your shoes once," he said evenly. "I know how hard it is to lose everything. And society doesn't make it easy to start over. Some guys make it. Some don't. The bitter ones never do. Neither do the ones who can't admit their mistakes. I figure you're gonna make it."

Scott felt a prickling behind his eyelids. For some reason this stranger's words of encouragement touched him deeply. "I figure I am, too."

"Reverend Young tells me you're a churchgoing man. That gives you a leg up right there."

"It also gives me hope."

"Hope is a good thing to have."

"It's the *only* thing I have right now."

"Maybe that's enough. For right now," Seth said sagely. "One thing you learn in this business. Patience. Things happen in their own time." He nodded toward a pot where new green leaves were just beginning to push their way through the dirt. "You take care of plants, give them light and warmth and water, and in time they'll flower. You can help the process along, but you can't make them bloom until they're ready. Same with a lot of things in life. Especially people."

Scott thought of Jess, and the slow, daunting task of trying to win back her love. "Yeah," he said heavily.

"But remember one thing. Spring always comes."

Scott looked at Seth, taken aback by the man's philosophical—and poetic—insight. No wonder Reverend Young had spoken so highly of him. "I like that thought."

Seth shrugged, the philosophical moment clearly over. "Good. Now go buy that coat. You'll need it tomorrow," he said briskly. A movement on the far side of the greenhouse suddenly caught his attention, and he turned. "Jason? Wait up!" he called. He looked back at Scott. "Gotta talk to him about the spring shipment of dogwood trees. See you tomorrow."

Scott watched the older man stride down the length of the greenhouse, impressed and encouraged by their encounter. This job was going to work out fine. He could sense it.

He turned up his collar and moved toward the door, bracing himself for the blast of cold air waiting for him on the other side. Seth was right, he thought wryly. The first order of business was a warm coat.

He was right about something else, too, Scott acknowledged as he stepped into the frigid February air and began the long, chilling trek to the bus stop.

No matter how cold, how inhospitable, how merciless the winter is, spring always comes.

It was a good thought, Scott reflected. An uplifting thought. And he resolved to hold on to it—no matter what lay ahead in the weeks to come.

Chapter Two

"Scott? Is everything all right?"

Scott smiled as his sister's voice came over the line. "Everything's fine. It just took me a couple of days to get settled."

"I can't believe Joe got appendicitis the day before you got out! We wanted to pick you up and help you get settled," she fretted. "Do you have a place to stay? Are you eating?"

His smile deepened. Karen had always been a mother hen, even more so since their own mother had died five years before. And her mothering instincts had intensified since he'd been in prison—for which he was deeply grateful. Other than Reverend Young, she'd been his lifeline, his only contact with the outside world for three long years. He would never forget her steadfast support and her willingness to stand by him despite the tragic mistakes he'd made— nor her long monthly trek to visit him. "Yes to both. How's Joe?"

"He'll live. It's you I've been worrying about. Why didn't you call sooner?"

"I did call. Almost as soon as I walked out the gates."

"But that was three days ago!"

"I've been busy ever since. I had to look at the apartments Reverend Young lined up, and I had an interview at the nursery today."

"Did you get the job?"

"Yes. It was the strangest interview I've ever had, but I have a feeling things will work out fine."

"Good. I know you were counting on that job." There was a slight pause, and when she spoke again he could hear the frown in her voice. "Listen, where are you?"

"In my apartment."

"So you have a phone. Give me the number." Scott complied, then Karen read it back to confirm. "Okay. I'm hanging up and calling you right back," she said briskly. "You can't afford this call."

"Karen, I'm fine. You don't have to—"

"I'm hanging up. Bye."

The line went dead and Scott shook his head, smiling with equal parts affection and exasperation. As a stay-at-home mom with three boys, Karen wasn't exactly rolling in dough, either. But when she got a notion in her head, there was no stopping her.

A moment later the phone rang and Scott reached for it. "That wasn't necessary, you know."

"Listen, big brother, do me a favor, okay? Let people help you if they want to. I just wish you'd come up here for a few weeks, like I asked you to."

"I appreciate the offer, Karen. I really do. But I need

to get back into the real world sooner or later. It might as well be sooner."

He could hear her sigh of frustration over the wire. "Look, Scott, you could use a break. You deserve it. I was there, remember? I saw you the first Friday of every month. You lost forty pounds in six months. You looked like death. I worried about you night and day. You never talked about life in there, but I know it was hell. I know how close you came to…giving up." She took a deep breath, and when she resumed speaking, there was a tremor in her voice. "Dear God, my heart bled for you every time I walked out the door and had to leave you behind. Do you know where I went when I left, after my first five or six visits? To the ladies' room to throw up. I just couldn't bear that you were in that place, and that I couldn't do anything to help you."

Her voice broke, and Scott felt as if someone had kicked him in the gut. Karen had never before even *hinted* at the emotional toll her visits had taken. Just the opposite. She'd always been upbeat and chatty, working hard to cheer him up by telling him humorous anecdotes about the family, passing on drawings the boys had done for him, sharing photos of the birthday parties and Christmases he'd missed. Those visits had been the only thing that kept him going in those early months. Because of her he had still felt connected to the outside world. Because of her he was able for a brief time to feel human again. But if he'd known the emotional toll it had taken on her, he would never have let her come. "I'm so sorry, Karen," he said, his voice anguished. "I had no idea."

"That was the intent." Her voice still sounded a bit shaky, but she quickly got it under control. "I know you, big brother. If you'd had any idea what those visits did to me, you'd have told me to stop coming. And I *wanted* to be there for you. But it's over now. I only brought it up because I want you to know that I realize how horrible it was. And I think you need to take some time to readjust. To rest. To decompress. That's why I wanted you to come up to Chicago and stay with us for a while. I still wish you would."

Scott felt overwhelmed by a rush of love and gratitude, and his throat tightened with emotion. Karen's love and support were blessings for which he would always be grateful. "I love you for offering, sis," he said, his own voice none too steady. "You don't know how much it means to me. Just like your visits. In case I haven't told you—and I probably haven't, because men aren't always too good at that communication thing— I want you to know that I wouldn't have made it without them. Knowing you were coming back, that I wasn't totally alone, that someone cared and was thinking about me, is the only thing that got me through those early months. You were my rock."

He heard Karen sniff over the wire. "Who says men aren't good at communication? You just got an A," she said tearily. She paused to blow her nose, and when she continued her voice was steadier. "Okay, now, enough of this mushy stuff. If you won't come up, then let me send you a little money to tide you over."

"I'm fine, sis."

"You can pay it back, okay? Consider it a loan."

"I have a job. And a place to live. I'm fine. Really."

Another exasperated sigh. "You are one stubborn man, you know that?"

He grinned. "I think it runs in the family."

"Very funny. Okay, have it your way. What's your address?"

He hesitated. "No money. Promise."

She muttered something he couldn't make out. "Fine. No money."

He gave her the information, and then glanced at his watch. "This call is costing you a fortune."

"Look, forget the money for a minute, okay? Indulge me. We've got three years of catching up to do *without* a guard standing over our shoulder. Which reminds me…do you think you'll be ready for a visitor soon?"

"You don't have to make a special trip down, Karen."

"Hey, just because you're out of prison doesn't mean you're going to shake me that easily. I'm heading down to check on you as soon as Joe's mother comes to visit in mid-March. She can help him with the kids while I'm gone. I'll consider it a vacation. Trust me—I deserve it. We've been decimated by the flu this winter, and guess who's been playing nurse?"

Scott chuckled. "When you put it that way, how can I refuse?"

"You can't," she replied pertly.

He glanced around the tiny furnished apartment, with its threadbare upholstery, worn carpeting and nicked furniture. He could just imagine what Karen would say about his living conditions. "Just don't expect the Ritz, okay?" he cautioned.

She gave an unladylike snort. "With three kids and twenty more years to go on the mortgage, the Ritz is out of my league, anyway."

But not this far out, Scott thought as his gaze once more traveled around the shabby apartment. She would *not* be happy to find him living in these conditions. But that was a battle for another day. "Tell Joe and the kids I said hi."

"Will do." There was a slight hesitation, and when Karen spoke again her voice was cautious. "Listen, I don't mean to be nosy, but…have you talked to Jess?"

Scott's smile faded. "Yes."

"Any luck?"

"She hung up on me."

Karen sighed. "I'm sorry, Scott."

"It's okay. I didn't expect her to welcome me with open arms."

"Hang in there, okay?"

"I will. Believe me, I'm an expert at that after the past three years. I've learned to take everything a day at a time."

"Not a bad philosophy. Listen, I'll call again in a couple of days. Promise to take care of yourself in the meantime?"

"Count on it."

"You'll let me know if you need anything?"

"Absolutely."

"Okay. I'll let you go for now. And Scott… welcome back."

As they said their goodbyes and Scott replaced the receiver, he thought about Karen's parting words.

Welcome back. They had a nice sound. And it felt wonderful to be back. To be free.

But the words he really wanted to hear were *Welcome home.* And those could come from only one person.

Jess slammed the car door shut with her hip, juggling a briefcase, a bag of groceries and a shoulder purse. She didn't usually work on Saturdays, but with the opening of the orchid show only a few days away she'd needed to tie up a few loose ends on publicity. The weather was too nice for indoor pursuits, though, she thought as she made her way toward her condo. The early-March day was unseasonably warm. Almost balmy, in fact. It was like a sneak preview of spring—and perfect for a nice long walk, she decided. As soon as she put away the groceries, she would change into her walking shoes and…

"Hello, Jess."

Startled, Jess came to an abrupt stop as the man who had once been the center of her world stepped out of the shadows of a spruce tree. The bag of groceries slipped from her grasp, and only Scott's quick reflexes kept it from hitting the sidewalk. He moved swiftly toward her and made a successful grab for it, which salvaged the canned goods—but dented her heart. Only inches away, his tangible, physical presence drove the breath from her lungs and she stumbled backward, desperately trying to put distance between them, unable to deal with the sudden, too-close proximity. She stared at him, wide-eyed, her hand moving involuntarily to her throat, frozen to the spot as she tried to process the impressions bombarding her senses.

There was no question that the man who stood motionless six feet in front of her, balancing the rescued grocery bag easily in one arm, was Scott. Absolutely no question. She would recognize him anywhere. Yet he was different. And it was more than the physical changes, though they were quite apparent, as well. For one thing, his dark hair now contained a sprinkling of silver at the temples. There were more lines on his face, which oddly enough seemed to suggest character rather than age. And he looked more toned than she'd ever seen him. His jeans fit his lean form like a second skin, and his T-shirt hugged a broad, muscular chest and revealed well-developed biceps. Scott had always been a handsome man. Now his virility was almost tangible.

But the physical changes weren't what gave Jess pause. It was something else, something almost indefinable. A sense of quiet calm, of acceptance, of surrender almost. As if he'd somehow found a way to deal with all of the tragedy and pain and horror, made his peace with it and moved on. In the depths of his brown eyes she saw serenity, and a wave of envy surged over her. How had he been able to achieve that when it had so utterly eluded her? she wondered resentfully. Nothing seemed left of his restless, driving ambition, which had grown stronger and stronger until it had become the center of his life and had driven a wedge into their marriage. In its place was a quiet, appealing gentleness.

But there were other things in his eyes as well, she

realized. Things that were even closer to the surface and equally disturbing in a very different way. Hunger. Need. And undisguised love. All of which left her completely off balance and confused.

While Jess struggled to come to grips with her volatile emotions, Scott took stock of the woman who had added so much joy to his life and filled his dreams for the past three years. She, too, was different than he remembered, and the changes troubled him. There was an unfamiliar tautness to her face, as if the skin was stretched too tightly over the fine bone structure beneath. And she seemed tense, tightly coiled, radiating an unsettling nervous energy that suggested she might snap at the least provocation.

Scott had known his unexpected appearance would upset her. But he sensed that Jess's tension went far deeper and was of a much longer-term nature. As if it was the norm rather than a momentary reaction. She seemed somehow…brittle, as if she would break at the slightest touch. And far too thin, he concluded with a sweeping gaze. The fluid silk blouse that hugged her upper body suggested angular lines and sharp edges rather than the soft curves he remembered, and the circumference of the belt of her black slacks seemed tiny. Jess had always been slender, but now she was just plain skinny. His gaze moved back to her deep green eyes, and there he noticed the greatest change of all. Gone was the sparkle of joy with which she had always greeted each new day. In its place was a deep-seated sadness that was clearly of long duration.

Scott's gut twisted painfully. He was well aware of

the pain he'd caused Jess. Had always recognized it on an intellectual level. But now, confronted with the physical evidence of it, he knew that the hell he'd been through in prison had been no worse than her own private hell, which had left her shattered and fragile and heartbreakingly vulnerable.

Scott wanted to go to her, to pull her into his arms and promise to take away her pain, to care for her, to never hurt her again. But he knew his words would fall on deaf ears. Because he was the *cause* of her pain. He *hadn't* been able to care for her in her greatest time of need. And there was no reason for her to believe that he would never hurt her again. Winning her back, he realized with a heavy heart, would be an even more daunting task than he'd imagined.

As he gazed at her, at the white-knuckled grip she had on her briefcase, at her face suddenly grown pale, he realized that she was trembling. Badly. She suddenly swayed ever so slightly, but when he instinctively took a step toward her she backed away in alarm, only to lose her balance as she tottered half on and half off the concrete walk. A moment later she lost her footing and found herself sprawled on the ground.

In a flash, Scott set the groceries on the walk and knelt beside her, his concerned eyes only inches from hers, his voice worried, his hand on her arm.

"I'm sorry, Jess. I didn't mean to startle you. Are you okay?"

She stared at him, hardly able to breathe. She looked at his hand—strong, gentle and achingly familiar—on her arm, and her heart stopped, then slammed into overdrive. Dear God, why was she being tormented this way? she cried silently. She'd never wanted to see this man again! She hated him! Hated how his ambition had eaten away at their marriage. Hated how he'd begun to turn to alcohol to relieve the tension of stress-filled days in the business world. Hated how he'd taken the deadly chance that fateful night that ruined her life and ended two others. And hated how, in his presence, she was confronted again by the "if only" that had hung like a dark cloud over her life ever since the tragic accident. The "if only" that said her daughter might not have died if she'd insisted on driving that night instead of letting Scott take the wheel.

Choking back a sob, she scrambled to her feet, filled with an urgent need to get away from Scott. For some reason she sensed danger. Not of a physical nature. But danger nonetheless. She had to get to the safety of her condo, where she could bolt the door against this intrusion on her life. Yet even as she slung her purse over her shoulder and reached for her brief-case, a sick feeling in the pit of her stomach told her that she couldn't bolt the door against this intrusion on her heart. That her life was once again about to be turned upside down. Blinded by tears, she groped for the grocery bag, but Scott beat her to it.

"Let me help." He reached for it and swung it up into his arm.

She hesitated for only a moment. Then, without a word, she turned and headed for her condo, half running as she dug through her purse for her keys, struggling to control the tears that threatened to spill from her eyes.

"Jess, please."

He was behind her. Following her. Harassing her. She walked more quickly.

"Please, Jess. I just want to talk to you."

Something in his tone made her step falter for a moment, but then, angry at herself for allowing the choked entreaty in his voice to affect her, she resolutely quickened her pace.

He didn't speak again, but she knew he was still behind her. Her hand was shaking so badly when she reached her door that she had difficulty fitting her key in the lock. Then, just when she thought she was home free, it slipped from her fingers and clattered to the concrete steps.

Before she could react, he reached down and retrieved it. Panic once more engulfed her. Now she was trapped. Tears of frustration spilled from her eyes, and she swiped at them angrily and desperately tried to figure out what to do. But her brain seemed to have shifted into neutral.

To her surprise, however, Scott didn't hold her hostage. After only a moment's hesitation he reached past her and fitted the key into the lock. It took him two tries, and she noted with surprise that his hands were almost as unsteady as hers. After he turned the key, he stepped back.

"I'll leave your groceries on the step," he said quietly.

She heard the rustle of the paper bag as he deposited the sack, and she reached for the knob, prepared to flee, planning to retrieve the groceries later. But then he spoke again.

"I never had a chance to say this in person, Jess. And I know it doesn't change anything. But I want you to know how sorry I am…about everything. I made a lot of mistakes. Tragic mistakes that I regret with all my heart. But the one thing that wasn't a mistake was loving you."

The raw pain, the passion, in his voice jolted her, compelled her with a force she couldn't ignore to turn and face the man she had once loved. He was standing a couple of feet away, his hands jammed into the pockets of his jeans, his face filled with such sadness and remorse that she couldn't doubt the truth of his words. But being sorry didn't change a thing, she thought bitterly as the tears she'd tried so hard to contain suddenly spilled out of her eyes.

Scott watched helplessly, feeling physically sick. He'd been prepared to face Jess's anger. But he hadn't been prepared to watch her crumble in front of his eyes. He lifted a hand in an imploring gesture, then let it drop back to his side. "Dear God, Jess, I'm so sorry," he repeated hoarsely, his voice choked.

She shook her head and reached again for the doorknob. "It's too late," she whispered brokenly. Then she slipped inside, shutting the door firmly behind her. A moment later he heard the bolt slide into place.

For several minutes Scott simply stood there staring at the closed door, struck by the symbolism. She was shutting him out of her life…and her heart. Her three words said it all. *It's too late.*

But Scott didn't believe it was too late. *Couldn't* believe it. Because it was impossible to envision a future without Jess. He needed her…just as he believed she needed him. They had linked their destinies once, for better, for worse, and Jess had abided by their vows despite the tragedy that had befallen them. Though they were married in name only at the moment, he clung to the hope that with God's help, Jess would eventually come to realize that he was a changed man. That his remorse was real. That his love for her had not only endured but grown during their long years apart. And that the joyous, vibrant, life-giving love they had once shared could live again.

As he turned away, Scott knew that his prospects seemed bleak. But he wouldn't give up. Because he believed in the truth of Seth's philosophy.

Spring always comes.

"Scott. It's good to see you." Reverend Young grasped Scott's hand warmly. "I was hoping you'd make it to services."

"It was a little tricky," Scott admitted. "The buses run on an entirely different schedule on the weekends."

The minister frowned. "I must admit I forgot about your lack of transportation. We'll find you a ride from now on."

"I don't want to put anyone out, Reverend. The bus worked out fine."

The minister laid a kindly hand on his shoulder. "There are a lot of good, Christian people out there, Scott. Give them a chance to put their beliefs into action."

Scott smiled. "It's pretty hard to refuse when you put it that way."

"Sometimes accepting help is much harder than giving it," he acknowledged. "So are you settled in? Everything going okay?"

"So far so good."

"How are you and Seth getting on?"

Scott grinned. "Fine. I think. He's not much of a talker."

Reverend Young chuckled. "True enough. But he's a good man. Fair and honest and dependable. He's not much of a churchgoer, but he really lives the golden rule. Is the work okay? I know he expects a lot."

"He does. But I don't mind hard work. Which is a good thing, because he's got a lot of commercial landscaping contracts and spring is a busy time. Let me put it this way…I rarely have any trouble sleeping." Except for the nights when even bone-weary fatigue couldn't overcome the longing in his heart for Jess, he added silently as a shadow swept across his eyes. Then he forced his thoughts in a different direction. "You have a nice church here, Reverend," he complimented the man, glancing around the grounds. "It's just like you described."

The minister nodded in satisfaction. "We've come a long way since this land was donated five years ago. Would you like to see the back?"

"Sure."

They made their way around the building, which stood on a slight rise that overlooked a small tree-ringed pond. Though it was in a suburban area, the grounds were quiet and secluded. "I come back here when I need a few moments to refresh my soul," the minister said. "It's a nice spot, isn't it?"

"Very. What's going on back there?" Scott nodded

toward the edge of the pond, where some sort of construction project was in progress.

"One of our members thought a gazebo would be a nice addition, and offered to build one."

"I agree." Scott eyed the terrain critically. "Have you thought about adding a meditation garden, as well? It's a perfect spot for one."

The minister looked at him in surprise. "Frankly, no. Though I have to say the idea has appeal."

"I'd be happy to draw up some plans for you. And if the church could afford to invest in some plants and trees, I'd be glad to do the work."

Reverend Young smiled. "You work all week, Scott," he reminded the younger man gently. "Everyone needs a day of rest."

Scott shrugged. "It would give me a lot of pleasure to create a place of beauty that people could enjoy. I wouldn't consider it work. And I have the time."

The minister studied him for a moment. "You need to take some time for yourself, Scott. And for Jess."

Scott stared out over the placid waters of the lake. Reverend Young knew his most intimate secrets and dreams, more so even than Karen. He'd tried to shield her as much as possible from his private demons, though clearly she'd picked up on far more than he'd realized. But with Reverend Young it had been different. The minister had been there when Scott was at his lowest ebb, when he'd given up on life, when he'd been able to see only darkness on the horizon. And he'd made the long journey to prison numerous times in those days just to see Scott, to walk with him through the valley of darkness, until light had finally begun to dawn on the dark horizon. If Karen had saved Scott by giving him abiding love, Reverend Young had saved him by giving him abiding faith.

"Things aren't going well with Jess," Scott said quietly.

"Have you talked to her?"

"Yes. The first time she hung up on me without saying a word. The second time I waited for her at her condo. But she couldn't get away from me fast enough. She just said it was too late and closed the door in my face."

"You knew it wouldn't be easy."

Scott sighed. "Yeah."

"Hate is a difficult thing to overcome, Scott. And forgiveness doesn't come easily for many people."

Scott frowned. "That's the odd thing, Reverend. I expected hate. And anger. But what I saw in Jess was more…I don't know. Confusion. Fear. Pain. It was almost as if the whole thing happened four days ago, not almost four years ago."

"I'm sure your release brought back all the memories. Made them seem fresh again. She may need some time to sort through her feelings now that you're back in her life. To deal with unresolved issues."

"So should I back off? Wait awhile?"

"You might want to move slowly," the minister counseled. "Even though I know that's hard to do. But I know the Lord will show you the way if you put your trust in Him."

Scott sighed and shook his head. "Patience is one of those virtues I'm still working on, Reverend."

The minister smiled sympathetically. "You and millions of other people." Then he turned back toward the lake, a thoughtful expression on his face. "You know, I think a garden would be just the thing for the gazebo. I'll run it by the church council at our meeting this week and let you know. Besides, gardening is a good way to develop patience," he added, his eyes twinkling as the two men headed back to the front of the church.

Scott grinned. "You sound like Seth."

The minister chuckled. "He's quite a philosopher, isn't he?" As they prepared to part, the minister laid a hand on Scott's shoulder, his eyes once more serious. "Hang in there, okay? I'll keep you in my prayers."

Scott took the minister's hand in a firm clasp. "Thanks. I can use them."

The minister smiled. "That's my job. You plant trees. I plant prayers. But both send out roots. We just need to do our part."

Scott thought about the aptness of Reverend Young's analogy as he headed back to his apartment. The visible signs of his relationship with Jess, the arching branches and beautiful blooms, had been ruthlessly chopped off at ground level. To the eye it had died. But Scott believed with all his heart that the roots were still there, filled with life. That with nurturing, tender new shoots would spring from the parched ground.

It was up to him to make that happen. And with the Lord's help and guidance, he would find a way.

Chapter Three

Jess glanced at her bedside clock and groaned. Three in the morning—only ten minutes later than when she'd last checked. Since going to bed four hours earlier, she'd logged all of thirty minutes' sleep, she calculated wearily. This was going to be one of those nights. Meaning tomorrow would be a very long day at work.

With a resigned sigh she threw back the covers, swung her feet to the floor and reached for her robe. Maybe a soothing cup of herbal tea would help, she thought hopefully as she padded toward the kitchen. Mechanically she filled the kettle, turned on the stove, dropped a tea bag into a mug. But her mind was elsewhere. Namely, on her encounter with Scott the day before.

She'd slept little last night and had spent most of today trying, with some success, to avoid thinking about Scott. But she had far less control over her *subconscious* thoughts, and they kept bubbling to the surface each time she began to drift to sleep.

The whistle of the kettle distracted her momentarily, and she automatically went through the motions of making her tea. Then she carried it to the living room and sank into a comfortable chair, letting her gaze rest on the photograph of Elizabeth prominently displayed on the coffee table. Her daughter's smile was infectious, her four-year-old eyes bright with enthusiasm and lively intelligence and the sheer joy of life so common in the very young. She would be almost eight now. Finishing up second grade. Looking far more grown-up than she had in this photo.

If.

Jess drew an unsteady breath. She knew it didn't do any good to keep rehashing the past. To keep asking the "what if?" questions. Her therapist had stressed that over and over again. You had to deal with the bad things in your life, then move on. And Jess had done that. She'd put the "what ifs" aside, learned to deal with her pain and then established a new career—and a new life. No, it wasn't totally "normal" yet. She still didn't sleep well. She didn't eat enough. And despite the support of her family, a deep, aching loneliness was still her constant companion. But no one knew that. In fact, few people outside her family would ever guess the trauma she'd been through. So yes, she had moved on. And she'd felt good about the progress she'd made.

Until now.

Because Scott's return had completely unsettled her, resurrecting doubts and emotions and questions that she thought had been laid to rest long ago. It had been easy to hate him, to blame him for everything, to think of him as cold and uncaring, when he was miles away. It was a whole lot harder when he stood three feet in front of her, his eyes filled with anguish and regret.

His physical presence also made her remember all too clearly the love and intimacy they had shared before ambition distracted his attention from the things that really mattered. It was one thing to dream about those things from the past, and a different thing altogether to have the subject of those dreams stand only an out-stretched hand away in the present.

And she certainly hadn't expected him to still love her. Not after the hateful things she'd said to him when Elizabeth died. Not after the cold, bitter note she'd sent him following the accident. Not after years of ignoring his letters. Nor had she expected his gen-tleness, or the quiet calm that seemed to reflect an inner peace and an acceptance of the past, as if he'd come to grips with what he'd done and found a way to live with it.

Her chaotic emotions, her sudden doubt and uncer-tainty, made her wonder whether she'd been deluding herself all along. Had she really dealt with the past, or simply ignored it, focusing on the *events* while burying the real *issues* deep in the recesses of her mind and heart unresolved—and still raw? If she had truly resolved her issues and put the past behind her, wouldn't she feel some of the quiet calm, the acceptance, that she'd seen in the depths of Scott's eyes? And if she had truly written Scott off, hated him as deeply as she'd con-vinced herself she did, wouldn't she have been able to sustain her righteous anger and dismiss him without a second thought? Wouldn't she have been able to ignore the love and regret in his eyes?

Wearily Jess let her head drop back against the up-holstered chair. The answer to those questions was obvious: yes. But in reality, she felt far from calm. She hadn't been able to dismiss him. And she hadn't been able to ignore the emotions she saw in his eyes. Like it or not, Scott's presence had disrupted her carefully re-constructed existence.

For more than three years, Jess had suppressed memories of the life she'd shared with Scott. But now she could no longer keep them at bay. So with a resigned sigh she let them flow.

Jess thought back to their first encounter, in a business meeting. They'd done no more than shake hands and say a few words, but the spark that leapt between them had made her nerve endings sizzle and left her stunned. He had looked equally dazed. So she hadn't been in the least surprised when he'd called the next day and asked her out.

From their very first date, Jess had known that Scott was the man she would marry. And when she'd walked down the aisle with him a year and a half later, her heart overflowing with love, she'd looked forward with joy to the life they would build together as husband and wife.

The first few years of their marriage had more than lived up to her expectations, she recalled wistfully. They cooked together, laughing over exotic new recipes. They gardened, a passion they both shared. They took weekend hiking trips. And when Elizabeth came, bringing a new joy and closeness to their relationship, Jess willingly gave up her public relations job to be a full-time mother. It was a decision she and Scott made jointly and with absolute conviction. Her joy seemed complete.

But as Scott began to climb the corporate ladder, things started to change. Slowly at first. In manageable increments. A late night at the office here. A missed family event there. Jess could handle those. She understood that there would be occasional conflicts between work and personal life. What she *didn't* realize was that those minor changes were only previews of the major ones to come. Because Scott had been "noticed" by the right people. His talents had been recognized. And as a result, career demands increased. "Rising young executives," it seemed, were expected to put their jobs first. Always. Period.

Jess tried to cope with Scott's increased absences and his growing distraction. She watched with alarm as his job became the center of his life. Between his cell phone, e-mail and pager he was never able to get away from the office. She kept telling herself that in time the demands would ease. But as the months, then years, went by and the pace only intensified, she realized that things would never change unless *Scott* changed them.

So Jess tried to talk to him about it. Repeatedly. But the conversations always followed the same script.

"What do you want me to do about it, Jess?" Scott would say impatiently. "In this business, if you're not on the fast track, you're not on *any* track. And I can't afford to be without a job. I'm the sole breadwinner.

Which is fine. We agreed to that. But I do feel more pressure now to provide us with a good living."

"Good is one thing, Scott," she'd reply earnestly. "But I don't need that huge new house you've been talking about. Or the new car. Or a diamond bracelet for Christmas. I'm perfectly happy with simple things. Maybe you could change agencies, find a less demanding job. One that would give us more time to spend together."

He would frown then, the conflict in his eyes apparent. "I know I haven't been around as much as you'd like, Jess. But people don't just walk away from jobs like this."

"Why not?"

The question was always met with a sigh of exasperation. "I worked too hard to give all this up now."

"Give what up? The country club membership? The designer suits? Is that what you're talking about?"

"Is there something wrong with those things?" he'd ask defensively.

"No. Only when they come at the expense of other, more important things."

"I'm doing the best I can to balance everything, Jess. I'll just have to try harder, I guess."

And that's where the conversation would always end. In a stalemate.

Two years into that lifestyle and after numerous dead-end conversations on the subject, Jess began to notice another disturbing change in Scott's behavior. He'd always enjoyed a glass of wine with a special dinner, a beer while cutting the grass on the weekend. But now he went for the harder stuff. A gin and tonic became his standard way to unwind at the end of a long day. And at social gatherings he drank far more than was prudent. It was one more worry for Jess to add to her growing list.

But there were good times, too. Scott was a wonderful father—when he was home. He never looked more relaxed or happy than when he was playing with Elizabeth. And she adored him, reaching out her small chubby arms to him and laughing with glee when he appeared. They had good moments as a couple, as well. In the small hours of the morning he would sometimes curl up behind her, stroke her body and whisper words of love that made her heart ache with tenderness—and with a bittersweet pang for the days when making time for love had been his first priority.

And then tragedy struck. The death of her beloved daughter. Bitterness. Recriminations. The end of their marriage in everything but name. The death of her dream for a happily-ever-after life.

Jess felt a tear trickle down her cheek, and she reached up to wipe it away. With an unsteady hand she raised the mug to her lips and took a sip.

But her tea had grown cold.

Just like her life.

"You look tired, honey. Are you feeling okay?"

Jess glanced at her mother. She usually enjoyed the weekly evening with her parents, but she'd dreaded tonight's dinner. She'd done her best to camouflage the dark circles under her eyes, the result of several almost sleepless nights, but obviously her makeup skills hadn't been up to the task.

"It's been busy at the office," she hedged.

"I'm looking forward to the iris show," Frank remarked.

"So am I," Jess said with a smile. Taking her parents to see the gardens when the irises were at their peak, followed by an elegant brunch in one of the downtown hotels, had become an eagerly anticipated annual outing.

"Speaking of flowers, I need to order some mulch for the rose beds. And I think I lost my Mr. Lincoln this winter. I'll have to replace that as soon as the shipments come in." He turned to Jess. "I'm planning to extend the back garden and add a few more bushes this year."

She smiled. Her father's rose garden was a neighborhood legend. "How many do you have now, Dad?"

"Forty-five."

"I don't know why you even bother going down to the botanical garden. You have your own right here."

He looked pleased. "Mostly roses, though. I like to look at all the other flowers, too."

"So have you been working longer hours?" Clare asked Jess, doggedly returning to her earlier line of questioning.

Jess toyed with the food on her plate, and took a deep breath. She might as well tell them about Scott's visit. After all, they were all adults. They could discuss the situation rationally. "Yes. And not sleeping very well for the past few days. Scott came by on Saturday."

Her father stared at her in stunned silence for a moment, then threw his napkin on the table and stood.

"That's it. I'm calling John Kane. We'll put a stop to this."

So much for rational discussion, Jess thought ruefully. This was the reaction she'd been afraid of. "I don't think that's necessary, Dad."

He planted his fists on his hips. "Are you telling me that you're not upset by these contacts?"

"No. But he'll get the message eventually."

"He'll get it a lot faster if he gets slapped with a re-straining order."

He'd also get in trouble. Probably big trouble, Jess figured. She doubted the criminal justice system showed much mercy to newly released prisoners who were accused of harassment. And after looking into his eyes, she just couldn't do that to him.

"Let it go for now, Dad," she said quietly. "I'll think about it if this keeps up."

Her father studied her appraisingly. "What did he say to you?"

She shrugged. "Not much. Just that he was sorry."

Frank snorted. "It's a little late for that."

"I told him the same thing."

"Did you also tell him to leave you alone?"

"More or less. I shut the door in his face."

"I don't like this, Jess," Clare said, clearly worried, "It's been a hard few years for you. You don't need to have your life disrupted again."

Jess didn't disagree. The trouble was, her life was already disrupted.

When she didn't respond, Frank spoke again. "Your mother's right, Jess. You've been through enough."

Jess looked at her parents. They'd always been overly protective of their only daughter. And while she deeply valued their support and understanding and unqualified love, this was a decision she had to make on her own. She'd been affected by Scott's return in ways she didn't quite understand. And until she did, until she made sense of her chaotic emotions and thoughts, she was reluctant to take any action.

"I appreciate your concern. But I want to give this a little time," she said firmly.

There was silence around the table for a moment, and then Clare spoke. "It's her decision, Frank. She'll let us know if she wants us to step in."

Jess sent her mother a grateful look, then transferred her gaze to her father. He frowned in disapproval and seemed poised to make another comment. But after a moment he silently took his seat instead, confining his response to a single sentence.

"I hope you know what you're doing," he said shortly.

So did she, Jess thought with a sigh.

"The welcoming committee's here!"

Scott grinned at Karen, who stood on the other side of his door bearing a pie carrier in one hand and a plate of brownies in the other. "I'm salivating already. I haven't had anything home cooked in years."

"There's more," she called over her shoulder as she sailed past. "The cooler in the trunk is filled with lasagna, meat loaf and a bunch of other stuff. Can you grab that while I take these to the kitchen?"

Scott did as requested, returning to find Karen surveying his apartment with a frown, her hands planted on her hips, her lips compressed into a thin line. Here it comes, he thought resignedly as he deposited the cooler on the kitchen floor. He took a deep breath and braced himself before turning toward her

"I appreciate all this food, sis. More than you know. But you didn't need to go to so much trouble. It must have taken you days to make all this."

"I'm glad I did. I just checked your freezer and your cabinets. Corn flakes, bread, instant rice, instant mashed potatoes, canned stew, eggs. Is that what you've been living on?"

"It beats prison fare," he replied lightly. "Was the drive down okay?"

"It was fine. But I'm not through talking about you yet." Her gaze swept over the apartment before returning to him, and she folded her arms across her chest. "This isn't acceptable, Scott."

"I warned you it wasn't the Ritz."

"It isn't even a cut-rate motel," she shot back.

"It's good enough for now."

"There was a lovely guest room waiting for you in my house. There still is."

"I need to be here, Karen," he said quietly.

She looked at him in silence for a few moments. "Because of Jess."

"Yes."

She sighed resignedly. "Well, I'm not going to argue with you about that. It would be a lost cause. But I'm not happy about this," she said with a sweeping gesture around the tiny apartment.

"I didn't think you would be."

"Is this really all you can afford?"

"For now."

"Does Jess know how you live?"

"No."

She bit her lip. "Look, Scott, I know you signed everything over to her when you went to prison, but don't you think you deserve *something*—just enough to give you a stake to get started again?"

"No," he replied flatly.

Karen shook her head in exasperation. "Okay, I'm not going to argue with you about this. Yet. Put on your coat. We're going out to dinner. My treat."

Scott frowned. "But there's plenty of food here."

"That's for you. After I go back." When he started to protest, she held up her hand. "Not open for discussion. Besides, after the long drive down here I deserve a night away from the kitchen."

Scott shook his head bemusedly. "Are you this bossy at home?"

She shrugged. "I happen to be a strong-willed woman."

"Bossy," he reiterated.

"Assertive," she corrected.

"Stubborn, too."

"If you keep insulting me I just might pack up my food and go home," she threatened.

Scott held up his hands in capitulation and then reached for his jacket. "Heaven forbid! You win," he said with a chuckle.

"I'm glad you see the light," she said smugly.

Not until they were seated in the quiet restaurant and had placed their orders did Karen once again bring up the subject of Scott's wife. "So tell me how things are going with Jess."

"They aren't."

"Are you giving up?"

"No. Regrouping. Trying to figure out how to break through the wall she's built between us." Suddenly Scott's eyes grew thoughtful as he studied Karen. "Hey, I just had an idea," he said slowly.

She gazed at him suspiciously. "I don't like that look in your eyes."

He ignored her comment. "Maybe *you* could convince her to talk to me."

Karen stared at him. "I haven't spoken with her in years," she protested. "Why would she listen to me?"

"Because Jess always liked you. And she won't hold *my* mistakes against *you*. I'm willing to bet that she'll at least be polite." He sighed and raked his fingers through his hair. "Look, I hate to ask you to do this. And I don't know if it will work," he admitted. "But I'm willing to try anything at this point. She's shut me out both times I've tried to contact her. I need someone to run interference for me."

Karen waited while their food was placed in front of them, her brow furrowed. "I'm not into confrontation, Scott."

He tried to smile. "You could have fooled me. You don't cut me any slack."

She made a face. "Very funny. You're my brother. That's different."

He looked at her steadily. "I know it's asking a lot, Karen. You've already gone above and beyond. But this means a lot to me."

Karen was silent for a moment, then she sighed deeply and picked up her fork. "I'll think about it, okay? Now eat your steak before it gets cold."

Jess glanced toward the door in surprise, then at her watch. Her pizza order had arrived in record time. Which was okay. For the first time in several days she was actually hungry. She reached for her wallet, then headed toward the foyer.

"You guys get faster all the..." Her voice trailed off as she stared at the petite, dark-haired woman facing her on the other side of the door. Scott's sister.

Karen nervously hitched up her shoulder purse and offered a tentative smile. "Hello, Jess."

Instead of responding, Jess glanced behind Karen, her gaze darting into the shadows of the deepening dusk.

"I'm alone."

Jess's gaze swung back to Karen, who looked as uneasy and uncomfortable as Jess felt. "Do you have a few minutes to talk?" Karen asked.

"I don't really think we have anything to say to each other, Karen." She was amazed at how cool and controlled she sounded, considering her insides felt like gelatin.

"I won't take much of your time."

Jess didn't budge. "Did Scott ask you to come here?"

Karen hesitated, then nodded. "Yes."

"Look, Karen, I don't have anything against you. In fact, I always liked you. But nothing you say will make any difference. I don't want Scott in my life. Period. I've made that pretty clear both times he's contacted me. I don't know what else I have to do."

Karen took a deep breath and held her ground. "How about five minutes?" she persisted. "That's all I ask."

Short of closing the door in Karen's face, Jess was faced with no option but to grant her request. Besides, she didn't want to hurt Karen. Or be rude. The woman had always been kind to her, and the two couples had shared some very good times. What could it hurt to give her five minutes? In fact, it might help. If Karen saw how resolute Jess was, maybe she would carry that message back to Scott and discourage him from further contact. It was worth a try.

Jess stepped aside and opened the door. "All right. Five minutes."

Karen moved past her, and Jess nodded toward the living room. "Would you like something to drink?"

"No, thanks," Karen replied as she settled on the edge of the couch. Jess perched on the arm of a chair across from her, folded her arms and waited.

Karen gripped her purse and took a steadying breath. "Look, Jess, I really don't want to be here. But I love Scott. I've seen what he's gone through these last few years. And I want to help him. He's had a really tough time."

"Forgive me if I can't feel too sorry for him."

Karen seemed momentarily taken aback by the sarcasm in Jess's voice. "I don't mean to imply you haven't, too, Jess. But prison is hell."

"So is tragedy. And loneliness. And grief. You don't have to be behind bars to taste hell," she replied tersely.

Karen nodded. "I realize that. But in addition to everything else, Scott also carried a heavy burden of guilt. He lost the two things he loved most in the world—Elizabeth and you. And it was his own fault. He lived with the anguish alone, day after day, locked in an eight-by-eight cell, with no one to talk to, no one to comfort him, no support system. It…it almost killed him."

For a moment Jess seemed taken aback. "What do you mean?"

"He wanted to die, Jess," Karen said quietly. "I came to visit him every month, and for the first year I was afraid every time I left that he would…do something. He lost forty pounds, and his hands shook all the time. And he always had this hopeless look in his eyes, even though he tried to act normal when I was there. But I know him too well. And he was far from normal. I worried every day."

Jess eyed her skeptically. "He looks fine now."

"He's better," Karen conceded. "But hardly fine. He believes there are unresolved issues between the two of you. And he'd like a chance to address them. That's why he wants to see you."

Jess couldn't argue about the unresolved issues. Not after spending too many sleepless nights thinking about the situation. But she didn't need to talk with Scott to deal with them. She'd work through them eventually. On her own. As she did everything these days. Her eyes grew cool and she shook her head.

"I don't think so, Karen."

For a moment Karen studied the woman across from her. Jess was almost like a stranger. An unhappy, unreachable stranger, whose eyes reflected disillusion and bitterness. "You've changed, Jess," Karen said quietly.

"Haven't we all."

"Yes. And that includes Scott. I wish you'd give him a chance to prove that to you."

Jess stood, her face impassive. "If he's changed, I'm glad. But that doesn't bring back Elizabeth. It doesn't bring back the judge who was killed. All it brings back is the pain. If he really cares for me, he'll leave me alone. I would appreciate it if you'd tell him that."

Karen hesitated a moment, then stood and walked toward the door. She paused at the threshold to look back at the other woman, her eyes sad. "I'm sorry I bothered you, Jess. And I hope you don't regret this decision. I have a feeling that you're making a big mistake."

As Karen walked away, Jess frowned and slowly closed the door. Was she making a mistake? Or was she being wise?

She didn't have a clue.

And when her pizza arrived a few minutes later, she realized that her appetite had vanished—just like her peace of mind.

"I'm sorry, Scott," Karen concluded with a sigh as she finished the report on her visit with Jess.

Scott tried to hide his disappointment. He'd known all along that it was foolish to hope that Karen's visit would make a difference. And it wasn't her fault that Jess had been unreceptive. "Don't be. You did your best. I knew it was a long shot."

Karen wrapped her hands around her mug and stared into the dark depths of her coffee. "Jess has changed a lot," she said carefully.

"Yeah. I know. She's way too thin. And too tense. And much more high-strung."

Karen nodded. "True. But she's different in other ways, too."

Scott frowned. "What do you mean?"

Karen shrugged. "I don't know, exactly. Jess used to be so open and full of joy. Now it's like she's shut down. Like there's no way to reach her. She has such bitterness and anger…." Karen shook her head in dismay. "Frankly, I don't know what it will take to get through to her."

"There has to be a way," Scott said resolutely.

Karen looked at him steadily. "And if there isn't?"

"I'm not willing to consider that yet."

"You know, sometimes people are physically hurt so badly that they can't be saved," Karen said softly. "I think the same is true of some relationships."

Scott rested his elbows on his knees and dropped his face into his hands. After a moment he drew a long shuddering breath, and when he looked at Karen a bit of light had gone out of his eyes.

"I'm not giving up."

"She doesn't want to see you, Scott."

"I respect that. But I believe that God is with me on this. Because I know, in my heart, that the marriage He blessed was meant to go on. And not just in name."

Karen's eyes were filled with compassion when she looked at him. "I hope you're right, Scott. But I think it will take a miracle."

"I survived three years of hell, Karen," he said, his gaze locked on hers. "I believe in miracles."

She had no rebuttal to that. "I wish I could help."

"You can. Pray."

"I already do. Every day."

"Then keep it up."

Because he knew he would need all the prayers he could get to bring about *this* miracle.

Chapter Four

At first glance, Jess wasn't sure. It *looked* like Scott from the back. In fact, as she studied the distant figure more closely, it looked enough like him to make her step falter. But surely she was wrong. Why would Scott be planting bushes in front of the hospital? she wondered in confusion.

Suddenly the man turned, and her suspicion became reality. It *was* Scott, she realized as her heart skipped a beat. For a moment he seemed as taken aback by her presence as she had been by his. Then he slowly set his shovel aside and walked toward her.

Jess thought about turning away, fleeing in the opposite direction. But she wasn't going to spend her life running. Since Scott lived in St. Louis, there was always a chance their paths would cross. She'd have to learn to accept that. And deal with it in a mature way. Which she was perfectly capable of doing, she told herself determinedly. After all, her first encounters with him had been upsetting only because they'd been so unexpected. Now that the initial shock had worn off, she was better prepared to deal with him.

Scott stopped a few feet away. Despite the chill in the air, he wore only jeans and a sweatshirt. There was a streak of dirt on his forehead, and he looked tired, Jess realized. As if he hadn't been getting enough sleep. The unfamiliar lines she'd noticed on his face at their first meeting seemed a bit deeper, too. Or maybe they were just more apparent in the harsh noonday sun, which also highlighted the sprinkling of silver at his temples. For the first time, Jess was consciously aware of the physical evidence of the hell Karen had said he'd endured. But she steeled herself against it. He had no corner on anguish, she thought harshly. Her lips compressed into a thin, unreceptive line and she stared at him mutely. Since he'd approached her, she waited for him to speak first.

Scott jammed his hands into his pockets, realizing that the ball was in his court. But he had no idea what to say. He was still trying to recover from the shock of seeing Jess so unexpectedly. Though his feet had automatically carried him in her direction, his brain hadn't yet kicked into gear. So for a moment he just drank in the sight of her. Her honey-gold, shoulder-length hair was pulled back at her nape with a barrette, and she wore tailored black slacks and a forest-green jacket with a black velvet collar. His gaze lingered at her neck, where a gold choker glinted in the sunlight and a rapid pulse beat in the hollow of her throat. Was she nervous, he wondered? Angry? About to let him have it—or about to give him a chance to plead his case?

Hoping her eyes might hold a clue, his gaze moved on, past her lips, past the dark shadows that indicated she, too, had been finding sleep elusive. But when his gaze reached her eyes, their green depths were cool and shuttered—and very unreadable. He'd just have to wing it, he realized. With an effort he swallowed past the lump in his throat and struggled to find his voice.

"Hello, Jess."

Her eyes were aloof as her gaze swept over his dirt-stained clothes. "What are you doing here?"

"Working." When she frowned, he nodded toward a landscaping truck off to the side. "I work for that company."

Jess's frown deepened. With Scott's experience, she'd just assumed that he was back in the marketing game. It had never occurred to her he would be working as a manual laborer. That sort of job would have been completely unacceptable to the Scott she remembered, who had come to value designer suits and power lunches, who had liked starched shirts and clean finger-nails. It didn't make any sense.

Of course, it was no concern of hers. She really didn't care what he was doing. Yet she couldn't stop the question that sprang to her lips. "What happened to marketing?"

He shrugged. "Ex-cons can't be picky. Besides, I don't have the stomach for it anymore. Or the heart. And I wanted an outdoor job."

She almost asked why, then thought better of it. The answer was obvious. If you'd spent three years of your life confined in the eight-by-eight cell Karen had described, she doubted a desk job in an eight-by-eight office would be very appealing.

"Why are *you* here?" he asked, interrupting her thoughts.

"Visiting a friend who just had surgery," she replied distractedly, still mulling over his response to her question. "I ran over on my lunch hour."

"And what are you doing these days, Jess?"

Jess snapped back to attention. The question was asked gently, with genuine interest. But she saw no point in prolonging the conversation. She glanced at her watch. "I'm running late. Goodbye, Scott." And with that she brushed past him, leaving a faint, appealing fragrance in her wake.

Scott watched her walk away and slowly let out his breath. After Karen's visit, he'd prayed for guidance about how best to approach Jess. He'd also talked with Reverend Young, who had wisely reminded him that patience was his friend in this endeavor and that the Lord would show him the way in His time—not in Scott's time. So Scott had put his faith in God. And now that faith had been rewarded. Best of all, Jess hadn't appeared upset. Or angry. And she'd actually said more than three words to him. Yes, the conversation had been strained and awkward. And no, she hadn't exactly been friendly. But it was a start, he thought with renewed hope.

For her part, Jess was more shaken by the encounter than she'd let on. Her heart was hammering in her chest, and as she punched the elevator button she realized that her hand was trembling. But at least she'd managed to remain poised and in control during their brief exchange, she congratulated herself. Her shock at coming upon Scott had been far less dramatic than at their first two encounters. In fact, she was more shocked by his job than by his presence. Manual labor seemed somehow inappropriate for a man of Scott's intelligence and abilities and experience. Why had he settled for such a job? There had to be higher-level jobs, even for an ex-con, that wouldn't require him to spend his whole day in a confined office. Yet he'd chosen to be a laborer. Jess frowned, recalling Karen's comment that Scott had changed. His job choice certainly seemed to bear that out, she acknowledged begrudgingly.

But if she was puzzled by Scott's choice of work, she felt good about her reaction to him. She hadn't fled, despite the temptation to do so. She'd kept her cool. She hadn't been swayed by the warmth in his eyes.

And the next time she saw him—if there was a next time—it would be even easier to walk away undisturbed, she thought with satisfaction.

Jess pulled into a parking place and glanced at her watch in frustration. If she hadn't been running late this morning, she wouldn't have walked out the door without the report she needed to present this afternoon. Skipping lunch to run home and retrieve it simply added to the pressure of an already stressful day.

Jess was halfway down the walk toward her condo when she noticed the man sitting on the ground, his back against a tree, his long legs stretched out in front of him. He was at right angles to her, engrossed in a book, and a crumpled brown paper sack and empty soda can lying on its side were beside him.

Jess's headlong rush slowed, then came to an abrupt halt. It was Scott again! Less than a week after she'd run into him at the hospital, she realized incredulously. The last encounter she had written off to chance. But you could stretch coincidence only so far. If he was going to start staking out her home, then she'd have no choice but to follow her father's advice and have a restraining order issued, she thought angrily.

Just then, as if sensing her presence, Scott looked toward her. Though his surprised reaction momentarily let some of the air out of her theory of a deliberate setup, she still couldn't buy pure chance. The odds against them running into each other twice in only a few days were too great. Taking a deep breath, she strode toward him.

"What are you doing here?" she demanded.

He closed his book and rose in one lithe movement. But instead of the defensive reaction she expected, his posture was relaxed, his gaze warm. A smile tugged at the corner of his mouth in the endearing way she had always loved, and she suddenly found it difficult to breathe. "Didn't we have this same conversation at the hospital?"

She folded her arms across her chest. "You didn't answer my question."

"I'm working." He shifted his book to the other hand and pointed to the Lawson Landscaping truck in the parking lot—which she'd have noticed if she hadn't been so rushed, she realized—then nodded toward a shovel and a flat of begonias a few feet away. "Now it's my turn. What are *you* doing here?"

She ignored his teasing tone. "I live here, remember?"

"I mean what are you doing here at lunchtime? We're always long gone before the eight-to-five crowd gets home."

She frowned in confusion. "You've worked here before?"

"Several times. Lawson has the groundskeeping contract for this complex."

The implications of his reply slowly sank in. He'd been in her neighborhood on more than one occasion. And he had made no attempt to contact her. So much for her father's harassment theory, she thought wryly.

"So what brings you home at lunchtime?" he repeated.

"I forgot a report that I need this afternoon."

A slow smile spread over Scott's face. "The Lord really does work in mysterious ways," he said softly.

She frowned again. "What's that supposed to mean?"

"I've been praying for our paths to cross again, Jess."

"This is just a coincidence," she scoffed.

"Oh ye of little faith."

The truth of the remark, said partly in jest, stung. "Since when have you gotten so holy?" she lashed out. "I seem to recall having to drag you to church when we were…" She stopped abruptly. "Well, a long time ago."

Suddenly his face grew serious. "I've changed, Jess. My faith is the main reason I survived the last few years."

She stared at him. "Do you really expect me to believe that?"

"It's the truth," he said simply. "You of all people should understand that. Your faith was always important to you. Now I know why."

But I don't, she thought silently. *Not anymore.* Her spoken words, however, were different. "Look, I don't have time for philosophical discussions," she said irritably. "I'm running late. You can believe whatever you want about these two meetings. I call it chance. Bad luck. Whatever. And I think it's highly unlikely to happen again. In fact, I hope with all my heart that it doesn't. Goodbye, Scott."

She lifted her chin and headed toward her condo. Though she purposely didn't look at him again, the title of the book he held somehow seemed to jump out at her as she passed. And for a moment her step faltered. It was the Holy Bible, she realized in astonishment.

As she picked up her pace once again, she suddenly—and much to her surprise—realized that she was envious. Because Scott had clearly found in *his* faith what she'd always claimed to have in *hers*. Trust in the Lord. A belief that no matter what happened, He was always with us. And a deep conviction that if we turned to Him for help, if we admitted our faults and asked for forgiveness, He would stand with us and welcome us home.

When she'd first seen Scott, she'd been struck by the deep inner peace in his eyes. Now she knew the source.

It was ironic, she thought with a bittersweet pang. In Scott's adversity, when he'd felt most abandoned, the

Lord had taken him in. Just the opposite had happened with her. In her adversity, she had walked away from her faith. Because she believed the Lord had abandoned her.

For the first time since Elizabeth's death, Jess acknowledged that the loss of her faith had made her the poorer. But she had no idea how to rebuild it. Or even if she wanted to. Because that would mean once more putting her trust in the Lord. And at this point in her life, she had very little trust to give.

To anyone.

"The garden's coming along beautifully, Scott."

Scott wiped his forehead on his sleeve as he gazed with satisfaction at the plantings that were transforming the area around the just-finished gazebo into a meditation garden. Dogwoods, Japanese maples, azaleas, boxwoods, lilies, hydrangeas, irises and banks of perennials now framed the slightly elevated natural wood structure. The layout was pleasing to the eye, and the plants had been chosen to provide a season-long display of color. "Thanks. I'm happy with the way it turned out," Scott concurred. "In a year or two, when everything is really established, this will be a lovely spot."

"It looks pretty good to me right now. And the board agrees. I'm sure they'll thank you officially, but in the meantime they wanted me to pass on their compliments."

"It was no big deal," Scott replied with a shrug. "I had the time, and it was a good chance for me to test my landscape-design skills."

Reverend Young smiled. "Well, if this was a test, you get an A." He held up a sack. "Mrs. Wagner dropped off some of her famous white-chocolate-chip macadamia-nut cookies. Think you could help me get rid of a few?"

Scott grinned. "I think that could be arranged." He laid his shovel aside and wiped his hands on his slacks before following the minister to the gazebo.

"Looks like spring's really arrived," the minister said as he settled onto one of the benches that rimmed the inside of the gazebo. He retrieved two cans of soda from the sack and handed one to Scott.

Scott took a long sip, then nodded. "That's for sure. Things are hopping at Seth's."

"I'll bet. Everything okay with the job?"

"Seems to be. Seth doesn't say much, but he's put me in charge of the crew a couple of times when the chief was sick. I take that as a good sign."

"I agree. Apartment okay?"

Scott smiled. "Not according to my sister. But it's fine for now."

"Still taking the bus everywhere?"

Scott reached for a cookie. "Yes. But I must admit that I'll be glad to get a car. I figure in another month or two, I should be able to swing it."

"I'd be more than happy to loan you the—"

"No." Scott cut him off firmly, then softened his tone. "I appreciate the offer, Reverend. But I want to do this myself."

"It's okay to accept *some* help, Scott."

"I need it more on another front," he replied with a sigh.

"Jess?"

"Mmm-hmm."

"How are things going?"

He shrugged. "I guess there's a little progress. We've run into each other a couple of times, and she's actually spoken to me."

"That's a start."

"Barely."

"Hang in there. And keep praying."

"I plan to."

The minister took a sip of his soda, then carefully placed the can on the wooden bench. "I'd like to ask a favor of you, Scott."

Scott looked at the man who had helped him find his way back to the Lord, who had given him a reason to live again. There was no way he could ever repay him for his kindness and caring. No favor would be too great. "Name it," he said promptly.

"Well, a group of area churches will be sponsoring a one-day retreat in a few weeks. The title is 'Coping with Adversity—Ask and You Shall Receive.' Some of the clergy will be giving talks and leading discussions, but we're also looking for people who are willing to give a firsthand account of how, in the face of tragedy, their faith helped them turn their lives around. You have a remarkable story to tell, Scott. We'd be honored if you'd share it."

Scott stared at Reverend Young. Bare his soul in front of a group of strangers? He couldn't even imagine it! He'd never been the kind of guy who went around talking about his feelings—even to people he *knew*.

Besides, he was no role model. His journey to faith had been a painful one, fraught with doubt and dead ends and despair. Hardly the stuff of inspiration. Yet he owed so much to Reverend Young. He hated to say no.

The minister smiled understandingly. "I can see you're surprised by my request."

"That's too mild a word." He raked his fingers through his hair and stared out at the placid waters of the pond for a moment before speaking. "It's not that I don't want to help, Reverend," he said slowly. "But I've made a lot of mistakes. I'm not sure I'm the best example to hold up to people. There are a lot of things I'm still struggling with. And even though I do have hope, I'm not where I want to be yet."

"That's precisely the point, Scott. Your hope will be inspiring to many people who are also struggling. And as for mistakes…that makes you human. Someone people can relate to. All of us have made mistakes, all of us have challenges in our lives. Generally not as big as the ones you've faced, thank God. But that's why your story will resonate with people. If you could find your way to God despite the problems that you had to shoulder, it gives all of us hope that we can do the same with our lesser struggles." He paused for a moment, then delivered his powerful closing argument. "Your witness could make the difference in some life teetering on the edge of despair, Scott."

Put that way, Scott realized that he was left with little choice. He had vowed to make his faith the center of his life, and here was a perfect opportunity to give something back to the Lord, who had sustained him through his trials. But it wouldn't be easy. He had never been comfortable sharing painful experiences. Even in the best days of his marriage he'd held back some of his doubts and fears from Jess, feeling that such an admission would somehow diminish him, make him less strong. Now he recognized that attitude, which still lingered, for what it was—a sin of pride. Funny. He thought the past three years had stripped away all remnants of his pride. Clearly, patience wasn't the only virtue he needed to work on, he acknowledged ruefully. Humility was right up there, too.

Scott took a deep breath. "You make it hard to say no. But this won't be easy for me, Reverend."

The minister laid his hand on Scott's shoulder. "Not much worth doing is, Scott," he said kindly. "But remember that when we have faith, we never do anything alone. And that knowledge should always give us the courage to carry on."

"Hey, Skip. What's up?"

Jess smiled at her brother's voice and headed toward a comfortable chair, switching the portable phone to her other hand. "Are you ever going to stop calling me that?" she complained good-naturedly.

"Why should I?"

"Because I don't skip anymore, for one thing. And for another, that nickname is too childlike for an adult woman."

"What's wrong with being childlike?" he countered. "Innocence and trust are good things. And you're never too old to skip."

"I disagree on all counts. If you have the first two, you get hurt. And my skipping days are over."

"More's the pity."

"So how are you enjoying Japan?" she asked, deliberately changing the subject.

"Okay, okay. I can take a hint. Japan was great."

"Was?"

"Yep. We wrapped things up and I came home a week early. I just got in a couple of hours ago, in fact. With a major case of jet lag," he added, stifling a yawn. "Let me tell you, fourteen hours on a plane is *not* my idea of a great time."

"So why aren't you sleeping?"

"That's the next item on my agenda. But first I want to hear about you. Why didn't you tell me Scott was out?"

Jess frowned. "How did you know?"

"Mom let it slip. So why didn't you tell me? I just talked to you last week."

"Because it doesn't matter."

"Yeah?"

"Yeah."

"That's not what Mom said."

"What do you mean?"

"She said you're rattled."

"I'm not rattled."

"You sound rattled."

"I'm not rattled!" she repeated more emphatically.

"Okay, okay! You're not rattled. Fine. So how is he?"

"How would I know?"

"Mom said you've seen him."

Jess sighed. "What else has Mom told you?"

"That there's talk of a restraining order. Is that true?"

"The talk part is. I haven't done anything about it yet."

"Is Scott bugging you?"

"Not really. He called once. And stopped by. Then he sent his sister to try and convince me to talk with him."

"Did she succeed?"

"No."

There was silence for a moment. "Do you want some advice?"

"No. But why do I think that won't stop you from giving it?" she said resignedly.

"Because you know me too well. Listen, would it hurt to talk to him, Jess? The man just spent three years in prison. Behind bars. Caged up like an animal. He's had a lot of time to think about what happened. Maybe he has some things he'd like to say to you."

"Maybe I don't want to hear them."

"Maybe you should."

Jess gave a frustrated sigh. "Nothing he can say will change anything, Mark. Our marriage is over, except in name. Elizabeth is dead. The life I knew with Scott is gone. I've started over. I see no point in rehashing old hurts."

"So how are you sleeping these days?"

At the abrupt change of subject, Jess frowned in confusion. "What?"

"How are you sleeping?"

"What has that got to do with anything?"

"Maybe a lot. Unresolved issues can prey on the mind."

"I don't have unresolved issues," she replied with more confidence than she felt.

"I don't buy that," he said bluntly. "I never have. I think you need to talk to Scott and work through this. Look, Jess, I know you've vilified him in your mind. But you loved him once. Doesn't that count for anything?"

"No," she said flatly.

Mark sighed. "Frankly, I don't buy *that,* either. I know how much you two were in love. At the risk of getting sappy, it was almost magic to watch you together. But putting all that aside for a minute, I knew Scott, too. I'm not saying he was perfect. Or that what he did wasn't wrong. But he was never a *bad* man. In fact, he had great integrity and principle. And he clearly believes that there are unresolved issues between the two of you. Deep in your heart, I think you feel the same way."

"Since when have you become a psychiatrist?" Jess said sarcastically.

He refused to be baited by her tone. "I think it's just common sense," he replied matter-of-factly.

"You're forgetting one thing, Mark." A tremor of anger and pain rippled through her voice, and she took a steadying breath. "Scott killed my daughter. And I can never forget that."

There was silence for a moment, and when Mark spoke again his voice was sober. "I understand that, Jess. But that doesn't mean you can't forgive."

Jess drew in a sharp breath, feeling almost as if she'd been slapped. "You expect me to forgive him?" she asked incredulously.

"I leave that up to you. But holding on to hate doesn't seem very productive. In fact, it usually holds us *back*. Sometimes forgiving is the only way to move on."

Jess had no response to that. Because, though her mind denied the truth of Mark's observation, her heart wasn't so sure.

"Are you still there?" Mark asked when the silence lengthened.

"I'm here," she replied stiffly.

"Listen, I'm sorry if I overstepped. But I care about you, Jess. I know talking to Scott would be difficult, but it also might free you once and for all from the anger that you've carried all these years."

Jess took a deep breath, and when she spoke she sounded weary—and spent. "I know you mean well, Mark. But this is something I have to deal with myself. And at this point I just don't want to talk to Scott."

"Will you at least think about it?"

She hesitated. "Maybe."

"Then enough said. Listen, I have *got* to get some rest. I'll call you again in a few days, okay?"

"Yeah."

"Take care, Skip."

A smile tugged at the corners of her mouth as the line went dead. Mark was incorrigible. But he was also smart. The "book" smarts she'd always known about, of course. You didn't get a Harvard MBA without superior intelligence. But his insights into her psyche surprised her.

Jess's grin faded and her face grew serious. Mark hadn't said much about the tragedy during Scott's imprisonment, and the few times he'd broached the subject she'd cut him off. So he'd let it rest. Until today. Now that Scott was out, and making his intentions clear that he'd like to talk with her, Mark had apparently become a man with a mission.

And much as she hated to admit it, a lot of what he said made sense. She did still harbor a deep-seated anger. It had bubbled to the surface with surprising force after Scott's first phone call, setting her on edge and bringing back memories of the pain and betrayal she had felt following the accident. It had also brought back her own guilt feelings. And her long-suppressed "what if" questions.

Mark was right about one thing, she acknowledged. There were unresolved issues in her life. Yet something held her back from talking with Scott. Until now, she'd thought it was anger and hatred. But suddenly, with startling clarity, she realized that her reluctance was fueled by something else entirely.

Fear.

And even more troubling, she had no idea why she was afraid.

Chapter Five

Jess turned off the engine and drew a shaky breath. She ought to stop coming here, she told herself as she gazed at the neat rows of headstones that surrounded her. Despite the peaceful, parklike environment, this annual trek always threw her emotions into turmoil. So much so that each year, when she left, she told herself it was her last visit. That she would end this heartbreaking ritual. And each year, when Elizabeth's birthday dawned, she found herself heading back again.

Maybe this time it would be easier, she thought hopefully as she reached for the pink sweetheart rose surrounded by baby's breath and fern. For a moment she gazed at the single, perfect blossom, then gently touched the delicate petals. Pink had been Elizabeth's favorite color, she recalled wistfully, her throat tightening with emotion. And the joyful, optimistic color had suited her. But today, the gray, overcast April sky better reflected her own mood, Jess acknowledged with a sigh.

As she began the trek to the painfully familiar spot where her daughter had been laid to rest, Jess thought back to another bleak, rainy day nearly four years before, when she'd followed this same path in the wake of the small casket carried by her father and brother. The ceremony had been private, just family and a few close friends, as she had requested. Though Scott had been out on bail, she had hoped he would honor her wishes and stay away. But when she arrived at the cemetery he had been there, along with Karen and her family. They stood on one side of the grave, she and her family on the other, the gulf that had separated them far wider than the narrow opening in the ground.

She'd glanced once at Scott—only once—during the brief service. The raw grief in his haggard face, the desperate apology in his eyes had been powerful enough to penetrate her own mantle of sorrow and momentarily touch her heart. But she'd quickly averted her gaze, refusing to be moved by his anguish. He deserved to suffer for what he had done, she'd thought, hatred welling up inside her. And she never wanted to see him again. At her lawyer's request, he had cleared his things out of their house while she was in the hospital recovering from the concussion she had sustained in the accident. By the time she returned home, there was little evidence that he'd ever lived there. She had no idea where he'd gone. And she didn't care.

When the minister finished his prayers, he'd walked over and offered words of condolence that echoed hollowly in her heart. She'd listened numbly until he'd said that the Lord would watch over her in her sorrow, and then anger had bubbled up inside her. It had taken every ounce of her willpower not to lash out at him, to ask where the Lord had been the night Elizabeth had died in a wreckage of twisted metal while Scott had walked away untouched. As if sensing her feelings, her parents had pressed close beside her, thanking the minister in her place. Then they had gently taken her arms, urging her to leave.

As she'd stumbled unseeingly across the grassy expanse, her eyes blinded by tears, she had taken one final glance over her shoulder. Karen and her family had moved off to one side, leaving Scott alone beside the small casket. He was crouched down, one hand resting on the smooth surface. As if sensing her gaze, he had looked up at her, his eyes bleak and lost and almost shell-shocked, as if to say, "How did this happen? How can Elizabeth be gone? And how have we come to this, you and I, we who were once so happy and so in love?"

But Jess had simply turned away, leaving him alone with questions to which she had no answers.

Jess choked back a sob as she now retraced her steps on this familiar path, digging in the pocket of her raincoat for a tissue. She still had no answers, nearly four years later. All she knew was that she wished she could go back to the time of Elizabeth's birth, before the seductive glamour of success had eaten away at the foundation of their marriage, when their three-person circle of love had been the center of their world. That had been the happiest time in her life.

Her eyes filled with tears, and she dabbed at the corners with her tissue, trying to clear her vision so that she didn't trip on the uneven turf or a ground-level headstone. In fact, she was so focused on her footing that she had almost reached Elizabeth's grave before she realized that someone was already there.

Jess stopped abruptly and stared at the familiar broad back. It was Scott, on his knees, sitting back on his heels, a discarded flowerpot and trowel beside him. One of his hands rested on the small headstone, and his head was bent.

Jess almost stopped breathing. She did *not* want to see Scott again! Especially here. For a moment panic overwhelmed her, but she forced herself to think logically. Her best plan was to make a quiet retreat, drive around for a few minutes, then return after he'd gone, she decided. Her heart hammering in her chest, she turned and began to walk rapidly away. But she'd gone only a few steps when his voice reached out to her across the stillness.

"Jess."

The intensity in his hoarse plea made her step falter.

"Please. Stay."

She wanted to ignore him. Wanted to keep walking. But something in his voice reached deep into her soul, compelling her to turn. And once she did, there was no way she could walk away.

Scott was still on his knees, his face raw with grief. Tears ran unchecked down his face, and the anguish in his eyes so closely mirrored what was in her heart that she could almost feel his pain as hers. At least in this one thing they still shared a tragic bond, she realized, her throat tightening with emotion.

They stared at each other in silence for a long moment, their gazes locked, and then Scott slowly rose, never breaking eye contact. Finally, with an effort, he tore his gaze from hers and transferred it to the flower she held.

"I see we both had the same idea," he said softly.

Jess glanced down at the grave to find that he had planted a miniature pink rosebush in front of the headstone. Her eyes blurred with tears, and she took several deep breaths, blinking rapidly to clear her vision. She would *not* break down, she told herself fiercely. She would cry later, in private, as she had been doing for the past four years. She was not going to share her grief with the man who had caused it.

When she finally worked up the courage to gaze at him again, she realized that Scott didn't seem to share her concern about revealing his emotions. With a jolt of surprise she noted that he'd made no attempt to erase the evidence of his tears. She stared at him, completely taken aback by this uncharacteristic behavior. In all the years she'd known him, she'd never seen him cry. He'd been stoic through sadness and through pain, priding himself on his strength to endure all that came his way. Now he stood before her in undisguised grief, seemingly comfortable with his vulnerability. Offering yet more evidence that he had truly changed, she acknowledged reluctantly.

Scott reached down to retrieve the pot and trowel, then stepped aside in silent invitation for Jess to come forward and place her own offering on the grave. For a moment she hesitated. What she really wanted to do was retreat to the safety of her car. She felt off balance, unsure how to react to this new Scott, no clue what he might do next. As if he understood her confusion and uncertainty, he backed off several paces to allow her to maintain a sense of personal space.

Jess realized that turning away at this point would be foolish. So she moved forward slowly until she stood directly in front of the headstone. She rested her hand on the smooth stone, as Scott had done, then knelt and gently laid the rose on the grave. After a moment she raised her gaze to her daughter's name, etched in granite, and with an unsteady hand ran her fingers over the letters. Elizabeth Grace Mitchell. Her gaze lingered on the name she and Scott had so carefully chosen to honor their mothers, a combination of their middle names. Then her gaze moved lower, to the dates of Elizabeth's brief life, and finally to the words at the end. "Cherished daughter of Jess and Scott Mitchell." At first she'd planned to put only her name in the inscription. But in the end, when it had come time to erect the headstone several months after the interment, she'd been unable to leave Scott's name off. For all his sins, she'd never doubted his love for Elizabeth.

"Thank you for that. I didn't expect it."

Scott's voice, raw with emotion, told her that the gesture had not been lost on him.

"I know you loved her, Scott," she whispered brokenly, her head bent as she fought the tears that threatened to spill from her eyes.

Scott's gut clenched painfully as he looked at the woman he loved, kneeling in grief on the grave of the daughter he'd killed, her slender shoulders hunched in anguish. Her hair had swung forward, hiding her face, but he could imagine the emotions that were reflected there. Because they were the same ones that were in his heart. A sense of loss that left you cold and empty inside. A dark despair that made you wonder if life would ever be bright again. A deep, aching loneliness that never went away. And for him there was guilt, as well. Deep, wrenching guilt that had almost driven him mad, until Reverend Young had helped him to believe in, and open himself to, the healing power of God. Though it had taken many months, he had finally made his peace with the Almighty. But in many ways, that had been easier than the challenge he faced with Jess, he realized with a heavy heart. Because God was always willing to give those who repented a second chance. The same didn't necessarily hold true for people. Even for those who have loved us.

Scott yearned to reach down and pull Jess into his arms, to hold her until the remorse and love in his heart seeped into the core of her being, until she knew beyond the shadow of a doubt that he had changed, that his love for her had never diminished and that with all his heart he wanted a second chance to prove to her that this time it would be different. No, he couldn't bring Elizabeth back. Dear God, he would give his life if he could! But he would do everything in his power to bring joy back into Jess's life and to be the husband she deserved, one who never forgot that the greatest of gifts was love.

Once more Jess laid her hand on top of the small monument and then made a move to stand. Instinctively Scott stepped beside her, reaching down to assist her. At his touch on her arm she turned, startled, and he almost backed off at the alarm in her eyes. But something told him to remain where he was.

"Let me help," he said quietly, holding his ground.

She stared at him wide-eyed. Even through her raincoat she could feel the firm, sure touch of his fingers. Her breath caught in her throat as memories came flooding back of the way his strong but gentle hands had always known how to work magic. To be comforting, sensuous, powerful, playful, depending on her mood or her need. He'd been so attuned to her emotions in the beginning that it had sometimes taken her breath away, she recalled with a pang. But that, too, had changed as ambition usurped his energy and attention.

For a long moment they simply looked at each other, their gazes locked, until the overpowering intensity finally compelled Jess into action. With Scott's assistance she rose shakily to her feet, then quickly stepped back, forcing him to drop his hold.

Scott seemed as shaken as she was by the brief touch. She saw his Adam's apple bob convulsively when he swallowed, saw him take a deep breath. Then he withdrew the Bible that had been tucked under his arm.

"Do you mind if I read a verse?" he asked in a voice that was ragged around the edges.

Jess shrugged, and when she replied her own voice was none too steady. "If you want to."

"Is there anything special you'd like to hear?"

"It doesn't matter."

He looked at her curiously. "You always had favorite verses. I'm sorry to say I don't remember what they were. I guess I never paid much attention in those days. But I'd be happy to read one if you'd remind me."

Her gaze cooled. "It really doesn't matter," she said more firmly. "I don't read the Bible anymore."

He frowned. "Why not?"

"I haven't kept up with my faith since…for the last few years."

His eyes filled with understanding and compassion. "It's hard to believe when things happen that don't make sense."

"That doesn't seem to be the case for you."

His eyes grew troubled. "Before I found my way back to the Lord, I had some pretty dark days, Jess," he said quietly.

She thought of Karen's comments about Scott's time in prison. How he had wanted to die. How he lost forty pounds in the first few months. How his hands had shaken so badly. How he'd always had a hopeless look in his eyes. And how she had worried about him every day. Apparently he had truly known some dark—and desperate—days. Which made Scott's return to the Lord even more remarkable, she realized.

"So what happened to renew your faith?" she heard herself asking.

"One of the prison chaplains took me under his wing. Made me realize that I wasn't as alone as I felt, that the Lord doesn't desert us even when we make terrible, tragic mistakes. I didn't buy it at first. But finally, after months of talking and prayer, I began to feel His healing power in my heart."

"Lucky you." Jess had meant to sound sarcastic. But underlying the sarcasm was an unmistakable wistfulness.

"It wasn't luck. It was a miracle," he said simply.

She had no response to that.

He held up the Bible again. "Do you mind?"

Silently she shook her head.

Scott opened the book and thumbed through it familiarly, stopping when he came to Psalms. And then, in a steady, measured voice he began to read a passage that Jess had once known by heart.

"'The Lord is my shepherd; I shall not want. In verdant pastures He gives me repose; beside restful waters He leads me; He refreshes my soul. He guides me in right paths for His name's sake. Even though I walk in the dark valley I fear no evil; for You are at my side with Your rod and Your staff that give me courage. You spread the table before me in the sight of my foes; You anoint my head with oil; my cup overflows. Only goodness and kindness follow me all the days of my life; and I shall dwell in the house of the Lord for years to come.'"

Scott slowly closed the book, then bowed his head. "Lord, we ask You to keep our Elizabeth in Your care on this, her birthday. We know she is wrapped in Your love, which far surpasses any joy that this world offers. But please help her know that she is loved and remembered by her mother and me, as well. And please give us who are left behind the grace and courage to carry on until the day we are all reunited in Your heavenly kingdom. Amen."

Jess looked at Scott's bowed head, his fervent prayer echoing in her heart, and suddenly she understood why she'd been afraid to talk with him. Somehow, intuitively, she had known that if she did, the wall of hatred she'd so carefully constructed would begin to crumble. Because she would be forced to admit that at heart he was a good man who had simply made tragic mistakes. Yes, the consequences of his actions had been terrible. But the actions themselves had not been undertaken with any malice. That acknowledgment, coupled with the striking changes in his personality, made it harder and harder to maintain the wall that separated them. And without that wall, she would be vulnerable again. To hurt. To betrayal. To loss. That was why she was afraid.

When Scott raised his head and glanced at Jess, his breath momentarily lodged in his throat. For the briefest second, in her unguarded eyes, he saw something that hadn't been there before. He wouldn't go so far as to call it warmth. But there was a…softer…look in her eyes. It was slight. It was very subtle. But it was there. And it gave him renewed hope.

Suddenly a gentle rain began to fall, and he tucked the Bible protectively in his jacket, then zipped it up. "I guess it's time to go."

Jess nodded. She glanced once more at the grave, where the pink flowers provided the only spot of color on this gray day. She hoped somehow that Scott's prayer had been heard, that her daughter would know that she was still deeply loved and sorely missed. "Happy birthday, Elizabeth," she whispered.

When she looked back at Scott, he was standing quietly, watching her. "You were a wonderful mother, Jess," he said hoarsely. "Just like you were a wonderful wife."

The unexpectedness of the comment took her off guard, and she had no idea how to respond. So instead she ignored it, confining her comment to a simple goodbye. Then she turned and walked toward her car.

She didn't look back, though she felt his gaze on her. And once in her car, hidden from his view, she sat for several minutes until her trembling subsided.

When she at last put the car into gear, she circled back toward the entrance, glancing once more at Elizabeth's grave in the distance. To her surprise, Scott was still there, though the rain had intensified. He seemed oblivious to the cold drops of water as he stared down at the grave, a solitary figure in the gray landscape, his hands in the pockets of his denim jacket. And somehow she knew that raindrops weren't the only moisture on his cheeks.

"Oh, Frank, look at this one!"

Jess and her father glanced toward Clare, who was standing in awe over a particularly stunning specimen of iris.

"I think I'll be adding another one to the list," he grumbled good-naturedly, taking a small notebook out of his pocket as they headed toward the older woman.

"Frank, write this one down," she said excitedly when they drew close.

"Sure thing," Frank replied, pausing to give Jess an

"I-told-you-so" look. "But honey, where are you going to put all of these? The bed is full already."

"I could say the same about your roses," she countered with an affectionate smile.

"Touché," he acknowledged fondly.

Jess smiled. Her parents' devotion to each other had always been an inspiration to her. Theirs was the kind of marriage she had always hoped to create, where love came first. Though her father had worked hard in a blue-collar job all his life, often coming home tired after a long day, he'd always made it a priority to spend time each evening with his wife and children. He'd rarely missed a school event or a dance recital, and each summer he'd pile the four of them into the family car, attach a pop-up camper that he'd bought second-hand, and they'd head out for a new adventure somewhere in the United States. Her mother had been equally devoted to the family, taking time each day when Jess and Mark arrived home from school to listen to their chatter over a glass of milk and cookies. It had been an idyllic childhood, and Jess would be forever grateful for the support and love her parents had lavished on their children.

Nor would she ever forget their support after Elizabeth's death. Without their intervention, she didn't know if she would have survived the dark days that followed. She'd lost a daughter, a husband and a whole way of life in the space of a few hours. For all intents and purposes, her world had come to an end. She, too, had walked through the valley of darkness mentioned in the Bible verse Scott had read at the cemetery . But unlike him, she had found no comfort in her faith. She owed her salvation to the love and support of her family.

"What do you think, Jess?"

With a start, Jess came back to reality. Her parents were looking at her questioningly, but she had no idea what they'd asked. "Sorry. I was daydreaming. What did you say?"

Her father nodded to two different irises. "Which one do you like better?"

She moved forward and studied the two delicate, frilly blossoms, one in shades of purple, the other white with a purple edge. "That one," she said decisively, pointing to the latter.

Her mother looked pleased. "I agree. Write that one down, Frank. I think I'll put that one in the…" Her mother's voice trailed off, and her eyes grew wide as she stared over Jess's shoulder.

Before Jess could turn to discover the source of her mother's distraction, a familiar voice spoke.

"Hello, Clare, Frank. Hello, Jess."

Jess's gaze moved from her mother's shocked face to her father's cold, contemptuous expression, then slowly she turned. Scott was standing just a few feet behind her, dressed in jeans and a long-sleeved shirt worn the way he'd always preferred, with the sleeves slightly rolled up. He was carrying what looked like a sketch pad, and his dark brown eyes gazed at her warmly.

"What are you doing here?" Jess asked, realizing even as she spoke that this was becoming her common greeting to Scott.

A smile tugged at the corners of his mouth, as if he had had the same thought. "The same thing you are, I expect. Enjoying a beautiful day at the garden. I often come on Saturday morning."

"Jess, isn't it time to leave for the brunch?"

At her father's terse question, she turned back to him. He was pointedly ignoring Scott, and she could see the anger smoldering in his eyes. It was far too soon to leave for the restaurant, but clearly Scott's appearance had ruined the garden for her parents.

"We should be okay, Dad," she replied, struggling to maintain an even, pleasant tone.

At her response, his mouth thinned. "I think we should go," he repeated more forcefully. "Your mother and I have seen enough here." He glanced pointedly at Scott, then turned away.

Jess knew how much her parents despised Scott for what he had done, but she was nevertheless taken aback by her father's uncharacteristic display of ill manners. She turned, an apology in her eyes, to find that a hot flush of embarrassment had crept up Scott's neck.

"I need to move on, too," he said quietly. "I'm heading for the Japanese garden. That's probably where I'll spend the next couple of hours." He was letting them know where he'd be so they could avoid him, Jess realized, struck by his thoughtfulness despite her father's rudeness. "It was good to see you again, Jess. Frank, Clare, enjoy the rest of your day."

With that he turned and walked away.

Scott was barely out of earshot when Frank spoke.

"Good riddance!" he said vehemently.

"Dad!"

"What?"

"He might hear you."

"So what if he does? I want him to know exactly what I think of him."

"He looks older," Clare said thoughtfully.

"He *is* older," Frank replied curtly.

"I just mean that prison must have been hard on him."

"Good."

Jess stuck her hands into the pockets of her slacks. "Don't you think you're being a little harsh, Dad?"

He looked at her stiffly. "Not particularly. He killed my granddaughter. And practically ruined my daughter's life. He deserves whatever suffering has come his way. I thought you felt the same way."

"I do," she replied, but her voice lacked conviction.

Clare gave Jess a troubled look. "Honey, has something happened? Is there something you haven't told us?"

Actually, there was. She'd never mentioned her unexpected meetings with Scott—at the hospital, her condo, the cemetery. Nor the unsettling effect they'd had on her. She needed to work through her feelings on her own, unbiased by the strong negative feelings her parents had about Scott.

She shrugged. "He seems different, that's all."

"Well, I expect he is, after three years in prison," Clare concurred.

"That doesn't absolve him from what he did," Frank maintained stubbornly. "Or change the consequences."

"No, of course not," Clare agreed.

Frank moved beside Jess and laid a hand on her shoulder. "Honey, you know we just want what's best for you," he said, gentling his voice. "And Scott isn't it. Maybe he's changed. I don't know. Frankly, I don't *want* to know. Because it doesn't matter. He's no longer a part of our life. I'm sorry we ran into him today, but he's really just a stranger to us now. He can't do anything more to hurt us. And as long as we keep shutting him out we're safe. Right?"

"Right," Jess responded automatically.

But in her heart Jess didn't feel safe at all.

Jess propped the bag of groceries on her hip as she retrieved her mail, then tucked it under her arm as she fitted her key in the lock. Once inside, she deposited the bag on the counter and quickly flipped through mostly ads and junk, shaking her head sympathetically for the overburdened mail carriers.

At the bottom of the stack was a flyer from her former church, and she gazed at it with a frown. She had no idea why she was still on the mailing list. She hadn't been an active member of the congregation for almost four years. She ought to just call and tell them to remove her name, she thought, glancing uninterestedly at the information about an upcoming retreat. She was just about to toss it into the trash with all the other junk mail when the last name listed under "speakers" caught her eye. Scott Mitchell.

With a frown, she glanced again at the theme of the event. "Coping with Adversity: Ask and You Shall Receive." It went on to say that a number of clergy would discuss the topic theologically, and that various individuals with extraordinary stories would talk about their personal faith experiences.

Slowly Jess sat down at the kitchen table, the groceries forgotten for the moment. Scott had shared a great deal with her during their marriage, but she couldn't recall a single incident when he'd opened up to other people. Especially about painful experiences or disappointments. How in the world had they talked him into this? she wondered incredulously.

Even more intriguing was the content of his talk. He'd said virtually nothing to her about his experiences in prison, referring only to "some pretty dark days." But what had actually happened? How dark was "dark"? And how had he found his way through the maze of despair back to faith?

Of course, there was no way she was going to attend this event, Jess told herself impatiently as she tossed the brochure onto the counter and turned her attention to the perishable items in her grocery bag. She wasn't *that* curious. And frankly, she didn't really *want* to know what had happened to Scott during his years behind bars. Partly because she felt he deserved whatever had occurred. But mostly because she was afraid that if she found out, the wall between them would crumble even more.

Chapter Six

"Excuse me…do you work here?"

Scott turned to find an older couple standing behind him. "Yes. Can I help you?" he asked pleasantly.

The man nodded toward the display of balled and burlapped dogwood trees in the nursery lot. "I'd like to get one of those for my yard, but I don't know much about trees. I need some advice."

Scott glanced around, but none of the retail staff was in the area. "I usually work on the commercial side of the business," he said hesitantly, unwilling to overstep the clear bounds Seth had set for his job. On the other hand, he doubted the owner would consider it good customer relations to leave this couple while he went in search of a salesperson. Especially when he could very likely help them. "I'll tell you what. Why don't you ask me your questions, and if I can't answer them I'll find someone who can."

"Fair enough," agreed the man. "My wife and I have

always liked dogwood trees, but we hear they're a bit temperamental. Any truth to that?"

"Well, they are subject to a few more problems than some trees," Scott verified, setting his shovel aside. "But a lot of ornamentals are like that. You'd need to watch for borers, which can eat away under the bark and eventually kill the tree. But it's easy to spot the signs, and the problem is relatively simple to treat. So I wouldn't let that stop you if you have your heart set on a dogwood. And they *are* a native Missouri tree, so they tend to do well here. What kind of sun exposure will it have?"

"We want to put it on the east side of the house. Lots of sun in the morning, but it's pretty shaded there in the afternoon."

Scott nodded. "That's good. Dogwoods don't handle full sun very well. They're also relatively slow growers. So while they have a spreading aspect, it will take a long time before you have much of a display, even with a fairly large tree. And it can sometimes take a year or two before they bloom."

"Hmm. Time isn't on our side, is it, Rose?" the man said, smiling affectionately at the older woman. "We aren't exactly spring chickens."

"If I could suggest something, then…"

"Certainly."

"You might want to plant a *grouping* of dogwoods. Maybe mix the pink and white. If you have a large enough area, that could work very nicely. And you'd have a lot more color a lot sooner."

"Well now, I hadn't thought about that. A grove."

The man considered that for a moment, then turned to his wife. "What do you think, Rose?"

"It sounds lovely."

"Is there any other landscaping in the area?" Scott asked as an idea began to take shape in his mind.

"No. We never did much on the side yard. But we just added a conservatory to the house, and now we have a great view of that part of our property."

"In that case, depending on your budget, of course, you might want to do a mulch bed that links the trees together. Maybe put in a few azaleas and some shade-loving perennials like hostas."

"This is sounding better and better," the man said enthusiastically. "Do you think you could come out to the house, take a look at the area, show us some ideas?"

Now Scott *knew* he'd overstepped his bounds. He was a laborer, not a landscape consultant—even if that *was* his long-term goal. But breaking the rules wasn't likely to move him in that direction. "Actually, I don't usually…"

"He'll be glad to."

Scott turned sharply at the sound of Seth's voice, and hot color stole up his neck. The owner stood only a few feet away and had apparently overheard the entire exchange.

"That would be great," the older man said.

"Why don't we go inside and take a look at the appointment book and we'll set something up," Seth told the man. Then he turned to Scott. "See me when you finish up here."

Scott nodded, a sick feeling in the pit of his stomach.

Seth had made the ground rules very clear when he started. Stick to your job. Ask for help when you need it. And don't confuse the two parts of the business—commercial and retail. Scott had clearly violated that rule. Which could not only derail his hopes of eventually moving into landscape design, but cost him his job. Reverend Young had warned him that Seth was a hard taskmaster who didn't tolerate insubordination. And that's exactly the way he might interpret Scott's action, though it certainly hadn't been the intent.

Scott finished shoveling the pile of mulch as quickly as possible, then headed for Seth's office, praying that the owner would at least listen to his explanation. Seth was on the phone when Scott arrived, and he motioned the younger man to take a seat.

"Look, Mike, we agreed on a Wednesday delivery, and that's when I need it," Seth said in a clipped tone. "I've got a commercial job starting on Thursday, and those boxwoods are a major part of it. What am I supposed to tell my customer? And who's going to pay the crew to stand around all day?" Seth chomped on his unlit cigar for a moment as he listened, his expression implacable. "Yeah. Yeah. Okay," he finally said. "Get me fifty of them Wednesday. I can hold off on the rest till Thursday. But no later. You got that?"

Seth dropped the receiver back into the cradle and turned his penetrating gaze on Scott. "So you want to tell me what that was all about?"

Scott took a deep breath. "I'm sorry if I overstepped. There wasn't anyone around to help those customers, so I thought it would be better if I—"

"Whoa!" Seth held up his hand, then leaned forward, propping his elbows on the desk. "That's not what I meant. Where did you learn so much about trees?"

Scott stared at his boss, taken aback. Apparently he wasn't angry after all. Relief flooded through him and he slowly let out the breath he hadn't even realized he was holding. "I've always enjoyed horticulture. And landscaping. I read a lot about it in prison, and I worked on the vegetable gardens and helped with the groundskeeping while I was there."

"You ever do any landscape design?"

"Not officially. But I've studied that, too, and I've done quite a few sketches."

"You still have them?"

"Yes."

"Bring them in tomorrow."

"I also designed and installed a meditation garden at Reverend Young's church," Scott offered.

Seth looked at him appraisingly. "When did you do that?"

"On Saturdays."

"Don't you do enough digging during the week?"

Scott shrugged. "I owe a lot to Reverend Young. I didn't mind."

Seth studied him for a moment longer, then consulted the work schedule. "Plan on going over to Mr. Hudson's house on Friday."

"I'm supposed to be on the crew over at the hospital then," Scott reminded him.

The older man waved the objection aside. "Laborers I can always find. Though not always as dependable as you," he added, giving Scott his first real—if back-handed—compliment. "People who know plants and have an eye for design are a lot tougher to find. So bring in those drawings. And I'll swing by that meditation garden on my way home." Seth reached for the phone, signaling the end of the discussion.

But as Scott rose and headed for the door, Seth stopped him with one final comment.

"You show promise," he said gruffly. "Keep this up, and things should work out just fine for you here."

A smile flashed across Scott's face. "Thanks."

As he left the office, Scott's heart felt lighter than it had in a long while. Somehow, earning Seth's respect meant more to him than all the bonuses he'd received in his former job. Because those were impersonal, determined by a formula that was revenue based. Seth's compliments, on the other hand—and his encouragement—seemed much more personal. And therefore more meaningful.

And best of all, if things went well with the Hudsons, maybe that project would open the door for Scott to begin building a new career.

Jess closed the folder, slid it back into her file drawer and glanced at her watch. She'd been in her office only twenty minutes, hardly long enough to justify a special trip into town on Saturday. Especially since she didn't have to give the presentation until the middle of next week.

Admit it, she told herself with a sigh. There was no legitimate business reason for this trip. Her *real* motives were purely personal, and to pretend otherwise was foolish. Since meeting Scott in the garden the week before, she'd been unable to forget his comment that he often came here on Saturdays. And deep in her heart, she wanted to see him again. Even though it made no sense.

She rose and restlessly walked over to the window, staring down unseeingly at the manicured grounds. For the past three months she'd gone out of her way to avoid him and, on the occasions when their paths *had* crossed, to make it clear that she wanted nothing to do with him. Yet now she was deliberately putting herself in a position to meet him. Which was probably a big mistake.

Her parents would certainly think so, she acknowledged. They considered any contact with Scott to be bad news. That was why she'd never told them about the times she'd run into him. Or about her plans for today. What would she say? That she was intrigued by the changes in him, driven by some powerful force deep inside to learn more about the transformation that had occurred during his time in prison? They would hardly be receptive to that message. Nor would they understand her change in attitude. And frankly, neither did she.

Jess sighed again. If she was smart, she would probably just turn around and go home. But she hadn't been feeling especially smart lately. Just unsettled. And going home was unlikely to change that. So she might as well follow her instincts.

Resignedly she reached for her purse, flipped off

the lights in her office and headed out into the garden. The cobalt-blue sky of early morning had given way to scattered clouds, but she took little notice of the weather—or the beauty around her. She was looking for only one thing—a tall, broad-shouldered man with a glint of silver in his dark hair. Nothing else registered in her field of vision.

Thirty minutes later, however, after a rapid but complete circuit of the grounds, she'd seen no sign of Scott. Which was probably good, she assured herself even as a feeling of disappointment swept over her. Trying to engineer a chance meeting had been silly. And not very smart.

She hitched her shoulder purse higher and resolutely headed toward the exit, rebuking herself for wasting so much of her day on a whim. She could have spent a lazy morning catching up on some reading, paying bills or doing something far more productive than…

"Jess!"

At the sound of the familiar voice, her heart ratcheted into triple time and she froze. So he was here after all. She forced herself to take a deep, calming breath, then slowly turned. He was striding toward her, dressed in exactly the same manner as last week, the same notebook under his arm, his expression surprised—and delighted.

"I thought it was you." His eyes smiled warmly into hers before he broke contact to glance cautiously around. "Are you alone?"

She nodded, struggling to find her voice. "Yes."

His smile broadened. "Good."

She couldn't blame him for his reaction, not after

their last encounter in the gardens. "Listen…about last week…my father…"

He smiled gently. "It's okay, Jess. I understand how he feels about me. He has a right."

Does he? she suddenly wondered as she stared into Scott's kind eyes. *Was* it right to hate in the face of true remorse and regret? At some point didn't hate become more destructive to the hater than the person hated? Wasn't forgiveness a part of healing, as her brother had inferred? But she voiced none of those troubling questions, tucking them away in her mind for later consideration. "Well, it was rude nonetheless."

"I'm used to a lot worse."

The words were said matter-of-factly, but she saw the flash of pain in his eyes. Clearly, the horrors of prison life had left an indelible mark, though he didn't dwell on the subject.

"Now I'm going to steal your question," he continued with an engaging grin. "What are you doing here?"

"I, uh, had to stop at my office. To go over a presentation."

He gave her a puzzled look. "So how did you end up here?"

"I work here."

He looked surprised. "At the garden?"

"Yes. In public relations."

"No kidding! That's great!"

"I like it." She knew her responses sounded stilted, but she couldn't help it. That's how she felt. Stiff. And awkward. And uncomfortable. Especially knowing that she had engineered this "chance" meeting.

"So are you leaving now?"

She nodded. "I just stopped in for a few minutes."

"Can I buy you a cup of coffee first? The outdoor café would be great on a day like this."

Jess stared at him. A casual meeting, a few words exchanged in passing were one thing. Spending time with him seemed somehow…wrong. As if by doing so she would somehow dishonor the memory of Elizabeth and be disloyal to her parents. At the same time, she thought about Mark's advice. He had encouraged her to talk with Scott, suggested that the only way to truly let go of the past was to face it. And more and more lately, she had begun to admit that he might be right.

Scott waited patiently for Jess's response, struggling to maintain a placid expression even though his heart was hammering painfully in his chest. He knew he was pushing things with his invitation, but what did he have to lose? At worst, she would say no. At best…well, that remained to be seen. But even a few minutes in her company, in this neutral setting of natural beauty, was bound to do *some* good. It *had* to. He'd prayed for guidance, for opportunity and for the right words when the time came. The Lord had certainly provided the first two. Now Scott hoped that He would come through on the last, as well.

As Scott waited for Jess to reply he used the moment to simply drink in the sight of her. For three long years he had had nothing but dreams to sustain him. Dreams of her kindness, her beauty, her joy. Of the way her eyes had once shone with love when they gazed at him. Of his hope of winning her heart all over again. Those were the dreams he had clung to.

And now Jess stood only a whisper away, no longer a dream but flesh and blood. She was close, so close. And yet so far. Reachable but not touchable, though the urge to do so grew stronger with each encounter. But until he saw welcome and warmth in her eyes, rather than the caution and conflict now reflected in them as she pondered his invitation, he knew that patience—and prudence—were his friends. Whether he liked it or not.

As the seconds ticked by, Jess realized she had to make a decision. But for some reason her brain didn't seem to be functioning. Her *heart,* on the other hand, had kicked into overdrive, urging her to follow her brother's advice and talk with Scott. And as she gazed into his warm brown eyes, her doubts somehow melted away. After all, it was only a cup of coffee. What harm could it do? In fact, if her brother was right, some *good* might come of it.

With sudden decision, she nodded. "All right. I have time for a quick cup."

If it wouldn't have attracted so much attention, Scott would have fallen to his knees on the spot. As it was, he simply sent a silent, heartfelt thank-you heavenward. "Great! Why don't you pick out a table and I'll get the coffee?" he suggested, struggling to contain the elation in his voice.

"Okay. Just a little cream."

He smiled then, that lazy, smoky smile that had always turned her knees to rubber. "I remember," he said softly. Their gazes connected for a brief second before he turned away, but it was long enough for her to see the heat simmering in the depths of his eyes. "I'll meet you on the terrace," he said over his shoulder.

Jess stared after him, caught off guard by the intimate, husky timbre of his voice and the look in his eyes, which had opened a floodgate of memories. She had never been a morning person, and when they were first married Scott had gotten into the habit of rising first to make coffee. Then he'd bring her a cup in bed, slipping in beside her to sip his as she slowly woke up. And sometimes, especially in the cold days of winter when neither wanted to leave their warm cocoon, they'd snuggle back under the covers for a few stolen moments. So yes, Scott knew exactly how she liked her coffee. And other things, as well.

A surge of longing suddenly swept over Jess, so strong and so unexpected that she gasped, causing a passerby to pause and gaze at her in alarm.

"Are you all right, dear?" the older woman asked in concern.

Jess felt her face grow red, and she nodded jerkily. "Yes. I—I'm fine."

The woman didn't appear to be convinced. "Are you sure? Would you like to sit down?"

"No, really, I'm fine."

An older man came up beside the woman and glanced curiously at Jess. "What's wrong, Ellen?"

"I thought perhaps this young woman was ill."

By now they were drawing inquisitive glances from those seated nearby, and Jess felt her color deepen. "I appreciate your concern, but…"

"Is something wrong?"

Jess turned to find Scott gazing at her with a troubled look, but before she could speak the older woman chimed in.

"Oh, are you with this young man, dear? Well, Harry, she's in good hands. I'm sure he'll see to her if she isn't well. You take care, miss," she said over her shoulder as they headed toward an empty table.

Jess closed her eyes, wanting to drop through the floor in embarrassment. How in the world was she going to explain that exchange to Scott? she wondered desperately. There was no way on earth she could tell him the truth!

"Jess?"

She forced herself to open her eyes and meet Scott's gaze. He looked even more concerned now, and a slight frown marred his brow. "What was that all about? Are you sick?"

Jess swallowed. "No. I'm fine. Where would you like to sit?"

Scott ignored her question, titling his head to study her face. "You look a little flushed."

But not because I'm sick! she thought silently, glad that he couldn't read her mind. "I'm fine, really," she repeated more firmly. "How about that table over by the railing? We can see the roses from there."

He hesitated for a moment, then much to her relief let the subject drop. In fact, he seemed a little distracted himself—which was okay with her. "That's fine," he agreed.

Scott followed her to the small café table, still

berating himself for his response to her comment about the coffee. He'd have to be more guarded in the future. He needed to avoid topics that would make him recall the intimate details of their marriage. Because a few more slips like that and he could easily scare her off.

"The roses are great this year, aren't they? Does your father still have his rose garden?" he asked with studied casualness as he deposited the cups and his notebook on the table.

She nodded. "Bigger than ever. It's become almost an obsession since he retired two years ago. He's got a couple of bushes right now that he's hovering over like a mother hen, in preparation for a show in July. So much so that he threatened not to go with us on vacation next week."

"A family vacation?"

"Yes. To Padre Island."

"Sounds nice."

"We've been going there the last few years. Mom and Dad really like it." But she didn't want to talk about her parents. Knowing how they felt about Scott, she could imagine their reaction to this little tête-à-tête. So she changed the subject, pointing to his notebook. "What's that for?"

"Landscaping ideas. I've done a lot of reading about the subject in the last few years, and I've dabbled in design. The botanical garden always inspires me, so I try to drop by on Saturday mornings whenever I can."

She looked at him curiously. "I thought you'd lost interest in that sort of thing years ago."

"Not really. I just didn't have the time to devote

to it. However, time hasn't been a problem these past few years."

The final comment was made lightly, but Jess suspected that for a man like Scott, who had always filled every minute of his day with activity, time must have hung very heavily on his hands in prison. However, that was ground she didn't want to tread on. "So what are you working on now?" she asked.

He hesitated, then reached for the notebook and flipped through a number of detailed drawings, stopping at one that was only partially finished. He handed it to her.

"That one's actually going to see the light of day," he said. "My boss has asked me to work with one of our customers to design this garden."

Jess glanced at him in surprise. There was an undercurrent of pride and excitement in his voice, a boyish enthusiasm, that she hadn't heard in many, many years. As if he truly loved what he was doing.

With interest she studied the detailed layout, drawn precisely on graph paper. It was a woodland cluster of plantings, with several dogwood trees as anchors. The design was pleasant to the eye and very natural looking, though the plotting of the plants and the groupings of perennials had clearly been carefully thought through.

"Very nice. May I?" she asked, nodding toward the notebook.

"Yes. But the designs are pretty rough. This kind of work is mostly done by computer these days, but I…well, I used what I had."

Jess looked again at the meticulous workmanship

and shook her head. "I wouldn't exactly call these rough," she disagreed. Each one had clearly been done with great care, and all were appealing. But the one she lingered over longest was a lakeside garden featuring a gazebo. There was something about it, some quality of tranquillity, that touched her soul. "This is lovely," she said softly.

Scott leaned over to see which drawing had caught Jess's eye. "As a matter of fact, that's the only design in the book that has actually been produced," he said, pleased she had singled it out. "It's for a meditation garden at my church."

Jess looked over at him. "You mean this garden really exists?"

"Yes."

She glanced down again, impressed by his talent, touched by a beauty that the black-and-white pencil drawing could only hint at. "I think you may have found your true calling, Scott," she said as she closed the notebook and handed it back to him.

"I think you may be right," he concurred with a satisfied nod. Then he set the notebook aside and smiled at her. "So now tell me about you. How did you end up here?"

She took a sip of her coffee and shrugged. "After… the accident I needed something to do. I volunteered here for a few months, and when the job became available, they offered it to me. It was a perfect fit with my public relations background, and they already knew me from volunteering. I've been here for almost two years."

"Do you like it?"

"Very much. It's pleasant work in a beautiful setting. And it keeps me busy, which is good. Also, since I sold the house I haven't had much opportunity to garden, and being in a place like this helps make up for that."

"Knowing how much you enjoyed working with flowers, I was a little surprised to find you'd moved to a condo," he admitted.

She took a sip of her coffee, gazing at him over the rim of her cup as she tried to discern whether he was upset that she'd sold the "trophy" house he'd once taken such great pride in. But he didn't appear to be disturbed. Just curious. She set the cup on the table and shrugged. "The house was too big just for me. Besides, I didn't feel capable of tackling the upkeep single-handedly. But I do miss having a yard, so I may get another house at some point. I don't know. I just sort of take it a day at a time for now."

He studied her silently for a moment, then sighed and glanced down at his coffee. "I can relate to that. Sometimes that's the only way to survive." When he looked at her again, his eyes were troubled. "Your parents watched out for you after the accident, didn't they?"

Though his tone was quiet, the intensity in his eyes told her clearly that this worry had been on his mind for a long time. She swallowed with difficulty, touched by the depth of his concern in a way she couldn't articulate, then averted her head and looked toward the rose garden. Dear God, yes, she had been alone—and lonely—despite her parents' best efforts to fill the gaps, she recalled, her throat tightening with emotion. Nevertheless, their love had made a huge difference. In fact, it was only because of them that she had survived.

She drew an unsteady breath, fighting for control, but when she spoke there was a catch in her voice. "They saved my life," she said simply, without looking back at him.

As Scott gazed at her stoic profile, his gut clenched painfully. Night after night in prison he'd lain awake staring into the darkness, praying that God would watch over her and keep her safe, that He would ease her pain. Jess had always been a strong woman. But when he'd seen her at the funeral, he'd known she was balancing precariously on the edge of an emotional breakdown. That only the support of her family, and God's grace, would keep her from falling into the abyss of despair and depression that had already sucked him in.

Clearly, she'd survived and gone on with her life, though it was equally clear that she'd been through hell in the interim. And the ordeal had obviously taken a lasting toll on her, he realized, noting the way her slender fingers were gripping the paper cup, so tightly that the shape was distorted. He longed to reach over and take her hand in a comforting clasp, to promise her that she'd never have to face such trauma alone again. But it was too soon. He knew that intuitively. He had to keep his distance. Physically, at least. But maybe he could put out some feelers on the emotional front.

"How are you *now,* Jess?" he asked gently.

She didn't turn back to him immediately. And when she did, she met his gaze directly with eyes that were dry—and slightly defiant. "I'm fine, Scott," she said as steadily, as convincingly, as she could. She forced herself to hold his gaze for a long moment, hoping he would buy her response—even though she herself was beginning to realize that it was a lie.

Scott didn't dispute her claim. But he didn't believe it, either. She was too fragile emotionally. Too thin physically. And too lost spiritually. She needed him as much as he needed her. But convincing her of that would take time. And he'd gone about as far as was prudent today. Reluctantly he took the last swallow of his coffee and reached for his notebook. "I'm glad things are going well for you, Jess. And it was good to see you today."

She looked at him in surprise, taken aback. He'd seemed so anxious to see her, to talk with her. So why was he was cutting their exchange short? But on the heels of that question came another, more disturbing one. Why should she care? And the answer was clear. She shouldn't. The fact that she *did* only made her angry. Letting Scott back into her life would just set her up for disappointments, she reminded herself. And she'd had enough of those. Abruptly she reached for her purse and stood.

"Thanks for the coffee," she said shortly.

If Scott noticed her change in tone, he gave no indication of it. "My pleasure," he replied, rising in a more leisurely way. "Can I walk you to your car?"

"It's not far."

"I don't mind."

She shrugged. It wasn't worth arguing about. "If you like."

They made their way silently through the main
exhibit building, and by the time they exited a light rain
had begun to fall. She glanced at the sky with a frown,
pausing under the overhang from the building. "You'll
get wet if you walk me to my car," she said. "Why
don't we just say goodbye here?"

"I'll get wet either way. It doesn't matter," he replied
as he withdrew a plastic bag from his pocket and
slipped his sketchbook inside.

"But if we each make a dash for our cars we'll only
get slightly damp," she persisted.

"I took the bus here, Jess," he said matter-of-factly.
"So where are you parked?"

She stared at him. Scott had taken a *bus?* He'd never
taken a bus in his life—except maybe in college. Certainly not since she'd known him. Why in the world
would he be doing so now?

"You took a bus?" she repeated in confusion.

"Yes."

"Why?"

"I don't have a car yet."

"Why not?"

He gave her a crooked grin. "Because car dealers
don't sell cars based on good looks. Although I'm not
sure that would necessarily help me even if they did."

Again she stared at him. Frankly, she had never even
thought about Scott's financial situation. Of course,
she knew he'd signed over his interest in all their assets
to her after the trial. Not that she'd asked him to. Or
cared one way or the other. At the time finances were
the last thing on her mind. She'd simply told her

attorney to deal with it and asked no questions. For the first six months she'd simply drawn on her accounts for day-to-day living expenses and counseling. And by the time she was able to take more control over her finances, she simply started from where she was. Her attorney was a trusted family friend with an impeccable reputation, and she'd never doubted his diligent management of her assets. But all along Jess had just assumed that Scott had kept *something* in reserve for himself. A cash account somewhere. Had she been wrong?

"I don't understand," she said, still confused. "Don't you have any money?"

He gave her an easy smile. "Sure. I have a decent job. Seth pays a good wage."

"No, I mean from before."

Now his face grew serious. "Didn't your attorney tell you? I turned everything over to you."

"I knew about the major assets, of course, but I...I guess I just assumed you kept something in reserve for...for when you got out," she replied, growing more and more flustered.

He shook his head. "I wanted you to have everything."

"But that isn't really fair. I mean, I have way more than I need."

"It's fair, Jess. Trust me." His gaze locked with hers, and she knew that this was one subject that was not open to discussion. "So do you want to make a run for it?"

She looked at the rain, which had intensified even

as they spoke. Scott would be drenched in a matter of minutes if he had to wait for a bus.

"Why don't you let me drive you home?" she said impulsively.

Scott looked as surprised by the offer as she felt.

"Are you sure?" he said cautiously.

No, she wasn't. In fact, she wasn't sure about a lot of things lately. But ignoring the issues wasn't going to make them go away. Just as avoiding Scott wasn't going to help her resolve her feelings about him.

"Honestly? No. It just…came out," she replied truthfully.

A shadow of disappointment briefly passed over his eyes, but he recovered quickly. "It's okay. I have to make a quick stop on the way home, anyway. It's better if I just take the bus. But thank you. Now, where's your car? I'll still walk with you that far."

She nodded to the right, and he fell in beside her as they rapidly crossed the asphalt. By the time they reached the door she had her key in hand, and she quickly fitted it into the lock and slid inside. She looked up at him to say goodbye, but the words died in her throat as she noted the rain already soaking through his cotton shirt, the lines of weariness in his face, the kindness in his eyes. And when she finally opened her mouth, entirely different words came out.

"I don't mind making a stop, Scott. Get in before you're soaked."

This time he didn't question her motives. After only the slightest hesitation, he simply closed her door and made his way around to the passenger side.

And as she reached over to unlock the door for him, Jess couldn't help but feel that she was opening the door to far more than her car.

Chapter Seven

Scott's physical presence somehow seemed magnified in the confines of Jess's compact car, and she nervously tucked her hair behind her ear before backing out of the parking spot. Somehow sharing her car with him seemed to move their relationship to a new, more personal level.

The significance of the moment wasn't lost on Scott, either. In the three and a half months since his release, his encounters with Jess had always been in public places where other people could see what they were doing and hear what they were saying. By contrast, the intimacy of her car gave them a degree of privacy they hadn't had in almost four years, providing an opportunity to talk about things best discussed behind closed doors. Considering her almost palpable tension, Jess was keenly aware of that, he surmised. She was probably having not just *second* thoughts about her offer of a ride, but third and fourth thoughts. So he needed to put her at ease, assure her he wasn't going to use the situation to introduce topics with which she was not yet comfortable.

"Nice car," he said, deliberately adopting an even, conversational tone. "And it sure beats the bus. Thanks again for the lift."

"No problem." Her voice sounded strained, and she lapsed into silence until they reached the parking-lot exit. "Which way?"

"Left. Then left again at the first light. There's a grocery store a few blocks down. That's where I need to stop."

She turned to him in surprise. "You're going grocery shopping?"

He smiled. "No. I just need to pick up a couple of things for someone."

As they drove the short distance, Scott purposely kept the conversation light. And by the time they pulled into the lot a few minutes later, she seemed to have relaxed slightly.

"Do you want to come in?" he asked.

She shook her head. "I'll wait."

"Okay. I'll only be a few minutes." He stepped out of the car, then leaned back down. "But lock the doors. This isn't the best part of town."

"I work down here, remember?" she reminded him wryly.

"I'll bet you never wander more than a block or two from the garden."

She conceded the point with a nod. "True."

"Good. Keep it that way, okay?" When her eyes widened in surprise, he grinned sheepishly. "Sorry. Some old habits die hard, I guess. I'll be right back." He locked the door before pushing it closed.

Jess watched him until he disappeared inside the

building, then slowly exhaled. She needed a few minute to decompress, to figure out what had happened back in the parking lot at the botanical garden. Because she'd certainly had no intention of offering Scott a ride. Not even *once*, let alone *twice*. Yet she hadn't taken him up on the out he'd offered. Why? There was no logical explanation for her behavior—except maybe that she was off balance because of all the strange things that had happened today, she reasoned, ticking them off in her mind.

First, Scott's invitation to stop at the café had come out of the blue. Given her reservations about merely exchanging a few words in passing, her acceptance made no sense.

Second, the unexpected eruption of intense longing in response to his comment about coffee had left her reeling. Despite the other problems in their marriage, the attraction between them had never diminished, she recalled, her mouth suddenly going dry. At least in that one respect, their marriage had been solid. But how could he still produce that kind of effect in her with just one intimate look and two simple words, when she'd spent the past four years hating him? That made even less sense.

Third, his abrupt ending to their impromptu coffee klatch had disconcerted her. Especially since he'd gone out of his way to look her up, making it clear that he wanted to talk with her, spend time with her. The fact that he'd cut their conversation short didn't make sense, either.

And finally, her impulsive offer of a lift had *especially* not made sense.

Then again, not much in her life *had* made sense these past few weeks, she acknowledged with a sigh. Feelings she thought she'd sorted out long ago had bubbled to the surface. Especially her feelings about Scott. With each encounter, she became less able to sustain the hate that her father, particularly, still harbored—and encouraged. She understood her parents' feelings, of course. Had shared them until recently. In fact, in many ways hate made life easier. Fix the blame, condemn and walk away unblemished. It was much neater than sorting through messy shades of gray. But in reality, most situations just weren't that simple. Particularly this one, Jess was beginning to realize.

She let her head drop back and wearily closed her eyes. Since Elizabeth's death, fatigue had been her constant companion. Hate might make life easier by dulling the pain of grief, but maintaining such a draining and nonproductive emotion took a lot of energy. Especially now. It had been much easier to despise Scott when he was far removed and locked behind bars. It was a whole lot harder when he stood inches away and she saw nothing but kindness reflected in his eyes. Her resolve to keep him at arm's length was definitely wavering, she acknowledged. But was it because giving Scott a hearing was the right thing to do, as Mark had suggested—or because she was simply too tired to fight his clear, if unspoken, determination to once more be a part of her life?

Jess didn't know. And there was no one she could turn to for advice. Her parents were too biased against Scott to view the situation impartially. Mark was too much of an advocate on the other side. Which left her stuck in the middle. And directionless.

There was a time, of course, when she could have turned to Someone else for guidance, she reflected sadly. But that had been years ago, when God's presence had been a real part of her life. The connection between them had been broken long ago, and restoring it seemed an impossible task at this point. She didn't even know where to start. And until she did, she was on her own, with nothing to guide her but her instincts. Which she didn't have a whole lot of faith in, considering where they had led her today, she acknowledged ruefully.

A sudden knock on the passenger window brought her abruptly back to reality, and her head snapped up. She reached to unlock the door for Scott, leaning over even farther to push it open when she saw that he was juggling a small bakery box and a bouquet of flowers.

"Sorry. Were you sleeping?" he asked as he slid inside.

His shirt was damp, and she wondered how long he'd stood in the rain debating whether or not to disturb her. "No. Just resting."

"Long week?"

"Busy," she amended.

He gazed at her, noting that the shadows under her eyes seemed even deeper than when he'd first seen her weeks before. "You look tired, Jess," he said gently. "Are you sleeping okay?"

She gave him a startled look, and her eyes shuttered slightly. *Too personal,* Scott chided himself. *Back off.* "Sorry. None of my business."

She reached forward and turned on the motor, ignoring his comment. "Pretty flowers," she said as she looked over her shoulder and began backing out of the parking space.

"Yeah. I think she'll like them."

Jess's foot slipped off the brake and she almost ran into the car next to her.

"Careful!" he warned in alarm. "You're pretty close on this side. It's a tight spot. Just ease back and I'll let you know when you're clear."

Jess forced herself to concentrate on the task at hand. She didn't speak again until she was safely heading for the exit, and then she chose her words carefully, fishing but trying not to be obvious about it. "Looks like you're going to a party," she remarked, nodding toward the box in which a small cake was revealed beneath a clear window.

"Hardly. The cake and flowers are for an old woman in my apartment building. Take a right," he instructed as she reached the exit, then waited until she was safely in traffic before continuing. "I found her crying this morning on the stoop. It's her birthday, and apparently there's no one left who remembers. Her husband died years ago, and she hasn't heard from her son in a long time. So I thought I'd surprise her with flowers and share a piece of cake with her. It's not much, and it won't make up for her being alone, but maybe it will brighten her day for a few minutes at least. Take a left."

Jess did as instructed, still processing the information Scott had just relayed. Though his tone had been low-key and matter-of-fact, his kindness was anything but, she conceded. He'd gone out of his way to remember a lonely old woman's birthday, spending money he obviously couldn't spare to give her a few moments of happiness. To let her know that someone cared.

Jess wasn't exactly surprised by Scott's thoughtfulness and generosity. He had always lavished gifts on her and Elizabeth—especially as the demands of his job left him unable to give them what they really wanted: his time. But his gifts had been well within their budget, given out of their excess. This gesture, on the other hand, was a gift out of his need. A living illustration of the widow's mite, Jess realized, deeply touched. Even more remarkable, it was for a woman who was practically a stranger, whose life had no connection to his beyond simple human compassion.

"This is it, the red one," he said, interrupting her thoughts.

Jess hadn't been paying much attention to her surroundings during the short drive to his apartment, but now she took a good look as she pulled up to the curb. And that's when she realized just how deep Scott's need was. The neighborhood he called home was not one she would feel comfortable in at high noon, let alone after dark. There was an abandoned building on the corner, and the apartments were housed in four-family flats that looked as if they'd been built at the turn of the century—and hadn't been updated since. Litter was strewn about on an abandoned lot across the street, and the lawn of the redbrick flat Scott occupied had more bare patches than grass. "Seedy" was the best way to describe the setting. "Dangerous" was a close second.

Jess stared at the neighborhood, appalled. This wasn't Scott. Not the Scott she'd married, whose wants were simple but who worked hard to provide his family with a decent standard of living. And certainly not the Scott who'd gone to prison, who had valued designer jeans and fine wines. Dear God, how could he live in these conditions? She turned to him in dismay, speechless, her shock clearly reflected in her eyes.

As their gazes met, Scott was instantly sorry he'd taken Jess up on her offer of a ride. The opportunity to spend additional time in her company—at *her* request—had simply been too tempting to refuse. But he should have anticipated her reaction. Should have known that it would be very similar to Karen's. His sister was *still* on him about the apartment, urging him to find other lodging. Offering to send him money. But as he kept telling her, it was good enough for now. In time, when he could afford it, he'd move. Until then, he'd sit tight and make the best of it. But Jess didn't need to hang around in a place like this, he decided, reaching for the door.

"Thanks again for the lift. And have a great time in Texas." He had already opened the door when her voice stopped him.

"Scott, wait. I…I didn't know that you…this is…" She glanced again at the shabby surroundings and her voice died.

"Serviceable," he supplied evenly.

"Awful," she corrected him vehemently, the revulsion in her eyes clear.

"It beats a cell, Jess," he said quietly.

The comment jolted her, and she stared at him in stunned silence as their gazes connected and held. For the first time she had a sense at some primal level of the horror of incarceration. Of being in a place where you had no control over your existence, where you were told what to do and when to do it, where doors clanged shut behind you every night, leaving you to face your private demons alone in the darkness of a cold, sterile cell. Suddenly she understood how, in light of that existence, this squalid apartment would be an improvement. And all at once, a place in her heart that had long been numb and lifeless began to stir.

Her throat constricted with emotion and she swallowed with difficulty. "Scott, I had no idea. I'm…" She stopped abruptly, realizing in confusion that she'd almost said, "I'm sorry." But why was she sorry? Hadn't she believed all along that no punishment was too severe for what he'd done to Elizabeth?

Scott saw the parade of emotions pass across Jess's eyes. Compassion. Sympathy. Confusion. But no coldness. Or hate. Not this time. Which was progress as far as he was concerned. And so was her shock at his living conditions, he suddenly realized. After all, if she didn't have *some* feelings for him, she wouldn't care where he lived—would she?

"It's okay, Jess," he said with a gentle smile, his heart suddenly lighter. "I'm fine here. Really. I'm free. And I'm a person again, not a number. That makes any place seem like a palace. Trust me."

Jess didn't trust anything at the moment. Particularly

her emotions. She had a sudden, desperate need to get away from here, to think this through alone, with no distractions. Especially the one sitting next to her.

"I have to go," she said in a choked voice, struggling to hold her tattered emotions together.

He studied her for a moment, his gaze penetrating and probing, and then he nodded. "I understand." Without further delay, he opened the door and stepped outside. "Thanks again, Jess. Take care."

She had no voice left to respond. She simply put the car in gear and drove away as quickly as she could, her stomach churning. But as she turned the corner, she couldn't resist the urge to look back. Scott was still standing where she had left him, watching her car disappear, holding the cake and flowers that would brighten an old woman's day. A ragged sob rose in her throat, and she had to blink rapidly to clear the sudden tears that blurred her vision. This was *not* the outcome she had expected from her encounter with Scott. Instead of helping her sort through her emotions, it had left her more confused than ever—and certain of only two things.

First, Scott *did* understand. Far too much. She'd seen it in his eyes. And that disturbed her greatly.

But even more disturbing was the fact that it had taken every ounce of her willpower to drive away and leave him alone in that dismal place.

"Now, that's what I call the life of Riley."

At her brother's teasing voice, Jess's eyes flew open. "Mark! You made it!" she said in delight, scrambling to her feet to throw her arms around him.

He returned the bear hug, then, still holding her hands, backed off slightly to look her over. "Well, I have to say the Texas sun seems to be good for you."

"Lying around on a beach being lazy in a gorgeous place like Padre Island would be good for anyone. How long can you stay?"

"Just until Wednesday. I barely got away as it is. It was touch and go up until the last minute."

Jess wrinkled her nose. "Three days isn't long enough to relax."

"Tell that to my boss."

"You work too hard, Mark."

"I like what I do."

"You need time for other things."

"Such as?"

"Family."

"I'm here, aren't I?" he said, spreading out a towel on the sand, then flopping down. "I always make it for at least a couple days of the annual family vacation. Speaking of which—remember all those trips we took in the camper?" he said with a chuckle.

"And all the times we put it up in the rain," she replied, smiling ruefully as she sat on her towel and wrapped her arms around her knees.

"Yeah. Listen, don't tell Dad, but I much prefer the condo," Mark admitted with a grin as he adjusted his sunglasses.

"I agree. Anyway, don't try to change the subject. You need time in your life for other things beside work."

"Like what?"

"A wife might be nice."

"There's plenty of time," he said nonchalantly. "Besides, I didn't come out here to talk about me. I want to hear all about you. And Scott. Mom doesn't seem to know anything, and you aren't exactly forthcoming on the phone."

Jess shrugged. "There's not much to tell."

He studied her for a moment, then shook his head. "Sorry. Don't buy it. We lived in the same house for more than twenty years. I can read you like a book."

"Baloney," she retorted, stretching out on the towel.

"Uh-uh," he said, leaning over to tickle the bottom of her foot. "You aren't getting off that easily."

"Stop that!" she said, swatting at him.

"Nope. Not till I get the truth."

She sat back up and crossed her legs. "How old did you say you were?" she demanded, trying to look stern.

"Thirty-one. Going on ten," he replied with an impudent grin.

"I believe it."

"So let's have the scoop on Scott. Have you taken my advice yet?"

"What makes you think I will?" she hedged.

"You'll bow to my superior wisdom in time," he said loftily, but the twinkle in his eyes belied his tone.

"You know, I think I'm beginning to understand why you're not married," she said sweetly, making a face at him.

"Hey! Let's not get personal!"

"I agree. Let's not." She lay back down and settled her sunglasses on her nose.

He gave her a moment's peace before trying a different tack. "Okay, fine. Have it your way. But how often do you get such a willing ear? Here I am, ready to put all my Listening 101 skills into action, and you're shutting me out."

She lifted her glasses and looked at him. "You aren't going to give up, are you?"

"Nope."

With a resigned sigh she sat up again. "So what do you want to know?"

"Everything."

"Let's not get too ambitious."

"Okay, okay. At least tell me if you've talked with him."

She eyed him warily. "First, a ground rule. This conversation stays between us. Agreed?"

"Sure."

She took a deep breath. "Yes, I've talked to him. Not about anything too serious. But our paths have crossed on a number of occasions—which Mom and Dad do not know about, by the way—and we've exchanged a few words. I also gave him a ride once. Now you have the whole story."

"How is he?"

Jess frowned. "He looks older. But he seems to have found…I don't know how to describe it, exactly. An inner peace, maybe. I do know that he's close friends with a local minister who's also one of the prison chaplains. He seems to have found a lot of comfort in his faith."

Mark's face registered surprise. "Really? I never thought Scott was all that religious. I mean, I know he went to church and lived a good life, but I never got the sense that he had a deep spiritual life."

"He seems to now."

"That's kind of ironic, isn't it?" Mark reflected. "In the midst of tragedy you lost God, and Scott found Him. Strange how life works. So how do you feel about this whole situation?"

"Honestly? Scared."

"I think that's probably normal."

Jess gazed out over the shimmering blue water. "I'm not sure I know what that word means anymore," she said wearily.

"I can tell you what it doesn't mean," Mark replied. "It doesn't mean keeping your feelings bottled inside. It doesn't mean ignoring issues. It doesn't mean pretending that everything's all right when it's not."

"You think that's what I've been doing?"

"I'd put money on it. How are you feeling about Scott these days?"

"Confused."

"Do you still hate him?"

"I keep trying to. But it…it gets harder and harder. Yet it seems somehow wrong to have anything to do with him. As if I'm…I don't know…dishonoring the memory of Elizabeth in some way."

"Maybe the best way to honor her memory is with joy and forgiveness, not bitterness and hate," Mark said quietly. "Scott loved her, Jess. Yet because of him, she died. He has to live with that every day of his life. Think of the pain and suffering he's already endured. What will it serve to add to that?"

"But I can't forget what happened, Mark."

"We don't have to forget in order to forgive."

"You make it sound simple."

"Hardly. But you'll find some good guidelines in that Bible peeking out of your beach bag. Try Ephesians, chapter four, verses thirty-one and thirty-two."

A flush rose on her cheeks, and she reached over and tucked the Bible out of sight. "I haven't opened it in years. I'm not even sure why I brought it with me," she said dismissively.

"Personally, I think it was a good idea. Try Colossians, too. Chapter three, verses twelve through fourteen."

She stared at him. "Since when have you become such a Bible scholar?"

He shrugged. "Let's just say that I've been on my own journey. And I want you to know that…" He shifted uncomfortably. "Well, along the way I've been praying for you and Scott."

Her throat constricted with emotion at this rare display of what her brother usually called "mushy stuff." "Thanks, Mark."

"Hey, what are brothers for?" he said with a grin as he stretched out on his towel, once more his irreverent self. "Call me for advice anytime."

"Let all bitterness, and wrath, and indignation, and clamor, and reviling, be removed from you, along with all malice. On the contrary, be kind to one another, and merciful, generously forgiving one another, as also God in Christ has generously forgiven you."

Jess read the words twice, then turned to the second passage her brother had suggested.

"Put on therefore, as God's chosen ones, holy and beloved, a heart of mercy, kindness, humility, meekness, patience. Bear with one another and forgive one another, if anyone has a grievance against any other; even as the Lord has forgiven you, so also do you forgive. But above all these things have love, which is the bond of perfection."

Slowly she closed the book and lay back on her pillow. She'd spoken truthfully to Mark when she'd said she had no idea why she'd brought her Bible on vacation. Especially since she hadn't opened it in almost four years. It had been a last-minute addition to her luggage, and she hadn't looked at it all week. But something had compelled her to include it.

No, that wasn't entirely true, she acknowledged. It wasn't some*thing,* but some*one.* Namely, Scott. He seemed to have found his way through the labyrinth of pain and grief of the past few years far better than she had. She could see reflected in his eyes the very things her soul desperately longed for. Acceptance of what life had dealt him. Understanding that gave clarity to chaos. A clear and confident sense of direction and destination. A perspective that tempered sadness with trust. He was clearly a man who had made his peace with himself and with his God and, in so doing, had found hope for tomorrow. And the Bible had apparently played a key role in his journey. Because that's where Scott seemed to go for comfort and guidance.

But he didn't just read the Bible. He clearly had an ongoing dialogue with the Lord, Jess acknowledged.

His words to God in the cemetery had been a relaxed conversation rather than a stilted, formal prayer, suggesting that he was accustomed to speaking to the Lord on a very personal level. Even when Jess had considered her faith to be at its strongest, she'd never reached the spiritual depth, the personal relationship with God, that Scott now seemed to enjoy.

Because of that relationship, she had a feeling that although he was probably as lonely as she was in many ways, he never felt truly alone. And she envied him that. Even the love of her parents hadn't been able to assuage the terrible, desolate sense of aloneness that had darkened her days for the past four years. Something was missing from her life, something more than her beloved Elizabeth or the husband she had once adored. The loss was even more profound than that, and she felt it at the very depths of her soul. It was a sense of isolation—and separation—from the one unchanging reality of life. From God.

Her throat constricted with emotion, and Jess closed her eyes. Mark had been right earlier in the day when he'd noted the irony that Scott, the less "religious" of the two, had found his way out of the maze of despair through faith, while Jess stumbled around in darkness, her bitterness toward God and her husband twisting her heart with a malignant anger. Scott had resolved his issues, while Jess's had simply festered. And he'd done it with the help of the God Jess had turned her back on. The God she had railed against in pain and anguish for taking her beloved daughter. The God she had abandoned as uncaring and unfair. Yet in his need, Scott had found in that very same God a loving, forgiving Father who stretched out His hand to those who called upon Him for help.

Jess knew that her rejection of the Lord had been motivated by anger and an inability to comprehend how a good and loving God could allow such tragic events to occur. She'd tortured herself over and over again asking "why?" and seeking answers where there were none. But as was slowly becoming clear to her, discerning the purposes of the Lord was a task far beyond the limited powers of the human intellect. After all, the Lord never called on us to understand His ways—just to accept them. And to trust in His abiding love.

That's what Scott had done. What Jess *needed* to do. Because she now realized that until she, too, found her way back to the Lord, she would never achieve the peace, and the healing, that Scott had found.

At the same time, she knew that it wouldn't be easy. Because the Bible verses Mark had recommended made it clear that though God was always ready to forgive us, He expected us to follow His example. Meaning that if Jess truly wanted to find her way back to the Lord, she needed to forgive, as well. And she would need a lot of help with that, she acknowledged. She needed God. But how did one begin to rebuild a relationship with the Almighty?

Jess turned back to the Bible and idly let it fall open. The words from James that met her eyes provided the answer to her question so clearly that for a moment she simply sat there in stunned silence.

"Draw near to God and He will draw near to you."

It sounded so easy, she thought. And perhaps it was. Perhaps it was as simple as what Scott had done in the cemetery, when he'd simply talked with the Lord. It was certainly worth a try. Jess drew in a steadying breath, then let her eyelids drift closed. And though she felt as tentative and awkward as a baby taking its first steps, she began to speak haltingly in the silence of her heart.

Dear Lord, I know that I've been away from You for…well, for too long. I don't know how to find my way back…only that I need to, because my soul is hungry for the peace that I see in Scott's eyes, a peace that I now know only comes from You. He's changed so much, Lord. For the better. And I believe with all my heart that it's because he found his way back to You. I'd like to do the same. I ask for Your help and Your grace, and for Your loving hand to guide me in right paths as I begin this journey. Most of all, I ask Your forgiveness for turning away from You in bitterness and anger. And I ask You to help me find in my heart the forgiveness that You so generously offer to all who seek it from You— and without which true healing can never occur.

When she finished her prayer, Jess drew a long, shaky breath. She knew that there was much more she could say. More that she could confess. More that she could ask. But this was a start.

Jess hadn't expected any immediate guidance. And none was forthcoming. Yet she no longer felt quite so alone. Because although the Lord's voice was quiet at the moment, she sensed that He was listening.

And she would do the same.

Chapter Eight

"Are you sure about driving me home, Dad? I can just stay in the cab and save you a trip."

"Don't even think about it, dear," said Clare. "Your father doesn't mind giving you a lift. We'll just transfer your luggage to our car."

"Welcome home, Clare, Frank. Hello, Jess. Did you have a good time?"

Frank paid the cabdriver, then turned to greet his neighbor. "Hello, David. Padre Island is always great. Everything okay here?"

"Just fine now, but we had a bad storm the day after you left. Saturday afternoon. Blew in here with a vengeance. We lost power for fourteen hours, and there were trees down all over the place."

Frank frowned, then turned to Clare and Jess. "I'll get the luggage in a minute. I better go check the roses."

"They're fine," David assured him. "They took a beating, but a nice young man came by bright and early

Sunday morning and cleaned everything up. You'd hardly know there was even a storm."

Frank's frown deepened. "Who was it?"

"Can't say I've ever seen him before," David replied. "Of course, Marge and I have only lived here a couple of years, but he said he'd known you for a long time. When I asked his name, he just smiled and said he was a Good Samaritan. I kind of got the impression that he'd just as soon have done his good deed and gone on his way without being noticed. But I figured you'd want to know."

Jess stared at the man as a suspicion began to niggle at her brain. Could *Scott* have been the Good Samaritan? Knowing how much her father's roses meant to him, and despite his less-than-kind treatment at the garden, had Scott nonetheless stepped in to help?

"What did he look like, David?" Frank asked.

"Tall. Good shape. Dark hair. A little silver at the temples, now that I think about it. So maybe he wasn't quite so young after all."

Jess's suspicion changed to certainty.

"I'll bring your mail over a little later," David continued. "Now I'll leave you folks alone to unpack and get settled."

"Isn't that odd, Frank?" Clare gave her husband a puzzled look as their neighbor strolled back to his house. "Who on earth would have done such a thing?"

Jess drew a deep, steadying breath. "It was Scott."

As she had expected, both heads swiveled in her direction and her parents stared at her in shocked silence for several long moments. Finally her father found his voice.

"What makes you say that?" There was a note of caution—and distance—in his tone.

Jess swallowed and nervously tucked her hair behind her ear. "I think maybe we better go inside so I can explain."

Frank nodded curtly and reached for two suitcases. "Good idea. No sense airing family business in public. If you ladies can get those carry-ons, we should be able to do this in one trip."

Once inside, Frank wasted no time getting back to the matter at hand. He dropped the bags in the living room, then turned to his daughter. "Okay, Jess. What do you know about this?"

"Why don't we sit down?" she suggested, her heart thumping painfully in her chest. She should have known that eventually her parents would find out that she had talked with Scott. It had been silly to keep it a secret. And it made things very awkward now.

"I don't feel like sitting," Frank replied, propping his fists on his hips. "You've been seeing him, haven't you?" he said accusatorily.

Clare stared at her daughter. "Is that true, Jess?"

Jess took a deep breath. "Not exactly. But our paths have crossed by chance on several occasions and…" A skeptical snort from her father made her voice falter.

"Frank, let Jess tell us the story," Clare admonished him before sitting down across from her daughter. "Go on, honey."

"Our meetings *were* by chance," Jess repeated more forcefully. "He works for a landscaping company, and I happened to be passing two of the job sites he was assigned to. I also ran into him at the cemetery on Elizabeth's birthday. And I saw him one day at the garden."

"I didn't know you still went to the cemetery," Clare said gently.

Frank brushed past that. "Do you mean you saw him at the garden other than the time we all ran into him?"

"Yes. About a week later. He asked about your roses, and I told him that you'd gotten into them in a big way. How you enter shows and everything. I also mentioned that we were leaving on vacation, so I guess he put two and two together, figured we were gone and decided to come over and attend to the roses after the storm. Which probably took a lot of effort, because he doesn't have a car. He must have taken the bus."

Frank frowned. "How do you know he doesn't have a car?"

"He told me. The day I ran into him at the garden." She frowned. "Dad, did you know that Scott turned everything over to me when he went to prison? Every dime?"

"Yes. It was the least he could do after ruining your life," Frank replied coldly. "We discussed it at the time."

Twin furrows creased Jess's brow. "I guess I didn't pay much attention. Money was the last thing on my mind. I always just assumed he kept *something* in reserve for when he got out. But he didn't. You should see how he lives."

Frank's frown of disapproval deepened. "How do you know how he lives?"

Jess felt hot color creep up her neck. She was getting in deeper and deeper. "I...I gave him a ride home from the garden. It was raining." She turned to her mother, hoping for an ally. "Mom, it's a terrible neighborhood. Run-down and dangerous looking."

Clare shook her head. "I don't know what to say, Jess," she replied helplessly. "I thought you hated Scott. But now…well, your attitude seems almost…sympathetic."

"Frankly, I don't know how I feel anymore," she admitted with a sigh. "He's changed so much. For the better. I can see it in his eyes. There's a remarkable humbleness and peace about him. And kindness. Look what he just did for you, Dad."

"He probably had an ulterior motive," her father replied brusquely. "Maybe he thought it was a way to get to *you*."

"That's a pretty cynical attitude."

"I'd call it cautious," he countered stubbornly. "Why else would he do me a favor, except to build up brownie points with you? I've made it pretty clear to him how I feel. So have you—at least, until recently. So what's his motivation?"

Love. He's doing it because he still loves me.

The thought came unbidden, and left Jess momentarily stunned—and speechless.

Suddenly Frank's eyes narrowed. "You know, if his living conditions are as bad as you say, maybe he's having second thoughts about turning all his assets over to you. Maybe he's after money."

The comment jolted Jess back to reality and she stared at him, appalled. "That's a terrible thing to say, Dad!"

"I wouldn't put it past him," he persisted, his voice laced with derision.

"But how can you think that?" Jess demanded in

dismay. "Scott made some bad *mistakes,* but he was never a bad *man.* Or mercenary. Or dishonest."

Her father's eyes grew cold. "No. He was just a murderer."

The bitterness in her father's voice was so venomous that Jess actually flinched. She knew her father hated Scott. But surely his hatred hadn't always been this virulent. Or had she simply been so caught up in her own pain that she'd never fully grasped the intensity of his feelings?

"Frank...those are pretty harsh words," Clare said in gentle reproach.

He turned to her. "Are you getting soft, too? That man killed your granddaughter, for God's sake! And almost ruined your daughter's life."

Clare flushed. "I know. But...well, he didn't do it on purpose, Frank. And he did go to prison."

"I suppose that makes up for everything," he replied sarcastically.

"No. But what would?"

Her mother's quiet, insightful question silenced her father for a moment, and Jess took the opportunity to reach for her purse and stand up. "I need to get home."

Frank nodded stiffly. "I'll get the car."

"Maybe I should take a cab, Dad."

Frank sighed and raked his fingers through his thick head of gray hair. "No. I'll drive you. No sense letting this thing disrupt the family. But I have a bad feeling about this, Jess. I think reestablishing contact with Scott is a mistake. You're opening the door to a lot of things that are best left buried."

She sighed. "That's the trouble, Dad. I'm beginning to realize that burying problems doesn't make them go away. And that maybe it's time I dealt with them."

Jess entered the dimly lit auditorium and made her way inconspicuously along the back wall, scanning the last few rows of the seemingly packed house for an empty seat. She'd had no idea that religious retreats were such a big draw, she thought incredulously. Then again, perhaps the theme was responsible for the crowd. Maybe a lot of people were seeking guidance on how to cope with adversity.

Though Jess hadn't planned to attend the event, something had compelled her to keep the flyer. Then, when she'd returned from vacation, she'd dug it out of the drawer where she had carelessly tossed it. Now that she had begun to pray for the courage and strength to forgive, it seemed like a good idea to hear what Scott had to say. Not that she intended to make her presence known. This was simply a fact-finding mission. A chance to hear his story from the anonymity of a darkened auditorium. An opportunity to view the situation from a different perspective and perhaps gain some insight that would help her understand her feelings.

So far, perspective and insight had eluded her, she acknowledged. Every time she'd seen Scott since his release, she'd been so busy trying to control her turbulent emotions, so focused on carrying on a rational conversation that she hadn't really been able to focus on *him*. She needed an opportunity to study him unobserved and unselfconsciously so that she could get a better handle on who he was now, this man who was still her husband and whom she had once known intimately, but who had changed in some dramatic, fundamental way. That's what tonight's outing was all about. She'd planned it down to the minute: arrive just in time for Scott's remarks, which were the last item on the agenda, sit in the back, then slip out unnoticed as soon as his talk ended.

Well, she'd arrived at the right time. But the sitting part didn't look too promising. However, just when she was about to give up she came upon a single empty seat in the last row. With a sigh of relief and a murmured apology, she edged past a couple of people and sank into the chair just as a sandy-haired, fiftyish minister with a kind face stepped to the podium.

"Ladies and gentlemen, for those of you who don't know me, I'm Reverend Keith Young," he said in a pleasant, well-modulated voice. "Let me add my own words of welcome on behalf of all the sponsoring churches, and thank you for your support of this wonderful event.

"For the last few hours, a number of highly respected Bible scholars have talked to us about the guidance offered in Scripture for dealing with adversity. And we've heard a number of amazing first-person stories about the healing and transforming power of faith. While all of the stories are inspiring, we've saved perhaps the most *dramatic* story until last.

"I met our next speaker, Scott Mitchell, about three years ago when he was in prison serving time for vehicular manslaughter. Scott had been involved in a drunk-driving accident in which two people were killed—a judge and his own four-year-old daughter."

A hushed murmur ran through the crowd, and the minister waited for it to subside before continuing.

"That night changed Scott's life forever. Today he has agreed to share with you his remarkable journey from grief and despair to redemption and hope. Please give Scott a warm welcome."

As the audience applauded, Scott rose from a seat in the front row and made his way to the slightly elevated platform, where the two men shook hands warmly. Then the minister placed his left hand on Scott's shoulder and said something quietly. Scott nodded, and as Reverend Young returned to his seat, Scott set the Bible he was carrying on the podium and reached for the microphone.

For a long moment he simply looked out over the group in silence, as if gathering his thoughts. Then he took a deep breath and began to speak.

"Once upon a time, in a different world, when I was a different man, I used to stand up in front of large groups of people all the time to give presentations on advertising campaigns and focus groups and consumer preferences," he said quietly. His voice was calm and in control, but Jess heard the husky undertones, a clear sign to anyone who knew him well that his emotions were close to the surface. Curiously, it wasn't a tone she had ever heard him use in public. He'd always been guarded about exposing his feelings to anyone except close family. Had he changed in that regard, too? she wondered, intrigued.

"In those days, I wore expensive suits and drove an expensive car and drank expensive liquor," he continued. "I traveled first class, ate in the best restaurants, mingled with the right people. Everyone thought I had it all. Including me. But my wife, Jess, knew better."

At the mention of her name, Jess drew in a sharp breath, and her heart began to thump painfully.

"Jess saw right through all the 'stuff' I grew to value so highly. She recognized it for what it was—a distraction from what really counted. Namely love. And friendship. And family. And simple pleasures. And faith. She tried to help me see that, too, because she recognized that our diverging values were causing problems in our marriage. But instead of listening, I started drinking. Not enough to be an alcoholic, but too much at times. Especially one particular time. The night my world ended."

Scott paused, and Jess saw his Adam's apple bob convulsively. The stark pain on his face was a window to the torment his soul had endured, and her throat constricted with emotion as memories of that night came swirling back to her as well, out of the dark recesses of her mind to which she'd banished them.

Scott moved to a stool in the center of the stage and perched on the edge, resting one foot on a rung. He drew a deep breath, and when he spoke again his voice was slightly unsteady.

"For the next few minutes I'd like to tell you what happened to me after that night. But I have to be honest with you. I didn't want to come here today. I'm not a man who has always been especially good at opening up to people and sharing my feelings. However, Reverend Young can be persuasive. He convinced me that maybe someone might be able to find in what I have to say a ray of hope that will give them the courage to carry on. And once he convinced me of that, I couldn't say no. Because I know how empty life can be without hope. So I'll give it my best."

And for the next forty-five minutes he did exactly that. He spoke of the horrors of the accident, in which he escaped unscathed while his wife suffered a concussion and two people died, including his beloved Elizabeth. He spoke of the surreal cemetery scene, choking up as he talked about kneeling beside the small white coffin as his world crashed in around him. He spoke briefly of the trial, how he went through the motions numbly, still in a state of shock.

He spoke at length about prison…of the suffocating feeling that accompanied the loss of freedom…of the degradation of being treated like a number instead of a person…of the long, empty days marked by rigid, repetitive routine. He spoke in a ragged voice of the pain and anguish and grief that struck fiercely once the numbness wore off. And he spoke of the crushing guilt that squeezed the life from his soul. Of the aching void left in his heart after the death of his wife's love. Of the hopelessness and despair and emptiness that drove him to such depths of depression that at times he felt suicidal. Of how he would lie in his dark cell at night, tears running down his face, praying for God to simply end his agony.

"I wanted to die," Scott said, his voice choked and

raw with emotion. "I'd lost my daughter. My wife. My freedom. My self-respect. My identity. I was as low as you could get. And that's when Reverend Young came into my life."

He stood again and moved to the edge of the stage, closer to the audience, taking a moment to compose himself. "My faith had never been especially strong," he continued. "Certainly not strong enough to withstand the nightmare my life had become. I couldn't fathom how a loving God would wreak such havoc on me and on the people I loved. I'd gone through a brief anger phase, but by the time I met Reverend Young I was at a point where I just didn't care anymore. About anything. So he had his work cut out for him. Because anger is actually a lot easier to deal with than apathy.

"He didn't give up, though. Week after week, sometimes twice a week, he'd show up. At first we didn't even talk about religion. But gradually he began to work that into the conversation. And one day he gave me this." Scott reached for the well-thumbed Bible and held it up. "He had marked a passage he thought I might find helpful, and even though I told him I wasn't interested, he left the book with me. Since time hangs heavy on your hands in prison, I ended up paging through it one day simply out of desperation for something to do. And the passage he had marked seemed to speak directly to me."

Scott opened the book and read. "'Only in God be at rest, my soul, for from Him comes my hope.'"

He paused for a moment, then closed the book and looked out at the audience. "Reverend Young, in his wisdom, had pointed me to the two things I needed most desperately—rest and hope. Guilt and self-re-crimination are terrible burdens that can eat away at you like a cancer and rob life of all peace and hope. But with Reverend Young's help, I eventually came to experience the healing power of God's forgiveness. To understand that He always stands ready to absolve us if we truly repent. And that He never deserts us. For as He told us, He is with us always, even to the end of time. And as He also promised, all things are possible with Him.

"I stand before you tonight as a living testament to the healing power of God's forgiveness and hope," Scott said with quiet sincerity. "I didn't reach this place overnight. It was a long, hard struggle, and I'm sure there were times when Reverend Young was ready to give up on me." He directed a brief smile toward the minister. "But I can tell you that the rewards are great for those who persevere, who seek the Lord with an open mind and open heart, and who are willing to put their trust in Him and listen to His words.

"When Reverend Young asked me to speak today, I told him that I wasn't sure I was the best choice. That I'd made a lot of mistakes and that I'm not where I want to be yet. I guess you could say my life is in a reconstruction phase at this point. When I left prison, I had two goals. One was to make faith the center of my life, and that has been easy. The other, however, has been much more difficult. And that's to win back the love of my wife."

As he paused to draw a deep breath, Jess suddenly felt as if all the air had been squeezed out of her own lungs.

"I realize that's an ambitious goal," Scott continued. "But I'm working on it. I've put my trust in the Lord, and I'm following the advice in Proverbs, which tells us, 'In his mind a man plans his course, but the Lord directs his steps.' Well, I know what my plan is. I love my wife with a passion and intensity that has grown rather than diminished through our years of separation, and I can't even imagine the rest of my life without her. So I trust that the Lord will guide me as I seek my goal.

"You know, a very wise man once told me that even on the coldest, darkest days of winter it's important to remember that spring always comes. I believe that with all my heart. And with the Lord's help, I have great faith that my life will once again bloom and bear fruit. Thank you."

There was a moment of silence, and then the auditorium was filled with thunderous applause as the audience rose to its feet in a resounding ovation. Jess followed suit, reaching up to self-consciously brush away the tears that were streaming down her face. But when she glanced around, she realized that she wasn't alone in her reaction. With his humble manner, painfully honest revelations and inspiring message of hope, Scott had clearly touched many hearts in this room. Including hers.

But beyond that, Scott's talk had also surprised her. Knowing how guarded he usually was when it came to talking about his feelings, she'd assumed that his presentation today would be a relatively straightforward account of his life in prison and a fairly sedate faith witness. Instead, he had spoken from the heart, exposing his deepest feelings and baring his soul to this room of strangers. Because of his willingness to share so openly, he'd connected with the audience at the deepest of levels, and in so doing had made every person in the room experience his pain and desolation in an almost tangible way. Likewise, his faith witness had been inspiring, offering hope that even the bleakest situation can be overcome through trust in the Lord.

Like everyone else in the audience, Jess had been deeply impressed and profoundly moved. But unlike them, she was suddenly afraid. Because if her previous encounters with Scott had shaken the foundations of the wall between them, tonight's revealing testimonial had knocked a gaping hole in it, opening a passage directly to her heart. And as the protective barrier she had erected between them crumbled, she felt increasingly exposed and vulnerable. It was risky business, this notion of reconnecting and forgiving, Jess realized, and she prayed that she had the strength to see it through.

When the applause at last died down and people once more took their seats, Reverend Young moved back to the podium. He paused to embrace Scott, and the warmth between the two men was unmistakable. Another first, Jess noted. Scott had always avoided public displays of affection, but he seemed totally comfortable with them now.

As the minister began to speak, Jess knew it was time to leave. She didn't want to run the risk of encountering Scott until she'd had time to sort through her turbulent emotions. With a murmured apology, she edged past several people and headed toward the exit, determined to make a hasty retreat. However, her step faltered when a ladies'-room sign caught her eye. She glanced uncertainly toward the stage, where Reverend Young seemed to be in the midst of his concluding remarks. Surely there would be time for a quick visit, she thought, changing directions.

But Jess had miscalculated. When she pushed the door open less than four minutes later the audience was on its feet, and quite a few people were already passing the ladies' room on their way to the exit. The minister must have wrapped up his remarks in record time, she realized in dismay.

Jess glanced toward the front of the auditorium. She could see the top of Scott's head above the crowd as he moved toward the exit. Not good, she realized in panic, quickly stepping back.

Even though she felt foolish about being a prisoner in the ladies' room, Jess couldn't see any way out of her predicament. She wasn't ready to face Scott. So her only option was to wait until the place cleared.

A few women stopped in the ladies' room on their way out, and Jess made a pretense of touching up her lipstick and combing her hair. But gradually the visitors tapered off and the din of the crowd subsided. Jess was just about to push the door open and peek out when voices on the other side stopped her.

"…was feeling worse and worse, so I told him to go home."

"No problem. I can catch a bus."

She froze. It was Scott. And Reverend Young.

"I don't know," the minister said skeptically. "It won't be easy at this time of day on a weekend. The schedule is so abbreviated." He sighed. "I didn't think this would be an issue when I sent Ray home. I planned to give you a ride myself until I got the page from the hospital."

"That's more important," Scott said firmly. "You need to be with that family. Don't worry about it. Trust me, I've gotten very good at this public transportation thing."

A third, unfamiliar voice joined the conversation, which moved to another topic. Jess frowned and took a deep breath. She had a feeling of déjà vu. Once more, Scott was without a ride—and she was in a position to help. But she didn't want to see him. Didn't want him to know about her presence at this event until she'd thought about all he'd said. At the same time, it seemed somehow selfish and uncharitable not to assist. As she wrestled with the dilemma, the third person said his goodbyes, once more leaving Scott and Reverend Young alone.

"You better head out, Reverend. I'll see you at services next week."

"All right, Scott. Thanks."

It was now or never. Without even giving herself a chance for second thoughts, Jess followed her instincts and pushed open the ladies'-room door.

The two men were standing about ten feet away, and both glanced in her direction. Reverend Young gave her a pleasant look, but Scott's expression went at warp speed from mild interest to shock to incredulity.

"Jess?" His voice was tentative, as if he couldn't quite believe his eyes.

"Hello, Scott." Her own voice was none too steady—and neither were her legs, she realized as she forced herself to close the distance between them. Her gaze connected with Scott's, and the delight and welcome in his eyes sent a flush of color to her cheeks.

When neither of them spoke, the minister stepped in. "Jess, I'm Reverend Young. It's a pleasure to meet you at last."

With an effort Jess tore her gaze away from Scott's and reached out to find her hand taken in a warm clasp. "Hello, Reverend."

"I've heard a great deal about you. All good things, I might add."

Jess's flush deepened and she glanced at Scott, unsure how to respond. So instead she changed the subject. "I couldn't help overhearing your conversation," she said a bit breathlessly. "And I—I'd be glad to give you a ride home."

He smiled, and the warmth in his eyes spilled into her heart. "I appreciate the offer, Jess. But it's too far out of your way."

She shrugged. "I don't have any plans for tonight anyway."

Reverend Young chimed in. "I'd take her up on it, Scott. Buses are few and far between at this hour."

Scott looked at her again. "Are you sure?"

She nodded, though in fact she wasn't sure at all.

"Then I accept. Thank you."

"And thank you again, Scott," Reverend Young said, placing his hand on the younger man's shoulder. "You gave a powerful talk that I know will help more than a few people find strength in their faith and better equip them to cope with their own adversity."

"I'm glad you think it was worthwhile. But I'm also glad it's over," he admitted with a grin.

The minister chuckled. "I'm sure you are. And I'll see you next week." He turned to Jess and once more extended his hand. "It was good to finally meet you, Jess. Feel free to join us anytime for Sunday services. You'd be most welcome."

Jess watched the minister stride toward the exit. She could feel Scott's gaze on her, but it took her several moments to gather the courage to turn to him. And when she did, she was momentarily distracted by the way his sky-blue cotton shirt hugged his broad, muscular chest, and by the small V of dark, springy hair that was visible at the open neck. He was tanned and fit and looked very, very appealing, she realized as her pulse accelerated. An almost tangible virility radiated from him, literally taking her breath away.

"It's good to see you, Jess," he said quietly, his eyes smiling warmly into hers. "I had no idea you'd be here today. Or that you even knew about it."

"I—I'm still on the mailing list at my church," she stammered, thrown off balance by her wayward thoughts. "I got a flyer."

He studied her for a moment. "I wish I'd known you were coming."

She looked at him curiously. "Why?"

"Because when a man professes his love for a woman, he usually likes to do it directly," Scott said softly, his burning gaze holding hers captive and making her heart lurch into triple time. "I didn't intend to tip my hand to you so soon about my intentions, but I guess God had different plans. So I'll have to go with the flow. I realize there's a lot that still divides us, and that it will take a miracle for you to forgive me, let alone find it in your heart to love me again. But I believe in miracles, Jess. And I have hope." He paused and took a deep breath. "So now you know how I feel."

She stared at him, taken aback by his sincere and straightforward declaration of love. She wished she was as clear about what *she* wanted and how *she* felt. But she was still confused and groping for answers. And she had no idea how to reply.

As if sensing her dilemma, Scott smiled gently. "I'm not asking for a response, Jess. Given what you heard today, I'm just grateful that you're willing to offer me a ride rather than telling me to take a hike. Shall we head out?"

Not trusting her voice, she simply nodded and led the way toward the exit. Scott fell into step beside her, and when they approached the door he reached past her to push it open. He was so close that his breath was warm on her temple and she could catch the distinctive male scent that was his alone. So close that a powerful surge of longing raced through her, catching her off guard and leaving her slightly breathless. So close that it reminded her of days long ago when a simple touch, or even a mere look, was enough to set off sparks that led to kisses—and often much more. Her mouth went dry, and when she risked a glance at Scott she found that the warmth in his gaze had been replaced by need. And unlike their encounter at the garden, when she thought she'd detected a flame of passion in his eyes before it was quickly masked, this time he made no attempt to hide it. He let her see exactly what was on his mind. Love. Attraction. Desire. Need.

Jess looked away quickly, more confused than ever. For years she'd thought that the passion she'd felt for Scott had died in the accident that robbed her of her cherished daughter. But she'd been surprised once in the garden, and again now, by its sudden and persistent resurgence. And she wasn't ready to deal with it. Or even think about it. Caution was the operative word here, she reminded herself. She knew exactly how Scott felt and what he wanted. Now she needed to logically figure out how *she* felt and what *she* wanted. She needed to analyze the situation rationally, without being influenced by hormones.

But unfortunately they were beginning to get in the way.

Chapter Nine

The ride to Scott's apartment was extremely awkward. At least for Jess. After thanking him for coming to the aid of her father's roses, she couldn't think of anything else to say. He, on the other hand, seemed to have no trouble making small talk, she thought enviously. Though she tried to take part, her responses sounded stiff and stilted even to her own ears.

All awkwardness and self-consciousness vanished, however, when Jess turned onto Scott's street and found their route blocked by emergency vehicles with flashing lights.

"This doesn't look good," she said with a frown as she pulled to a stop.

An officer from a nearby police car walked over, and Jess rolled down her window.

"Can I help you, ma'am?" he asked.

Scott leaned over. "I live near the end of the block, Officer." When he gave the address, the man frowned.

"I'm afraid that's where the problem was. Faulty

wiring in one of the flats started a fire. Fortunately, it was contained to one unit, but *unfortunately* I think it was yours." He took a notepad out of his pocket. "Are you Scott Mitchell?"

"Yes."

"I'm sorry, sir. There's not much left," he said sympathetically. "If you'll pull over to the curb, ma'am, I can give you some more information."

Jess did as he directed, and the officer rejoined them as they stepped out of the car. "The fire's been out for a couple of hours, so we're just about to wrap up here. We've moved everybody out temporarily."

"Was anyone hurt?" Scott asked in concern.

"No. Which probably wouldn't be the case if this had happened at night. This kind of fire catches quickly, and smoke inhalation is a real danger. So if there's a bright side, that's it. I can let you have a look if you'd like to try and salvage anything," he offered.

"Yes, thanks. I'll be right with you." The man nodded, and as he walked back toward his patrol car Scott turned to Jess. "Well, this is certainly an exciting end to the day," he said with a rueful smile. "But to be honest, dealing with a fire isn't half as bad as getting up in front of that roomful of people."

She stared at him, amazed at his calm acceptance of the situation and distraught by the unexpected turn of events.

"Hey, don't look like that," Scott said softly. He lifted his hand as if to reach out and touch her face, then let it fall back to his side. "Everything will be fine. So don't worry about it, okay? And thank you again for the ride. I appreciate it more than I can say."

She continued to stare at him. Did he actually think she was just going to go merrily on her way? His home—if such a generous term could be applied to his shabby flat—had just burned down! He had apparently lost everything. *She* was upset, even if he didn't seem to be. There was no way she could walk out on *anyone* in those straits. Especially Scott. Not after she'd listened to his story today. Not after everything he'd already gone through. Not after he'd made it clear that he loved her.

"I'll stay for a few minutes," she said. Before he could reply, she reached into the car for her purse and slung it over her shoulder.

When she turned back to him, the look in his eyes spoke more eloquently than words of his gratitude—and love. Silently he stepped aside to allow her to follow the officer, then fell in beside her, his hand protectively at her elbow. The light touch of his fingers on her bare skin was like an electric charge, and she tightened her grip on her purse, struggling to control the tremors that ran through her body. Scott might have tipped his hand today about his feelings, but she wasn't yet ready to acknowledge her own—to him, or to herself.

The officer stopped at the edge of the taped-off area and nodded toward what had been Scott's apartment. "The floors are okay, and structurally the building is still sound. These old places were built to last. But the walls and ceilings in your apartment are scorched and there's not much left of the contents."

"I'll just take a quick look around." Scott turned to Jess. "Will you be okay here for a few minutes?"

"I'll stick close," the officer promised.

"Thanks. Hang on to this for me, okay?" He handed Jess his Bible, then turned and strode toward the burned-out apartment.

"Tough break," the officer said, shaking his head sympathetically. "But he seems to be taking it okay. I hope he didn't have anything too valuable in there."

Jess doubted it. Mostly because he didn't seem to *have* anything valuable. At least not in a material sense.

The officer's radio crackled to life, and after a murmured "excuse me," he moved a few feet away to handle the call, leaving Jess alone to stare at the vacant building where most of Scott's unit had been reduced to ashes—just as his life had been, she thought, struck by the symbolism. She glanced thoughtfully down at the Bible she held in her hands, which had provided him with the comfort and courage to overcome tragedy and go on with his life—and with the perspective to understand what really counted. Maybe that's why the fire seemed of so little consequence to him, she mused. It had destroyed only things, which were replaceable. It hadn't destroyed anything of real value.

When Scott emerged a few minutes later he was carrying only a few items, and she looked at them curiously as he approached. There was a family picture of herself, Scott and Elizabeth, which had miraculously survived even if its frame had not; a small metal cross; and two books on horticulture that were a bit charred at the edges. That was it. Her throat tightened with emotion, and when her gaze rose to his, she had to forcibly resist the urge to reach up and wipe away a smudge of soot on his cheek.

He smiled at her, but she could see the weariness in his face, smell the acrid scent of smoke on his clothes. "The officer was right. There's not much left. I'm pretty much down to the clothes on my back."

"I'm sorry, Scott," she whispered.

"Hey, it's okay," he reassured her, forcing his lips into a smile. "I salvaged the only things that were really important to me. And I'm getting used to this starting-over thing. I'll be fine." He glanced toward the apartment, and it was clear when he spoke that the symbolism wasn't lost on him, either. "Maybe I'll be like the phoenix. Maybe something new will rise out of the ashes," he said quietly. He was silent for a moment, and when he turned back to her his grin was genuine. "Anyway, Karen won't be sorry. She hated this place."

"I can't say I blame her."

Scott shrugged. "It met my needs."

"Did you find anything worth saving?" the officer interrupted as he rejoined them.

"Not much," Scott admitted.

The man sighed. "I didn't think you would. Listen, you're welcome to use my phone if you need to call someone or arrange a place to spend the night."

"He can use my cell phone," Jess interjected.

"Okay. Then I just need to ask you a few questions for our report," the officer said to Scott. "I've got the paperwork in my car. Ma'am, you can wait in your car if you'd like. This won't take long."

She nodded, and they made their way silently back down the block. Scott opened her door for her when they reached her car, and after she slipped into the driver's seat he leaned down.

"You don't need to wait, Jess. This might take a while, and I'm sure you have better things to do than hang around here."

She looked at him, this man she had long ago said goodbye to in her heart. Scott had been as dead to her as Elizabeth, their sacred marriage vow reduced to a union in name only. But like the phoenix, he had returned, transformed. And God help her, she *liked* the new Scott. Enough that even the fear of what lay ahead couldn't compel her to just walk away. She drew a shaky breath, and when she spoke her voice was slightly unsteady. "I don't mind waiting."

He studied her for a moment, and then his eyes grew soft. "Thank you," he said quietly. "I'll wrap this up as quickly as I can."

Jess watched as he made his way over to the police car, still juggling the few meager items he had salvaged. In addition to the soot on his cheek, there were now smudges on his shirt, as well. Did he have the money for new clothes? she suddenly wondered. And how would he get to the store to buy the immediate necessities? Almost no buses ran after eight o'clock at night.

More important, where was he going to sleep? From what she'd seen, he couldn't spare much money for a hotel. His sister lived in Chicago, so that wasn't a possibility. Reverend Young might be able to put him up for a couple of days, but the minister could be at the hospital—and unreachable—late into the night. Perhaps Scott had kept in touch with some of his friends, she thought, though that seemed unlikely. Most of his "friends" in the years before the accident had been business associates, men who would have little loyalty to a friendship once it outlived its utility. So who was he going to call?

"All finished."

Startled, Jess turned to find Scott once again at her window. "That was quick."

He shrugged. "There wasn't much I could tell him. And I didn't lose anything of value, except some clothes."

She nodded. "Why don't you get in while I dig out my phone?"

Scott hesitated and glanced at his soiled hands and clothes. "I'll get your car dirty."

She reached down and pulled her trunk release. "There are some rags in the back. Help yourself."

When he joined her a few moments later, his salvaged items were neatly wrapped and tucked under one arm but he was still wiping his hands. "This soot is insidious," he said ruefully.

"You've got a streak on your face, too."

He flipped down the visor mirror, then reached up to scrub his cheek. "Thanks."

Jess watched him for a moment, trying to gather the courage to follow through on a plan that had been slowly taking shape in her mind. She was well aware that it flew in the face of caution—which only an hour ago had been her operative word. But somehow caution seemed less important than compassion at this point.

"Scott…"

"Mmm-hmm." He was still focused on erasing the smudge on his cheek.

"Where are you going to stay tonight?"

There was an almost imperceptible hesitation in his movement, and then he resumed rubbing. "I'm not sure yet. I'll work something out," he said lightly.

Jess drew a shaky breath, knowing that what she was about to say could change her life forever. "I—I have a spare bedroom."

His hand stilled, and slowly he turned to face her. His gaze locked with hers, intense, searching—and cautious. "Are you offering me a place to stay?" he asked carefully, as if he couldn't quite believe what he'd just heard.

She nodded jerkily, not trusting her voice.

Scott stared at Jess, momentarily speechless. Even though he believed in miracles, never in his most optimistic moments could he have envisioned an offer like this. For a long moment he gazed into the eyes that he adored, and his heart contracted with tenderness. He knew those eyes so well, knew every nuance of their expression. During their years together, he'd seen them sparkle with joy, glow with passion, shine with enthusiasm. He'd watched them flash with anger, glint with laughter, glimmer with mischief. He had learned to read her moods simply by looking into their green depths. Since his return, though, her eyes had been so guarded that he'd rarely had a clue to her feelings. But now he saw plenty of emotions. Doubt. Confusion. Caution. Fear. And most important, the glimmer of something more.

Not love, certainly. Or even affection. It was more like…willingness…openness…receptivity. He couldn't quite put his finger on it. All he knew was that it represented a quantum leap forward. And suddenly his spirits soared.

Scott turned to gaze again at his ruined apartment, viewing it with new eyes. He didn't care about the contents, but the fire *had* disheartened him, and in the silence of his heart he had cried out, "What next, Lord?" The hassle of finding a new apartment, the expense of replacing his clothes when he was just getting enough cash together for a used car, the problem of emergency housing—it had all seemed overwhelming at first. And yet, in a way, the fire had been the answer to his prayer, he realized. Because by prompting Jess's offer, it had given him the opportunity to interact more closely with her and prove that while he was a new man in many ways, his love for her had never changed. Perhaps his words about the phoenix had been prophetic after all, he reflected.

Jess studied Scott's profile as he stared at the flat he had called home for the past four months. Already she was having second thoughts about her impulsive offer. Learning to forgive was one thing—but sharing her home with the man who had once shared her bed? That was rushing things. And definitely not very prudent. But how did she gracefully retract her invitation? she wondered in sudden panic, her mind racing. Should she just be honest? Say that the arrangement would probably be uncomfortable for them both, that a motel would be better for a night or two? It wouldn't set him back that much financially, she reassured herself. And it would certainly provide more peace of mind. For her, at least.

Jess was just about to voice her thoughts when Scott turned back to her, and for a moment her resolve faltered––giving him the opening he needed. Because he took one look at her face, saw the panic in her eyes and knew she was on the verge of taking back her invitation. Up until now he'd given her a chance to change her mind on every offer she'd made. But this was an opportunity he simply wasn't willing to give up––even if he had to play on her sympathy to make it stick.

"I appreciate your offer more than I can say, Jess," he said quickly, jumping in before she could speak. "I'm not sure I can reach Reverend Young tonight, and my so-called friends more or less vanished after I went to prison. I could dip into my car fund for a motel, but I hate to do that. Frankly, the bus is getting a bit old." Then he played his trump card. "But if it's too much of an inconvenience, I could always go to a homeless shelter for a few nights."

Jess's retraction died on her lips. Scott in a homeless shelter? she thought, appalled. No way! She'd be more uncomfortable thinking about him in an environment like that than coping with him in her guest room. She had to see this through. "Like…like I said, I have a spare bedroom," she said.

His smile warmed her all the way to her toes, making her feel a little better about her decision. She'd done the right thing after all, she assured herself as she put the car in gear.

She just wasn't sure it was the *safe* thing.

* * *

They made only two stops on the way home. One at a discount store so Scott could pick up a change of clothes and some toiletries. The other at a Chinese restaurant for take-out food. Nevertheless, by the time they reached her condo it was after nine.

Jess nervously hitched her purse higher on her shoulder as they approached her door. Scott was juggling both bags, so she prayed he wouldn't notice how badly her hand was shaking as she struggled to fit her key in the lock. When at last it clicked, she gave a relieved sigh and pushed open the door.

But her relief was short-lived. Because as they stepped over the threshold, the full impact of what she'd done slammed home. If she'd once been nervous because her *car* seemed too intimate, how in the world was she going to cope with living under the same roof with a man she had once loved—and who still filled her with longing?

Jess had no idea, she realized numbly as she led the way to the kitchen. But keeping her distance—both emotionally and physically—seemed like a good plan, she reasoned as she headed toward the cabinets to retrieve glasses and utensils.

"Do y-you want to clean up before we eat?" *Don't stammer,* she berated herself. *Acting nervous will only make this situation worse.* She forced herself to take a deep breath before she spoke again, and this time her voice was steadier. "I can always nuke the food if it gets cold."

"I'd like that, thanks. These clothes really absorbed that smoke smell."

She reached for a glass from the cabinet. "Okay. I'll show you where…oh!"

She watched in dismay as the glass slipped from her fingers and shattered on the tile floor. So much for not acting nervous, she thought in disgust as she bent to retrieve the shards.

"Be careful, Jess," Scott warned as he moved toward her. "Those pieces can cut like—"

"Ouch!" Jess jerked her hand back from a jagged shard. Already blood was dripping from her finger.

She heard his muttered oath as he moved beside her. "Let's get that under water." Without waiting for her to respond, he reached for her hand, drew her to her feet and led her toward the sink. He turned on the water and gently cradled her hand under the steady stream, letting her blood wash over his own hand as he leaned over to examine the cut.

Jess stared down at her delicate fingers resting in Scott's sun-browned hand and for a moment she thought her lungs were actually going to explode. So much for physical distance. Not only were they physically close, they were actually *touching*. Which was *not* good. She was losing control here, she realized. And that was scary.

Instinctively she made a move to pull her hand away. But just as instinctively Scott's grasp tightened and he turned to her, his eyes troubled.

"I'm sorry. I'm trying not to hurt you, Jess, but I need to see how deep this cut is."

Jess allowed him to put her finger back under the water. It was simpler than trying to explain that her reaction was caused by fear, not pain, she decided resignedly.

After what seemed like an eternity Scott turned off the faucet and looked down at her. "It's pretty deep, but I don't think it needs stitches. Do you have any bandages?"

She nodded. "In the bathroom. I'll get them." The words came out in a croak.

He frowned and looked at her worriedly, then took her arm and led her over to the table, where he gently pressed her into a chair. "I'll find them. Sit here until I come back. Your finger will just bleed more if you move around."

Jess didn't argue. The day's emotional overload had apparently short-circuited her brain, and she was too numb even to think. So she simply sat there until Scott reappeared with bandages and antiseptic.

"Okay, I think we're set," he said as he dropped into the chair next to her and extended his hand. "Let's have a look."

Jess gazed down at his waiting hand. The lean fingers were familiar, but the callused palm momentarily jolted her. Blue-collar hands, work roughened and sun browned, had replaced the neatly manicured, white-collar hands she remembered. Yet there was an earthy strength to them, a steadiness and sureness that hadn't been there before.

Jess's gaze flickered back to his. He was watching her, waiting patiently, but the look in his eyes disconcerted her. There was encouragement and tenderness in their depths, but also a flicker of apprehension, as if he was unsure whether she would willingly give him her hand. And, on a deeper level, her trust.

Jess hesitated for a moment, aware of the symbolism. Then, with sudden decision, she followed her heart and reached out to place her hand in his.

Scott hadn't even realized he was holding his breath until his lungs suddenly started working again. He knew Jess was second-guessing her invitation, and he'd been afraid that she would get cold feet at any moment and send him packing—until this simple gesture of trust, which reassured him that at least for tonight he was safe from eviction.

But not necessarily from temptation, he realized as he transferred his attention to her hand. His mouth went dry as he looked at the delicate fingers that had once touched him with such tenderness and love. A surge of longing swept over him, almost painful in its intensity, and it took every ounce of his willpower to remain still when what he really wanted to do was pull Jess into his arms and hold her. To feel her soft curves against the hard lines of his body. To bury his face in her fragrant hair and inhale her essence. To run his hands over her silky skin.

Scott drew a ragged breath, praying for control as he attended to the cut. Now that she knew his intentions he needed to move with extreme caution, he reminded himself. Patience, restraint and discipline were essential. He didn't want to make her even more nervous than she already was. To the point that she might very well ask him to leave. So he needed to appear calm and cool, even if he was anything but.

He cleared his throat and secured the end of the bandage. "All done," he pronounced. "Just leave the glass on the floor and I'll clean it up in a few minutes. But I could sure use a shower first."

"I'll get you some towels," she said, rising.

He followed more slowly, taking cover behind the bag of clothing and toiletries he'd purchased.

"You can pretty much use this bath exclusively," Jess said, striving with limited success for an even tone as she placed clean towels on the counter. "I have an attached bath in my bedroom. The guest room is across the hall. I keep it ready, because Mark visits occasionally when he's passing through town. If you need anything, let me know. I'll be in the kitchen when you're finished." And with that rush of words, she made a fast exit.

Scott took a long, cold shower, and by the time he returned to the kitchen Jess had cleaned up the floor. He thought about saying something, but decided to let it pass. "The food smells great," he pronounced.

At the sound of his voice, the pulse rate Jess had just gotten under control once again accelerated. And when she turned from the sink, it slammed into high gear. Scott was standing in the doorway, and he looked… *fabulous* was the word that came to mind. His damp hair was slicked back, and though his clothes might not be designer brands, they fit as if custom made. The jeans hugged his slim hips and outlined his long muscular legs, and his black T-shirt revealed impressive biceps. Jess nodded jerkily toward the table, where she'd set two places. "I reheated everything," she said a bit breathlessly. "Have a seat."

"Can I help with anything?"

Her eyebrows rose in surprise. That wasn't an offer she was used to hearing. Even in the early days of their marriage Scott hadn't been into housekeeping-type duties. He'd taken care of the outdoor chores, leaving indoor jobs to her. "No. Everything's ready. What would you like to drink?"

He glanced at the glasses of water on the table. "This is fine."

Jess scooped the food onto platters, then joined him at the table. He eyed it hungrily and smiled. "I haven't had any really good Chinese food in a long time," he said, reaching for a serving spoon.

"Even since…in the few months?"

He shook his head. "I usually eat in."

Because it was cheaper. The words were left unsaid, but Jess could read between the lines. "Well, I think you'll like this. I found this place shortly after I moved in here, and I go so often we're on a first-name basis now."

Scott ate as if he hadn't seen food in a week, clearly savoring every bite. "You don't cook anymore?"

"Not much."

"I thought you enjoyed it."

"I did. Once upon a time. But cooking for one isn't much fun. I just…got out of the habit."

They ate in silence for a few moments, then Scott gestured toward his surroundings. "I like the condo. And you've done a nice job decorating it."

"Thanks."

It was a perfunctory reply to what she clearly con-sidered to be a perfunctory compliment, so Scott tried again. "I mean it, Jess. It's comfortable and homey, but not cluttered. I like the clean lines and colors."

She looked at him in surprise, and this time her tone was warmer. "Thank you. Actually, I haven't devoted too much attention to the place. I just wanted something simple and uncomplicated to come home to at the end of the day."

"A haven from a world that usually isn't either of those things," he said quietly.

She gave him a thoughtful look, struck by his insight. "I hadn't thought of it that way," she said slowly. "But you're probably right."

"Simple is good," he reflected. "That's why I wasn't very upset by the fire. Almost everything is replaceable. And I salvaged the things I really wanted. The horticulture books were given to me by Karen and Reverend Young, so they have sentimental—and practical—value. The cross was made by a former inmate who became a good friend. He sent it to me a few months ago, after he got out. And the picture—well, that's been with me ever since I…since the accident. I'll clean it all up later."

She nodded. "I put everything in the laundry room. And feel free to use the washer and dryer."

"Thanks. I'd also like to call Karen to let her know where I am, if that's okay. She can ring me right back so we don't run up your bill."

She waved his offer aside. "Don't worry about it."

"Thanks." Scott scraped up the last bite of chicken broccoli and then gave a sigh of satisfaction. "That was great." He nodded toward her plate, well aware that she'd spent more time pushing her food around than eating, which probably explained why she was so thin. "Are you finished?"

"Yes."

He reached for her plate and stood. "I'll take care of the dishes." At her astonished look, he chuckled. "I told you I've changed," he reminded her with a wink. Then he glanced at his watch and gave a low whistle. "Hey, this is way past your bedtime! Why don't you turn in? You're going to have trouble getting in your eight hours tonight as it is."

Which was nothing new, she thought. Five or six hours were about the most she could manage these days. But she let the comment pass. "All right. Thanks. See you in the morning."

She got as far as the door before his voice stopped her.

"Jess."

She paused and slowly turned. Though they were several feet apart, she could feel the warmth in his gaze as if it was a caress.

"Thank you again for doing this," he said quietly.

"You're welcome," she whispered. And then she fled.

"Karen? Sorry to call you so late."

"Scott? What's wrong?"

"Nothing. I'm fine. Relax," he hastened to reassure her. "I'm at a different phone number for the next couple of nights, and I just wanted to give it to you in case you need to reach me for any reason."

"Why are you at a different number?"

"Just take it down, then call me back and I'll answer all your questions." He gave her the number, then hung up. When the phone rang a moment later, he snatched it up immediately so Jess wouldn't be disturbed.

"Okay, what gives?" Karen demanded without preamble.

"There was a fire at my flat, and—"

"Are you hurt?" she asked in alarm.

"No. I'm fine. I just need to find a new place to stay."

"What happened at the flat?"

"Faulty wiring."

He heard her unladylike snort across the wire. "Why am I not surprised? Well, as far as I'm concerned, good riddance. That place was a dive."

"Oh, come on. Don't hold back. Tell me how you really feel," he teased her.

"Ha ha. So where are you staying?"

"Jess's condo."

For once, his sister was struck dumb. At least for a moment. "Do you want to explain that?" she asked when she finally found her voice.

He chuckled. "I thought you'd be surprised."

"That, my dear brother, is a gross understatement."

"Remember the retreat I told you about, the one where I was going to speak?"

"Yes. It was today. I was going to call you tomorrow and see how it went."

"It went fine. No surprises. Except one. Jess was there."

"You're kidding! You never told me she was coming!"

"Because I didn't know. Anyway, I don't think she planned to tell *me*, either, but as she was leaving she happened to overhear Reverend Young and me talking. The guy who was supposed to give me a ride got sick, so she stepped in and offered to take me home."

"You're kidding!"

"You said that already. And no, I'm not."

"Well, go on," she said impatiently. "How did you end up at her condo?"

"When we got to the flat, there were emergency vehicles all over. The building had been evacuated, and she offered me her guest room."

"Wow!" Karen breathed in awe.

"Yeah, wow."

"You know, this is all too much to be coincidence," she said thoughtfully.

"That thought did cross my mind."

"It looks like your prayers are being answered. Make that *our* prayers."

"Looks that way. But do me a favor, okay?"

"Sure."

"Keep praying. Because now that I have my foot in the door, literally and figuratively, one wrong move could blow the whole thing."

"Keep the faith, Scott. I don't think the Lord would have brought you this far to slam the door in your face."

"I hope not. But one thing I've learned, Karen. Never take anything for granted. And always be prepared for the unexpected."

Chapter Ten

Jess turned to squint at the illuminated dial of her bedside clock and groaned. Two-thirty. In four hours she'd have to get up. And so far she'd had virtually no sleep.

Restlessly she turned on her side and scrunched her pillow under her head. She hadn't heard a sound out of Scott since she'd closed her door for the night, so she couldn't blame her sleeplessness on a noisy house guest. No, it was the house guest *himself* who was keeping her awake. If she didn't sleep all that well on a *typical* night, she might as well throw in the towel tonight, which was about as far from typical as they came, she thought wryly.

With a resigned sigh, Jess swung her legs to the floor and stood, hitching up the shoulder on her oversize T-shirt as she stretched wearily. Maybe a cup of herbal tea would help her doze, she thought hopefully. Four hours of rest wasn't enough, but it would be better than nothing.

Jess moved to her door and cracked it slightly, listening intently. Silence. She glanced at the guest-room door. Closed. Scott was obviously asleep. Lucky him, she thought enviously as she opened her door and padded quietly down the hall.

Normally she made her tea the old-fashioned way, in a kettle, but tonight she settled for the faster and quieter microwave. As she waited for the water to boil, she glanced around the spotless kitchen. True to his word, Scott had washed their dinner dishes. She peeked into the laundry room. His personal items were gone, so apparently he'd cleaned up those, too.

Jess removed her mug from the microwave and dipped her tea bag in the hot water, mulling over all that had happened in the past eight hours. If anyone had told her this morning that Scott would be spending the night at her condo, she would have laughed in their face. And yet here he was, sleeping only a few feet away.

Jess drew a shaky breath and wandered into the living room, stopping in front of the photo of Elizabeth. It was slightly out of position, and as she reached for it she suddenly knew that Scott had also held it in his hands tonight. What had gone through his mind? she wondered with a bittersweet pang as she sank into an overstuffed chair and tucked her feet under her. Had he thought about all that might have been, as she so often had? Of the two of them watching their daughter grow? Of brothers and sisters joining the family? Of school plays and piano lessons and soccer games? Of first dates and graduations and, eventually, weddings? Of stolen romantic moments that kept the love between the two of them young and vibrant? Of grandchildren, who would add sunshine and youth to their days as they grew old together? And in the end, of looking back on a long life together and finding contentment and satisfaction in the circle of love they had created that would go on long after they had departed this earth? Had he thought of all those things? she wondered. And if so, had his stomach knotted painfully—as hers always did—making him feel physically sick to know that they would never be?

Suddenly Jess realized that tears were streaming down her face, and she reached up to wipe them away, hugging Elizabeth's picture to her chest. She set the mug down, then let her head drop back on the chair, struggling to control the feeling of bleakness and desolation that always swept over her when she allowed herself to think about the "what ifs." It wasn't a healthy thing to do. She knew that from counseling, so she rarely indulged herself. But the emotional events of today, the fact that the man who had destroyed her dreams was sleeping a mere few feet away, made it impossible not to think about what might have been. And to wish, vain though it was, that they could go back in time and start over.

Jess closed her eyes wearily. Scott seemed intent on making a fresh start. Seemed to believe that it was possible to begin again. But she wasn't as optimistic. They had too much baggage. The hate she'd felt for four years wouldn't turn into love overnight, even if she *was* impressed by the changes in him. Even if she had, in fact, grown to like this new Scott. Nor could she seem to get rid of her own guilt, the thought that if she'd insisted on driving the night of the accident things might have turned out differently. The one thing they did have going for them, she admitted, was chemistry. Amazingly, that was just as powerful as it had always been. But it wasn't enough to sustain a relationship over the long term. The baggage had to be dealt with, too.

Mark had told her that seeing Scott might help her do that. So she was making an effort. Like going to the retreat today. And hearing Scott talk candidly about his mistakes, his regrets and his hopes *had* helped. She understood for the first time—maybe *let* herself understand for the first time—the pain and desolation he had suffered, which had been no less than hers. And—even harder to admit—perhaps worse. Because *he* was the *cause* of hers. Scott had never been a man who wanted to cause anyone pain, least of all his family. That's why he'd struggled so hard trying to juggle the often conflicting demands of his job and his family. Why he'd seemed so often frustrated. Why he'd turned to alcohol to ease the stress.

And for that, too, Jess felt guilt, she acknowledged. Perhaps if she had been more understanding they wouldn't have begun to drift apart. Perhaps he wouldn't have needed the alcohol. Perhaps the accident would never have happened.

Once more tears trickled out of the corners of her eyes. And this time she made no attempt to wipe them away. Mark was very likely right when he'd suggested that she had simply buried her issues instead of dealing with them. But doing so had allowed her to cope, to go on living what *appeared* to be a normal life. Even if that life was a pretense, it had given her something to cling to, allowed her to stay afloat.

But now she was adrift—and sinking fast.

Scott opened his eyes, instantly awake, his heart racing. He stared at the dark ceiling, momentarily disoriented, and tensed, suddenly on guard—a reflex born of an environment where being ready for anything was the only way to survive. But then the events of the preceding day came rushing back, and his coiled muscles slowly relaxed. He was in Jess's condo. And it wasn't just a dream.

For several moments Scott lay quietly, savoring the feeling of freedom, of safety and, most of all, of proximity to the woman he loved. She was just a few feet away, he thought in wonder, swallowing past the lump that suddenly appeared in his throat. So many times in prison, when he'd awakened in the middle of the night overcome by a crushing sensation of desperate loneliness, he'd closed his eyes and forced himself to pretend that he wasn't really alone. That Jess was nearby.

And now she was.

Impulsively he swung his feet to the floor, closing the distance to the hall in three long strides. It might be silly, but he just wanted to look at her room. To stare at her door and imagine her sleeping just on the other side, curled on her side, her hair spilling over her pillow, her chin tucked into her shoulder in the endearing sleep position she favored. Often he'd awakened and found her in that pose. And sometimes, in the early days of their marriage, he'd been so overcome by gratitude for the gift of her love that a rush of tenderness would sweep over him as he watched her sleep, so strong it brought tears to his eyes. But as the demands of his job increasingly sapped his energy and attention, he'd become too preoccupied to notice such things. Or appreciate them.

Those days were over, however. Never again would he take such blessings for granted, he vowed.

Scott quietly opened his door and looked down the hall, frowning when he realized that Jess's door was wide open and her bed empty. He glanced over his shoulder at the illuminated dial of the bedside clock. Three in the morning. She had always been a sound sleeper. What was wrong? Was her finger hurting? Had it started to bleed again? The cut had been deep—maybe she should have had stitches, he thought worriedly.

Scott eased his door shut and strode toward the chair where he'd draped his clothes, reaching for his jeans and stepping into them in one rapid, fluid motion. Then he returned to the hall, pulling on his T-shirt as he walked, and quietly made his way to the kitchen, only to find the room dark—and deserted. His frown deepened, and he turned to the living room, which was faintly illuminated by a low-watt lamp. And that's where he found her.

She was curled in an overstuffed chair, a half-empty mug on the floor beside her, a framed photo pressed against her chest. And judging by her even breathing, she was asleep. Slowly he moved closer, until he stood directly above her. Though the light was dim, he could see the evidence of tears on her pale cheeks, the dark shadows under her eyes, the troubled frown on her face that even sleep didn't erase. His gut clenched painfully and he drew a ragged breath. She looked so fragile. So vulnerable. So alone.

Scott thought about the Jess he had known in happier days—strong, vibrant, in love with life. Certainly the strength was still there. She couldn't have survived these past few years if it hadn't been. But she'd paid a price for her survival. There was an unnatural tension about her, a nervous energy that spoke of long-term stress. She now seemed more focused on making it through the day than on *enjoying* the day. And her vibrant personality was now subdued, her joy replaced by a deep, abiding sadness that whispered even at the edges of her infrequent smiles.

Hardest of all to bear was the knowledge that he was the cause of her distress. And his heart wept yet again for the havoc his misguided priorities and tragic lapse in judgment had wreaked on the woman he loved more than life itself.

Suddenly Jess's eyelids flickered open, and she looked up at him sleepily, momentarily confused. "Scott?"

For a second he was disconcerted by her unexpected awakening. But he recovered quickly, forcing his lips into a smile as he squatted beside her. "Bingo. What are you doing out here in the middle of the night?" he asked unevenly, his eyes only inches from hers.

Her vision suddenly cleared as the last vestiges of sleep vanished, and she straightened up abruptly. Her rapid movement caused the neckline of her T-shirt to slip and the hem to creep up, giving Scott a quick glimpse of a creamy shoulder and a long length of shapely thigh. She gasped and made a frantic grab for both ends of the garment, dropping the picture in the process.

Scott bent to retrieve it, struggling to control the surge of longing that left him suddenly way too warm. She, on the other hand, seemed cold—or, more likely, nervous—he noted when he turned back to her. She was visibly trembling, one hand clutching the neckline of her T-shirt, the other pulling the hem as far down as it would go. He set the photo back on the coffee table and headed across the room toward the couch to retrieve a throw, which he silently draped over her—for both their sakes.

She snuggled under it gratefully, covering every possible bit of exposed skin. Only then did she look up at him, and when she did her mouth went dry. How could a man with uncombed hair and stubble on his face look so appealing? she marveled. With an effort she tore her gaze from his face and let it drop lower. He wore the same T-shirt he'd had on at dinner, she noted, and his jeans had obviously been hastily pulled on, sans belt. He hadn't even bothered with socks or shoes, she realized, staring at his bare feet far too long before she found her voice. "Th-thank you."

"My pleasure." The rough, whiskeylike quality in his voice drew her gaze back to his. "So what are you doing up at this hour?"

"I—I couldn't sleep."

He sat on the ottoman in front of her and rested his forearms on his knees, clasping his hands in front of him. "Something you ate?"

She shifted uncomfortably. "No. I—I just don't sleep very well anymore."

He frowned. "Since when?"

"For a while," she hedged.

"Since when, Jess?" he persisted, gazing at her intently.

She sighed. Why hide it? "Since the accident."

He let his breath out slowly. "Almost four years," he said quietly. "No wonder you always look so tired. How much sleep do you get?"

"I don't know. Five, maybe six hours a night."

He glanced at his watch. "Or less." He looked at her worriedly. "That's not enough."

"It's as much as you ever got."

"I don't need as much sleep as most people."

"Even so…why are *you* up? Three o'clock is late even for you."

He raked his fingers through his hair. "I don't know. Strange place. Strange noises. I'm a pretty light sleeper now."

She looked at him curiously. "That's a switch. You may not have needed *much* sleep, but when you did sleep it took practically an earthquake to wake you."

At the intimate reference, his lips quirked briefly into a smile, but when he spoke his voice was sober. "Prison does strange things to you. You learn to be on alert pretty much all the time."

"Why?"

He looked at her silently for a minute. "Let's just say that it's not a very nice place, Jess. Or a safe one," he said quietly.

She stared at him, suddenly feeling sick. As open as he'd been in his talk at the retreat, there were obviously a lot of things he hadn't revealed. Bad things.

"I'm sorry," she whispered.

"Hey, I survived," he said reassuringly. "It's over. And good came out of the experience, for which I'm grateful. Now it's just a matter of putting the bad behind me."

She gazed at him, and the wistful look in her eyes tugged at his heart. "How will you do that?"

He drew a deep breath. "By focusing on the good," he replied simply. "One thing I learned, Jess. You can't forget the past. God knows, I tried. I'd still like to erase the memory of the bad days in our marriage, of the accident, of the trial, of prison. But I can't. It's part of me, both the good and bad. And that's true for everyone. So eventually you have to accept the past, learn what you can from it, then leave it behind and move on."

"That's not an easy thing to do," she whispered.

Without even thinking, he reached over and took her hand, cradling it between his. In the quiet of the night he heard her sharply indrawn breath, but she didn't pull away. "I know," he said hoarsely. "Dear God, I know!" He glanced toward the picture of Elizabeth, and when he spoke his voice was choked with emotion. "I used to lie awake wondering what she would have been like as she grew up. Would she have liked soccer? Gymnastics? Chess? Would she have taken ballet lessons? Would she have been good at math? I even tried to imagine the holidays and the birthday parties and the proms we'll never share with her." He drew a ragged breath, clearly struggling for control. "Sometimes I still think about all that. But mostly I try to think of the joy she brought to my life. Of her enthusiasm and her infectious smile and the way she could make me feel warm inside, and important, with just a look. She gave me so many gifts in her short life, Jess. I can't bring her back, but neither can anyone take away those gifts. That's what I try to remember."

When he looked back at Jess, tears were once more streaming down her face. He reached over and gently brushed them away, blinking back his own. "I'm sorry," he whispered brokenly, his eyes anguished. "Dear God, I'm so sorry for all the pain I caused you!"

Jess looked down at their entwined hands. The impulse to reach for him, to let him take her in his arms and hold her until the world went away with all its grief and guilt and regrets, was so strong that it frightened her. Her need for comfort was always most intense in the quiet, dark, early-morning hours when she invariably felt most alone, and the temptation to simply follow her impulses was powerful. But in the light of day she would most likely regret such a rash action, she cautioned herself. It was too soon. And even though she believed that Scott's remorse was genuine, it couldn't restore the life she had known.

Carefully she disengaged her hand from his, struggling to ignore the disappointment in his eyes. "I'm working on forgiveness, Scott," she told him. "But I— I can't make any promises."

"I'm not asking you to. I'm just asking you not to shut me out. To give me a chance."

She sighed. "I don't seem to have a lot of choice in the matter, considering how life seems to be throwing us together."

"Maybe that's a sign." The soft chime of a clock sounded in the darkness, and Scott glanced at his watch, angling toward the light that barely illuminated the room. "Three-thirty! You need to get some sleep."

"What about you?"

Sleep was the last thing on his mind. "I think I'll have some coffee first."

"All right. There's instant decaf in the cabinet by the stove." She wrapped the throw more tightly around her and stood. "I'll see you tomorrow."

And as she disappeared down the hall he let her parting comment echo in his mind, savoring the most wonderful words he'd heard in a long, long time.

"Here you are, sir." Scott handed the customer his change, and the man folded the money together with the rest of his cash before shoving the roll of bills into his pocket. "Now let me help you get everything to your car."

Scott moved to the other side of the counter and reached for the two trays of annuals while the man picked up a hanging basket of fuchsia.

"Looks like you're going to have a nice garden," Scott commented as they made their way across the parking lot.

"My wife used to do all the gardening, but her arthritis has slowed her down considerably. So now she supervises and I plant," he said good-naturedly. "But I don't have her green thumb."

"Well, impatiens and begonias are pretty forgiving, so they were good choices," Scott said as the man opened his trunk and placed his plants inside. "You should be fine."

"Thanks again for your help."

"My pleasure."

Scott turned and headed back toward the main building, only to pull up abruptly a few feet from the car when his gaze came to rest on a stack of folded bills that looked suspiciously like the ones the customer had just shoved into his pocket. Scott bent and picked up the money, flipping through it. There was more than two hundred dollars in the roll, he realized, recalling the days when that amount of money was just pocket change to him. Now it was a fortune. And it would certainly beef up his car fund—if he was the kind of man to be swayed by such temptation. But it just wasn't in his nature. He turned back to the car, flagging the customer down as he pulled out of the parking spot.

"I think you dropped this, sir," he said, handing the roll of bills through the window.

The man frowned and reached into his pocket. "Good heavens! You're right. Thank you so much!" he said gratefully as he took the money. "I guess there are still some honest people around after all."

Scott grinned and stepped back. "A few. Enjoy the flowers."

"I will. And thanks again."

Scott watched the man drive away, then turned back toward the main building—only to find Seth watching the scenario from a few feet away, fists on his hips, chomping on his ever-present unlit cigar. For a moment Scott's step faltered. Though the nursery owner never said much, Scott had developed great respect for him as a businessman—and a person. Seth had not only given him a chance when few were willing to take on an ex-con, but had steadily increased Scott's responsibility. After Scott's first design project went well, Seth had moved him permanently into the retail side of the business and funneled more such projects his way. He'd also given him a nice bump in salary. So even though Seth didn't offer much verbal praise, his actions spoke loud and clear. But right now Scott wasn't quite sure how to read the enigmatic look on the man's face. And he certainly wasn't expecting the man's first words.

"I think I found you a car."

Scott stared at him, his expression momentarily blank. "A car?"

Seth gave a quick nod. "I have a friend who's a mechanic. I asked him to keep an eye out for you. He thinks he's got a good one." Seth gave Scott the particulars, including the attractive price. "You can trust Les. He's a good man. I told him you might stop by on your lunch hour to take a look."

"I'd like to," Scott said with a frown. "But I'm already short on hours today." His work day had started with an apology to Seth for his late arrival because of the unfamiliar bus schedule from Jess's condo.

Seth waved his comment aside. "You work harder in

eight hours than most people do in twelve. Don't worry about it. I have to run an errand at lunch time, so I can drop you off at his shop and pick you up on my way back."

Scott hardly knew what to say. So he settled for a simple but heartfelt "Thank you."

"Meet me in the office at eleven-thirty," Seth said gruffly, turning toward the main building. As Scott watched the nursery owner stride away, his throat tightened in gratitude. Reverend Young had been right about Seth. The man might not practice much formal religion, but he lived the Christian values more fully than many churchgoing people Scott had met. Though Scott had been warned to expect the stigma of his prison record to follow him, it had still been a shock to experience reactions ranging from caution to distrust to aversion when people found out he was an ex-con. Even people at church. Some had been wonderful, of course, accepting him fully and welcoming him into their midst. But in the eyes of others he'd seen judgment and condemnation, as if his mistakes had tainted him forever. Those were rough moments. Discouraging moments. But thank God there were good people, too. Like Seth. And Reverend Young. People who believed in him and were willing to give him a chance.

Now, if only he could convince Jess to do the same.

The doorbell interrupted Scott's perusal of the real estate listings, and he set the paper aside with a discouraged sigh. Finding a reasonably priced apartment was proving difficult—especially since he'd promised

Karen he would upgrade his previous lodgings. But he'd have his car tomorrow, and then he could check out a few places in person—which should expedite things, he thought as he walked toward the door.

Fortunately, after seeing the long hours he worked and the time it took to travel by bus, Jess had told him that she didn't mind if it took him a few days to find a place to stay. He didn't intend to take advantage of her generosity, of course—but neither did he plan to rush. This time with her was a blessing, and he didn't want the opportunity to see her on a daily basis to end any sooner than necessary. It was too close to heaven, he thought, his lips curving into a smile.

The smile was still on his face when he opened the door a moment later, but it froze when he came face-to-face with Jess's parents. Their own smiles quickly gave way to shock, and from there her father's expression degenerated to hostility.

"What are you doing here?" Frank asked curtly, his face growing ruddy.

Scott's stomach twisted into a knot. "Hello, Frank. Clare. There was a fire at my flat, and Jess offered me her guest room until I found a new apartment."

"Where is she?"

"On her way home, I suspect. She should be here any minute. Would you like to come in and wait?"

"No, we would not."

"Is there anything I can help you with?"

"Yes. You can leave Jess alone!" Frank said furiously.

Scott felt a hot flush creep up his neck, and he struggled to maintain a cordial tone when he spoke. "I think that's between me and Jess."

Frank's face grew redder. "Really? Well, I don't. Not after what you did to her. Not after you left her mother and me to pick up the pieces. Good God, man, don't you think you've done enough damage? Do you have any idea how long it took her to get back on her feet after the accident? To be able to make it through a day without shaking so badly that she had to take medication? Do you know how many months she spent in counseling? And now you waltz back into her life and turn it upside down all over again! Don't think her mother and I haven't noticed the changes in her since you came back, either. Or that we haven't spent sleepless nights worrying that she'll end up on the verge of a nervous breakdown again. If you cared for her at all, you'd leave her alone. You'd walk out of her life and never come back."

By the time Frank finished his furious tirade, Scott felt almost physically sick. He had known just by looking at her that the past few years had taken an immense toll on Jess. But apparently the trauma had been even worse than he'd imagined. He'd had no idea she'd come that close to a nervous breakdown. Was Frank right? he wondered. Had his return caused more harm than good? Would Jess be better off without him?

With a weary sigh Scott raked his fingers through his hair and gazed at Jess's parents. "The last thing in the world I want to do is hurt Jess again," he said with quiet sincerity, his eyes troubled. "I love her. I always have and I always will. I realize I've made some bad mistakes. And I spent three long, lonely years in prison thinking about them. But the one thing that wasn't a mistake was marrying Jess. She's always been the best part of my life. It may have taken a tragedy for me to realize that, but now that I have, I want to spend the rest of *my* life filling *hers* with joy. I just don't see how that could be bad for her. Or for us."

There was silence for a moment while the two men stared at each other. Then Frank turned away. "Come on, Clare. Let's get out of here," he said coldly.

Scott transferred his gaze to Jess's mother, whose eyes were far less hostile than her husband's. She looked at him for a long moment, then held out a foil-covered dish. "I was going to drop this off for Jess," she said softly. "She likes my pot roast, and we had extra. There's enough for two."

Gratitude filled Scott's eyes as he reached for the container. "Thank you."

She nodded, then turned and joined her husband, who had moved a few feet away. He took her arm stiffly, and without a backward glance they walked away.

Slowly Scott closed the door and tiredly made his way to the kitchen, feeling suddenly drained. He slipped the casserole dish into the oven, then sank into one of the kitchen chairs and let his head drop into his hands. For the first time since his release he was actually tempted to have a beer. Working outdoors in the heat and humidity of the St. Louis summer had taken its toll physically, and the encounter with Jess's parents had taken its toll mentally. Yeah, a beer would taste good about now, he thought. Except he didn't drink anymore. Not even beer. He'd had enough trouble with alcohol to last ten lifetimes.

The phone rang, and Scott automatically reached for it. "Hello."

There was silence for a moment, and Scott frowned. He wasn't in the mood for games. Or for recorded phone solicitations, he thought irritably. He was just about to hang up when a voice on the other end spoke.

"Scott?"

Scott's irritation changed to puzzlement. No one knew he was here, except Seth and Karen. And this voice belonged to neither. "Yes?" he replied cautiously.

"I thought it was you. Sorry. It just took me by surprise. This is Mark."

Scott closed his eyes and groaned silently. Great. Just what he needed. A browbeating by yet another member of Jess's family. "Hello, Mark," he said coolly.

"So Jess finally took my advice, I see."

Scott's frown reappeared. "What are you talking about?"

Mark chuckled. "I can see she didn't give her brother credit for his brilliant counsel. By the way, welcome back."

At Mark's friendly tone, the tension in Scott's shoulders eased. As did his frown. "Thanks. What advice?"

"When she told me you were out and trying to talk to her, I told her to listen. She's kept everything bottled up inside for too long. And while *she* may think she's dealt with her issues and moved on, *I* know better. You guys had a good thing going for a long time. Frankly, I think you still do. The trick is convincing her."

Scott felt the last vestiges of tension vanish, and he expelled a relieved sigh. "Thanks."

"For what?"

"For not hating me. For trying to convince Jess to give me a chance. For calling when you did—right after I opened the door and gave your parents the shock of their lives."

"Ouch. I take it they didn't know you two have been talking?"

"They might have. But they didn't know I was staying here."

There was silence for a moment, and when Mark spoke his voice was cautious. "You want to explain that?"

Scott smiled. "It's not what you think. Unfortunately. There was a fire at my flat a couple of days ago, and Jess offered me her spare bedroom."

"No kidding! So how are things going?"

"I'm still here."

"Yeah. Good point. I'd call that progress," Mark said encouragingly. "Is she around?"

"Not yet. She should be here any minute."

"Okay. I'll get back with her later. In the meantime, hang in there. I have a good feeling about this. I know my sister. Even when she thought she hated you, she didn't. She just hated what you *did.* In fact, I'd go so far as to say that she still loves you. But hey, enough of this mushy stuff. I gotta run. If you need to hear a friendly voice, though, just give me a ring. Anytime."

The line went dead, and slowly Scott replaced the receiver, his expression thoughtful. Could Mark be right? he wondered. Did Jess still love him?

He wasn't as sure about that as Mark. But he did agree that her invitation to stay was definitely progress. And for right now, that was good enough.

Chapter Eleven

Scott had been listening for Jess, and when he heard her key in the lock he rose and headed for the foyer. He wasn't looking forward to telling her about her parents' visit, but he would rather she heard about it from him first.

"Someone's been cooking," she said with a surprised look, sniffing appreciatively as she leaned down to deposit her briefcase and purse on the floor. "It kind of smells like my mom's pot roast."

Scott took a deep breath. "It is."

Jess froze for a second, then slowly rose and turned to him in dismay.

"She and your dad stopped by a little while ago to drop it off."

Jess reached up to tuck her hair behind her ear, her eyes troubled. "I'm sure that wasn't very pleasant for you."

He shrugged. "I survived. Frankly, I'm more worried about *you*."

"Don't be. I can handle it."

She was putting up a good front, he acknowledged, but her voice lacked conviction and she was clearly agitated. He watched as she moved into the living room and stopped to stare unseeingly out the window, one hand on her hip, the other massaging her temple.

"It's my own fault for waiting to tell them," she said with a sigh. "I was going to break the news when I went to their house for dinner on Thursday, hoping that in a relaxed atmosphere they might be a bit more receptive. But that was just wishful thinking. They have strong feelings on the subject. Especially Dad." She turned to Scott with a frown. "What did they say?"

"Your mother was pleasant enough," he hedged.

"Which means Dad wasn't," she said flatly, dropping onto the couch. "Why am I not surprised?" Wearily she passed a hand over her eyes. "Nothing's ever easy, is it?"

Scott watched her silently, read her inner struggle in her eyes. It wasn't fair to make her choose between him and her parents. He didn't have the right to impose that burden on her. Much as he wanted to extend his stay, he couldn't do so if it made life more difficult for her. He jammed his hands into his pockets and took a deep breath. "I don't want to cause you any more problems, Jess. I can be out of here in an hour."

She frowned. "Did you find an apartment?"

"Not yet. But it's only a matter of days."

Slowly she shook her head, and her chin tilted up ever so slightly. "No. I offered you a place to stay, and I'm not backing down. It's my decision, not theirs," she said defiantly. "As much as I love Mom and Dad, they're wrong about this. It's my life. I have to live it as I think best, whether they agree or not." She rose and strode toward the door, pausing only to reach for her purse. "I'll be back in a little while. It's time Mom and Dad and I talked this thing out."

It had not gone well, Jess thought despondently as she got into her car. Actually, "abysmal" might be a better way to describe the encounter with her parents. Although her mother had been somewhat receptive, her father had stubbornly refused to listen to anything that conflicted with his firmly entrenched opinions, summarily dismissing the notion that Scott might truly have repented and changed. When their "discussion" degenerated to the point of becoming a shouting match, Jess had simply walked out.

She drove aimlessly for a time, too upset to return to the condo and face Scott but with no other destination in mind—until she suddenly thought about the meditation garden he'd designed for his church. She'd made a point to note the name of the church on his drawing, thinking that she might stop by sometime to see in person what she had so admired on paper. And suddenly this seemed as good a time as any. A contemplative, quiet place to think was just what she needed.

When Jess pulled into the deserted parking lot a few minutes later, dusk was starting to descend. A slight breeze gently stirred the warm air, giving the illusion of coolness, and the birds were just beginning their twilight song. She made her way toward the back of the church, pausing in admiration when she turned the corner. The rough pencil sketch had hardly done justice to the garden Scott had designed, she realized as her appreciative gaze swept over the scene.

A natural-wood gazebo stood gracefully on a small rise and was reflected in the surface of the placid lake beside it. A curving path led to the structure, weaving in and out among banks of glorious flowers that spilled down in welcoming array. As Jess slowly made her way toward the lake, she felt enveloped in color and harmony—the result of expert design, she realized. And by the time she stepped into the gazebo, her tension had eased considerably.

Jess sank onto the wooden bench that rimmed the inside of the structure and thought about the creator of this oasis of peace and harmony and tranquillity. Her husband. The man she had once loved with a passion that had seemed destined to endure for all time. But in the end, it hadn't been strong enough to survive hardship and tragedy. Oh, the passion had been. No question about that. But the love…that was different. Love was so much more than just hormones. It was trust and consideration and respect and communication and sharing and commitment. It was putting the other person's needs above your own. It was supporting them and believing in them even when the world didn't.

And it was forgiving.

Jess drew a long, shaky breath. The Scott who had emerged from the gray walls of prison was a man who, under other circumstances, she could easily fall in love with, she acknowledged. But they weren't beginning a relationship from scratch. They had a history together, one filled with pain and loss and tragedy. And so their future very much depended on forgiveness. Hers.

"Jess?"

She turned, startled. "Reverend Young!"

The minister closed the distance between them, pausing at the edge of the gazebo. "I'm sorry. Am I disturbing you?"

She managed a wry smile. "Relatively speaking, no."

"May I join you, then?"

"Of course."

He stepped up into the gazebo and sat across from her, gazing out over the lake. "This is a great spot, isn't it? I usually come back here for a few minutes to refresh my soul whenever I stop by the church. Scott did a great job." He paused for a moment to savor the view, then turned back to her. "By the way, I spoke with him a little while ago," he said. At her surprised look, he smiled. "We stay in close touch. I told him when he got out that I would always be available as a sounding board, and I'm happy to say he takes me up on the offer regularly. He told me about his encounter with your parents. And that you had gone to talk with them. I'm sure that wasn't easy."

Jess sighed. "No." Now it was her turn to gaze out over the lake. "They're having a hard time understanding why I've let Scott back into my life. And frankly, so am I. I've hated him for four years, and yet I invite him to stay at my condo." She shook her head, bewildered. "It doesn't make any sense."

"It might," Reverend Young said mildly.

Jess turned to him with a frown. "What do you mean?"

"Well, it all depends on whether the Scott you invited to stay at your condo is the same Scott who went to prison."

She looked at him thoughtfully. "In some ways, yes," she said slowly. "But he's changed quite a bit, too. For the better."

"Then maybe your invitation does make sense."

"Tell that to my parents," she said with a sigh.

"What do *they* think you should do?"

"Tell him to get lost. They still hate him for what he did to Elizabeth—and to me."

"And what about you, Jess? How do you feel about him?" he asked gently.

"I don't know." She rose restlessly and moved closer to the lake side of the gazebo, pressing her palms flat on the railing as she stared out over the water. "I used to hate him. But I'm tired of hating. And I—I'm not sure anymore that everything I blamed on him was all his fault, anyway." She paused, trying to gather the courage to speak what had long been in her heart. "The thing is, I shouldn't have *let* him drive that night," she said slowly. "If I'd been behind the wheel, maybe Elizabeth and the judge wouldn't have been killed. And if I'd been more understanding about his pressures at work, maybe he wouldn't have turned to alcohol in the first place."

She was afraid that when she turned she would see censure and recrimination in the minister's eyes. Instead, they reflected kindness and compassion.

"Guilt can be a terrible burden," he said quietly. "It can rob our lives of joy and hope and peace. We all do the best we can under the circumstances in which we find ourselves. Sometimes we make good choices. Sometimes we don't. That's part of being human. And we can't spend our lives beating ourselves up over the bad choices. At some point we have to accept the mistakes we've made, forgive ourselves and move on."

"You sound like Scott." She forced her lips into the semblance of a smile. "Or maybe he sounds like you."

Reverend Young chuckled. "The concept may have started with me—or, more accurately, with the Lord," he admitted. "But Scott took it to heart, though he'll be the first to admit that he struggled mightily with it. Sometimes it's easier to forgive others than to forgive ourselves, you know. But in the end, he felt the healing power of God."

Jess looked at him wistfully. "I wish I could."

"You can. You just have to ask for forgiveness—and most important, be willing to follow His example by forgiving others."

She drew a deep breath. "Even if that leads into dangerous waters?"

He eyed her shrewdly. "Anything that requires a leap of faith involves a certain amount of danger, Jess. That's true of forgiveness. And trust. And love."

Jess turned and gazed out again over the placid lake, wishing some of its serenity would seep into her soul. She tucked her hair behind her ear and drew a steadying breath. "Can I tell you something in confidence?"

"Of course."

"Sometimes I—I think I'm falling in love again with Scott," she whispered.

"Is that bad?" he asked gently.

She looked at him in confusion. "I don't know. It feels wrong somehow, like I'm dishonoring the memory of Elizabeth by accepting back into my life the man who caused her death."

Reverend Young studied her for a moment. "You know, Jess, I visited Scott regularly when he was in prison. We had a lot of long talks. Many of them about Elizabeth. And I lost track of the number of times he broke down and wept bitterly over her death. I can tell you with absolute certainty that no man ever loved his daughter more than Scott. Her loss was as devastating to him as it was to you. So I don't really think there's a conflict between your feelings for Scott and your love for Elizabeth. In fact, I believe that one of the best ways for you to honor the memory of Elizabeth would be to love her father—who loved her with all his heart."

Jess stared at Reverend Young. Could he possibly be right? she wondered in shock. Was loving Scott respectful of—rather than a violation of—the memory of Elizabeth? Or was the minister telling her this just because he was looking out for Scott's best interests? Yet she saw only conviction and honesty in the man's eyes. Dear God, she wanted to believe him! Desperately! Because if she did, there would be one less worry on her mind. One less obstacle to forgiveness. And she would be one step closer to making peace with her past.

"You don't have to make any decisions until you're ready," Reverend Young reassured her with an understanding smile. "Just think about it. Pray about it. And answers will come—in God's time." He stood and reached out to take her hand in a warm clasp. "I'll keep you in my prayers. And now I'll leave you to enjoy this beautiful spot in peace."

Jess watched the minister disappear down the flagstone path, then turned back to the quiet lake. Peace. Even the word had a lovely sound, she thought wistfully, savoring the echo of it in her mind. For four years it had been absent from her vocabulary. And from her life. In fact, she'd begun to believe that it had disappeared forever.

But suddenly, for the first time in a very long while, she felt the stirrings of hope in her heart. Reverend Young's comments had given her new insights and new options about how to deal with her situation. And if he was right, maybe she would find—through reconciliation—the peace that had been so elusive.

Now she just needed the courage to follow her heart.

"…heard the latest about Scott Mitchell?"

"I knew he got out."

"That's not the half of it. Get this…he and Jess are living together!"

Jess stopped abruptly, hidden by a bank of greenery from the women whose conversation she had inadvertently overheard at the restaurant where she was meeting Scott for lunch. She recognized the voices—the wives of two of Scott's former business associates with whom she and Scott had gone out socially on a number of occasions.

"You're kidding! Why in the world would she take up with him again? He's an ex-con, for heaven's sake!"

"I have no idea. She could certainly do better than that. I mean, what can he offer her? His career is toast. Brian saw him planting flowers at an office building downtown. He must work for a nursery or something. Manual labor—do you believe it? Which probably pays dirt—pardon the pun."

The other woman chuckled. "Cute. Anyway, that's probably all he could get. After all, who'd want to hire an ex-con?"

"Yeah. So much for the good life. No more power lunches or country clubs or filet mignon for him."

"Not exactly the fast track."

"Not exactly *any* track."

"Oh, I don't know. Maybe one day he could move up to shrubs. Or even shade trees. Or maybe Jess could support him."

Jess had become increasingly incensed as she listened to the conversation, but the two women's laughter was what drove her over the edge. Without even stopping to think, she stepped around the greenery.

"Hello, Jennifer. Susan." It was a struggle, but somehow she managed to maintain a civil tone.

"Jess! Why…we were just talking about you," one of the women replied, clearly flustered. She exchanged a guilty look with her companion, and both women's faces grew pink.

At least they had the grace to look embarrassed, Jess thought, gritting her teeth. "I know. I couldn't help overhearing. And I wanted to set the record straight on a few things. First of all, Scott and I are not living together—at least, not in the way you think. Second,

Scott understands that material things aren't really what life's about—and that they have nothing to do with what a person has to 'offer.' So the amount of money he makes isn't that important to him. It's too bad more people don't have their priorities straight," she said, glancing pointedly at the diamond rings on the women's fingers and the BMW key chain lying on the table.

"As for manual labor," she continued, "it's a lot more honest than the backbiting politics of the corporate world. And finally, I would suggest you think about your attitude toward ex-cons. You know one now. So you ought to realize that they don't all fit the same mold. Writing people off, denying them a chance because of a stereotype—be it race or gender or age or a prison record—is just plain wrong." She paused and took a deep breath. "Enjoy your lunch, ladies."

Jess didn't wait for them to reply. She simply turned and walked toward her table, her head held high. Only when she sat, her back to the women, did she realize that her legs felt like rubber and her hands were trembling. In-your-face confrontation just wasn't her style, she acknowledged, drawing a shaky breath. She generally avoided it at all costs, unless she felt passionate about a subject.

Which ought to tell her something, she suddenly realized with a jolt. Because her last two confrontations had involved defending Scott.

Scott's throat tightened with emotion and he moved farther back into the shadows as he watched Jess walk to her table. He, too, had overheard the conversation between the two women they'd once considered friends. Frankly, he was getting used to dealing with that kind of garbage. It rarely bothered him anymore. What did bother him was that their derogatory comments hadn't been confined to him. By association, Jess had been tainted, as well. Which was something he simply hadn't considered when he'd thought about them reuniting.

Scott jammed his hands into his pockets as he studied Jess's profile. She was clearly upset. He could see it in the rapid rise and fall of her chest, in the way she tucked her hair behind her ear, in her white-knuckled grip on her water glass. But intuitively he knew she wasn't upset because of the women's disparaging comments about *her*. She was upset because of what they'd said about *him*. Which made him feel good. And bad.

On the plus side, her vigorous defense of him was clear evidence that her feelings for him were deepening—whether she realized it or not.

On the minus side, today was only a preview of what she'd have to deal with if they got back together. Scott recalled her father's comment a few days earlier. "If you cared for her at all, you'd leave her alone. You'd walk out of her life and never come back," he'd said. Scott hadn't believed him then. But suddenly a seed of doubt crept into his mind. Was it fair to subject Jess to the bias that would likely follow him the rest of his life? he wondered, a troubled frown furrowing his brow. He'd just seen the effect of it firsthand. Her righteous anger told him that she was able to deal with such prejudice publicly. But as he studied her now, he was also aware that it had bruised her heart. This time, on his behalf. But eventually she would feel the hurt for herself, as well.

"Excuse me, sir…can I help you?"

Scott turned to find a waiter at his elbow. "No, thanks. I'm just getting ready to join my party."

As the man disappeared, Scott took a deep breath. Hiding in the shadows wasn't going to give him any answers. If he'd learned anything at all over the past four years it was to acknowledge problems and deal with them head-on. So, forcing his lips into a smile, he stepped into the sunlight and made his way toward Jess.

She looked up as he approached and returned his smile, though he could still see evidence of strain on her face as he took the seat across from her.

"Sorry I'm a few minutes late," he apologized. "A long-winded customer."

"That's okay. It gave me time to make a quick trip to the ladies' room."

"That's what I figured. The hostess said you'd been seated on the patio, but you were nowhere to be seen when I got here. So I waited under the grape arbor."

She shifted uncomfortably and glanced over her shoulder toward the table where the two women had been seated.

"They made a fast exit after your conversation."

Her gaze swung back to his. "How much did you hear?"

"Enough. And I'd like to thank you for your spirited defense."

Her face colored slightly. "I can't believe the things they were saying! How can people be so...so..."

"Unkind?"

Her eyebrows rose. "I had a stronger word in mind."

A wry smile pulled at the corners of his lips. "I'm getting used to it, Jess. It goes with the territory of being an ex-con."

"Well, it shouldn't."

"I agree. But it does. And unfortunately, the stigma is transferred to people who associate with ex-cons. Frankly, I don't care what those women said about me. But I do care very much about their derogatory comments about you."

She looked at him blankly. "What do you mean?" she asked, confirming his suspicion that she hadn't even noticed their snide remarks about her. He hated to call attention to them, but she needed to be aware of what she would face if the two of them got back together.

"Their implications were pretty clear," he said soberly. "You must be crazy to take up with an ex-con. It was beneath you. There's nothing I could offer you. You might even end up supporting me."

She stared at him. "I heard some of that. Not all."

"Trust me, it was there. Ex-cons become very sensitive to those kinds of things."

She looked at him, appalled. "Do you run into this all the time?"

He shrugged. "I was warned about it, so I was prepared. For myself, anyway. But not for you," he replied, evading her question.

She dismissed his concern with an impatient shake of her head. "I can handle that kind of garbage," she said brusquely.

"I know. I saw you in action. But I'd rather you didn't have to. And unfortunately, if you hang around me you'll have to," he said evenly, his gaze locked with hers.

Though his manner was outwardly relaxed, Jess could feel his tension. Clearly, he was deeply concerned about the scene that had just transpired—and even more concerned that it would likely be repeated in the future. Far more concerned than she. And he needed to know that. She returned his gaze steadily, and when she spoke her voice was filled with quiet resolve. "I'm not going to live my life to accommodate other people's prejudices. If people are so shallow they can't look past stereotypes, that's their problem, not mine. And if they can't accept me for who I am—the choices I make, the people I…" She had almost said "love," she realized in shock, her breath lodging in her throat. She stared at Scott, who was watching her intently, and quickly changed direction. "The people I choose to include in my life—then I don't want to have anything to do with them. And as for people like Jennifer and Susan— frankly, they're not even worth wasting breath on."

Scott studied her, warmed and encouraged by her response. Clearly, her feelings on the subject were strong. But were they strong enough to stand repeated attacks? he wondered. Including those from her own parents? Would she eventually become disheartened— or would her convictions intensify in adversity? Unfortunately, Scott didn't know the answer. He'd just have to trust his heart on this one, he realized—and pray that the Lord would offer him guidance.

"Can I take your order?"

Jess and Scott simultaneously looked at the waiter, then at each other.

"I'm ready, but you've hardly had a chance to look at the menu," Jess said.

He glanced down and scanned it quickly. "Go ahead. I only need a second."

Jess turned back to the waiter. "I'll have a chicken Caesar salad."

Scott looked at her with a frown. To get her to accept his invitation for this "thanks-for-your-hospitality" lunch, he'd had to overcome her protests that it was both unnecessary and too expensive. Though she'd finally capitulated, the cost was clearly still on her mind. "Don't you want something more substantial than that?" he said.

"This is plenty, really. I usually just have yogurt for lunch, so this is a big meal for me," she replied truthfully.

For a moment Scott hesitated, but then he let it pass and gave his own order. "Actually, as it turns out, this lunch is not only a thank-you but a celebration," he said as he handed his menu to the waiter.

She looked at him in surprise. "How so?"

"I have some good news. I found an apartment."

Jess stared at him. If his news was so good, why had her stomach suddenly dropped to her toes? she wondered. "Th-that's great," she replied, striving for an enthusiastic tone.

"I stopped in to see it this morning on my way to work. I think even Karen would approve. There is one problem, though. It won't be ready for occupancy for a week."

Though she quickly masked it, Scott saw the relief in her eyes—and suddenly felt the same emotion sweep through his heart. She didn't want him to leave!

"You're welcome to stay on at my place," she replied, confirming his assessment.

He smiled at her, and the warmth that radiated from his eyes sent a flush of heat sweeping over her. "I was hoping you'd say that. Because there's nowhere else I'd rather be. Thank you." He reached over and covered her hand with his.

Her breath caught in her throat as she looked at his lean brown fingers resting on hers. It took a concerted effort to tear her gaze from their hands, but when she finally did the undisguised hunger in his eyes not only made her mouth go dry—it curled her toes.

And made her wonder if she'd just made a big mistake.

"Wow! Something smells great!" Scott called as he stepped through the front door. "I hope I got what you wanted. I had no idea ginger came in—"

"Happy birthday!"

Scott paused, speechless, on the threshold of the kitchen. Today had *started* with a surprise, when Jess had said she'd like to go to church with him. And now it was *ending* with one, as well. The significance of the day had fleetingly crossed his mind when he'd awakened this morning, but then he'd forgotten about it. Frankly, his birthday had passed pretty much without notice for the past four years, except for a card from Karen and her family. He'd certainly never expected Jess to mark the occasion. And yet she had obviously gone out of her way to make the day special, to the point of contriving an errand so she could prepare a surprise while he was gone.

His gaze moved from the table set with crisp linens and good china to the chocolate cake on the counter dotted with far too many candles, then on to the gaily wrapped package beside it. Finally it returned to Jess, who was watching him anxiously, her face slightly flushed.

A rush of tenderness washed over him, and he reached up to brush the back of his hand across his suddenly damp eyes. "I can't believe...I never expected... This is so..." He paused and cleared his throat. "So much for eloquence," he said with a shaky laugh. "What I'm trying to say is thank you."

Jess smiled nervously. "You're welcome. I made pork tenderloin. I know you used to like it. I hope it's okay. I haven't made it in...for a long time."

If he was a man given to impulse, Jess would be in his arms by now, Scott thought. But he was still treading on somewhat shaky ground, and a wrong move could blow all the progress he'd made so far, he reminded himself, silently repeating the mantra he'd adopted over the past few days as logic and need duked it out in his heart. *Don't rush her. Wait until she reaches out to you. Be grateful for whatever she offers.* It was sound advice. But it was getting harder and harder to follow.

"Pork tenderloin sounds wonderful," he said huskily.

She tucked her hair behind her ear. "Well, have a seat. It's ready."

He did as instructed, and though the meal started off a bit awkwardly, his light banter quickly put her at ease. By the time they got to the cake, she was completely relaxed.

"I think you put too many candles on this," he protested with a smile as she placed it in front of him. "It's going to set off your fire alarm."

She chuckled. "I don't think so. Now make a wish."

It was what she'd always said on birthdays. But the last word faded out as their gazes locked. Because Scott had only one wish. And they both knew what it was. Without breaking eye contact he slowly leaned down and blew until every candle was out.

Again he was tempted to reach for her. Again he refrained. But it took every ounce of his self-restraint.

There was silence for a moment, and when she spoke her voice was a bit too bright—and breathless. "Well… that was impressive. I could say something about lots of hot air, but I won't." She lifted the cake to the counter behind her, turning her back as she cut it. "Why don't we take our cake and coffee into the living room?"

"Okay." He stood as well and reached for their plates. "I'll just clean up a little first so we don't have this mess to come back to."

She turned, the cake knife in her hand. Since becoming her house guest he'd made it a point to take on clean-up chores after meals, but tonight she shook her head. "Not on your birthday," she said firmly.

He hesitated, then grinned and put the plates back on the table. "Since you have a knife in your hand, I don't think I'll argue. Can I at least carry the cake into the living room?"

She nodded, handing him the two plates. "I'll get the coffee."

When she joined him a moment later carrying two mugs, she also had the wrapped package under her arm. She handed him his coffee, then sat beside him on the couch and held out the present.

"You didn't have to do this, Jess," he said, hesitating.

She shrugged. "I wanted to. Go ahead. Open it."

He reached for the package then, and she scooted closer to look over his shoulder as he tore off the wrapping to reveal a comprehensive landscaping book.

"I asked some of the horticulturists at the garden to recommend a good reference book," she said anxiously. "This was their unanimous choice. I—I hope it's all right. I can return it if you don't think it will be helpful."

Scott ran his hand lovingly over the dust jacket, trying to swallow past the lump in his throat as he vainly attempted to think of something he could say that would adequately express what was in his heart. But finally he gave up. Mere words couldn't capture the depth of his feelings for this special woman, for her thoughtfulness and her kindness and her incredibly loving heart.

He turned to her, and her eyes were so close he could see the gold flecks in their irises. So close that he began to drown in their green depths. So close that logic somehow seemed less important than listening to his heart. And his heart was speaking loud and clear, telling him to forget about words and express his feelings in the silent language of love.

It was time, his heart said with quiet certainty.

And Scott listened to his heart.

Chapter Twelve

Slowly, ever so slowly, Scott set the book aside and reached out to gently touch Jess's cheek. He heard her breath catch as his fingers made contact, and then she went absolutely still, like a tensed deer unsure whether to linger or bolt. Warning bells went off in Scott's mind, but he was powerless to heed them. Now that he'd touched Jess, there was simply no way he could back off.

Lightly, brushing her skin with only the tips of his fingers, he began to stroke her cheek. Her eyes fluttered closed, and though a tremor ran through her she didn't pull away. Even when he let his fingers travel to the curve of her neck, when he gently pushed aside her soft hair to trace the delicate curve of her ear, she remained unmoving. Only when his fingers returned to her face and whispered across her soft lips did she jerk back with a gasp, her eyes wide.

Jess stared at Scott. She'd known all along that the chemistry between them was as potent as ever. She'd tried to ignore it, tried to dance around it, tried to pretend she could control her reaction to it. But that was no longer possible. Scott's undemanding, gentle touch had ignited a feeling that simply could not be ignored. Every nerve in her body was tingling, and her pulse rate was off the scale. She wanted this. Needed this. But she was scared.

Reverend Young had said that anything that required a leap of faith involved a certain amount of danger, she recalled. And there was certainly danger here—because they were at a turning point. She could walk away, insulate herself in the relatively safe but lonely world she'd created, or she could take that leap of faith, trusting that her heart—and the Lord—would guide her steps.

As she looked into Scott's deep brown eyes, she knew what she *wanted* to do. She wanted to melt into his embrace, let his strong, sheltering arms carry her to a world where only the two of them existed. Where they could soar together to a place of joy and peace and harmony. Where nothing mattered but the love that bound them together. That's what she wanted—if she could just get past the doubt and fear.

With an effort she pulled her gaze from his and transferred it to the picture of Elizabeth. Fear hadn't been part of her daughter's vocabulary, she recalled with a wistful pang. Elizabeth had always wanted to climb to the highest spot on the jungle gym while her mother watched in trepidation from below, ready to cushion her fall if she lost her balance or took a wrong step. Jess had repeatedly cautioned her to be careful, a warning that

usually fell on deaf ears. But suddenly, as clearly as if
it had been spoken yesterday, the response her daughter
had once made to that admonition came back to her.

"I *am* being careful, Mommy. But if you're too
careful you can never touch the sky," Elizabeth had
said matter-of-factly, in all of her four-year-old wisdom.

Tonight Jess wanted to touch the sky. Or at least take
the first step up the jungle gym. But there was no one
waiting to catch her if she fell, as there had been for her
daughter. Yet she knew beyond the shadow of a doubt that
the lack of a safety net wouldn't have stopped Elizabeth.
So the question was, did she share her daughter's courage?

Scott watched Jess as she gazed at the picture of their
daughter, fully aware that she was struggling with a
decision that would have dramatic implications for both
of them. He remained motionless, barely daring to
breathe, his hand resting in his lap where he'd let it drop
when she'd abruptly backed off. For four long years
he'd dreamed of the moment when he would again hold
the woman he loved in his arms, the moment she would
come to him willingly and say, if not "I love you," at
least, "I'll give this a chance." And now the moment
seemed near. So near that he began to tremble. And to
pray.

Jess took a deep breath, trying vainly to control the
uncomfortable pounding of her heart as she looked
back at Scott. His gaze captured hers compellingly, revealing a myriad of emotions. Tenderness. Love. Encouragement. Hope. Passion. Most definitely passion,
she acknowledged as her mouth went dry. The banked
fire in his eyes was carefully held in check, but she

knew that it would burst into a consuming flame at the slightest provocation. Yet he didn't say a word or make a move. He simply waited, leaving the outcome in her hands.

Jess thought again of Elizabeth, always reaching for the sky. Never letting fear get in the way. And with sudden decision, she slowly, tentatively reached out and touched his face.

His eyes darkened, and now it was his turn to suck in a sharp breath. But he remained otherwise motionless—which gave Jess the courage to continue.

Lightly, gently she let her fingers move over his face, revisiting the familiar contours, learning the changes. His brow was no longer as smooth as it had once been, she realized. But worry and pain and sorrow could do that to a person. A muscle in his cheek clenched as her hand drifted lower to graze the taut skin over his cheekbones. Then her fingers moved lower still to trace the line of his strong jaw. It was just as she remembered it, complete with the slightly rough texture that signaled the beginning of evening stubble—a tactile sensation that had always given her pleasure. Only when her fingers approached his lips did she hesitate.

Jess's touch had been pleasurable torture, and it had taken every ounce of Scott's willpower to remain unmoving as she explored his face. But now that she'd hesitated, he reacted. Slowly, deliberately he reached for her hand and guided it to his lips, placing an exquisitely tender kiss in her palm. When he raised his gaze to hers, he made no attempt to hide the love in his eyes.

Nor could she hide the longing in the depths of hers, though doubt still hovered at the edges. But he wasn't going to give doubt a chance to get the upper hand. Not tonight. Not when he was a whisper away from making a reality of the dream that had sustained him in prison.

So before she had a chance for second thoughts he reached out to her, cupping her face with both hands, letting his callused thumbs gently stroke her satiny skin. He could feel her quivering, and he knew that she was afraid. But he also knew that fear alone wasn't the cause of her reaction. And that gave him hope.

As he drank in the sight of her beautiful face and felt her soft skin beneath his fingers, a wave of gratitude and tenderness and love washed over him, so intense that tears pricked his eyelids and his throat tightened with emotion. "I love you, Jess," he whispered hoarsely. "I always have and I always will."

He watched her eyes grow luminous, then fill with answering tears. And when he pulled her close, pressing her soft, supple body tightly against the hard, muscular planes of his own, she offered no resistance. He buried his face in her soft hair, and for a long time he simply held her, savoring the moment that for four long years had been only a fantasy. He could feel her trembling—or was it him? he wondered. He felt as shaky as a teenager about to experience his first kiss. Except the stakes were a whole lot higher in this case.

At last he eased back far enough to search Jess's slightly dazed eyes. Doubt had been replaced by yearning. And invitation. And need. And so he did what he'd been wanting to do ever since he'd seen her that first day outside her condo. He lowered his mouth to hers to taste the sweetness that only her kiss could offer.

As Scott's lips moved over hers, gently at first and then with growing urgency, Jess's world spun out of orbit. For four long years she'd stifled memories of the radiant joy of being in Scott's embrace. Of the way his strong arms would mold her pliant body to his, firmly, surely, possessively, but with infinite tenderness even at the moments of greatest passion. Even now, after four lonely years, when he must be yearning for so much more than this simple kiss, his touch was demanding but not forceful. She could taste his hunger, feel his need, and she knew what he wanted. But she also knew that he would be grateful for whatever she was willing to give. And that made her feel safe. Which, in turn, only made her want to give more.

Scott knew the precise instant at which Jess let down her guard and gave herself to the moment. He could feel her surrender in the subtle change in muscle tension, in the way her body melted against his. And as she proceeded to meet him kiss for kiss, as her hands moved convulsively over his back, up to his neck, urging him closer and closer, only one rational thought penetrated his consciousness—the dreams that had sustained him in his cold, sterile cell didn't even come close to actually holding Jess's warm, responsive body in his arms.

When Scott at last drew back, they were both breathing fast. Too fast. For several long seconds that was the only sound in the room as they both struggled to regain their equilibrium. But slowly they came back to earth. And as they did, Scott saw the doubt and uncertainty creep back into Jess's eyes. And heard it in her voice.

"Scott, I…I didn't plan for…I mean, I don't want you to think that… I'm still not sure…" Her voice trailed off, and warm color suffused her face.

He studied her for a moment, then reached over and took her hand. "Let me put your mind at ease," he said, his voice slightly unsteady. "I don't consider tonight a promise or a commitment. Just a first step. Okay?"

Relief flooded her eyes, and she nodded jerkily. "Okay." She drew a deep breath, then looked at the table. "I—I'm afraid our coffee got cold. And we didn't eat our cake."

He looked at her steadily. "No. But I got my wish."

As for the coffee, it was the only thing in the room that *had* grown cold, he thought wryly as his remark sent another becoming blush across Jess's cheeks. And suddenly he was glad he'd found an apartment. Because he knew he still needed to move slowly. And after tonight, that was going to be very, very difficult. Especially when he wanted to share so much more than a roof with the woman he loved.

"Got a minute, Scott?"

Scott looked up from his clipboard to find Seth standing at the entrance of the tropical house. "Sure. I'm about done with the inventory in here anyway."

"Let's sit for a minute, then." Seth nodded to a teakwood bench tucked under a display of palms.

Scott watched in surprise as the older man headed

toward the bench. The only time Seth ever sat was in his office, and even that was a rarity. The man seemed to have an inexhaustible supply of energy, and he was constantly on the move. Unless he had something serious to discuss.

Scott frowned. Had his boss noticed his preoccupation this week? he wondered as he followed him to the bench. Because ever since his birthday, he'd been distracted. Big time. There'd been no more kissing, but the tension between him and Jess fairly sizzled. It took every ounce of his willpower to keep his hands to himself, and on the few occasions when he simply hadn't been able to resist the urge to reach out and touch her, sparks had flown in all directions. Keeping himself in check had become a major battle.

Adding to that had been other, more practical concerns that he'd pushed aside until now. Like the need to contribute financially to a relationship. Like making enough money to support a family, if the Lord were to bless him with other children. Seth had been good to him and he loved the work, but even if he kept moving up at the nursery, it would be a long time before his wages would be sufficient to provide for a family. And the idea of reentering the corporate world—even if that was possible—held no appeal.

As Scott sat on the bench, Seth leaned back, chewing speculatively on his cigar. "In case I haven't said it already, I want to thank you for the marketing advice. Those ads you put together with that agency are paying big dividends. Gross revenue is up twenty percent since they started running. Which means we're twenty percent busier. Too busy for me to handle alone. I could use a partner. You interested?"

Scott stared at the older man, dumbfounded. He had grown accustomed to the owner's abrupt style and rapid-fire delivery, but today's bombshell left him reeling.

Seth's eyes glinted with amusement and the corners of his lips quirked up. "I guess maybe that was a little too blunt. But I'm not a man who likes to waste words. Get to the point and get on with it is my motto. Good thing I didn't go into politics, I guess." He leaned back on the bench and crossed his arms over his chest.

Usually Scott appreciated the man's wry wit and dry sense of humor. But he was so busy trying to assimilate Seth's first comment that he barely heard the second one. "You want me to be your partner?" Scott said incredulously when he finally found his voice.

"That's right."

"But…why me?"

Seth chomped on his cigar and eyed him shrewdly. "You're smart. You're a hard worker. You're honest. You have a knack for this business. Seems like a winning combination to me. So are you interested?"

Scott raked his fingers through his hair as a wave of excitement washed over him. Maybe he had a future here after all. Seth's offer would allow him to do the work he loved for the rest of his life *and* provide him with a decent standard of living. But Scott's euphoria quickly faded as a strong dose of reality suddenly kicked in. Partnerships cost money. Which he didn't have, he acknowledged with a sigh. "I'm definitely interested. But unfortunately I can't afford to buy into the business," he said regretfully.

Seth shrugged. "We can work things out. I could put together an equity deal that would let you work toward half ownership over time."

Once again Scott stared at him, completely taken aback by the man's kindness and generosity. "You're serious, aren't you?"

"Wouldn't have said it if I wasn't," Seth replied gruffly, though the affection in his eyes belied his tone. "But don't make any snap decisions. This is a hard business. Takes a lot of energy and stamina to keep things on an even keel. It's a good business, though. Working with living things, creating places of beauty—that's healthy for the soul. Keeps you in touch with God's creation. So think about it overnight. And if you're still interested in the morning, we'll talk about the particulars."

Seth stood, and Scott followed. The older man was slightly shorter than Scott, and much more wiry in build. But there was strength in his muscles, and character in his face. Their eyes met, Seth's startlingly blue, Scott's deep brown. And though they came from entirely different backgrounds, each man recognized in the other a kindred spirit. Each knew that their shared values and mutual respect would provide a solid foundation on which to build. And Scott also knew that he could never form a partnership with a finer man. He held out his hand, and Seth took it in a firm grip.

"Thank you." The words were simple but heartfelt.

"It's my pleasure, Scott. Good people deserve good things. I'm just doing my part."

* * *

Scott flipped on the evening news, then headed for the kitchen. Jess had called to say she'd be a little late, and she'd sounded so tired that in a moment of madness he'd offered to start dinner. Though he'd gotten very good at most household chores, cooking was definitely not one of them, he acknowledged ruefully. Still, he could at least get the salad going. After all, how much damage could he do to lettuce?

As he absently withdrew the ingredients from the refrigerator he thought back to Jess's reaction when he'd told her about Seth's offer, and a smile tipped the corners of his lips. She'd clearly been delighted for him—and proud. It had been a good moment. One that had led to a spontaneous kiss—of joy and congratulations and celebration rather than passion, but a good kiss nonetheless. One that was comfortable and natural and warm. The kind that couples often shared after years of marriage. The kind *they* had once shared—and which had sometimes led to other ways of celebrating. This one hadn't. But it was another step forward. And it gave Scott hope that Jess was on the verge of stepping out of the past and into the future—with him. Though he would be moving in two days, he was optimistic that before long their separation would be history. That they could once again…

"…identified as Juan Ruelas, who was released from prison in April after serving ten years of a fifteen-year sentence for involuntary manslaughter. More on this story when we return."

With a frown, Scott left the salad fixings on the

counter and moved into the living room. He knew Juan Ruelas. They'd served together. The man had been a loner, rarely talking to other inmates, but for some reason he'd taken a liking to Scott. Maybe because they both came from St. Louis. But more likely because Scott was willing to listen when the man wanted to vent about his growing-up years in the slums, about his absentee father and alcoholic mother, about stealing food when he was nine years old because there was nothing to eat in the house, about his bitterness toward a society that seemed to offer little hope and even fewer opportunities. He would pour out his feelings in a rush of words, like water suddenly released from behind a dam. Scott could do little to ease his pain—except listen. But that had often seemed to be enough.

Scott had known Juan might be released in the spring and that he, too, planned to return to St. Louis. He'd meant to follow up, to let the troubled man know that he still had a friend if things got tough. But his own transition back into society had been fraught with more challenges than he'd anticipated and he'd never gotten around to looking Juan up. Now it appeared to be too late. Though he'd missed the first part of the teaser for the news, if Juan was the lead story he was in big trouble.

The commercial break ended, and the anchorman came back on the screen. "Earlier this afternoon Judge Walter Johnson was taken hostage at his office in the county courthouse by a man he sentenced to prison ten years ago. According to witnesses, Juan Ruelas gained access to the courthouse about four o'clock this afternoon through a service entrance and made his way to Judge Johnson's office. He released the judge's secretary, who told police that Johnson had two handguns and that he appeared extremely agitated. He is demanding one hundred thousand dollars in cash, an airline ticket to Mexico and safe passage to the airport in return for the release of Judge Johnson. The police have been negotiating with him by phone, but so far there has been no progress. We'll keep you informed as developments occur.

"In other news tonight…"

With a troubled frown Scott reached over and slowly turned off the television. The police would get nowhere with Juan. He hated authority figures of any kind, particularly those in law enforcement, whose mere presence seemed to incite his already volatile emotions. Only someone he trusted would have a chance of reaching him, of convincing him to give up this crazy scheme. Only someone like Scott.

"Is something wrong?"

He turned, startled, to find Jess hovering in the doorway. He hadn't heard her come in, but he could tell from her expression that she'd been standing there long enough to sense that something was *very* wrong. Her hand was white-knuckled on the door frame, and every line of her body was tense.

Scott drew a shaky breath. *Dear God, why?* he cried in silent anguish as the full impact of the news story suddenly hit home. *Just when I'm about to regain my life, I'm faced with a situation where I might lose it. And yet I can't just walk away. Not when another life hangs in the balance. A life I might be able to save. If Juan is*

*as agitated as it sounds, there's no one else who even
stands a chance of calming him down enough to talk
him out of this plan. It's up to me. And I could very well
fail. Please, Lord, give me the courage to do what I have
to do. And please help Jess understand why I must.*

Slowly Scott walked toward Jess—and the closer he
came, the more scared she got. There was pain in his
eyes. And fear. And resignation. But there was also
love. Deep, abiding love that reached all the way to the
depths of her soul. She clung to that love as Scott
reached out and took her cold hands in his.

"Did you see the story about the judge?" he asked
quietly.

She nodded mutely, not trusting her voice.

"I served with the man who took him hostage. In a
sense, I became his confidant. He's a troubled soul,
Jess, with a lot of anger inside. I don't know what made
him do this, but I do know that he must be desperate.
And he's not going to listen to the police. He'll only
listen to someone he trusts."

The knot in her stomach tightened convulsively, and
her voice was strained when she spoke. "His social
worker, maybe?"

Scott shook his head regretfully. "Unfortunately,
no. He or she is part of the 'system' Juan hates. It has
to be a friend."

Jess drew a shuddering breath. She knew where this
was leading. Had known almost since she'd stepped
into the room. "You can talk to him by phone, can't
you?" There was a touch of desperation in her
voice now.

Scott saw the fear in her eyes, and it matched that in his heart. He wished he could just walk away from this, pretend he'd never heard the news story. But it wasn't in his nature. "We can try that first," he said carefully, knowing that wasn't what she wanted to hear, but reluctant to make any promises he might not be able to keep. Because he doubted that a long-distance conversation would have much impact with Juan. But he would try. For Jess's sake. And his own.

Jess took refuge in the protective circle of Scott's arms as he made his call to the police, drawing comfort from the solid strength of his lean body. She watched him as he spoke, his voice calm, his resolution firm. And although she was deathly afraid, she was also proud. Of his caring. His convictions. His compassion.

And suddenly, as if a veil had been lifted, she realized that all her doubts about this special man were groundless. Over and over again during the past few months he'd demonstrated how his life had been transformed by the power of God's grace, had proven that he was a man worthy not only of forgiveness—but of love. Jess had simply been too blind—or perhaps too hard-hearted—to recognize that the changes in Scott were real, just as his remorse was. And now that she had, it might be too late.

Scott replaced the receiver and turned to her, taking both her hands tenderly in his. "They're sending a squad car. I'll be back as soon as it's over," he said gently.

She shook her head. "I can't just sit here and wait for the phone to ring. I'm going with you."

He frowned. "I'll feel better if you're here."

"But I won't. I'm going."

The stubborn set of her chin told him that argument was useless. And he didn't want to spend these last few moments arguing, anyway. Silently he reached for her, and she went willingly into his arms, hugging him fiercely.

"Oh, Scott, why did this have to happen now?" she asked brokenly, her voice muffled against his shirt.

"I don't know," he admitted, his lips in her hair, his own voice none too steady.

They clung to one another silently, all too aware that in a few minutes Scott would walk into a situation fraught with danger and uncertainty. And equally aware that he might not walk out. For Jess, it was like a replay of the nightmare events of four years before. Now, as then, her life was in chaos, pummeled by forces she didn't control. But this time, instead of closing herself off from the Lord she reached out to Him, praying for the strength and courage to accept His will.

When the doorbell rang, a sob rose in Jess's throat and she instinctively hugged Scott even more tightly. Only at the second, more insistent ring did he ease back and look down at her. Tears were running freely down her face, and the anguish and fear in her eyes tore at his heart. "I have to go," he said gently.

"I know," she whispered brokenly. She reached up to lay her hand against his cheek for a moment, then cupped his neck and drew his head down to hers. And in the instant before their lips met in a last, desperate kiss, he heard her whisper four beautiful words.

"I love you, Scott."

* * *

"We told him you were on the way. He's on the line. Good luck."

As Scott took the phone from the officer he glanced toward the cordoned-off courthouse, where a man's life hung in the balance. *Please, Lord give me the words— and the courage—to see this through,* he prayed fervently.

"Juan?"

"Hey, Scott, is that really you, man?"

Juan's voice was so agitated that Scott hardly recognized it. He had seen the man rant and rave on numerous occasions, but from his high-pitched, frenzied tone it was clear that Juan was over the top today, high on either drugs or fear. Though his heart was hammering in his chest, Scott kept his voice as calm as possible when he responded. "Yeah. It's me. What's going on?"

"I got me a judge."

"So I hear. What do you want a judge for?"

"I don't want him, man. He's just a ticket out of here. I'm heading for Mexico."

"I thought you were going to go straight when you got out."

"Yeah, well, it didn't work out that way," he said bitterly. "Nobody wants an ex-con around. They treat you like dirt. Like you still got the smell of prison on you. Ain't no such thing as a second chance, man."

"There might be, if you let the judge go. I can talk to the police for you."

A brief, harsh laugh came over the line. "Who you

tryin' to kid, man? They'll throw me back in that hole and I won't never see the light of day again. I can't go back there. This is my only—" A click sounded on the line, and Juan stopped talking for a moment. "Hey, man, what was that noise? Is somebody listening in?" he asked suspiciously.

"No. It's just me and you."

"Yeah, well, I'm not talkin' on the phone anymore. You wanna talk, you come up here. Alone."

The line went dead.

Slowly Scott handed the phone back to one of several police officers who were now clustered around him. "He wants me to come up."

"No!" The panic in Jess's voice—and eyes—was almost palpable as she reached out to clutch his arm.

"I agree with the lady, Mr. Mitchell," one of the officers said. "That guy's on the edge. And he could slip over at any moment."

"He won't hurt me," Scott said with more confidence than he felt.

One of the higher-ranking officers stepped forward. "I don't think it's worth the risk. We could end up with two dead men instead of one," he said bluntly.

Scott heard Jess gasp, and he reached for her hand and held it tightly. But he didn't look at her. If he did, his courage would fail. "He won't hurt me," Scott repeated. "I know Juan. He trusts me. And there's a chance he'll listen to me. If he doesn't, you're no worse off than you are now. You really don't have anything to lose."

The officer looked at him skeptically. "You mean

you think he'll just let you walk out of there after your little chat?"

Scott's gaze locked with his. "I'm betting my life on it," he replied steadily.

The man studied him for a moment, then brushed a weary hand across his eyes. "I don't know what else to try, other than rushing the building. And we're bound to have some casualties if we do that." He sighed and turned to one of the officers. "Okay. Get Ruelas on the phone again. Tell him his friend is coming up." Then he turned back to Scott and pointed toward the building. "It's the corner office. Second floor. The one with the broken glass. He took a potshot at us earlier. I guess he wanted to let us know he was serious."

As Scott glanced toward the window that had been shattered by a bullet, his courage faltered. Dear God, he didn't want to do this! But the cup had been given to him. He had no choice but to accept it. Slowly he turned to Jess, and his gut clenched painfully as his gaze took in her pale face, trembling hands and shock-filled eyes. He reached for her and pulled her close, cradling her head with his hand as he pressed her cheek to his chest, wanting to spare her this but knowing he couldn't.

"I'll be back," he whispered, his voice muffled in her hair.

And then, before she could respond, he gently extricated himself from her arms and strode toward the building, leaving his fate in the hands of the Lord.

From the moment Scott disappeared inside the courthouse, time crawled for Jess. Five minutes felt like an hour. Ten minutes felt like a year. Twenty minutes felt like an eternity. After half an hour, she was so distraught that one of the officers brought her a bottle of water and urged her to sit down. But she refused both. Her throat was too tight to swallow, and she was too hyper to remain still. So she paced. And prayed. And kept her gaze fixed on the second-floor window.

After forty-five minutes, even the police were getting uneasy. There'd been no communication from the building, and a phone call to the judge's office had gone unanswered. Jess's nerves were ready to snap, and she was just about to demand that the police do something—*anything*—when at last the silence was broken.

By a single gunshot.

Jess's heart stopped, then lurched on, and she felt physically sick. Pandemonium broke out around her as the officer in charge snapped out orders and several uniformed men prepared to rush the building. But the frenzied activity came to a sudden stop when the police phone rang.

For a moment everyone froze. And then, at the second ring, the commanding officer reached for the receiver. He listened for a moment, then nodded. "Okay. Sit tight. Help is on the way." He replaced the receiver and turned to the assembled group. "Ruelas turned the gun on himself. Let's get a doctor up there on the double and move in. Johnson and Mitchell are okay."

Jess heard the words. Processed them. And then she did something she'd never done before.

She fainted.

* * *

Jess heard the voice calling her name from a long way off. The voice she'd been afraid she would never hear again. And as her eyelids flickered open and she saw the face that matched the voice, she knew the nightmare was over. Scott was safe.

"She's coming around."

At the sound of the unfamiliar voice, Jess transferred her gaze to a uniformed figure on her other side with a stethoscope around his neck. A paramedic. Only then did she realize that she was lying on the ground. "Did I faint?" she asked in surprise.

The worried frown on Scott's face eased and he squeezed her hand. "You've been out cold for ten minutes."

"The vitals all seem to be okay," the paramedic said. "How do you feel?"

Jess looked at Scott, and tears of relief flooded her eyes as she reached out to touch his weary face. "Grateful to have my husband back," she replied in a choked voice.

Scott covered her hand with his own, and their gazes locked in silent communication that spoke more eloquently than words of the love that filled their hearts.

"We can take you in and have you checked out just to be safe," the paramedic offered.

Jess's gaze never left Scott's. "I'm already safe," she said softly.

And as Scott reached for the woman he loved and tenderly took her in his arms, his heart overflowed with joy. For he knew that at long last he had truly come home.

Epilogue

"You look beautiful. Don't touch a thing."

Jess set the comb back on the counter and slowly turned to Scott. She had never seen him look more handsome—even on their *first* wedding day. His dove-gray suit sat well on his broad shoulders, and his silver-and-maroon tie looked elegant against his starched white shirt. The silver flecks in his hair added a distinguished touch, and the fine lines in his face that had appeared over the past few years spoke of character and caring rather than age.

But it was his eyes that set her heart racing. Because they were the eyes of a man deeply, irrevocably in love—who was making no attempt to hide his love as his gaze moved leisurely, appreciatively over his wife.

"I like the dress."

Jess blushed and self-consciously smoothed a non-existent wrinkle out of the sleeveless, knee-length ivory lace sheath that flattered her slender figure. Though it had been hastily purchased, it was clear from Scott's expression that she'd made a good choice. "Thank you." She reached for the boutonniere that lay next to her bouquet. "Do you need some help with this?"

"Absolutely."

She stepped toward him and reached up to his lapel, all too aware of his almost tangible—and overpowering—virility. The distinctive, masculine scent of his aftershave filled her nostrils, and they were so close that his breath was a warm caress on her cheek. Suddenly she began to quiver. Not in fear, but in anticipation. For soon they would once again be man and wife in the fullest sense of the word.

It took her fumbling fingers several tries to secure the boutonniere, but at last it was firmly in place. She made a move to step back, but Scott grasped her upper arms and held her in place, forcing her to meet his eyes. His gaze searched hers, incisive, assessing. "Any second thoughts?" he asked.

She looked at him steadily and shook her head. "None."

He studied her for a moment longer, as if to reassure himself, then lowered his head to claim her lips in a lingering kiss that was filled with passion and promise.

"No more of that until *after* you renew your vows," a voice interrupted teasingly.

Scott and Jess turned to find Reverend Young in the doorway, and Scott grinned. "Then let's get this show on the road."

The minister chuckled. "My sentiments exactly. I'll meet you in the gazebo."

Scott retrieved Jess's bouquet, then reached for her hand and laced his fingers with hers. "Ready?"

She smiled, and when she spoke her voice was quiet but confident. "Yes."

With an encouraging squeeze of her hand, Scott led her outside. And as they began their walk through the garden he had so lovingly created, she thought about her answer. Yes, she was ready. Ready to let go of the past. Ready to move forward, into the future, with the man she loved. Ready to touch the sky.

Scott, too, was ready. To start a new chapter of his life with the woman he cherished. And he was glad they'd chosen to begin this way. Though their marriage had never actually ended, he and Jess had felt that it needed an official new beginning. And they'd wanted to share this moment with the people who meant so much to them.

As they walked down the path toward the gazebo, he let his gaze travel over the group assembled by the lake. Karen and her family were there, and even from a distance he could tell that his sister, always a sucker for happy endings, was already misty-eyed. Seth had come as well, looking slightly uncomfortable—but remarkably distinguished—in a suit. And Mark was there, grinning from ear to ear, clearly elated that his sister had at last taken his advice. Even Jess's parents had come. It had been touch and go with her father until the last minute, but in the end his love for Jess had outweighed his feelings about her husband. Scott knew he still had fence-mending to do with Jess's father, but he took Frank's presence today as a hopeful sign.

When they reached the gazebo and stepped up to join Reverend Young, Scott glanced down at Jess. Their gazes met and held, and her eyes reflected what was in his heart—gratitude for this second chance at love, and absolute trust that the Lord who had brought them back together would continue to stand by them and give them the strength and courage to face whatever challenges might lie ahead. And in that moment of silent communion their hearts pledged what words would reconfirm in just a few moments.

Reverend Young began to speak, and as Scott transferred his gaze to the minister he was filled with a feeling of absolute peace and completeness. For he and Jess had now come full circle. They'd survived the dark, bleak winter of pain and separation and loss. Now they stood poised on the threshold of a new day, a new season, one filled with the promise of hope and joy and love.

And as he and Jess prepared to renew their vows before God and their families and friends, he suddenly recalled the words Seth had said to him the first time they met. And he knew that they were true.

Spring always comes.

* * * * *

Dear Reader,

As this book goes to press, my parents are celebrating their forty-eighth anniversary. What an accomplishment in a world where half of marriages end in divorce. And what a shining example of the enduring power of love! Through good times and bad, in sickness and in health, they have faced life together, always knowing that their love would see them through.

In comparison to their forty-eight-year union, my marriage is a mere child at twelve years. But I already have a sense of how tough it can be to keep that "for better, for worse" vow. So many things take a toll on marriage. Demanding careers that leave couples little time—or energy—for each other. Unexpected disappointments that change the direction of your life together. Well-laid plans that go awry. Hurts that only time and a change of heart can heal.

Fortunately, few marriages have to overcome the kind of tragedy that Jess and Scott face in *Never Say Goodbye*. Instead, most are simply worn down by the petty annoyances of daily life. And in a world of "I-have-to-take-care-of-myself-first" attitudes and values that change from situation to situation, there is little to encourage the stick-to-it-iveness that is the glue of marriage. It's easier to just give up when trials and tribulations replace romance and roses.

But what a loss that is. Because it's the enduring power of love that gives marriage its depth and dimension. For there is incredible peace and joy in knowing that whatever happens, you'll still be together. And that your love will burn with an unquenchable flame that is steady and sure and strong all the days of your life. Just as my parents' has for nearly half a century.

Happy anniversary, Mom and Dad. I love you. Always.

Irene Hannon

CROSSROADS

You changed my mourning into dancing; you took off my sackcloth and clothed me with gladness.
—*Psalms* 30:11

To my precious niece, Catherine Moira,
who has been such a blessing in our lives.
May all your tomorrows be filled with joy and love.

Chapter One

Bruce Lockwood banged the door and stormed into the kitchen, his eyes flashing. "Mr. Jackson is a—"

"Bruce!" Tess gave her fourteen-year-old son a stern warning look. She knew exactly what he was about to say, and she didn't allow that kind of language in the house.

"—creep!" Bruce finished more tamely, slamming his books onto the table.

Tess cringed. She hadn't exactly had the best day herself, and she wasn't sure she was up to another tirade about Southfield High's principal. She took a deep breath, willing the dull ache in her temples to subside.

"Do you want to tell me what happened?"

Bruce gave her a sullen look. "He's just a creep, that's all." The boy withdrew a card from his pocket and tossed it onto the table. "He wants you to call and make an appointment with him."

Tess frowned and reached for the card, her stomach clenching. The adjustment from small-town school in Jefferson City, Missouri, to big-city school in St. Louis had been difficult for him, particularly midyear. If there had been any way to delay their move until the end of the term, she would have. But the unexpected merger of her newspaper with a larger chain had left her a victim of downsizing, and the offer from a community newspaper in suburban St. Louis had seemed the answer to a prayer. She'd been able to find a comfortable apartment near the office in a quiet suburb, and had hoped that the small-town feel of the area would ease the transition to their new environment. It had worked for her, but not for Bruce.

Tess glanced down at the card. "Mitch Jackson, principal." Her frown deepened. Parents weren't usually contacted unless there was a good reason. The ache in her temples began to throb, and she looked over at her son. He was watching her—his body posture defiant, but his eyes wary.

"Why does he want to meet with me?"

"I didn't do anything wrong," Bruce countered.

Tess folded her arms across her chest, her lips tightening into a thin line. "I didn't say you did. I just asked why he wants to see me," she replied, struggling to keep her temper in check.

"Because he's a creep!"

"That's not an answer."

"It's true! Ever since I transferred to that dumb school he's been watching me, just waiting for me to mess up. He should still be a cop, the way he's on me for every little thing."

Tess held the card up. "What 'little thing' prompted this?"

Bruce glared at her. "You're as bad as he is. Always asking questions, always breathing down my neck. Why can't people just leave me alone?"

Tess stared at her son. How had her relationship with Bruce deteriorated in two short months? There was a time when they used to talk, when he shared things with her. But since coming to St. Louis he'd withdrawn, shutting her out of his life and his thoughts. She'd tried to draw him out, but the demands of her new job had left her too little time to spend with her son during this critical transition period. Whatever his problems at school, she knew she shared the blame. Slowly she sat down on the kitchen chair, drew a steadying breath and looked up at him.

"Maybe because people care."

Bruce gave a dismissive snort. "Mr. Jackson doesn't care. He's just nosy."

"I care."

He was disarmed by her quiet tone and steady gaze, and his expression softened briefly. But a moment later the defiant mask slipped back into place. "You're too busy to care."

His words cut deeply, and Tess's stomach again contracted painfully. "That's not true, Bruce. You always come first in my heart. But I have to put in a little extra time at the beginning to learn the ropes. You know I need this job."

He shoved his fists into the pockets of baggy slacks that hung on his too-thin hips. "Yeah. Thanks to…Dad." His tone was bitter, the last word sarcastic. He turned away and stared out the window, his shoulders stiff with tension. "I wish we still lived in Jeff City," he said fiercely.

Another painful tug on the heartstrings. "I do, too. But this was the best offer I had. I'm still here for you, though. You know that, Bruce. I may be your mom, but I'm also your friend."

He shrugged. "I have other friends."

And you aren't one of them. The message was clear. And it hurt, even though she was glad that he'd finally connected with a group at the school, where cliques were already well established. But she was also a bit uneasy. He never talked about his friends, never brought them home, never even introduced her to any of them. "I'd like to meet them," she replied.

"They're *my* friends, Mom," he said tersely, turning back to her. "Do I have to share everything?"

She looked at the gangly teenager across from her and wondered not for the first time where her sweet young son had gone. She missed the endearingly protective little boy with the touching sensitivity and wise-beyond-his-years perceptiveness. She'd always known Bruce would grow up. She'd just never expected him to grow *away,* she realized, her eyes misting.

When Bruce spoke again, his voice was gentler. Maybe the sensitivity wasn't gone entirely, Tess thought hopefully.

"I'm okay, Mom. Really. You don't have to worry about me."

Tess fished in the pocket of her slacks for a tissue. "Worrying is part of the job description for motherhood," she replied, dabbing at her eyes. "Look, Bruce, I need to know what Mr. Jackson wants to talk to me about. I don't want to be blindsided. You've been avoiding the question, and I need an answer."

He shrugged dismissively. "It was nothing to get excited about. Some of the guys had been smoking in an empty classroom, and Mr. Jackson showed up. He could smell the smoke, and he said he was going to put us on report and talk to our parents."

Tess stared at Bruce. "You were smoking?"

He looked at her in disgust and reached for his books. "See? Even *you* jump to conclusions. I said *some* of the guys were smoking. Not *me*. Why does everybody always think the worst?"

Tess watched with a troubled expression as he strode down the hall and disappeared into his room. She'd heard that many adolescents developed an attitude, but somehow she'd never expected it of Bruce.

Wearily she rose and set the kettle on the stove. A soothing cup of tea would help, she decided, though what she really needed was someone with whom she could share her concerns and frustrations about single parenthood and adolescent boys. She'd tried prayer, which usually anchored her. But this time her prayers hadn't had their usual calming effect. She still felt unsteady—and unsure. About a lot of things. Was Bruce's behavior normal for his age—or was it indicative of more serious problems? Did all teenage boys get involved in minor infractions as they tested their wings? Did they all shut out their parents? Would it help if he had a father figure?

Tess poured the water into a mug and carried it back to the table, propping her chin in her hand as she absently dunked the tea bag. That last question had popped up over and over again during the past six years, and always she came to the same conclusion. Yes, it would help if he had a father figure. But only if it was a *good* father figure. And her ex-husband, Peter, certainly hadn't been it. Not by a long shot. She'd stayed with him far too long as it was. Might still be there if she hadn't found…

Impatiently Tess dismissed that line of thought. Peter was history. He'd done so much damage to his son's self-esteem that Tess still spent sleepless nights wondering if it could ever be truly undone. As for her own self-esteem…he'd done a number on that, too. At least she'd been older and, with her strong faith, better equipped to deal with it. She was a survivor. Even so, years later, the scars remained with her, as well. Peter had destroyed her confidence, leaving her unsure of her intelligence, of her talents…of herself as a woman. The only things she *had* been sure about were her mothering skills.

Tess's gaze fell on the principal's card, and slowly she picked it up, her spirits nose-diving.

She *had* been sure. Until now.

"Have a seat. Mr. Jackson is just finishing up another meeting. He'll be with you in a moment."

Tess nodded at the receptionist in the small anteroom outside the principal's office and headed toward a chair in the far corner. As she sat, she took a deep breath and nervously hitched her shoulder bag into a more secure position. Thanks to her son, she'd received the dreaded summons of her childhood. She'd been called to the principal's office.

Memories came flooding back of stern-faced Mr. Markham, whose very presence had intimidated even the most self-assured students, let alone someone like bookish, shy Tess. She'd lived in fear of committing some transgression that would call her to his attention and result in a humiliating penalty. Strange how those childhood fears could sweep back so compellingly. In a way, she felt as if she was ten years old again. And she didn't like it.

Suddenly the door to the inner office opened, and Tess's heart began to hammer painfully in her chest. She took another deep breath as her fingers clenched around the strap of her shoulder bag. *This is ridiculous,* she admonished herself. *You're an adult. He can't do anything to you. Calm down!*

A bored-looking woman in a suit that Tess figured cost more than she made in a month crossed the threshold, followed by a slightly balding man. He glanced impatiently at his watch, then turned back to speak to someone just out of sight inside the doorway.

"We'll consider your suggestion," he said coldly.

"I told you all along that a private school would be better for Jerome. I never did think he'd do well in a…public…environment," the woman said with undisguised disdain.

She swept out without a backward glance, followed by the balding man.

The receptionist watched them leave, then glanced at Tess. Her raised eyebrows and the slight shake of her head spoke more eloquently than words.

"I take it sometimes the parents are worse than the

kids," Tess commiserated with a rueful smile, hoping some levity might quell the butterflies in her stomach.

The woman rolled her eyes and rose. "That's putting it mildly. I'll tell Mr. Jackson you're here."

The woman stepped up to his door, knocked softly, then entered. As she disappeared inside and closed the door, Tess took a deep breath and braced herself.

Inside the office, the receptionist regarded the tall, broad-shouldered man who stood gazing out the window. "Tess Lockwood is here, Mitch," she said. "Think you can handle one more parent today?"

Mitch turned, and the late-afternoon sun highlighted the glints of auburn in his dark hair. "That depends on her mood," he said with a sigh.

The woman tilted her head consideringly. "I'd say she's nervous. Maybe even a little scared. Actually, she doesn't look much older than some of your students. My guess is she was one of those good kids who always went out of her way to avoid being called to the principal's office, and is none too happy—or comfortable—about finding herself in one at this stage in her life."

One corner of Mitch's mouth twitched up. "You missed your calling, you know that? You should have been either a psychologist or a psychic."

She grinned. "No ring, either. And she's alone. Single-parent household."

"Or a detective."

"I'll remind you of those many career options next time I ask for a raise. So should I send her in?"

Mitch hesitated. "Give me five minutes, okay? I

want to make a few notes about that last meeting—or should I say confrontation?" he added with a grimace.

"That bad, huh?"

He reached up and massaged the back of his neck. "Karen, let me ask you something. Was I too hard on the King boy?"

She gave an unladylike snort. "I don't think you were hard enough. I would have expelled him."

Mitch smiled. "Thanks for the reality check."

"You're welcome." Karen tilted her head and studied him for a moment. "You look tired."

"Goes with the territory."

"Nope. Don't buy it. You push yourself way too hard. You worry about these kids like they were your own. That's way above and beyond the job description for principals."

He shrugged. "Somebody has to worry about them. And parents don't always do the best job."

Karen shook her head. "I admire your commitment. The world could use more principals like you. Only do me a favor, okay? Try not to take their problems home—at least not every night. You need a life, too."

"I have a life."

"Right," she said dryly. "You spend your days—and a lot of nights—here, then help your uncle on his farm every weekend. Some life."

"It works for me."

She rolled her eyes. "You're a lost cause, Mitch Jackson."

As she closed the door behind her, Mitch shoved his hands into his pockets and turned back to the window, his gaze troubled. Karen was right. He didn't have much of a life. And he wasn't sure his sacrifice was making much difference. Since switching careers from law enforcement to education, he'd run into far too many parents like those who had just exited his office. Overprotective. Unwilling to admit their offspring might be wrong. Blaming the system for their child's problems.

There were good parents, too. But in his job he saw mostly the ones who really didn't care. Or who were too busy to pay much attention to what their kids did. Or who were so absorbed in their own lives or careers that their priorities were screwed up. Or who abdicated their parental duties by treating their teenagers like adults instead of like the kids they were—desperate for guidance despite their facade of confidence and bravado. They were the same type of parents he'd run into as a cop. Only in his previous career, he'd usually run into them when it was too late—because that's when the law generally got involved. He knew that firsthand—not only as a cop, but as a parent.

The sudden, familiar clench in his gut made him suck in his breath, and his hands knotted into fists as memories came flooding back. Nightmare memories that haunted his dreams and far too often jolted him like an electric shock during his waking hours. He closed his eyes as the pain washed over him. *Dear God, will it never go away?* he cried in silent anguish. The searing pain was as fresh as it had been six years before. A pain so intense it had motivated him to switch careers. Had driven him to try to catch kids' problems at an early stage, before it was too late. Had compelled him to transform the job of principal from deskbound administrator to one of hands-on involvement and intervention. His atypical methods had raised more than a few eyebrows. But they were often effective. And those successes were what made his job worthwhile, what gave his life meaning.

A discreet knock on the door interrupted his thoughts, and he glanced toward it as Karen stuck her head in.

"Ready?"

No, he wasn't. But he couldn't put if off any longer. After the meeting with Jerome's parents, Mitch wasn't optimistic about that boy's future. But maybe Bruce had a better support system. That was one of the big differences between his job and his personal life, he reflected as he drew a deep breath. There was always another chance with his job.

"Yes. Send her in."

As Karen ushered in Tess Lockwood, Mitch did a rapid assessment. His secretary had been right about the woman's appearance. Though she had to be in her mid-thirties, she could easily pass for a college student. Her boxy pantsuit couldn't quite hide her slender curves, nor could the staid barrette at her nape successfully restrain her shoulder-length russet hair. A few tendrils softly framed her face, which would be lovely if it wasn't so tense. But even the strain in her eyes couldn't take away from their vivid green depths, framed by a thick fringe of lashes.

Karen also seemed to be on target about Ms.

Lockwood's attitude. She obviously didn't want to be
here, and she was clearly nervous. But why? Was it due
to legitimate worry about her son, inconvenience to
herself or anger at a system that she believed was the
real cause of the problem, as Jerome's parents did?

Mitch didn't know, but he'd find out soon enough.
And in the meantime, some subtle nuance that he
couldn't put his finger on told him to handle this woman
with kid gloves. Maybe it was the fine lines of fatigue
around her eyes. Or the death grip she had on her purse
strap. Or the caution in her eyes, which seemed to speak
of past hurts that had left her unwilling to trust. He had
no idea why the warning bell had gone off in his mind.
But his instincts had saved his life on more than one
occasion when he was a cop, and he wasn't about to
question them now.

He smiled and stepped forward, extending his
hand. "Ms. Lockwood? I'm Mitch Jackson. It's a
pleasure to meet you."

Tess placed her cold fingers in his firm, warm clasp,
and for a moment she simply stared at the tall man in
front of her. *This* was Bruce's ogre? she thought incredulously. This dark-haired man with the compassionate,
deep brown eyes and cordial manner, whose face reflected character and humor and intelligence? *This* was
the hated principal? She'd prepared herself for another
Mr. Markham, someone pinched-faced with beady eyes
and an intimidating demeanor who, with a single look,
could make her feel nervous and incompetent as a
parent. She had *not* been expecting a handsome contem-
porary with kind eyes and the rugged physique of an

athlete, who radiated virility—and who suddenly made her feel nervous and incompetent on a very different level.

Tess realized that he was waiting for her to reply, and somehow she found her voice. "Th-thank you. Please excuse me for staring," she stammered. "It's just that you aren't exactly…that is, I had a different image of…well, from what Bruce said…" She felt hot color steal onto her cheeks. So much for eloquence and poise. She sounded like an idiot!

But if the man across from her thought so, he was gallant enough not to show it. Instead, a smile twinkled in his eyes as he gestured toward a seating area next to his desk. "Let me guess. From what Bruce said, you expected a monster with eyes in the back of his head, a fire-breathing dragon intent on burning anyone who comes close, an evil version of a Superman/Santa Claus with X-ray vision and a checklist of bad deeds—or all of the above."

That description pretty much fit her image of Mr. Markham, for whom nothing less than absolute compliance and perfection had sufficed. Thank heaven Mitch Jackson seemed to be cut from different cloth, Tess thought with relief as she sat in one of the upholstered chairs. For one thing, he didn't appear to take himself too seriously. For another, he seemed warm and personable.

"You just described the principal at my grade school," she confessed with a smile.

For a moment Mitch was stunned by the transforming effect of her smile. She looked even younger now, her features relaxing as they softened. Though she wore almost no makeup, her face had a natural loveliness and a certain intriguing—and appealing—wistful quality. Her eyes radiated warmth and intelligence, and for just a moment he found himself drowning in their depths. It was an unexpected—and disconcerting—experience. So he forced himself to focus on the shadows beneath those amazing eyes instead. Shadows that didn't appear to be the result of one sleepless night, but spoke more of long-term strain, stress, overwork—or all three. For some reason, those shadows bothered him more than they should. Which was odd. And way off the subject, he reminded himself.

"I think we all have a principal like that somewhere in our memory bank," Mitch commiserated, struggling to regain his balance.

He had an engaging dimple in his left cheek when he smiled, Tess noted distractedly, trying to focus instead on the conversation. "Though they probably weren't quite as bad as we remember," she admitted.

"Maybe not. But I'm certainly not the most popular man on campus with some of *my* students. Bruce happens to be one of them."

"Why not?" She hadn't meant to be quite that direct, but this man was easy to talk to, and the words were out before she could stop them. Fortunately Mitch didn't seem to mind.

"For a lot of reasons. Number one, I enforce the rules. Number two, I care about my students, and I make it a point to keep my eye on the ones who seem to need a bit of extra supervision. Number three, I used to be a cop, and I can spot trouble—and the potential for trouble—pretty quickly. That's why I've been watching Bruce. He seems to be a basically good kid who just needs a little more help than most to stay on the straight and narrow."

Tess stiffened at what she perceived to be criticism. "You make it sound like he's on the verge of becoming a delinquent. Don't you think you're overreacting to one little smoking incident? Which Bruce tells me he didn't even participate in, by the way. Most kids experiment with cigarettes at some point or other. I don't approve, but I don't think it's necessarily a sign of serious trouble."

Mitch frowned. "Is that what he told you? That this meeting is just about a simple smoking incident?"

Now it was Tess's turn to frown. "Isn't it?"

Mitch rose to retrieve a folder from his desk. As he rejoined her, he flipped it open. "The smoking situation was only the latest in a series of incidents," he informed her, the seriousness of his tone and demeanor in sharp contrast to his initial conversational manner. "Though even that was more than you've been led to believe. Those guys weren't smoking cigarettes. They were smoking a joint."

Tess stared at him incredulously. "You mean marijuana?"

He nodded. "Yes. There was no sign of it when I showed up. But the odor is unmistakable—and lingering."

"Marijuana?" Tess repeated the word in shock. "Drugs? You mean Bruce is involved with drugs?" Now there was a note of panic in her voice, and her fingers tightened convulsively on her purse.

Mitch wished he could bring back her smile of moments before, erase the twin furrows of worry on her brow and ease the tension that had made her skin go taut over the fine bone structure of her face. But his job wasn't to make parents feel good, he reminded himself. It was to help kids.

"I don't think he's into drugs," he replied carefully. "At least not yet. But he hangs around with a rough, older crowd, and sooner or later they'll pull him down to their level. Kids like Bruce are easy prey, Ms. Lockwood. He doesn't seem to have a lot of self-confidence, and it's tough to break into established cliques, especially midyear. That makes him vulnerable to groups that are on the fringe. They offer a haven of friendship that can be very powerful—someone to sit with in the cafeteria, a sympathetic ear, somewhere to belong. A 'home,' if you will."

"Bruce has a home," Tess protested, a tremor of fear running through her voice.

Mitch studied her for a moment. He knew he was venturing onto shaky ground, but the more information he had, the more likely he could help. "May I ask a question?"

Tess eyed him cautiously. "What is it?"

"Is there a father figure in Bruce's life?"

Tess's eyes went cold. "No."

"Any friends outside of school?"

She swallowed and shook her head. "Not that I know of. It's…hard for him to make friends. His self-esteem isn't…isn't all that high."

"Why not?"

She took a deep breath, and her eyes shuttered. "That's a long story, Mr. Jackson."

"And not a pleasant one, I take it."

"No."

The answer was terse—and telling. For a long moment there was silence, and then Tess spoke again.

"Look, Mr. Jackson, I do the best I can. I'm a single mom who has to work full-time to keep a roof over our heads and food on the table. I try my best to be mother, father and friend. Lately Bruce has been shutting me out. He obviously didn't tell me the whole truth about the smoking incident." She paused and took a deep breath, bracing herself. "You said there were others?"

Mitch nodded and consulted his file. "We haven't caught the perpetrators, though we have strong suspicions. And in all cases I suspect that Bruce was involved, either as a participant or bystander. Five weeks ago we found obscene graffiti on the wall in one of the boys' rest rooms. The next week several cars in the parking lot were vandalized during a basketball game—tires slashed, rearview mirrors ripped off, long scratches on the sides. Two weeks ago some software disappeared from the computer lab. The smoking incident is the latest problem."

Tess began to feel ill. "But you said you have no proof that Bruce was involved in those other things," she pointed out faintly, a touch of desperation in her voice. "Why do you think he is?"

"Because of the group he hangs out with. I won't go so far as to call it a gang, but it's borderline."

The principal had just confirmed the suspicion that

had been niggling at the edge of Tess's consciousness for the past few weeks, and her spirits slipped another notch—as did her confidence. She was trying so hard to juggle the demands and responsibilities of her life. But clearly her best simply wasn't good enough. She was failing Bruce, the only person in the world who mattered to her. And she didn't know what to do about it.

Mitch watched the play of emotions on the face of the woman across from him. Pain. Despair. Panic. On one hand, he hated to put her through this. On the other hand, he felt a sense of relief. The presence of those emotions told him that she cared—truly cared—about her son. She might not know how to help him, but she wanted to—and that was the key. He could work with parents like Tess Lockwood. Because they were generally willing to work with him.

"I'm sorry to upset you, Ms. Lockwood. But it's better to find out now rather than later. And we can work this out, I'm sure."

At the man's gentle tone, Tess's gaze flew to his. She'd expected to be read the riot act from a stern disciplinarian with a shape-up-or-ship-out stance. She *hadn't* expected warmth, caring and the offer of assistance.

Tess's throat tightened and her eyes filmed over with moisture at this stranger's unexpected compassion. She glanced away on the pretense of adjusting the shoulder strap on her purse, willing herself not to cry. She blinked several times, fighting for control, and when she at last looked up, her voice was steady, her gaze direct.

"I agree that sooner is better. I just hope we're soon enough. Bruce is a good boy at heart, Mr. Jackson. And I've tried to be a good parent. But I can see now that I need help. Obviously, parenting isn't one of my talents, and I'd appreciate any advice you can offer."

Mitch caught the glimmer of unshed tears, clearly held in check by the slimmest of control, and frowned. His gut told him that she really was trying her best. But she was clearly stressed to the limit. "I didn't mean to imply that you aren't a good parent, Ms. Lockwood. On the contrary. I can see you care deeply about your son's welfare."

"But that's not enough."

The despair in her voice went straight to his heart, and he had a sudden, unexpected impulse to reach out and take her hand, to reassure her that she wasn't quite as alone as she seemed to feel. But that kind of gesture would be completely inappropriate, he reminded himself sharply. So before he could act on it and embarrass them both, he rose abruptly and walked over to his desk.

The flyer he wanted was right on top, but he made a pretense of shuffling through some papers, buying a moment to compose himself. For some reason, this woman had touched a place deep in his core, nudged feelings that had long lain dormant. He wanted to help her, and not just because it was his job. Which was crazy. After all, he'd just met her. Besides, he wasn't in the market for personal involvements of any kind—especially with mothers of troubled students. And he'd better remember that.

The expression on her face when he turned back

almost did him in. Clearly, his abrupt movement had disconcerted her. She looked vulnerable and uncertain and in desperate need of comforting. It took every ounce of his willpower to calmly walk back to his chair and simply hand her the flyer he'd retrieved.

"Caring is the most important thing, Ms. Lockwood," he said, his voice a shade deeper than usual. "But sometimes it does take even more. You might want to attend this meeting next week. Chris Stevens, one of our counselors, is going to talk about the pressures teens face and how parents can help. There'll also be an opportunity for discussion and questions. I think you'll find it worthwhile."

Tess glanced down at the sheet of paper. It had been a long time since anyone had offered a helping hand, and once more her throat constricted with emotion.

"Thank you. I'll do my best to make it." She folded the paper and put it in her purse, then rose. Mitch was instantly on his feet, and when he extended his hand, she once more found her fingers enveloped in his warm grasp.

"In the meantime, I'll keep my eye on Bruce. And don't hesitate to call if you have any other concerns."

Tess gazed up into his kind eyes, and for the briefest moment allowed herself to wonder what life would have been like if Bruce had had a father figure like Mitch Jackson in his life these past few years. Somehow, in her heart, she knew that things would have been a lot different. For him—and for her.

Suddenly afraid that he would read her thoughts, she withdrew her hand and lowered her gaze. "I appreciate your interest," she said, her voice quavering slightly as he walked her to the door.

"It goes with the territory. Goodbye, Ms. Lockwood. And try not to worry. I have a feeling that things are going to improve."

She gazed at him directly then, and once more something in her eyes reached to his very soul. "I hope so, Mr. Jackson. And thank you for caring."

Mitch watched her speculatively as she walked across the reception area and disappeared out the door. Unlike the parents from his previous conference, Tess Lockwood seemed to have taken his comments to heart. He had a feeling that she wouldn't easily dismiss their encounter.

And for reasons that had nothing at all to do with her son, Mitch didn't think he would, either.

Chapter Two

"Okay, let's talk."

At Tess's no-nonsense tone, Bruce looked up from his desk, his eyes wary. "About what?"

She moved to the side of his bed and sat down. "Guess."

"I suppose Mr. Jackson told you a lot of garbage."

"'Garbage' is a good word for the behavior he discussed."

"I haven't done anything wrong," Bruce declared defensively.

"You know what? I believe you. But from what I heard, you're heading in the wrong direction."

"Mr. Jackson just wants to get me in trouble."

"Wrong. He wants to *keep* you from getting in trouble."

Bruce looked at her defiantly. "So now you're on his side."

"That's right. Because he happens to be on *your* side."

"That's a bunch of—"

"Bruce!"

He clamped his mouth shut and stared at her sullenly.

"That's exactly the kind of behavior I'm talking about. Since when did you start using language like that?"

"Like what?"

"Come off it, Bruce. You've let enough slip these last few weeks for me to realize that you've expanded your vocabulary. And I don't like it."

"Words don't hurt anything."

"I disagree. They hurt your character. And they can also give you a juvenile record if you scratch them on the walls in the boys' rest room."

Bruce's face grew red. "I didn't have anything to do with that."

"I didn't say you did. And I don't believe you vandalized the cars or stole the computer equipment."

"I wasn't smoking, either."

"Maybe not. But when it comes to drugs, the cops bust you first and ask questions later."

He looked at her in confusion. "What are you talking about?"

"Mr. Jackson gave me a few more details about the smoking incident."

He still looked confused. "What does that have to do with drugs?"

Tess stared at him, and slowly the light began to dawn. He honestly didn't know! Relief coursed through her and the tension coiled deep inside eased ever so slightly. "That wasn't just a cigarette, Bruce," she said gently. "It was a joint. Marijuana."

His face blanched. "Who told you that?"

"Mr. Jackson."

"I don't believe it! Besides, how does he know? He didn't see anything."

"He was a cop, remember? He could tell from the smell. You're lucky he contacted *me* instead of the police."

Bruce frowned. "He didn't have a case, anyway," he said slowly, some of his cockiness returning. "There wasn't any evidence. And the smell would have been gone by the time the police got there."

Anger flashed in Tess's eyes. "Maybe the next time you won't be so lucky."

Bruce glared at her defiantly. "I can take care of myself."

"Really? So what are you going to do when they pass around the next joint?"

His gaze skittered away. "I don't have to smoke. They'll be my friends even if I don't."

"They're not your friends *now,* Bruce. They're bad news, and they're going to drag you down with them. Can't you see that?" she pleaded, a note of desperation creeping into her voice.

"No! I like them! They're nice to me! They're the only ones who *are* at that dumb school. Do you know what it's like not to have anyone to sit with at lunch? It su…it stinks! I sat by myself every day until they invited me. I owe them," he said fiercely.

An ominous chill went down Tess's spine. The scenario Bruce had just described was exactly the one Mitch Jackson had used as an example. By drawing him in, by accepting him, the group he'd hooked up with had evoked not only a sense of gratitude, but of obligation. Which could be very dangerous.

"You don't owe them a thing," Tess shot back, but she could see that her words fell on deaf ears. She rose, trying to control her panic. "Okay. Until further notice, you're to come home right after school."

Bruce sent her a venomous look. "You're grounding me?"

"You got it."

"Why? I haven't done anything wrong. You said you believed me."

"I do. But I think you're on dangerous ground."

"So you're going to lock me up? I bet that was Mr. Jackson's idea," he said angrily.

"As a matter of fact, it wasn't. I thought it up all by myself."

"I'll still see the guys at school," he countered defiantly.

"That's true. But I think Mr. Jackson will be keeping his eye out for you there."

"I should have figured you two would team up," he said bitterly. "Adults always stick together."

Instead of responding, Tess simply left the room. Once out of sight, she leaned against the wall, struggling to control the tremors that ran through her body. *Please, Lord, help me!* she prayed desperately as another wave of panic washed over her. She had no idea how to deal with this situation. But she knew she needed help. The counseling session Mitch had invited her to couldn't come soon enough. Because Bruce was in way over his head.

And so was she.

* * *

"Morning, Tess. Have I got a story for you!"

Tess glanced up at the managing editor and smiled. Caroline James was about the same age as Tess, but she was light years ahead of the paper's newest reporter in terms of sophistication and polish. Why someone with Caroline's experience, abilities and contacts was content to be the managing editor of a suburban news-paper was beyond Tess's understanding. She was just grateful to have the chance to hone her skills under the guidance of a true pro.

"Hi, Caroline. What's up?"

"A great coup for our little paper, that's what." Caroline sat on the single chair in Tess's cube and crossed her legs, revealing their shapely length under her fashionably short skirt. As she leaned back, her silk blouse shimmered in the overhead light, as did her simple but classic gold necklace. Style. Class. Poise. Caroline had it all, Tess thought wistfully. In her tailored slacks and baggy sweater, Tess felt dowdy and plain by comparison. Not to mention awkward. Even on her best days, Tess didn't move with the lithe grace that came so naturally to Caroline. Yet her boss was completely down-to-earth, without a pretentious bone in her body, and she had gone out of her way to make Tess feel at home on the paper. It was hard to be envious of someone so nice.

"Sounds promising," Tess replied.

"More than promising. A sure thing. It seems we have a man of great distinction right here in our midst."

"Really? Who?"

"One Mitch Jackson, local principal."

Tess stared at Caroline in shock. "Mitch Jackson?"

"Yeah." Caroline tilted her head and gazed at Tess. "You look funny. Do you know him?"

Tess nodded and cleared her throat. "Yes. Sort of. That is, we've met. Briefly. He's the principal at my son's school."

"Great! A connection! That will make it even easier to scoop the daily. Hopefully he'll give us first crack."

"At what?"

"A feature profile. He's just been chosen to receive the governor's award for excellence in education. He's introduced some really innovative programs at the school. We've tried to do a story on him before, but apparently he prefers to stay out of the limelight."

Tess tried to calm the sudden pounding of her heart. "So what makes you think he'll be any different this time?"

"The school board," Caroline informed Tess smugly. "My sources tell me they've been after him for quite a while to be more forthcoming with the press about his programs. Good publicity for the school district, which is handy when it comes time for funding. They aren't going to let him get away with a 'no comment' this time, I guarantee it. Besides, if you know him, we already have an in."

"I don't really know him, Caroline. We only met once."

"That's okay. He'll remember you."

Tess frowned. "Why do you say that?"

"Because you are one attractive gal. You have terrific eyes, gorgeous hair, a great figure—even if you do hide it under oversize clothes—and you're single. What guy wouldn't notice?"

Tess felt hot color creep onto her cheeks. "I think maybe you need to get your contacts changed," she said with an embarrassed smile.

"Trust me on this," Carolyn said with a grin. "By the way, I understand he's single. Not to mention handsome, if you can believe this picture that just came over the wire." She tossed a clipping onto Tess's desk. "Probably make a great catch."

"Maybe *you* should interview him," Tess suggested. "I'm not in the market."

A shadow passed over Caroline's eyes, so brief Tess almost missed it. "Me, neither. I already had my taste of heaven," she said lightly, but Tess heard the whisper of sadness in her voice. "Anyway, personal stuff aside, you're one of our best feature writers. You'll be able to do this story justice. What do you say?"

Tess frowned. She hadn't counted on another opportunity to spend time one-on-one with Southfield High's principal. In fact, she was still recovering from their last encounter. She'd lain awake far too many nights thinking about Mitch Jackson. And that was based purely on a meeting that had focused on *Bruce*. Now she was being asked to get "up close and personal" with *him* for a profile. The mere thought of it sent a delicious, anticipatory tingle down her spine. Which was silly, of course. She would be dealing with him in a purely professional capacity, much as he'd dealt with her the last time.

Yet the yearning to see him again was inexplicably

strong. For some reason, just being in his presence made her feel…*tingly* was the word that came to mind. For the first time in years she'd felt more like a desirable woman than a mom. And it was renewing, quenching a place in her heart that had long been parched and lifeless. Though she wasn't in the market for romance, she was enough of a romantic to want to have that feeling again, if only for the duration of one more meeting.

"Don't think so hard, Tess," Caroline advised her with an understanding smile. "I can see you're interested in the story—and maybe in the man. Just go for it." Before Tess could reply, Caroline stood and made her way to the door, pausing on the threshold. "In case I haven't told you lately, we're really glad to have you aboard here. Not only are you an excellent writer, you're smart and intuitive, and you have a warmth that makes people open up. We're lucky to have someone with your talent. So give this a shot, okay?"

Tess watched Caroline walk away, then slowly reached for the clipping and studied the grainy picture of Mitch Jackson. Her boss was right—he was one handsome man. But he was also much more. She had seen and felt firsthand things that the picture didn't reveal. The caring and compassion in his insightful eyes. His ability to make you feel that *your* problems were *his* problems. The innate strength and sense of honor that seemed to radiate from his very core. His total dedication and commitment to his students. None of those things could be captured by a picture.

Nor could his almost tangible virility. It awakened

yearnings in her that had long lain dormant, yearnings she thought had slowly withered up and blown away like a once-beautiful autumn leaf. It was frightening— and intimidating—to discover that those yearnings could so unexpectedly be brought back to life. Not that it mattered, of course. Despite what Caroline had said, someone like Mitch Jackson would never give her a second look. Even if she wanted him to. Which she didn't, she told herself firmly. The last thing she needed in her already complicated life was another complication. Or distraction. And she knew instinctively that Southfield High's principal could definitely be both.

Tess deliberately shifted her attention to the sketchy text that accompanied the photo. There wasn't much in it that she didn't already know. He'd been a cop earlier in his career, had moved to St. Louis two years ago, was a hands-on principal who believed in getting involved in the lives of his students. The only new piece of information she gleaned from the write-up was that prior to coming to St. Louis he'd lived in Chicago.

Tess's face grew thoughtful. Clearly there was a whole lot more to Mitch's story. Whether or not he'd reveal it, however, remained to be seen. But she did seem to have a knack for getting people to open up and reveal more about themselves than they'd planned to. And she liked challenges, especially intriguing ones.

Tess glanced back at Mitch's picture. *Intriguing* was a good word for Southfield High's principal. Other words came to mind as well, but she chose to ignore them. She didn't have the time or inclination for romance, she reminded herself. What she did have was

a son to raise—a job that required her full-time attention. And she would do well to remember that.

Tess glanced around the crowded meeting room,
relieved to see that other parents also seemed to feel the
need for more information about raising teenagers. It
helped a bit to know that she wasn't alone.

Her quick scan revealed few available seats, but she
spotted one in the middle of the last row and quickly
made her way toward it. As she carefully edged past
those already seated, trying not to step on toes as she
went, she glanced at her watch. She'd made it with two
minutes to spare.

Tess was still settling in when a familiar voice over
the microphone drew her startled gaze. She hadn't
expected Mitch to extend his workday by attending the
evening meeting. Once more she was impressed by his
dedication.

"Good evening. For those of you I haven't met, I'm
Mitch Jackson, the principal," he said, looking completely at ease in front of the crowd. "I'd like to
welcome you to tonight's program and thank you for
taking time out of your busy schedules to attend. I think
you'll find it very worthwhile. As you know, we are extremely fortunate to have Chris Stevens on our staff,
and even more fortunate that she agreed to make this
presentation tonight. Let me review her credentials for
you and I think you'll agree."

As he did so, the resonant, well-modulated timbre
of his voice reflected both warmth and competence.
Despite his casual attire of open-necked shirt and sport

jacket, he radiated a quiet confidence and authority that marked him for leadership and engendered respect. He seemed to be a man in absolute control of his life, who had found his place in the world and had his act together, Tess reflected.

"And when Chris is finished, we'll both be happy to answer any questions you might have," he concluded, once again surprising Tess as he took a seat in the front row. Not only had he kicked off the meeting, he intended to be there when it finished. Did he always work such long hours? Tess wondered, filing the question away for the hoped-for interview. Since receiving the assignment that morning, she'd simply been too busy to call and discuss it with him. Perhaps she'd have a chance tonight, she mused. Though it would probably be difficult to single him out in this crowd.

An hour later, when the presentation ended, Tess realized she'd just spent one of the most worthwhile evenings of her life. Chris Stevens was good, just as Mitch had promised. She had touched on many of the fears and uncertainties that Tess had been feeling. Clearly Tess's experience with Bruce wasn't unique. But just as clearly, kids that age needed a strict set of rules and lots of one-on-one discussions with a caring adult. Chris had hammered home those points throughout her talk.

Which only made Tess realize just how remiss she'd been on both counts since coming to St. Louis. In Jefferson City, Bruce had never seemed to need rules; he'd just done the right thing without prompting and had always hung around with a wholesome group of friends. As for one-on-one talks, she'd never had to earmark certain times. They'd always eaten breakfast and dinner together, so those talks had evolved naturally.

Things had been different since they'd moved to St. Louis. For one thing, since Tess was the new kid on the block, her job schedule was somewhat erratic. She was frequently assigned stories that required coverage at undesirable times—evenings, weekends, holidays. As a result, dinners with Bruce were infrequent. And he'd stopped eating breakfast, so that talk time was gone, too. She'd also been too lax on rules.

Tess resolved to make some immediate changes, both in her life and Bruce's. He wouldn't like it, but if what Chris said was true—and Tess instinctively sensed that it was—kids actually did better when there was more rather than less parental intervention in their lives. Not so much that you stifled them, but enough to let them know that you cared deeply and had standards by which you expected them to live. It was clearly a tough line to walk, but Tess was determined to find it.

When the applause died down, Mitch stood and rejoined Chris at the front of the room, and for another twenty minutes they adeptly answered questions, concluding with an invitation to stay for coffee and a snack.

As Tess gathered up her purse and notebook, she wearily glanced at her watch. Nine-thirty. It had been another long day. Late in the afternoon she'd had to cover a story that had run much longer than she expected, and she'd come to the meeting directly from there. Her stomach rumbled ominously, reminding her that she hadn't eaten anything since lunch, when she'd grabbed some yogurt and an apple. She gazed longingly toward the coffee table, where a crowd was now gathering. Sweets weren't exactly a healthy dinner, but she knew by the time she got home she'd be too tired even to nuke a microwave dinner, let alone eat it. A cookie or two would have to suffice, she decided.

The food line inched along slowly, and by the time she reached the table the crowd had thinned considerably. She hesitated at the display of sweets, debating the merits of chocolate chip versus oatmeal cookies, when a deep, rich chuckle distracted her.

"Take both. I am."

She turned to find Mitch smiling at her, and her heart did a little somersault.

"Are you planning to eat and run, or would you like to sit for a minute?" he asked.

Tess looked at him in surprise. "I, uh, hadn't actually thought about it."

"Well, I for one don't do especially well when I have to juggle coffee in one hand and food in the other. Seems like you need a third hand to eat. Would you like to join me over there?" He nodded toward a couple of unoccupied chairs against the back wall.

"Sure."

"I'll get the coffee. Just pile some cookies on a plate, and I'll meet you," he said, flashing her a grin as he headed for the coffeepot at the other end of the table.

Tess automatically did as he asked while she tried to figure out why he had approached her. Had something else happened with Bruce? she suddenly wondered in panic. After tonight's presentation, it was clear that she'd made some bad mistakes. And she intended to correct them. But maybe it was too late. Maybe Bruce had done something that…

"You must be hungry," Mitch teased, interrupting her train of thought as he settled into the folding chair beside her.

Tess glanced down, and a flush rose on her cheeks at the sight of the tall pile of cookies on her plate. "Good heavens, I don't know what I was thinking," she said faintly.

"Don't worry, I can help you put a dent in them," Mitch assured her as he handed her a cup of coffee and reached for a cookie. "Dinner was a long time ago. Probably for you, too."

"Actually, this *is* dinner," she admitted with a wry smile as she reached for a chocolate chip cookie.

He frowned. "Seriously?"

"Yes. I don't make a habit of this, but some days there just doesn't seem to be time to eat."

His frown deepened as his discerning gaze briefly swept over her. Last time he'd seen her she'd worn a boxy pantsuit that revealed little of her figure. Tonight she had on an oversize sweater that again effectively hid her curves. But her slender hands and the clearly defined bone structure in her face suggested to him that his original assessment of her as slender might need to be modified to too thin.

Tess was embarrassingly aware of his discreet perusal and sought to divert his attention. "I have a feeling you know what it's like to be time-challenged," she remarked. "You've obviously had a long day, too."

His gaze returned to her face. "True. But I *always* find time to eat," he added with an engaging smile as he bit into his cookie.

He wasn't bringing up his reason for singling her out, Tess realized. Perhaps he was trying to lead up to it gradually, as he had in his office. But at this point she preferred the bad news up front. She took a steadying breath and gazed at him directly.

"Has something else happened with Bruce, Mr. Jackson?"

Mitch noted her tense grip on the coffee cup and looked at her quizzically. "Not that I know of."

Her brow wrinkled in puzzlement. "Then why...? I mean, there are a lot of people here who would probably like to talk with you, so...well, I guess when you took me aside I just assumed that there was a problem," she finished, flustered.

Mitch looked at the woman across from him, a faint frown marring his own brow. Why *had* he sought her out? If he'd had any sense he would have left as soon as the group of parents around him had dispersed. He was beat, and the weekend ahead at his uncle's farm would be taxing. In fact, he'd planned to make his exit as quickly as possible. So what was it about Tess Lockwood that had made him suddenly change his mind when he'd seen her in line for coffee?

For one thing, she'd been on his mind a lot since their meeting, he admitted. Though he'd tried, he hadn't been able to explain—or dismiss—the odd effect she'd had on him that day. He'd gone to sleep more than once with her vivid but troubled green eyes as his last conscious image. It was oddly unsettling, considering that over the past few years he'd built up a pretty thick skin when it came to women. Yet somehow Tess had gotten under it. But he couldn't very well say that, he realized, struggling to come up with a suitable response.

"I figured you wouldn't know anyone here, and I wanted to make sure you felt welcome," he replied at last, striving for a conversational tone.

"Oh. Well, I appreciate that. And thank you for telling me about the program. It was very good."

"Chris does a terrific job," he agreed, relieved to be back on safer ground.

Tess suddenly realized that this was as good a time as any to broach the subject of the interview, so she took a deep breath and plunged in.

"You both do. In fact, I understand that you've just won the governor's award for excellence in education."

He looked at her in surprise. "How did you know?"

"It came over the wire at the newspaper where I work."

"Ah. No secrets from the press, I guess."

"Actually, the write-up wasn't very detailed."

He shrugged. "It was enough for most people."

"That's not what my editor thinks."

He eyed her speculatively. "What do you mean?"

"She'd like me to do a feature story on you."

He took a moment to respond, and she was suddenly afraid that he was going to turn her down flat. Instead, his reply was noncommittal. "I usually stay away from publicity."

"So we've heard," she admitted. "But when I mentioned that we'd met, my boss was hoping you might agree to talk with me. She thought you might feel more comfortable with a familiar face."

Mitch took a slow sip of his coffee as he considered the request. Frankly, he wasn't all that comfortable—with the story or the woman. He was a private person, for good reason. Few people knew the painful details of his past. Few people *needed* to know. He'd have to sidestep a lot of questions if he agreed to this interview, and that could be uncomfortable. So would being one-on-one with Tess Lockwood. She had already touched his heart in places that were best left undisturbed, and he barely knew her. Further contact could only be more disruptive to his peace of mind.

At the same time, he suspected that she was working hard to build a new career and a new life in St. Louis. Having to go back to her editor and say that she'd failed to nab an interview couldn't be good for her. It would just add more stress to what already appeared to be a stress-filled life. And he couldn't bring himself to do that.

"All right, Ms. Lockwood. Let's give it a try," he agreed.

Tess smiled. There was relief—and something else he couldn't quite identify—in her eyes. "Thank you."

"Call me tomorrow and we'll set something up. I may live to regret this, but at least the school board will be happy," he said with a lopsided grin.

"So will my editor." She shifted her purse onto her shoulder, and Mitch reached over to relieve her of her plate and cup.

"I'll take care of these."

"Thanks. And thank you again for telling me about this meeting. And for agreeing to the interview." She tilted her head and gave him a rueful smile. "I guess I'll be in your debt big time."

He smiled, and his gaze deepened and connected with hers in a way that left her a bit breathless. "I'll remember that."

For a moment she actually felt lost in his eyes, and the buzz of voices around her seemed to recede. It was only with great effort that she finally dragged her gaze away from his, mumbled goodbye and beat a hasty retreat.

As Tess made her way to her car, she tried to figure out what had just happened. Or, more accurately, she tried to figure out *if* anything had happened. She'd probably read far too much into a simple look, she told herself. After all, there was nothing about her to rate any special attention. She was just one more parent with a troubled teen. Bruce was Mitch's main concern. And that was exactly as it should be.

Tess knew that. And accepted it. But it didn't stop a sudden surge of bittersweet longing from echoing softly in her heart.

Chapter Three

"How about a cup of coffee to go with that pie?"

Mitch looked up at the older man and smiled. "You spoil me, Uncle Ray."

"No such thing. Your visits give me a good excuse to visit the bakeshop in town. Course, their pies aren't as good as Emma's. But they're sure a sight better'n mine."

"I do miss Aunt Emma's pies," Mitch agreed.

"Me, too. And a whole lot more," Uncle Ray said, his eyes softening briefly before he turned away to fiddle with the coffeemaker.

Mitch glanced at his uncle, still spare and straight at seventy-six. Only a pronounced limp, the result of a bad fracture from a severe fall over two years before, had slowed him down. Mitch knew the older man found the limp burdensome, though he never complained. And he still tried to put in a full day in the fields. Mitch had been trying to convince him to slow down, but as Uncle Ray always reminded him, farming was his life. He liked working the land.

Besides, Mitch reflected, the land had been the one constant in a life that had known its share of loss and grief. So he couldn't bring himself to force the issue. Instead, he'd found a job in St. Louis and spent his spare time helping out on the farm. It was the least he could do for the man who had been his lifeline six years before, who had shown him the way out of darkness step by painful step, who had helped him reconnect with his faith and find solace in the Lord. He owed his life—and his sanity—to Uncle Ray, and whenever the work began to overwhelm him, he only had to think back to that nightmare time to realize just how deeply in debt he was to this special man.

"So what's on the schedule this weekend?" Mitch asked when the older man turned to place a cup of coffee in front of him.

"There are still a couple of fields that need to be turned over," Uncle Ray said as he sat down across from Mitch. "I figured I'd get to them during the week, but I don't move quite as fast as I used to."

Mitch frowned. "I thought we agreed that we'd do the heavy work together, on weekends?"

Uncle Ray shrugged. "I have time to spare, Mitch. You don't. What little free time you have shouldn't be spent out here on an isolated farm with an old man."

"We've been through this before, Uncle Ray. I told you, I like coming out here. It's a nice change of pace from the city."

"Can't argue with that. It is a great place. Nothing beats the fresh air and open spaces. But you need some time to yourself, son. Companions your own age. You aren't going to find those things out here."

"I have everything I need," Mitch assured him. "My life is full. I have no complaints."

Uncle Ray looked at him steadily. "You know I don't interfere, Mitch. I learned my lesson on that score the hard way years ago." A flicker of sadness echoed in his eyes. "But I care about you, son. I don't want you to be alone."

Mitch reached over and laid his hand over his uncle's slightly gnarled fingers. "I'm not alone."

"That's not what I mean."

Mitch sighed. "I know. But I had my chance once, Uncle Ray. And I threw it away."

"You're a different man now."

"Maybe. Maybe not. I can't risk it."

"Well, it's your life, Mitch. I can't tell you how to live it. I just want you to be happy."

"I am happy, Uncle Ray."

"Can I ask you one other thing?"

"Sure." Mitch's reply was swift and decisive. In a friendship forged in pain, there were few secrets and even fewer off-limit questions.

"In all these years, has there ever been anyone… special in your life?"

Mitch took a sip of his coffee and forced his lips into a smile. "I assume you mean a woman."

"That's what I had in mind."

Mitch thought of all the women he'd met in the past six years who had made it clear that they were available if he was interested. But he hadn't been. Not even remotely. Not after… His pretense of a smile faded and he shook his head.

"No."

"Hmm." Uncle Ray pondered that for a moment as he scooped up another bite of pie. "So no one's ever caught your fancy, made you second-guess your decision to stay single?"

For some disconcerting reason the image of Tess Lockwood suddenly came to mind, and Mitch frowned. How odd. He barely knew the woman. They weren't even on a first-name basis. True, she'd somehow managed to touch a place in his heart that he'd carefully protected all these years. But it had to be just some weird quirk. What else could it be when they were essentially strangers? Mitch looked over at his uncle to find the older man gazing at him quizzically.

"What's wrong, son?"

Mitch shook his head. "For some strange reason the mother of one of my problem students just came to mind."

"A friend of yours?"

"Hardly. We've only met twice. She's a single mom who's got her hands full with a troublesome teen and a new job. I'm not sure why I thought of her just now."

"The mind works in mysterious ways," Uncle Ray said noncommittally. "Well, I just don't want to take up all of your free time. I can try to find one of the local boys to help me out."

"We've been down that road before," Mitch reminded him. "They're either all working on their family's farm or they don't know one end of a plow from the other."

"Good help is hard to find," Uncle Ray conceded.

"So let's just go on as we have been," Mitch concluded, savoring the last mouthful of pie. "It works for both of us. You get a farmhand, I get three square meals and fresh air, and we both get great conversation." He wiped his mouth and grinned as he laid his napkin on the table. "And if you ask me, that's a pretty good deal all the way around."

The building was hot. And still. And ominous. A prickle of apprehension skittered across the back of his neck, and he tightened his hold on the gun. Something was wrong. Very wrong. He could sense it. And he'd been a cop long enough to respect his senses. Especially in abandoned warehouses.

At least he wasn't alone. Jacobsmeyer was circling in the other direction, only a shout away. And his partner was good. The best. Mitch drew a deep breath. Whatever was wrong, they'd find it. And fix it.

He stopped at a closed storage door, listening intently. Nothing. He tried the knob. Unlocked. Carefully he eased it open. Darkness. An even stronger feeling of foreboding. He swept the beam of his flashlight over the floor. Trash. Empty cans. A sport shoe protruding from a pile of boxes. A beat-up shopping cart. Some... He suddenly went still, then slowly swung his light back to the shoe, his stomach clenching. God, let me be wrong! he prayed. *But his eyes hadn't lied. The shoe was attached to a leg.*

He sucked in his breath, his heart hammering in his chest. He'd been here before, and it was never pretty. But it was his job. Steeling himself, he picked his way over the trash to the boxes. Hesitated. Took another breath. Slowly let the arc of light travel up the body. Hesitated again. Finally moved it up to the face. Felt his world tilt. Crash. Shatter into a thousand pieces. And then he screamed. And screamed again. And again. And...

Mitch jerked bolt upright in bed, shaking violently. Dear God, the nightmare was back. Just when he'd begun to believe that it had released its hold on him. But now it had returned, stronger than ever.

"Mitch? You okay?"

Uncle Ray's concerned voice came from the other side of the door, and Mitch sucked in a ragged breath. "Yeah. I'm...fine," he called hoarsely, his voice as tattered as his nerves.

"You need anything?" Though his uncle's voice was calm, it was laced with worry.

Mitch took another deep breath, forcing air into lungs that didn't want to expand. "No. I'm okay, Uncle Ray. Sorry I woke you."

"I wasn't really sleeping anyway. Try to go back to sleep."

"Yeah, I will. Thanks."

Slowly Mitch eased himself back down, damp with sweat. He'd put his uncle through this drill more times than he could count. But the older man never seemed to mind. He'd been through his own hell. He understood.

Mitch wanted to let go of the nightmare. Wanted to find a way to put it behind him and move on, as Uncle Ray had. He'd always hoped that in time the memory would fade. But he was less and less convinced that it would. Because while both men shared a legacy of regret, only Mitch's included an unspeakable horror.

And no matter what he had done in the intervening years to make amends, no matter how often he'd prayed for release from the guilt and the pain, deep in his heart he knew that he didn't deserve a reprieve from the traumatic memory of that night.

At the sound of a knock, Mitch looked up. "Come in."

Karen opened the office door. "Ms. Lockwood is here."

Mitch glanced at his watch, then at his piled-high desk. As usual, the day had flown by and he'd finished only half of what he'd set out to accomplish. "There aren't enough hours in the day, Karen," he lamented with a sigh.

"That's because you take on too much."

He leaned back in his chair and steepled his fingers. "True," he conceded agreeably. "But what do you suggest I eliminate from my schedule? Tony Watson, who's picked me for the father figure he so desperately needs? The live teen chat room I host twice a week? The meetings with parents of problem kids? The budget?" He paused and tilted his head thoughtfully. "Actually, I could do without the budget, but I don't think the school board would approve."

Karen made a face. "I see your point."

He smiled and leaned forward again. "I thought you would. Okay, show Ms. Lockwood in. I might as well get this over with."

She hesitated and looked at him quizzically. "In the interest of curiosity, how in the world did she get you to agree to this? You hate publicity."

He shrugged. "I guess she caught me at a weak moment."

Karen planted her hands on her hips. "You don't have weak moments."

"Has anyone ever told you that you're an opinionated woman?" he teased.

She tilted her head thoughtfully and counted off on her fingers. "Let's see. My mother. My husband. My kids. The guy at the car repair shop. The director of the—"

"Enough!" Mitch interrupted with a laugh. "Just show Ms. Lockwood in."

Karen grinned. "You got it, boss."

Mitch smiled and shook his head as he repositioned the stacks of papers on his desk. He'd inherited Karen when he'd taken on this job, and she'd been a godsend, serving as secretary, administrative assistant, sounding board, reality check and mother hen all rolled into one. Not to mention comic relief. He couldn't have gotten along without her.

"I hope that smile is a good omen for our interview."

Mitch glanced up, and the perfunctory greeting died on his lips. He knew the woman in the doorway was Tess Lockwood. He would recognize those eyes anywhere. But everything else about her was different. Her hair hung loose and free, softly brushing her shoulders. She was wearing makeup—not much, but enough to enhance her already lovely features. And her clothes—gone were the boxy suit and baggy sweater. They'd been replaced by a short-sleeved silk blouse that clung to her curves and a sleek black A-line skirt that emphasized her trim waist and shapely legs. The transformation was stunning.

The seconds ticked by, and Mitch suddenly realized that he was staring. A hot flush of embarrassment crept up his neck, and he cleared his throat, struggling to recover.

"Come in, make yourself comfortable," he said, gesturing toward the chairs they'd occupied at their first meeting.

Tess made her way across the room, well aware of Mitch's reaction to her new look, though he'd recovered admirably. But while that brief, slightly dazed expression had done wonders for her ego, she suddenly regretted her impulsive purchase of the stylish new outfit. She'd been out of the dating game far too long to remember the rules, she realized in panic. What if Mitch actually…well…*did* something about that look in his eyes? Like ask her out. What would she do then? Bruce already thought she'd sided with the enemy. She could imagine his reaction if Mitch and she saw each other socially. Her relationship with her son was strained as it was, especially after their long talk this weekend about the new house rules. Good heavens, what had she been thinking? she berated herself. She should have just stuck with her serviceable, if dowdy, wardrobe.

But as she sat down and turned to Mitch, her doubts and uncertainties melted in the warmth of his eyes.

"I hope you won't take offense if I say that you look especially nice today," he said as he sat across from her, intrigued by her becoming blush—a reaction more typical of a schoolgirl than a once-married woman.

The husky quality in his voice did odd things to her stomach. "No, not at all," she replied a bit breathlessly.

He leaned back and propped an ankle on his knee. "Okay. Where do we start? I'm new at this, so you're going to have to walk me through it step by step."

Tess smiled and reached for her notebook. She might not be comfortable in the role of desirable woman, but she was quite comfortable in the role of reporter. "I like to think of an interview as simply a conversation. Except I get to ask most of the questions. Why don't we start with the award? Tell me what led to it."

He did so easily, talking about the innovative intervention programs and one-on-one involvement he encouraged between students, parents, administration and teachers. Under Tess's astute questioning, he revealed his passionate commitment to the kids, his concern about societal pressures on teens and on the American family, and the satisfaction he found in his work.

"I'm impressed, Mr. Jackson," she said honestly. "The world could use more people who care so deeply. And I'm also curious. I understand that you were once a police officer—in Chicago, I believe. This is quite a career switch. What prompted you to make the change?"

Tess sensed his sudden, almost imperceptible withdrawal.

"I saw a lot on the street," he said carefully, his words slower and more guarded. "Almost always too late for prevention. I wanted to find a way to intervene earlier. This kind of work seemed to offer that opportunity."

Tess's job had taught her to be attuned to nuances, and there were plenty here. There was something very important that he wasn't revealing, and she was both curious and intrigued. But pushing usually just made a wary subject back off more. And she didn't really need to go any deeper for this interview. So, regretfully, she moved on. "What brought you to St. Louis?"

She could sense his slight easing of tension. "My uncle. He has a farm about an hour south of St. Louis, and a little over two years ago he had a bad fall that left him with a limp. I came that summer to help, and when it was obvious that he'd need ongoing assistance with the farm, I got a job here."

"You must have been there this weekend," she said with a smile.

He looked at her in surprise. "How did you know?"

"Your tan. When I saw you Thursday, your face didn't have nearly as much color."

He grinned. "Your powers of observation are admirable, Ms. Lockwood. You're right. We worked in the fields this weekend. I spend most of my free time there, especially in the nice weather."

"Any other family locally?"

"No."

"How about back in Chicago?"

An intense flash of pain ricocheted across his eyes. "No. My parents are both gone and my…my wife died seven years ago."

Mitch frowned. He hadn't meant to say that. Hadn't intended to reveal anything about Dana. Wasn't sure why he had.

"I'm so sorry," Tess said softly, taken aback by that fleeting glimpse of anguish. "I had no idea…." Her voice faltered. She'd wondered about a wife, found it difficult to believe someone like Mitch would have remained single all these years, had speculated there might be a divorce in his past. But she hadn't expected this. "I didn't mean to bring up painful memories," she apologized.

He took a deep breath. "It's okay." And surprisingly, it was. It didn't hurt nearly as much to talk about it as he'd expected. "It was cancer. It hit out of the blue and, mercifully, took her quickly. But it was still a terrible thing to watch. For a long time afterward I was…lost." For a lot of reasons, he thought, his gut twisting.

"I can understand that," Tess empathized. "I went through something similar with my father five years ago." She paused and took a deep breath. "It's awful to watch someone you love slip away."

"Yes, it is. But it helps to have a support system. I had my mother and Uncle Ray. How about you?"

"I had Bruce. And my faith, which was a great comfort."

"What about Bruce's father?"

Tess looked at him in surprise. She almost brushed aside the question, but for some reason decided to answer it. "We divorced six years ago."

His gaze softened in sympathy. "I'm sorry, Tess. Divorce can sometimes be as painful as death."

"More so, in some ways," she said sadly. "And don't be sorry. The divorce was long overdue." She tilted her head and forced herself to smile. "Now, how did things get turned around? I thought we were talking about you?"

He grinned. "You already know the story of my life."

Hardly, she thought. The man across from her had secrets, which he clearly didn't intend to reveal, she realized. Besides, she had plenty of material for her story. It was time to wrap things up.

Tess smiled and closed her notebook. "Well, at least enough for my story," she amended.

"You know, this wasn't nearly as bad as I expected," Mitch admitted as they both rose and walked toward the door.

"I'm glad to hear it." She paused on the threshold and turned to hold out her hand. "And thank you. My editor will be very pleased."

He smiled as he took her hand in a firm grip. "I hope your readers will feel the same way. I'm afraid they might be bored by the story of a dull school principal."

At first Tess thought he was kidding, but as they said their goodbyes she realized he was dead serious. Dull? she thought incredulously. Mitch Jackson? No way. Intriguing would be a more apt description, she decided as she walked down the hall. She'd thought that by the end of the interview she'd know all the important things about the principal. But she had a feeling that she'd barely scratched the surface of this fascinating man. Instead of satisfying her curiosity, today's interview had made her want to find out more.

Unfortunately, there wouldn't be much opportunity for that, she admitted with a pang of regret. Any future contact with the principal would be related to Bruce. Because to Mitch, she was just another mother dealing with a problem child.

Except at the end of the interview he had called her "Tess," she realized suddenly, stopping abruptly. That was a good sign. Wasn't it? Didn't it mean he thought of her as a person in her own right, not just as a mother?

Tess wasn't sure. Wasn't even sure if she *wanted* him to think of her that way. It was too scary. And complicated. And probably unwise.

She knew all that intellectually. And accepted it.

But for some reason, her heart just wasn't listening.

"So how was your day?"

"Okay."

Tess sighed. So far the new dinner-hour-together rule hadn't spurred the conversation and sharing she'd hoped for with Bruce. It was the old "You can lead a horse to water…" scenario. And Bruce wasn't drinking. But she wasn't going to give up.

"Did you look into the art club?" she asked, trying again. Chris Stevens had run through a list of supervised after-school activities at the meeting, and Tess had suggested the club to Bruce, who'd always shown strong artistic aptitude and interest.

"They're a bunch of geeks."

"How do you know?"

At his disgusted look, she let it drop.

They ate in silence for a few moments before she

worked up the courage to introduce a new subject. "Guess who I interviewed today?" she asked, her tone a little too bright. When he didn't respond, she plunged in. "Mr. Jackson."

That got his attention. "Why?"

"He just received the governor's award for excellence in education."

"You're kidding!"

"No. He's doing good work at the high school."

Bruce gave a disdainful snort. "Right."

"So you don't think he's a good principal?"

Bruce shrugged. "He's too 'in-your-face.'"

"Meaning?"

"He's always hanging around with the kids. And watching what we're doing. I thought principals were supposed to stay in their office and run the school."

"Maybe he's trying to change the rules."

"Why?"

"I asked him that in the interview."

"Yeah?" Bruce looked interested. "What did he say?"

"He said that when he was a cop, he saw a lot of kids on the street who were in trouble. But by the time the police got involved, it was usually too late. He said he wanted to find a way to help kids before they got to that point. That's why he became a principal. And why he's changing the rules, I expect."

"He was probably a better cop than he is a principal," Bruce said.

"Do all the kids think so?"

He shrugged. "The geeks seem to like him. The guys

I hang around with don't. Except maybe Tony Watson. But he's got problems. I think he figures Mr. Jackson can help him."

"What kind of problems?"

"Stuff at home. His parents don't get along. I think his dad drinks, and his mom's never around. She travels a lot for her job."

"Doesn't sound too great," she agreed. "So what does Mr. Jackson do?"

"He just talks to him. After school sometimes. Tony seems to be okay for a while after that. But it never lasts long. I feel sorry for him."

"Maybe you could invite him over some time."

Bruce gave her another disgusted look and changed the subject. "I saw your name on the sign-up sheet for the food booth at the school carnival. Did you really volunteer?"

"Yes."

"Why?"

"I thought we could spend some time together there." Which was true enough. But she'd hoped it would also give her a chance to meet some of his elusive friends.

He looked appalled. "Mom! Even if I go, I was going to hang around with the guys."

"I don't expect you to spend the whole day with me, Bruce. But I thought we could have a hot dog and soda or something when I finish working. And what do you mean, *even* if you go?"

"I'm not sure about it. I have to check with the guys."

"But what do *you* want to do?" she pressed. "You used to like carnivals, especially the rides."

He shrugged. "That's kid stuff."

But that's what you are! she wanted to cry out. *Just a kid.* Instead, she reached for his empty plate. "I don't know. *I* still like carnivals, and I'm no kid," she said, striving for a conversational tone.

He considered that. "Well, I might go. For a while."

"I hope so. It would be fun. And you know what else I was thinking? Maybe this weekend we could go to the art museum. I hear it's great, and there's an exhibit right now that I thought you might especially like. It's on the—"

"I'll have a lot of homework this weekend," Bruce cut her off.

"You have to have some time for fun, too."

"Joe's having a party Saturday night at his house. Maybe I could go to that," he said hopefully.

"Maybe. Will his parents be home?"

"Oh, Mom!"

"Yes or no?"

"I don't know."

"If you give me his phone number, I'll call and check."

"Forget it." He shoved his chair back and stood. "Can I dry the dishes later?"

"Sure."

Tess sighed as he disappeared down the hall. So far, she didn't seem to be making much progress. But things would change eventually. She was sure of it.

She only hoped the change would be for the better.

Chapter Four

If she never saw another funnel cake in her life it would be too soon, Tess concluded, wrinkling her nose in distaste as she poured the batter through the namesake cooking implement and watched it coil around unappetizingly in the hot grease. After making the fat-laden sweets for the past hour, Tess couldn't believe that anyone would actually eat them. But they'd been selling like the proverbial hot cakes to the students at the school carnival.

Tess lifted the golden, cooked pastry onto a paper plate and liberally sprinkled it with powdered sugar before handing it to the parent who was filling orders at the front counter. She glanced at her watch, noting with relief that her shift was almost over. In ten minutes she'd be free to have the agreed-upon hot dog and soda with Bruce.

If he showed up, she amended, her worried gaze scanning the school grounds. So far he'd made himself scarce. Since their arrival she'd caught only a fleeting glimpse of him in the distance, and his friends were nowhere to be seen. So much for any hopes she'd harbored about meeting his elusive companions, she conceded with a resigned sigh.

"How's business?"

The familiar, husky voice close to her ear made her jump, and she dropped the funnel into the vat, gasping in pain as hot grease splattered and sizzled on the back of her hand. She heard Mitch's startled oath, and a moment later he ducked under the rail and took her hand, cradling it in his as he frowned at the shiny red patch of burned skin.

"This needs attention." His gaze met hers, contrite and troubled. "I'm sorry, Tess."

There was something about the way he said her name, his voice roughened with some emotion she couldn't identify, that made her own voice quaver.

"It—it wasn't your fault," she assured him. "If I'd been paying more attention this never would have happened. And I'm fine, really."

Instead of responding, Mitch called over her shoulder, "Hank, Tess burned her hand. She needs to go to first aid."

The older man in charge of the booth joined them, a concerned look on his face. "A casualty already?"

"It's nothing, really," Tess insisted, trying to tug her hand free. But when it was obvious that Mitch didn't intend to release it, she stopped struggling.

Hank peered down at the injury with a troubled expression and seconded Mitch's diagnosis. "That's a bad burn. You go on, Tess. We have plenty of help. And your replacement will be here any minute."

Tess glanced down at her hand. The burn did look nasty. But she found herself focusing more on Mitch's strong, capable fingers and his tender touch, which were playing havoc with her respiration. She forced herself to take a long, steadying breath before she spoke. "All right. You both win. Where's the first aid station?"

Mitch's hand dropped to the small of her back and he guided her out of the booth. "I'll go with you."

Tess knew she should protest. She was perfectly capable of finding her own way. And Mitch was a busy man. But she liked the feel of his hand at her waist, even if it was just a polite, impersonal gesture. Tess couldn't remember the last time she'd been touched in such a protective way. And whatever Mitch's intent, his touch satisfied a need deep inside her, one that often surfaced during the long, solitary nights, or when the demands of single parenthood overwhelmed her. It was a touch that made her feel as if she wasn't quite so alone. As if someone cared. That feeling, long absent from her life, was one to be savored, if only for a brief moment.

"Here we are. It's not exactly the Mayo Clinic, but they should be able to handle this," Mitch said with a smile, putting an end to her momentary flight of fantasy.

The school nurse quickly saw to the burn, and within a couple of minutes Tess was free to go.

"Can I buy you a soda?" Mitch asked as he lifted the flap for her to precede him out of the tent.

Tess's heart gave a little leap, and an inexplicable feeling of happiness washed over her. "You don't have to do that," she protested halfheartedly.

He flashed her a crooked grin. "True. But I'd like to. After all, you were hurt, in part, because of me. It's the least I can do."

So his offer was just part of the job. Tess's spirits quickly nose-dived, but she forced her lips into a smile. "I'm sure you have other things to attend to, Mr. Jackson. But thank you."

Mitch almost accepted her answer at face value—as a brush-off. He wasn't the type to force his company on anyone, man or woman. But for some reason he hesitated. Her refusal somehow didn't ring true. In his gut he sensed that she *wanted* to spend more time with him. So what was holding her back?

For a long moment he studied the woman across from him. Today she was dressed in form-fitting jeans and a cotton T-shirt that softly hugged her curves. She had the body of a twenty-year-old, Mitch noted appreciatively—not to mention gorgeous eyes. A man could drown in their delicious green depths. But there was hurt in them, too, and wariness. Tess Lockwood struck him as a woman who had learned through adversity to be strong and capable and independent, who was used to tackling the challenges of life single-handedly. But he also sensed that somewhere deep inside she yearned to be less alone. Not that she needed a man to lean on. Just that she would welcome someone with whom to share the triumphs and tragedies of life. Yet something—or someone—had made her cautious. Unsure. Even a little skittish. It was uncertainty, not unwillingness, that was holding her back from accepting his invitation, Mitch suspected. So he decided to make one more attempt.

He stuck his hands into the back pockets of his jeans and gave her his most persuasive smile. "First of all, the name is Mitch. I believe I've been calling you Tess for quite some time, so turnabout is fair play. And second, I don't have anything else to attend to. So would you reconsider?"

Tess's breath caught in her throat, and her spirits rebounded. He really did want to spend more time with her! He wasn't just being polite! The warmth and sincerity in his disarming smile convinced her of that. She drew a deep, unsteady breath and nodded. "All right. Thank you."

His smile broadened. "Good. I hate to drink alone."

A couple of minutes later, sodas in hand, they found a table in the sun. Tess closed her eyes and lifted her face to the balmy rays, enjoying their caressing warmth.

"Mmm. This is great," she said, her lips curving into an appreciative smile.

Mitch took a sip of his soda and let his gaze rest on those lips—soft and supple and made to be kissed. She was more relaxed than he'd ever seen her—and far more appealing than was healthy for either of them, he realized with a start as his gaze swept down the slender column of her throat and lingered on the bare expanse of creamy skin at her collarbone. He swallowed with difficulty and looked away, firmly reminding himself that he wasn't in the market for romance. And neither was the lady, from all indications.

When he glanced back she was looking at him, her chin propped in one hand, her slender fingers playing with the soda straw. "You got lucky, you know that?" she remarked with a smile.

Her words jolted him momentarily, until common sense kicked in. Tess couldn't possibly be talking about the fact that they'd met—even if that was the first thought that had come to *his* mind. "How so?" he asked, striving for a casual tone.

"The weather," she replied matter-of-factly. "Mid-March can be awfully nasty in Missouri. It takes a lot of courage to plan an outdoor carnival for this time of year."

He let his breath out slowly, willing his racing pulse to slow down. "Not courage," he corrected her. "Tradition. Southfield High's been having this carnival on the same weekend for years. And I think they've only had bad weather once."

"Well, someone's doing something right. But I was surprised to see you here. I thought you went to your uncle's on weekends."

"I do. I'm heading out there as soon as I leave here. But I had to put in an appearance."

Tess's fingers stilled and she frowned. "So I *am* holding you up."

He shook his head. "I wasn't going to leave until after—"

He broke off abruptly to look over Tess's shoulder, and she turned to find Bruce glaring at her.

"I waited by the food booth for ten minutes," her son said accusingly, shooting a venomous glance at Mitch.

A crestfallen look swept over Tess's face. "Oh, honey, I'm sorry!" she apologized contritely. "I burned my hand and Mit…Mr. Jackson walked me over to first aid. We stopped to have a soda on the way back. I just lost track of the time."

He shrugged stiffly. "It doesn't matter. The food here stinks, anyway. I'd rather go out with the guys for pizza. If that's okay."

Mitch saw the distress on Tess's face and stood. "I was just leaving," he said easily. "Why don't you stay and have something to eat with your mom, Bruce?"

Bruce glared at him. "I don't have to do what you say when I'm not in school."

"Bruce!" Tess reprimanded him, shocked by his defiant tone. "Apologize to Mr. Jackson!"

"Why? I didn't do anything wrong," he countered sullenly.

Tess rose, bristling with anger. "You most certainly did. You were rude and insolent. There was no call for that tone. I raised you better than that. Now, apologize."

Their gazes locked for a moment in a silent battle of wills. But though they were equal in height, he was no match for her maternal authority. At last his gaze fell and he studied the toe of his sport shoe.

"I'm sorry," he mumbled begrudgingly, refusing to meet Mitch's eyes. Then he looked at Tess. "So can I go with the guys for pizza?"

Tess debated silently. She'd blown it just now by not showing up on time for the "date" with her son. And she'd added insult to injury by allowing Bruce's nemesis to be the cause of her tardiness. She needed to make it up to him, and this might be the way. After all, his request wasn't unreasonable. And she had been keeping him on a pretty tight leash. She longed to turn to Mitch, ask his advice, but that would only make things worse with Bruce. She was on her own.

"Where are they going?" she stalled.

"Just down the street. To Little Italy."

Tess knew the place. It was a popular—and safe—hangout for high school kids. "Okay. But I want you home by seven."

"Seven! But Mom, it's Saturday night!"

"And you're fourteen." She ignored his dirty look. "Do you want me to pick you up?"

His expression said, "Get real," but his spoken words were different. "I can walk."

The restaurant was only a few blocks from their apartment and the area was safe, so Tess nodded. "Okay. I'll see you at seven. No later, Bruce. Got it?"

"Yeah."

Tess watched as he disappeared into the crowd, then turned to Mitch, her shoulders drooping. "So did I blow it?" she asked heavily, clearly distressed by the confrontation.

He shook his head. "You can't keep kids under lock and key all the time. And you can't always be there to watch over their shoulder. Little Italy is okay. And you set a clear curfew. You did the right thing, Tess."

She wanted to believe him. Desperately. She'd made a lot of mistakes in her life, but she was determined not to make any more when it came to Bruce. Mitch's reassurance was comforting. But more important, it was credible. He wasn't the type to lie just to make someone feel good. Especially when a kid's future was at stake. She'd learned enough about him to know that. The knot in her stomach eased slightly and she slowly exhaled. "Thanks."

Mitch glanced at his watch, and Tess took the cue. She reached for her purse and slung it over her shoulder. "Thanks for the soda, too. I'm sure you're anxious to get on the road."

Her statement was true enough. Mitch had planned to arrive at the farm before dark. He could still make it if he left now.

"Actually, since your meal plans fell apart, I thought maybe we could grab a bite first. The food here isn't quite as bad as Bruce implied."

Judging by the faint flush that rose on her cheeks, the invitation surprised her as much as it did him.

"I don't want to hold you up," she said hesitantly.

She'd given him an out. Which he should take, he told himself firmly. Spending time with an attractive mother of a problem student wasn't in his plans. Nor was it safe. He knew that at some intuitive level. The logical thing to do was grab a carryout and take off. But somehow his heart wasn't listening to logic.

"We both have to eat anyway. Unless you make a habit of cookies for dinner."

She smiled. "No. That was a rare exception. I much prefer real food."

"Two orders of real food coming up, then. What would you like?"

"Surprise me."

"No hated foods I should steer clear of?"

She grinned. "Only funnel cakes."

He chuckled, a deep sound that resonated pleasantly in her ears. "I don't blame you. Okay, sit tight and I'll be right back."

When he returned a few minutes later laden with bratwurst, potato salad, coleslaw and brownies, Tess arched her eyebrows. "So did you invite everyone in line to join us?" she teased.

"Hey, we eat hearty on the farm," he countered as he divided up the food. "You need a lot of energy to drive tractors and mend fences and pitch hay."

"So what excuse do *I* have for eating all these calories?"

His gaze swept over her, swift but discerning. "I don't think you need to worry."

Though his tone was matter-of-fact, his words caused an odd flutter in her stomach. She watched him surreptitiously, admiring his strong profile as he squeezed mustard onto his bratwurst. He was a man who could easily let his good looks go to his head, could take advantage of his innate charisma. Instead, he was down-to-earth and genuine. Though he was clearly used to being in charge, his authority was tempered by kindness—and something else she couldn't quite put her finger on. But it was there, in his eyes. Something had happened to Mitch Jackson somewhere along the way that had changed him irrevocably. Tess knew that as suddenly and surely as she knew that for the first time in years she actually found herself attracted to a man.

At just that moment Mitch looked at her, and she felt herself dissolving in the warmth of his dark brown eyes. A sudden surge of longing swept over her, setting off warning bells in the recesses of her heart and sending shock waves rippling through her. For a woman who thought she'd tamed her physical needs, who had convinced herself that she'd built up an immunity to their power, it was extremely disconcerting to discover that it had simply taken the right man to reawaken her long-dormant desire. The fact that she wasn't in the market for romance—nor, she suspected, was he—didn't seem to matter. The attraction was real and seemed to have a life of its own, which scared her. And made her want to turn and flee. In fact, she intended to do just that at the first opportunity. In the meantime, she needed to focus on something else.

"So tell me about the farm. How big is it?" she asked, grasping at the first thought that came to mind.

If Mitch was surprised by the abrupt change of subject, or noticed the slightly breathless quality of her voice, he didn't let on. "It's a nice spread," he replied easily. "About five hundred acres. Uncle Ray leases most of it to a tenant farmer now, but he still works about a hundred acres. It's enough to keep us busy."

"Do you spend all your free time there?"

He shrugged. "Pretty much. It's a nice change of pace."

"I have some friends who own a farm near Jefferson City," Tess told him. "It's smaller than your uncle's—probably a couple hundred acres, mostly fields, some woods. Bruce and I used to go out there sometimes on the weekends. He always enjoyed it. Of course, that was in the old days. I doubt that a farm would hold much appeal for him now. It wouldn't be cool." She sighed. "It seems like sometimes…sometimes I hardly know him anymore," she confessed in a disheartened tone.

Her face grew sad and forlorn, and Mitch fought a powerful impulse to reach over and take her hand. He deliberately reached for the potato salad instead. "Adolescence is tough on everyone," he commiserated, purposely adopting a clinical tone. "But most kids get through it unscathed. Some just need a little more help than others."

Tess nodded. "Like Bruce. How do you spot kids like him?"

He shrugged. "I pay attention, especially to midterm transfers. They often have problems adjusting and finding their niche. It's not rocket science."

"No. It's more difficult than rocket science," Tess declared emphatically. "Because human beings aren't as predictable as rockets. Especially adolescents."

"They can be just as volatile, though. But there are patterns of behavior that pretty consistently indicate trouble, if you know what to watch for."

"Which clearly you do. How did you learn so much about kids, Mitch?"

It was an innocent question. But his gut twisted painfully, and he found it difficult to swallow the bite of potato salad he'd just taken. They were dangerously close to off-limits territory, and he bought himself a moment to formulate an answer by taking a long, slow drink of his soda. "I was young once," he replied at last, aware that his response was incomplete and unsatisfactory. But it was all he was prepared to offer.

Before her reporter skills could kick in, prompting her to ask a follow-up question, he turned the tables. "You mentioned in our first meeting that Bruce has a problem with self-esteem. As Chris pointed out in the meeting you attended, self-image is a big part of what drives adolescent behavior. Kids who have issues in this area are often susceptible to peer pressure. But it's a bit unusual to find that problem in teenagers who have at least one very loving, involved parent in their life—which Bruce does. It's more common when kids come from homes where the parents are apathetic or even abusive." He hesitated, and when he spoke again his tone was more personal than professional. "Can I ask you something, Tess?"

She broke off a piece of her brownie and let it crumble through her fingers. She knew where this was leading. Peter. She'd never talked about her relationship with her ex-husband—to anyone. Had never felt the need to dredge up those unhappy memories. Until now. Suddenly she wanted to share the trauma—at least some of it—with this man whose kind, sympathetic eyes seemed to invite confidences. *Please, Lord,* she prayed silently, *help me find the courage to share this hurt I've held so long in my heart. And the courage to trust my instincts about this man, who seems so compassionate and caring.*

Her heart thudding painfully in her chest, she drew a deep breath and spoke quietly. "You want to know about Bruce's father."

"I *have* wondered where he fits into the picture," Mitch admitted, his eyes watchful, his tone careful.

"He doesn't."

Mitch looked surprised. "There's no contact at all?"

"No. Unless he happens to remember to send a check

to Bruce at Christmas. But the lack of contact isn't a negative in this case." Tess took another deep breath and gazed at him directly. "Peter—my ex-husband—was a lousy father. It's as simple as that. When we first got married, he said he didn't want children right away. When Bruce came along two years later—quite unexpectedly—I accepted it. Peter didn't. I thought he'd eventually come around, but he never did. He resented Bruce for intruding on our lives, and he held him to impossible standards. Bruce tried so hard to please him—" her voice broke, and she forced herself to take a deep, steadying breath "—but nothing he did was good enough. In the beginning I tried to make excuses for Peter, but kids are smart. Bruce knew how Peter felt about him. Yet he still kept trying to win his love. Only, Peter didn't have any to give—to Bruce or, as I finally realized, to me."

The next part was even harder, and Tess dropped her gaze to stare at the mangled brownie on her plate. When she spoke her voice was so soft that Mitch had to lean closer to hear. "I married Peter when I was twenty. He was the first man I'd ever seriously dated, and I mistook infatuation for love. He was handsome and ambitious and successful, and I was flattered when he took a fancy to me. It was only later that I realized what the real attraction was—my father's political contacts. Peter was a lobbyist for the theme park industry, and my dad was a state senator. He had the connections Peter wanted. I was just…just the means to an end."

Even after so many years the admission hurt, and Tess paused to draw a shaky breath before venturing a look at Mitch. Instead of the pity she'd been afraid of finding in his eyes, she saw something else entirely. Something surprising. Anger. Controlled, but simmering just below the surface.

"He was an idiot." Mitch's voice was low, but intense.

Tess's eyes widened at the unexpected comment, but before she had time to analyze it, he spoke again. "How long were you married?"

"Too long. Ten years chronologically, but it felt like a lifetime. Frankly, our marriage began to deteriorate almost immediately, and it disintegrated after Bruce was born. But I kept hoping things would improve. Even when I went back to school to finish my degree, I still did all the things that were expected of the wife of someone in Peter's position. I kept thinking that if I just did a better job as a wife, he would learn to love me—and Bruce."

"I take it that never happened."

She shook her head sadly. "No. I stayed far longer than was healthy for anyone. We were all miserable. Not that anyone would have guessed. Peter put up a good front publicly. In his profession, it was in his best interest to keep up the pretense of being a solid family man." Tess gave a brief, bitter laugh. "What a joke. We were a family in name only."

"What finally made you decide to leave?"

Tess gazed at him, into eyes that beckoned her to open her heart and share her pain, to tell this final secret. She *wanted* to. Wanted to exorcise the ghosts of that final humiliation. But even now, years later, the words wouldn't come. The memory still hurt too much. No, she couldn't talk about that final degrading moment, the turning point when only one option had been left to her. Not even to this man, who she suspected would treat her disclosure with understanding and gentleness.

"I was worried about Bruce. About the damage that had already been done, and the damage that would continue to be done if we stayed. And Peter had an offer to move on to bigger things in Washington. The time was right for us to go our separate ways." Which was the truth. Just not the *whole* truth. But it was enough. For now.

Tess crumpled her napkin with hands that weren't quite steady and forcibly lightened her tone. "So now you don't have to wonder about Bruce's dad anymore. He's out of our life. Which is no great loss. And we're doing fine on our own. Better, really. I just wish I could erase the scars he left with Bruce. But I'm working on it."

And what about the scars he left with you? Mitch wondered silently. Though he suspected she would deny it, they were there. He could see them in the sadness and disillusionment in her eyes, which spoke eloquently of her own pain as well as the pain she felt on behalf of her son. Yet she had spunk. And spirit. And strength. She was a survivor. She had made a courageous decision, and then done what was required to create a new life for herself and Bruce. But she'd also clearly paid a price. In stress. Uncertainty. Tension. Emotional distress.

Mitch's throat tightened and he was again tempted to reach over and take her hand. Again he held back, afraid of where that simple touch could lead. He'd vowed years ago to stay away from personal involvements. Friend, adviser, counselor, confidant—he could handle those roles. But nothing more. Yet more was exactly what his heart wanted from Tess Lockwood. So he needed to keep his distance. For both their sakes.

"I'm sorry, Tess."

It was a simple but heartfelt comment. And it was all that needed to be said.

"Thanks. I am, too. Frankly, I never thought I'd end up being a single mom at thirty-six. I really believed in that 'till death do us part' vow we took before God, you know?"

The wistful note in her voice tugged at his heart, and he could no longer resist the temptation. He reached over and covered her hand with his. "Don't stop believing in it, Tess," he said huskily. "It can happen."

His gaze locked with hers, and for just a moment she stopped breathing. And started believing.

"Can I tell you something, Mitch?" she said impulsively, her throat tight with emotion.

"Of course."

"Your wife was one lucky woman."

Tess wasn't surprised that Mitch seemed taken aback by her personal comment. She was taken aback herself. But she *was* surprised by the raw pain that seared through his eyes. And by his response.

"Dana wasn't all that lucky, Tess," he said flatly. "Frankly, I wasn't the best husband."

She gave him a skeptical look. "I have a feeling you're being too hard on yourself."

He brushed her comment aside impatiently. "No. It's true. I was too caught up with being a cop, working long hours and weird shifts. I loved Dana—but my job always came first. And a lot of things suffered because of that." He gazed at her directly, his face somber. "There are a lot of regrets in my past, Tess."

"You don't have a corner on that market," she said gently. "I guess all we can do is learn from our mistakes and move on."

The ghost of a smile touched the corners of his lips. "You sound like my uncle. He's always telling me the same thing."

She smiled in return. "And have you taken his advice?"

"I'm trying."

"That's all any of us can do. That, and put our trust in the Lord. My faith was the one absolute in my life for a long time. Even when my world was falling apart, I knew that I wasn't alone."

Mitch sighed. "I wish I could say the same. There was a time in my life when I felt totally abandoned and lost. But thanks to my uncle, I found my way back to my faith. That's one of the things I'm most grateful to him for."

"Speaking of your uncle…" Tess reminded him gently.

Mitch glanced at his watch. There was no way he'd make the farm before dark. But somehow he didn't care. His gaze connected with hers again, and there was an intensity in his eyes, a message in their depths, that made her pulse suddenly trip into double time. "He'll understand. Besides, can I tell you something,

Tess? When it comes to regrets, the past hour with you isn't one of them. Except for that." He reached over and gently tapped the edge of the burn with a whisper-soft touch of his finger.

Tess gazed down, trying to still the staccato beat of her heart. She couldn't very well say it, but she'd gladly burn the other hand for another hour with this special man. Not that it could ever lead anywhere, she reminded herself. Her first priority was Bruce, and the last thing she needed to do was complicate her relationship with her son by starting one with his enemy.

"I enjoyed it, too," she replied softly. "And the burn will heal."

But not her heart, she thought as they said goodbye. For just a brief moment she'd had a taste of something she'd never experienced, even in her marriage—a meeting of souls. She and Mitch had connected at some elemental level—physically, mentally, emotionally, spiritually. In other circumstances, there would be great promise in this relationship. But she had to put her relationship with Bruce first. And it didn't look as if she could have both. Which meant only one thing.

She would have to add yet another regret to her already long list.

Chapter Five

By seven-thirty Tess was angry. By eight o'clock she was getting worried. When there was still no sign of Bruce by eight-thirty, she was beginning to panic.

And by the time the phone rang at nine o'clock, she was frantic. Her voice was shaking as she struggled with a simple hello.

"Ms. Lockwood?" The male voice was unfamiliar.

"Yes."

"This is Sergeant Roberts of the Southfield Police Department. We have your son here at the station. He was a passenger in a car that was involved in an accident."

Tess's stomach plummeted to her toes, and her lungs stopped working. "Is he all right?"

"He's scared. But not hurt. Only the driver was injured. A laceration above his eye that needed stitches. I'll be happy to give you the details when you come to get your son."

"I'll be there in fifteen minutes."

Tess replaced the receiver and sank onto a stool by

the counter as her legs suddenly gave way. She forced herself to take a long, slow breath and then buried her face in her hands. She wanted to cry—with relief… frustration…anger…fear…and a depressing feeling of helplessness. She'd been afraid that Bruce was heading for a run-in with the law. But she'd hoped that she'd intervened in time to keep that from happening. At least this call wasn't related to lawbreaking, she consoled herself. But the next time it very well could be—unless she quickly figured out a way to get her son to see the light and straighten up.

As it turned out, the summons to the police station wasn't quite as innocent as Tess had assumed. Sergeant Roberts was waiting when she arrived, and once she was seated across his desk he didn't waste any time getting to the point.

"Ms. Lockwood, are you aware that your son was drinking this evening?" he asked bluntly.

She stared at him, her eyes widening in shock. "What?"

The sergeant grunted and pulled a sheet of paper toward him. "I guess that answers my question." He consulted the document in front of him. "According to his statement, he and several friends went to Little Italy and got a take-out pizza, which they washed down with beer. Then they switched to gin and went cruising. Eventually they drove into a tree. The driver's blood alcohol level was well above the legal limit. Frankly, they got lucky. They could have killed someone. Or been killed themselves."

During the officer's recitation of the facts, Tess felt the color slowly drain from her face. When he finally looked up, his stern expression eased slightly and his voice lost its clinical tone.

"Would you like a drink of water?"

Tess shook her head jerkily. "No. Thanks." She took a deep breath and met the officer's gaze directly. She didn't want to ask the question, didn't want to believe it was possible, but she had to have all the facts.

"Was…was Bruce drunk, too?"

The man shook his head. "We could smell the gin on his breath. He claims he only took one drink of beer and a sip of the gin. Frankly, I'm inclined to believe him. We did a Breathalyzer, and he was clean."

Tess swallowed with difficulty and closed her eyes. Though he'd made some very bad choices, he'd somehow found the strength to temper his response to peer pressure when it came to drinking. *Thank You, Lord, for that,* she prayed fervently. But the police officer was right. Things could have been so much worse.

When she finally opened her eyes, the sergeant's gaze was more sympathetic. "Has he been in trouble before, Ms. Lockwood? Some of the other kids are familiar to us, but I don't recall seeing Bruce before."

"We've only been here since the first of the year. Bruce has had some adjustment problems at school, but I've been addressing them. I'd hoped we were making some progress, but…" Her disheartened voice died away.

The man frowned. "Look, ma'am, we see a lot of kids in here who are heading down the wrong path. But the fact that Bruce didn't drink with his buddies is a good sign. Trust me. It's tough to say no in that situation. I wouldn't give up on him yet."

Tess sent him a grateful look and straightened her shoulders. "Thank you. I don't plan to. Just the opposite, in fact. If he thought I was being tough before, he's in for a real shock now. Is he being charged with anything?"

He rose. "Not this time. He was just a passenger, and the Breathalyzer was negative. But we put him in a holding cell. More for effect than anything else," the man said, flashing her a quick grin. "I'll take you back. And just so you know, I read him the riot act and put the fear of God into him. I think it made an impact."

He paused outside a door, entered a security code, then ushered Tess through. "Do you want me to give you a few minutes back here, or just let him out?"

Tess looked around—at the sterile, unfriendly walls, the security cameras, the barred windows, the stripped-down furnishings. "I'll take the few minutes back here," she said firmly.

He nodded and stopped beside another door with a small window. Tess glanced inside, and her heart contracted painfully. Bruce was huddled in the corner, sitting on a cot, hugging his knees to his chest. His head was down, and his shoulders were hunched and tense. She could almost feel his fear.

Sergeant Roberts fitted a key in the lock and swung the door open. "He's all yours. I'll be back in fifteen minutes," he said quietly.

Tess took a deep breath and stepped inside. A moment later she heard the door shut and lock behind her. But her attention was focused on her son, who was now staring at her with wide, wary and very scared eyes. Her first impulse was to rush over to him, take him in her arms as she had when he was a child with a nightmare, and reassure him that everything would be all right. But he wasn't a child anymore. And this nightmare was real. As for everything being all right—she couldn't guarantee that. It wasn't in her power. *He* had to help. And so she held her ground silently, waiting for him to speak first.

After several long seconds he drew a shuddering breath. "Aren't you going to say anything?" he asked in a subdued tone.

Tess willed her voice to sound calm and in control, even if her insides were churning. "Like what?"

He shrugged. "I don't know. Mother stuff. Tell me it was wrong to miss the curfew. And to ride with the guys when they were drinking."

"You said it for me."

He sighed. "I guess I'm grounded for life."

"Certainly for the foreseeable future."

He looked at her steadily. "I just tasted the beer and only had one sip of gin."

"That's what the sergeant said you told him."

"It's true."

"How old are you, Bruce?"

He eyed her warily. "You know."

"And what's the legal drinking age?"

"I know what it is, Mom." He dropped his head to his knees and turned away.

Tess took another steadying breath and moved to the straight chair beside the cot, praying that she would find the right words, words that would make an impact on her son. At this proximity, she could see the tearstains on his colorless face, and once more she wanted to simply pull him into her arms and comfort him. But the time wasn't right. Not yet.

"Let me tell you something, Bruce. It took a lot of guts not to drink more than a sip. Peer pressure can be pretty powerful, and I admire you for saying no. But that wouldn't have saved your life if the accident had been worse. You needed to say no sooner. Drinking and driving don't mix. You know that. Fortunately, only the driver was injured. And his stitches will be out in a couple of weeks. But he won't get rid of his juvenile record so easily."

Bruce turned to her, and she saw the fear in his eyes intensify. "Are the police going to…to book me?"

Tess let him sweat it out for a moment before she shook her head. "No."

His relief was palpable. "So I can go home?"

"Yes. But take a look around you while we wait for the sergeant to come back, Bruce. And remember it. Because whether or not you end up back here is up to you."

Bruce studied the small cell, distaste written all over his face. And when they finally heard the key being inserted in the lock, he was on his feet instantly.

Sergeant Roberts opened the door and then silently escorted them back to the reception area.

Tess held out her hand. "Thank you, Sergeant."

He took her fingers in a firm grip, then turned to Bruce. "You've got a good mother. Listen to her."

The ride home was silent. Tess glanced toward Bruce a couple of times, but in the dim light she couldn't read his expression. Had tonight had any impact at all? she wondered. Would it be a turning point—or only make things worse? Had she handled the situation the right way—or only widened the gulf between them? Unfortunately, Tess didn't have the answers to those questions, she acknowledged, deeply discouraged and suddenly bone weary as she pulled into a parking place near their apartment.

Bruce followed her to the door, head down, hands in his pockets. But she saw him take a deep breath when they stepped inside, heard his relieved sigh, could feel the almost palpable easing of tension. Tess dropped her purse on the couch and turned to him. "Are you hungry?"

He looked at her in surprise, his gaze wary. "Yeah."

"How about an omelet?"

"Okay."

"Why don't you go change while I make it?"

He didn't need any urging to shed the clothes he'd worn in jail, Tess noted. In fact, a moment later she also heard the shower running. Maybe his visit to the police station *had* made an impact, she thought hopefully.

She joined him at the table, sipping a white soda as he devoured the food.

"Aren't you going to eat anything?" he asked between bites.

She shook her head. The thought of food made her stomach even more queasy than it already was. "I had something at the carnival."

"With Mr. Jackson?"

"Yes."

He thought about that for a minute. "Are you going to tell him about this?"

"He won't need me to tell him. The police let the school know when any of the students get into trouble."

Bruce looked at her. "How do you know?"

"Mr. Jackson told me during the interview for the story."

"Is that legal?"

She almost laughed. "I think it's an informal thing, Bruce. Not an official report. Mr. Jackson used to be a cop, remember. He's got contacts there. They talk. Things come up."

"Yeah." His face fell. "He'll really be on me now."

Tess reached over and touched his hand. He seemed surprised, but he didn't pull away. "He cares about his students, Bruce. And I care about *you*. Can you imagine how frantic I was tonight when you didn't show up? And when the police called…." She choked and paused, struggling for control. "That's every parent's worse nightmare."

Bruce looked at her, the contrition in his eyes sincere. "I'm sorry, Mom," he said softly. "I didn't mean to worry you." He patted her hand awkwardly.

She looked at her son, tall now, the soft features of childhood giving way to the angular lines of adolescence. Lately she could see in his face the man he would soon become. Where had the years gone? she wondered in disbelief. It seemed like only yesterday that he was climbing onto her lap for a bedtime story. So much had changed in the intervening years, she thought wistfully.

But one thing hadn't changed. She still wished for him exactly as she had as she held him so tenderly in her arms the day he was born—a full and happy life, filled with love and satisfaction and contentment and a deep, abiding faith that would see him through adversity. She had vowed that day to do everything in her power to make that wish come true, and she had tried mightily through the years to honor that vow. That was why these past few weeks had been so difficult, she realized. They had reminded her that even deep maternal love couldn't shelter a child from the pain of loss or the consequences of mistakes. But she *could* stand by him. She *would* stand by him. And he needed to know that. To believe it.

"I know you didn't, Bruce. And I know you're going through a tough adjustment right now. I just wish I could put a bandage on the situation and make it better, like I did when you used to fall and scrape your knee. But I can't. You're old enough now to make a lot of your own decisions. All I can do is let you know that I'm always here for you. And that no matter what happens, I'll always love you. Will you remember that?"

Bruce nodded. "Yeah. And…I love you, too, Mom." Embarrassed now, he pushed his chair back and stood. "I guess I'll head to bed."

"Me, too." She stood as well and reached for him, closing her eyes against the world as she held him tightly for a long moment in a bear hug. "Sleep tight."

It was what she used to say as she tucked him in at night, and Bruce finished it for her. "And don't let the bedbugs bite."

"Things will be okay, Bruce," she told him fiercely, pulling back to look up at him. "Tomorrow can be a new beginning."

His eyes clouded, and the troubled expression he'd worn for the past few weeks slipped back into place. "Maybe," he replied noncommittally. "Good night, Mom."

Tess watched him disappear down the hall, tension coiling in her stomach once again. "Maybe" wasn't good enough. She wanted guarantees. But as she'd learned long ago, life didn't come with them.

Tess frowned, then highlighted the last few sentences in the article she'd written about Mitch and hit Delete. The closing was way too subjective. For the first time in her career she was having a hard time keeping her personal feelings out of her writing. And she was having lots of personal feelings. Too many, in fact. They kept intruding on her thoughts no matter how hard she tried to keep them at bay. And she was really trying. But it was a losing battle, she admitted with a resigned sigh.

The phone rang, and she reached for it distractedly, her gaze still on the screen.

"Tess Lockwood."

"Tess? It's Mitch. I heard about what happened Saturday night, and I just wanted to call and make sure everything was okay."

Tess's heart began to beat double time as the familiar, husky voice came over the wire. Suddenly it was no problem to transfer her attention from the screen to the phone.

"Hi." She berated herself for the sudden breathless quality of her voice, praying he wouldn't notice. "Your timing is impeccable. I'm working on your story."

"Then you can probably use a break from the boredom."

She heard the self-deprecating humor in his voice and smiled. "Don't sell yourself short."

"Hey, I'm just a guy doing his job. Nothing more. But tell me about Saturday," he prompted, diverting the attention from himself. "I saw Bruce earlier today, and he seemed to have survived. What about you. Are you okay?"

Tess felt her throat tighten with emotion. Which was silly, of course. The call was nothing more than a follow-up with the mother of a problem student. But she was touched nonetheless.

"I'm fine," she replied. "And thank you for checking. I'm sure you're busy enough just keeping up with the students, let alone their parents. But that's probably why you're so good at what you do—and why you win awards."

Mitch frowned. Tess had assumed his call was professional. But was it? He hadn't stopped to analyze his motives when he'd decided to contact her. All he knew was that he wanted to reassure himself that Saturday's trauma hadn't rattled her too badly. But he knew that Tess was a strong woman. She didn't need him to check up on her. Yet he'd made the call anyway. Which led him to believe that it was motivated by reasons that had nothing to do with his job. And to let her think otherwise wasn't honest.

"Actually, I'm not always this good about follow-up with parents," he admitted.

There was silence on the other end of the line for a moment while Tess digested that comment. Was he implying a personal interest? Or just letting her know that Bruce's case needed more intervention and involvement than most? Tess had no idea. So she played it safe and stayed neutral.

"Then I especially appreciate the call. It's nice to know I'm not in this thing with Bruce completely alone."

Mitch's frown deepened. Did her polite, impersonal remark imply that she wanted to keep their relationship on a professional basis? Or was she still just running scared? Connected only by voice, with none of the visual cues he'd had at the carnival, Mitch was uncertain. And frustrated. Unfortunately, a phone conversation was not the way to get clarity. Which he would be wise not to seek anyway, he reminded himself firmly. Relationships had been off his radar screen for seven years. And it would be best if they stayed that way.

"Well, if I can help in any way, don't hesitate to call," he said, matching her impersonal, polite tone.

"I won't. And Mitch…thank you again."

The sudden warmth in her voice washed over him like a tropical wave, and his own voice heated up in response. "You're welcome. Goodbye, Tess."

As Tess slowly replaced the receiver and turned regretfully back to her computer, she realized that Caroline was standing in the doorway, grinning.

"I take it the interview went well."

Tess felt hot color steal over her cheeks. "How did you know?"

"I assume that was Mitch Jackson on the phone. I only caught the tail end of the conversation, but from your tone of voice I gather you two clicked."

"He was very…nice," Tess conceded self-consciously. "I should have the story wrapped up before the end of the day."

Caroline folded her arms across her chest and leaned against the edge of the cubicle wall. "Is that all I'm going to get?" she teased, her eyes twinkling.

Tess's flush deepened. "There isn't any more to tell."

"Hmm." Caroline studied her for a moment. "So why did he call?"

"I had some trouble with Bruce Saturday night. He heard about it and wondered if everything was okay."

Caroline frowned and straightened. "Is it?"

Tess nodded. "For the moment." She gave her boss a quick recap of the evening's events, then sighed. "These last few weeks have really been a challenge. I'm lucky Mitch Jackson has taken such an interest."

Caroline eyed her speculatively. "I know he's committed to his work, or he wouldn't be winning awards," she conceded. "But I doubt he makes a habit of checking to see how the parents of his students are doing. Unless his interest is more than academic."

Tess stared after Caroline as her boss turned and disappeared around the corner. She wasn't sure the managing editor was right. But the possibility sent a tingle down her spine. However, her priority was Bruce.

Period. Getting his life turned around would require every bit of her energy and attention.

With an effort Tess forced her attention back to the words on the screen. Recalled something Mitch had just said in their conversation. And suddenly had the ending to her story.

"I'm just a guy doing his job. Nothing more," Tess typed, attributing the quote to Mitch. Then she continued. "Clearly, the governor's office doesn't agree. Mitch Jackson isn't just a man doing his job. He's a man with a mission—doing a great job. And Southfield High is a better place because of it."

Tess leaned back. Mitch *was* a man with a mission. Because he cared so much about the kids, he did his job with focus, commitment and passion.

And suddenly Tess couldn't help but wonder what it would be like if Mitch devoted that same focus, commitment and passion to some lucky woman.

The answer came immediately to mind. And it was all contained in one word.

Heaven.

Uncle Ray finished the article, took off his glasses and carefully lowered the newspaper to the kitchen table. "That's a mighty fine story, son. I'm proud of you."

Mitch felt his neck grow hot. "Thanks, Uncle Ray. I thought you'd like to see it. But frankly, I'm a little embarrassed about the whole thing. I didn't get into this line of work to be in the limelight."

"I know that. And I think it came through real clear

in the story. The reporter…" He picked up the paper again and looked for the byline. "Tess Lockwood. She sure seems to have caught your personality. And all in one interview, too."

Mitch wrapped his hands around his coffee cup. "Actually, we'd met before that. You remember the woman I mentioned when I was out here a few weekends ago? The one who's the mother of one of my problem students?"

Uncle Ray nodded. "I seem to recall something like that."

"Well, she works for the community newspaper. She did the story."

"Is that so?"

Mitch saw the sudden gleam in his uncle's eyes and held up his hand. "Don't jump to any conclusions, Uncle Ray. All of our meetings have been strictly professional."

The older man nodded sagely. "I'm sure they have. How is the boy doing, by the way?"

Mitch frowned. "Everything's been quiet for the past week. But there was an incident last weekend." He explained the car accident to the older man, who shook his head.

"Sounds like that boy needs a good talking-to."

"He does. Te…his mother is doing her best, but I think she may be in over her head on this one. Fourteen is a tough age, especially without a father figure. Bruce seems like a good kid, but he's in with the wrong crowd. Things worked out okay last weekend, but next time he may not be so lucky. I'm intervening where I can, but there's only so much I can do. I only see him during school hours. And even then, I doubt I'm having much impact. To him, I am definitely the enemy with a capital *E*."

"Hmm. That is a problem. Especially if you've taken a particular interest in this boy." Uncle Ray reached for his mug and took a sip of coffee. "You know, you might have more luck getting through to him if you could get him one-on-one outside of school. Let him see you in a different light. Might help him to see you more as a friend than an enemy."

Mitch considered that. "You could be right," he agreed.

"Why don't you invite him to come down here to the farm with you for Easter?"

Mitch stared at his uncle. "Are you serious?"

The older man shrugged. "Why not? Plenty of room. And the fresh air might do him some good."

Now that the initial shock was wearing off, Mitch began to warm to the idea. "You know, that just might work," he said slowly. "His mother told me that when they lived in Jeff City, Bruce used to love visiting the farm of some friends of theirs."

"There you go."

Mitch regarded his uncle silently for a moment. "I think you might be on to something, Uncle Ray. But what made you think of this? I've had lots of problem students through the years, and you've never suggested anything like this before."

He shrugged. "Can't say. Just seems like you've taken a special interest in this boy. And it sounds like he could be at a crossroads. I sort of fancy helping you help him pick the right route. Do you think his mother would agree to this?"

Mitch nodded. "She wants to do whatever's best for her son." Then he frowned. "But I hate to take him away from her on a holiday weekend. They only have each other, so she'd be alone."

"Well, bring her along."

Mitch stared at the older man. His uncle was full of surprises tonight. "Bring her along?"

"Sure. Like I said, plenty of room. Be nice to have the house full of people on a holiday for once."

While Uncle Ray was kind and generous to a fault and such a gesture was characteristic of him, there was something more going on here than mere philanthropy, Mitch deduced. Like maybe a bit of matchmaking. He took a sip of his coffee and carefully set it on the table.

"Uncle Ray, you wouldn't by any chance be trying to play Cupid here, would you?"

The older man could have won an Academy Award for the innocent look he gave his nephew. "Cupid? I think I'm a little old for that, don't you?"

Mitch grinned. "You're not too old for anything."

The hint of a smile touched Uncle Ray's lips. "How about some more coffee?" Without waiting for a response, he rose and walked over to the counter to retrieve the pot.

"You're avoiding the question," Mitch accused.

Uncle Ray looked over his shoulder and eyed his nephew shrewdly. "How did it come up, anyway? One minute I'm trying to be a good Christian by opening my home to a troubled youngster, and the next you're thinking about romance. And you think *I'm* the one who's got Cupid on my mind?"

Mitch frowned at his uncle's back. Somehow this conversation had gotten all turned around. Had he over-reacted to Uncle Ray's generosity, read too much into it? Was he the one with cupid on his mind?

If he was honest, Mitch knew that the answers to those questions were *probably* and *definitely*. He couldn't deny that there was something about Tess Lockwood that had gotten under his skin. Or that she was invading his thoughts—and his heart—more and more. But why? And what was he going to do about it?

Uncle Ray had very adeptly avoided answering his question about Cupid, Mitch realized as the older man refilled his cup. But it didn't matter now. Because the questions he'd just asked himself were much more im-portant, though the answers were just as elusive.

Chapter Six

"This is a really dumb idea. Why can't we just stay home for Easter?"

Tess looked up as her son entered the living room and unenthusiastically dumped his duffel bag next to the couch. "Did you pack something nice for church on Sunday?"

"Do I have to go?"

"It's Easter."

"Big deal."

"Yes, it is," Tess replied firmly. "We've never missed church on Easter. The only reason we don't go every week now is because of my work schedule. But I miss it. A lot."

"I don't," Bruce shot back. "It's boring." He slouched into a chair, stretched out his long legs and scowled. "Why did you say yes to this, anyway?" he groused. "Three days with an ex-cop principal and an old man—some holiday."

Tess counted to ten—slowly—as she walked down

the hall to retrieve her suitcase. When she reached the sanctuary of her room, she took a deep breath and sat on the edge of the bed. She hadn't answered Bruce's question. Mostly because she didn't know the answer. The invitation had come out of the blue, taking her by surprise. And Mitch had said all the right things when he'd issued it. Things that made it hard to turn down. Like how beneficial it could be to his relationship with Bruce to let the boy see him in a different setting. And how good it might be for Bruce to get back to the country environment he'd once enjoyed so much, in simpler days. The rationale had seemed to make a lot of sense at the time. She was desperate to help Bruce, and Mitch had positioned this weekend in a way that made it sound almost therapeutic.

But that wasn't the only reason she'd accepted, Tess admitted. Yes, she was touched by Mitch's willingness to go the extra mile for Bruce. And yes, she believed that Mitch was sincerely convinced that a weekend in the country might be good for Bruce. But though Mitch was a dedicated principal who went above and beyond for his students, she really didn't think he invited most of them—and their mothers—to spend a holiday at his uncle's farm. Which meant that maybe, just maybe, part of his reason for asking was that he wanted to spend time with her. And even with her teenage son and his elderly uncle as chaperons, that thought sent a shiver of excitement through her.

Tess knew she wasn't being wise. After all, romance was *not* among her priorities. Her roles were clear and straightforward—mother and breadwinner. Period.

But in her heart she knew it wasn't quite that simple. Because she was a woman, too. And that part of her, those needs, had been suppressed far too long. Which hadn't been much of a problem, frankly, until Mitch came along. He made her feel like a desirable woman again, whether that was his intent or not. She had no idea of the depth of his interest in her, only that it had to be there, at some level, or this invitation would never have come.

Tess knew she shouldn't get carried away with romantic fantasies. But for just one weekend the temptation had been too great to resist. And what harm could it do? Bruce might very well benefit from the trip. As for her, a weekend with Mitch might help satisfy the longing in her soul for male companionship, even if only temporarily. It seemed to be a win-win situation all around. *If* she could get Bruce to cooperate, she reminded herself with a sigh as she hefted her suitcase.

The doorbell rang just as she reached the living room, sending her heart jumping to her throat. She glanced at her son, hoping he would buy her a moment to compose herself by answering the door, but he clearly had no intention of budging from the couch. She took a deep breath, willing the uncomfortable hammering of her heart to subside, but her body just wasn't cooperating, she realized helplessly.

A second ring from the bell and Bruce's curious look finally compelled her into action. She wiped her palms on her jeans and made her way to the door, praying for a modicum of composure. *Please, Lord, just let me get through the first few moments,* she pleaded.

Let me look cool and composed and in control. Let something clever and witty trip from my tongue.

But that was not to be. Because when she opened the door and caught her first sight of Mitch, her pulse went off the scale and her voice deserted her.

He was dressed more casually than she'd ever seen him, in well-worn jeans and a forest-green shirt that hugged his muscular chest and broad shoulders. His dark hair was slightly windblown, and despite a slight chill in the air, he exuded warmth. As Caroline had noted, he was one handsome man.

But it was actually his smile that did her in. Compelling. Engaging. Intimate. It somehow seemed to reach deep inside her, to a place no one had touched for a long, long time. Her breath caught in her throat, and the greeting she'd finally mustered died on her lips.

For a moment their gazes connected and sizzled in silence. When Mitch finally spoke, the husky quality of his voice made her knees go weak, and her grip on the door involuntarily tightened. "Good morning, Tess."

"Hi." Her voice cracked, and she wanted to sink through the floor. So much for being cool and witty. She sounded like some schoolgirl with a crush on the principal—and would probably be taken just about as seriously, she thought, her spirits drooping. Mitch was far too worldly to be interested in someone who acted more like a lovesick student than a desirable woman. And even if she wasn't in the market, it would be nice to have someone look at her, just once, with fire in his eyes. The smile on her lips suddenly felt stiff, but she struggled to keep it in place.

Mitch could feel the tension in the air. The catch in her voice communicated her nervousness, and he didn't doubt that she'd had second thoughts about this weekend—just as he had. But now that he stood just inches away from her, any lingering doubts vanished. He not only *wanted* to spend time with this woman, he *needed* to, because at some very basic level he was drawn to her. Not just because she was beautiful, though he certainly appreciated her physical attributes. His gaze flickered over her quickly, discreetly, but his keen eyes missed nothing. Long, shapely legs eased into worn jeans that fit like a second skin. A waistline that seemed small enough for his hands to span. A soft, pink cotton shirt, open at the neck, that subtly molded her curves and revealed the pulse beating rapidly in the hollow of her throat. She was scared, nervous, uncertain…attracted?

He felt his own pulse accelerate as his gaze moved swiftly back to her eyes, past soft, slightly parted lips that seemed made to be kissed. And suddenly he was the one who was nervous.

"W-would you like to come in?" She stepped aside, and Mitch crossed the threshold, taking his time—and a long, slow breath—as he scanned the small but cozy room. Tess had done a good job with the apartment, he realized, noting the homey touches throughout. It was a friendly, welcoming place—except for the expression on Bruce's face, Mitch amended as his gaze connected with his problem student.

Mitch steadily returned the young man's hostile glare. This was the one part of the weekend he was *not* looking forward to. Getting through to Bruce, trying to put their relationship on a different footing, wasn't going to be easy. But it was important. Bruce was on the edge, and unless someone pulled him back soon, he could end up like…

As always, Mitch's gut clenched painfully, and he blocked out that image. He wasn't going to go there. Not today. But he was going to do everything in his power to keep Bruce from making the same mistakes. Just as he had for every troubled student who'd come his way ever since that night.

Despite the teenager's antagonistic look, Mitch smiled. "Hello, Bruce."

Bruce waited a long moment before mumbling a barely audible "Hi." Then he turned his attention back to the TV, pointedly ignoring the two adults by the door.

Tess frowned, but Mitch's smile was reassuring. "Everything will be fine," he said softly.

She gave him a worried look and spoke in a low voice. "I hope so. Bruce hasn't exactly been enthusiastic about this. I don't want him to ruin your holiday weekend."

"He won't."

She sighed. "I wish I could be so sure."

"Trust me on this."

She tilted her head and looked at him quizzically. "Do you know something I don't?"

Actually, he did. But he couldn't very well tell her that as long as she shared his holiday it was bound to be a good one. "Let's just say I'm an optimist," he offered. "And that I don't intend to let anything ruin this weekend."

Tess gave him a weary smile. "I like your attitude."

"It beats the alternative," he replied with a grin. "So are you ready? It's too pretty a day to waste in the city." He reached for her bag.

"We're all set. Bruce, help Mitch take the bags out to the car while I get the food."

Though Mitch had protested that it wasn't necessary, she'd insisted on contributing her homemade lasagna and cinnamon streusel coffee cake to the weekend's festivities. As she headed to the kitchen she glanced again toward Bruce, who was still slouched in front of the TV. "Now, Bruce," she said pointedly in a tone that brooked no argument.

By the time she returned from the kitchen, there was no sign of Bruce. She gave Mitch a quizzical look as he reached over to take the cooler of goodies.

"He's in the car," he replied to her silent question.

"Did he say anything?" Hope and fear mingled in her voice.

"No. But he'll loosen up."

She sighed. "I don't know. He's gotten pretty good at shutting people out."

At the pain and discouragement in her voice, Mitch felt his throat contract with emotion. Parenting an adolescent was never easy, even for two people. Doing it single-handedly while coping with a new job, a new town and a son having difficulty adapting to a new school made it even tougher. He knew that Tess was doing her best, and he was tempted to reassure her that things would work out. But he couldn't guarantee that. And he'd learned a long time ago not to make promises he couldn't keep.

"Maybe the change of scene will give him a new perspective," Mitch said encouragingly. "If nothing else, it will brighten up my uncle's holiday. He's really been looking forward to this. He doesn't have much company these days."

"I still can't believe he was willing to invite two total strangers to stay with him," Tess said, shaking her head. "He must be a very generous man. Will you tell me about him on the drive?"

"Sure."

By the time they pulled into the gravel drive leading to the modest, two-story frame farmhouse that Uncle Ray had called home for forty-five years, she'd learned a lot about the older man. His beloved wife had died eight years before, and his only son had been killed in Vietnam. Though his uncle had coped with those losses, relying on a deep-seated faith to see him through, Mitch confided that he often worried about the older man spending so much time alone. Yet his uncle never complained, saying that he was too busy to get lonely.

"Uncle Ray really is amazing," Mitch told her, the admiration clear in his voice. "Even though he's spent his life on a farm—and trust me, no one knows more than he does about corn and wheat and soybeans and soil and weather…you get the idea—his interests go far beyond the world of farming. And he's a voracious reader."

According to Mitch, he fancied biographies and, interestingly enough, romance novels, citing their optimism and happy endings as tonic for the soul in a world where the concept of lifelong love and commitment had somehow lost favor. Tess liked him already.

She'd also learned a lot about Mitch during their hour-long drive. It was clear that he felt a deep sense of responsibility toward his uncle—more, perhaps, than required by mere kinship. She sensed that these two men shared some sort of special bond, though Mitch revealed nothing that would verify that hunch. When he spoke of his uncle his voice held unmistakable affection, and if he ever resented spending his rare free time working with the older man on the farm, he gave no indication of it. Generosity, it appeared, ran in the Jackson family.

Tess glanced into the back seat a couple of times during the drive, hoping to pull Bruce into the conversation, but he was hunched into the corner, his eyes closed. He might be sleeping, but more likely he was simply making a statement that he had no intention of participating in this weekend, she speculated resignedly.

"There's Uncle Ray."

Tess transferred her gaze to the house at the end of the gravel drive they'd just turned into, where an older man stood on the porch, waiting to greet them. Tall and spare, with fine, neatly trimmed gray hair, he radiated strength and tenacity—as if he had weathered the storms of life much as the huge oak tree in his front yard had weathered the storms of nature.

As they pulled to a stop by the front porch, he made his way a bit stiffly down the three steps. During the drive Mitch had told her more about the accident that had predicated his own move to St. Louis, and she could now see firsthand the lingering effects of it. She knew it must be difficult for Mitch's uncle, an independent man who was used to doing things on his own, to have to rely on help from others to keep up with the farm.

Mitch set the parking brake and smiled at her. "Welcome to my home away from home. Sit tight and I'll get your door."

She didn't protest, waiting as the two men shared an uninhibited bear hug as they met in front of the car. She caught a glimpse of Bruce in the visor mirror and saw that he was awake—and watching the exchange. Good. Seeing Mitch in this caring context, relaxed and removed from his official capacity, was exactly what Bruce needed. Maybe in this environment he would realize that the principal truly had his best interests at heart, that his concern was genuine. And then maybe…just maybe…he would allow Mitch to get close enough to give him some guidance. Tess prayed that would happen soon. Because she knew that she desperately needed help with her son, just as she intuitively knew that Mitch could provide it.

A moment later Mitch opened her door and reached down to take her hand, drawing her toward his uncle.

"Uncle Ray, I'd like you to meet Tess Lockwood. Tess, this is my uncle."

He released her hand, and Uncle Ray engulfed her slender fingers in a work-worn grip. His voice was warm and welcoming when he spoke, and his cobalt-blue eyes were kindly—and as sharp and insightful as those of his nephew. "It's a pleasure to meet you, Tess. Mitch has told me quite a lot about you, and I've been looking forward to this weekend."

She mulled over that nugget of information as she returned his greeting, trying to focus on the older man's words rather than the delicious memory of Mitch's hand momentarily holding hers. What exactly had Mitch told his uncle? Nothing bad, obviously, because the man appeared to be genuinely glad to make her acquaintance. In fact, more than glad. There was a gleam of interest in his eye that somehow seemed to go beyond mere hospitality. But before she could analyze it, he'd turned his attention to Bruce, who had gotten out of the car and now stood somewhat awkwardly behind the adults.

"And you must be Bruce. Mitch tells me you're new at school this semester. Must be hard, makin' that kind of transition in the middle of the year. Never did like changes, myself. But the good Lord just keeps dishin' 'em out. That's life, I expect, whether you're a senior in high school or a senior citizen like me. Hope you like farms."

Bruce seemed somewhat taken aback by the older man's lengthy greeting. "Uh, yeah. I do."

"Good. I'll show you around later. But first, let's get everybody settled."

Tess found herself in the guest room, while Bruce was given the room once occupied by Uncle Ray's son. The older man planned to give Mitch his room, but his nephew insisted on taking the couch in the den.

Once they were all settled, they regrouped in the cheery country kitchen for lunch.

"I hope this is all right," Uncle Ray said anxiously as he passed around the plates. "I'm not much versed in entertaining. That was always my wife's department, and since she passed on eight years ago, I haven't had many people over. 'Cept Mitch, of course. He's a regular. Best farmhand I ever had, matter of fact. And not too picky when it comes to eating. Good thing, too. My repertoire is limited. That's why I got some fancy store-bought food for lunch. I heard city folks like quiche."

"Don't let him fool you," Mitch warned, his eyes twinkling. "He makes a mean meat loaf. And the best beef stew I've ever tasted."

"Can't take any credit for those," Uncle Ray said as he eased himself into a chair at the head of the polished wooden table. "After Emma passed on, I got to craving some of her specialties, so I dug up her old cookbooks. Took some practice, but I finally mastered a few. Matter of fact, we're having one of my favorites tonight. Tuna casserole. Nothing fancy, but real tasty."

"Bruce is a great fan of tuna anything," Tess told him.

"Well, then I picked the right thing, I guess," the older man said. "I've been partial to it myself since I was a teenager. How old are you, son?"

"Fourteen."

"Is that right? I would have guessed sixteen."

That seemed to please Bruce. "I'm tall for my age."

"I'd say so. Probably top six feet by the time you stop growing. Why, you might even pass Mitch."

That seemed to please him even more. "I'd like to be tall."

"Why is that?"

Bruce shrugged. "People can't push you around as much if you're bigger than they are."

Uncle Ray nodded thoughtfully. "I suppose that's true. Course, bein' tall isn't the only way to get respect. There was a man lived down the road a piece when I was younger. Couldn't have been more than five-five, five-six. And nobody ever pushed him around. Looked up to him, in fact."

Bruce polished off the last bite of his quiche and looked at Uncle Ray with interest. "Why?"

"I suppose it was because he always did the right thing. And I mean *always*. Not to mention the fact that he lived by the golden rule. Never turned anybody away who was in need, and was always the first to help in times of trouble. Amazing thing, too, considering a lot of the people he helped weren't so nice to him when he was young. Called him 'shorty' and 'stubs' and lots of other things, from what I hear. Treated him pretty bad, sort of like an outcast." Uncle Ray shook his head. "Kids can be real mean sometimes."

Out of the corner of her eye Tess saw Bruce's nod of affirmation.

"But he never let it turn him bitter or spiteful or mean. He just went about his business, doing his best. Never gave anyone a lick of trouble, though I expect if he'd wanted to get even with some of the kids who were giving him a hard time, there were opportunities. But eventually all those boys grew up, and then they recognized what a fine person Roger was. The girls did, too, by the way. In fact, Roger married the prettiest girl in town and raised three fine sons. He passed on to his reward twenty, twenty-five years ago now, but nobody who ever met him forgot him. And you know, when I think of him now, I remember him as one of the tallest men I ever knew."

Bruce pondered that for a few moments. "It wasn't fair, what those guys did to him when he was young. He couldn't help being short."

"That's a fact," Uncle Ray agreed.

Mitch's uncle had hit on a theme that was near and dear to Bruce's heart. How many times had she heard the sometimes plaintive, sometimes bitter expression "But it's not fair" in the past few months? More than she could count. And considering the frown on her son's face right now, he was wrestling with the concept yet again. She wished she'd been able to come up with an explanation for the vagaries of the world, but in her heart she knew there wasn't one. Bottom line, that was just how life worked. So maybe Uncle Ray's response was best. Just acknowledge it rather than try to explain it. Bruce seemed to respect that.

"How about a tour of the farm, Uncle Ray?"

Mitch's voice broke the brief silence, and she smiled at the older man. "Yes, that would be lovely."

"Mitch knows the place as well as I do. Why don't you two go on and we'll catch up with you? Me and Bruce are gonna have some more of that fancy quiche. What do you say, Bruce? It's pretty good for store-bought stuff."

"Yes, sir."

Tess stared at her son. She hadn't heard him call anyone "sir" in—well, not since they'd moved to St. Louis. Amazing.

Tess studied the older man as he rose to cut two more

slices of quiche. He'd given little indication since their
arrival that he knew the extent of Bruce's problems. But
Tess expected that Mitch had filled him in pretty thor-
oughly. And she also suspected that the casual conversation about fairness and respect might have been
carefully orchestrated by Uncle Ray. Which impressed
her.

But what impressed her even more was that Bruce
was listening. For some reason, he seemed to have connected with Mitch's uncle. That wasn't exactly what
she'd expected this weekend—nor hoped for, if she
was honest—but if Bruce bonded with Uncle Ray
rather than Mitch, so be it. As long as it helped him get
his act together, she was all for it.

Uncle Ray returned to the table with two more
loaded plates, and as Bruce began to ply the man with
questions about the farm, Mitch grinned at Tess. "I
don't think we'll be missed here. How about that tour?"

"Sounds good."

As they stood, Uncle Ray looked up at them. "You
two take your time. Bruce and I have plenty to talk
about."

Tess gave Mitch a "Do you believe this?" look and
followed him outside. Neither spoke until the door was
firmly closed behind them, at which point Mitch voiced
her exact thoughts.

"I see signs of progress already."

Tess looked up at him. "How in the world did your
uncle do that?" she asked wonderingly as they strolled
toward the barn.

Mitch shook his head. "If I knew that, I'd be ten

times more successful with my students. He has an amazing ability to empathize with people. Young or old, rich or poor, man or woman, he has this uncanny knack of knowing exactly the right things to say to draw people out. And he listens well. I hadn't really thought about him and Bruce clicking, but something is going on in there, that's for sure. In fact, I feel a bit like the odd man out," he teased.

Tess smiled. "Hardly. If it wasn't for you, we'd be spending the holiday in a cramped apartment instead of this glorious place." She paused at the edge of a field and leaned on the fence. The freshly turned earth was rich and dark, and a pond shimmered in the distance. Puffy white clouds billowed lazily in the deep blue sky, and the silence was interrupted only by an occasional bird call or the distant moo of a cow. She closed her eyes and lifted her face to the sun, feeling the tension melt away from her. "This is the perfect antidote for a weary soul," she said with a sigh.

Mitch angled toward her and propped one arm on the fence. She looked at peace for the first time since he'd met her, he realized, as the bright, midday light turned the reddish highlights in her hair to glints of fire. The fine lines of strain around her eyes were dissolving under the caressing warmth of the sun, and he watched as she drew in a deep, cleansing breath. Since her eyes were still closed, he took the opportunity to let his gaze leisurely trace her upturned profile, drinking in the smooth brow, perfect nose, full lips, firm chin and the delicate, slender column of her throat. Her loveliness alone would attract any man, but coupled with what he already knew of her character, he couldn't help but think again what a fool her husband had been. Even if he'd married her for the wrong reasons, how could he have failed to eventually realize what a treasure he'd found? And how could he not love the son she'd borne out of their union? It boggled his mind.

And it made him angry. Very angry. Bruce's father had hurt his son in ways that Mitch could clearly discern. And in throwing away the love of the special woman who now stood beside him, her husband had hurt her in ways that Mitch could only begin to imagine. Ways he wished with all his heart he could erase.

Tess chose that moment to open her eyes, and the expression on Mitch's face made her heart stop, then race on. He was gazing at her with such intense tenderness that it took her breath away. No one had ever looked at her like that, as if she was someone precious to be cherished and protected. Her lips parted in surprise, and she unconsciously lifted her hand to her throat.

At her movement, Mitch very deliberately—and with obvious difficulty—altered his expression from tenderness to simple friendliness. She watched his Adam's apple bob convulsively, and his voice was noticeably husky when he spoke.

"We haven't made much progress on our tour. Come on, I'll show you the barn."

He took her arm as they traversed the uneven ground, and Tess hoped he wouldn't feel the tremors that ran through her. Maybe they hadn't seen much of the farm, but she'd learned a lot more than she'd bargained for a few moments ago, when she'd turned to him and caught his unguarded expression.

Tess wasn't very worldly. She hadn't had much experience with men other than her husband, and she'd been out of the dating game for a very long time. But she knew enough to recognize when a man was interested. And Mitch was definitely interested.

The question was, did he intend to pursue his interest? And if so, how was she going to handle it? Because unless he and Bruce established a truce, any involvement she had with the boy's enemy could make her son bond more closely with the gang that had become his adopted family. And that could only lead to disaster.

Tess's spirits took a nosedive. Her current dilemma confirmed what she already knew. Life was filled with difficult choices. And as Bruce had recently discovered, it often wasn't fair.

Chapter Seven

"Hey, Uncle Ray, that ship-in-a-bottle is cool! Where did you get it?" Bruce handed the older man his glasses, which he'd volunteered to fetch from the bedroom, then sat beside him in front of the computer in the den.

Uncle Ray took the glasses and adjusted them on his nose as he turned on the computer. "My son, Jeff, made that for me many years ago."

"No kidding! How did he get all those big pieces in there?"

"With a great deal of patience and skill. He was good at that kind of thing. Would have made a fine surgeon, I think. That's what he wanted to be."

There was a momentary pause, and when Bruce spoke again his voice was tentative. "On the way down here I heard Mr. Jackson tell Mom that he got killed in Vietnam."

"That's right."

"You must have been real sad."

Uncle Ray took off his glasses and swiveled away

from the computer to look directly at Bruce. He studied the boy for a moment, as if debating how to respond. "That's a fair statement, son. It's real hard when someone you love dies, especially when they're so young. And when it didn't have to be."

Bruce frowned. "What do you mean?"

Uncle Ray sighed and carefully set his glasses next to the computer. "I was once a very stubborn man, Bruce," he said quietly. "After I made up my mind about something, I couldn't see things any other way. That's how it was about that war. When I was growing up, young men went to war when they were called. Maybe they didn't like it, but they went anyway, because it was the right thing to do. But Jeff didn't see it that way. Not for that war, anyway. He didn't believe in what we were doing in Vietnam. In fact, he felt so strongly about it that he wanted to go to Canada to avoid the draft."

"Could he have done that?"

"Yes. Some young men did."

"Was that wrong?"

Uncle Ray gazed into the distance. "I thought so at the time. And I told Jeff so. Plus a lot of other things. I told him that he was being unpatriotic. That I'd always thought he had guts, but I wasn't so sure anymore. And that I was ashamed of him."

The answer was plain, straightforward and painfully honest, given without excuses and unsparing in its harshness. But the raw regret and deep sadness in the older man's voice eloquently communicated his anguish. Instinctively Bruce reached over and touched his arm.

Uncle Ray looked at Bruce and laid his work-worn fingers over the boy's hand. "I'm sure you can guess the rest, son. Jeff loved me so much he couldn't bear for me to be ashamed of him. So he put aside his own convictions and went when he was drafted. He was only over there two weeks when we got word he'd been killed in an ambush in the jungle."

Bruce's voice was hushed when he spoke. "I'm sorry, Uncle Ray."

The older man patted his hand. "Thank you, son. I am, too. I still miss Jeff every day, even after all these years. And I still regret that he never got to be that surgeon. Could have done a lot of good for a lot of people, I think. It was such a waste." He sighed and shook his head. "Took me a long time to learn to live with myself after that. Had a lot of conversations with the Lord about it. Didn't seem fair, him gone, me still here, when it was my mistake. 'Cause the fact is, I was wrong about that war."

Bruce looked at him curiously. "It's kind of weird to hear an adult admit they're wrong."

Uncle Ray smiled gently. "Let me tell you something, Bruce. Admitting mistakes, having the courage to say you're wrong, is a sign of growing up. Trouble is, a lot of people never learn to do that. Or they learn too late. Like me. I didn't get a second chance with my mistake. But lots of times people do, and if we're smart, the next time we do better."

"I guess everybody makes mistakes," Bruce said slowly, his brow creased with a frown.

"That's a fact. Important thing is to learn from them."

Uncle Ray picked up his glasses and settled them back on his nose. "Okay, that's enough heavy stuff for today. Let's surf."

"Man, he is one cool dude."

Tess gave the spaghetti sauce one final stir and turned to Bruce. Instead of the perennial scowl he'd worn for the past few months, his face was animated and eager. Uncle Ray had certainly made an impression. Bruce had talked of little else since their visit to the farm a week before.

"What's the latest?"

Bruce straddled a kitchen chair. "He just sent me an e-mail about this great Web site he found on the Pilgrims, to help me with the research for my history paper. Did you know that they landed at Plymouth Rock because they ran out of beer?"

Tess chuckled. "Can't say that I did. Are you sure about that?"

"Yeah. The Web page has part of a journal from the ship, and it says they had to land because they ran out of food and stuff, especially beer. Mr. Landis knows a lot about history, but I bet he doesn't know that."

"You could be right."

Bruce rose and helped himself to some cookies from the jar on the counter.

"You know, Mom, Uncle Ray could use some help on the farm and I was thinking…well, I've got spring break coming up in two weeks, so I thought maybe…if he wanted me to…I could spend the week with him."

Tess looked at him in surprise. "Did he invite you?"

"No. Not exactly. Not yet. But I think he would, if I volunteered to help him."

Tess reached over to stir the spaghetti sauce again, buying herself a moment to think. A week on the farm was certainly preferable to a week with the group he'd been hanging around with at school. And Bruce and Uncle Ray had certainly seemed to hit it off. They'd been e-mailing daily. It was a completely unexpected turn of events, but Tess was nonetheless grateful. Bruce had seemed more like his old self ever since their visit to the farm, and she was willing to support anything that made a positive impact. But she wasn't willing to take advantage of the older man's generosity, even though the temptation was great.

"It would be okay with me, Bruce," she replied finally. "But Uncle Ray might not want two week-long house guests."

"Two?"

"Mitch will probably be there, too."

Bruce's face fell. "Yeah. I forgot about that."

"I'll tell you what. I'll ask Mitch to talk to Uncle Ray and see if he's willing to take on one more farmhand for the week."

Bruce frowned. "I don't know. When we were there for Easter, I kind of had Uncle Ray to myself. It wouldn't be the same this time."

"Maybe it would be better."

He gave her a look that said, "Get real."

"Why is that so unlikely?" she persisted. "You haven't had any trouble with Mitch at school lately."

"He's still the principal."

"He could also be your friend, if you'd let him."

"Like he's yours?"

The unexpected question, delivered in an accusatory tone, startled her. "What do you mean?"

Bruce shrugged stiffly. "You call him Mitch. And you two seemed real friendly at Uncle Ray's."

Tess felt hot color steal onto her cheeks, and she bent down on the pretense of looking for a lid in the cabinet. She'd tried to keep her growing feelings for Mitch in check, but apparently Bruce had picked up some undercurrents. Had Mitch, as well? The thought made her cheeks grow even warmer, and she rummaged even more vigorously in the cabinet. *Get a grip,* she admonished herself tersely. *You could be overreacting here. Play it cool.*

"Well, I guess we have become friends," she said, striving for a conversational tone as she straightened up. "He's a very nice man, Bruce."

"Yeah. Right."

Tess folded her arms and leaned back against the counter. "You may not want to believe that, Bruce, but it's true. He cares about people. Especially his students. He could be your friend if you let him."

"I have enough friends."

They were moving onto dangerous territory, and she didn't want to get into an argument that could propel him back into the arms of his so-called friends. Since Bruce had been grounded after the car accident, his contact with his "group" had been limited to school hours. Interestingly enough, he hadn't complained much. Nor had he talked about his brief visit to jail.

Maybe she was being naive, but Tess had a feeling the events of that night had had a big impact. As had the trip to the farm. With things going so well, she didn't want to rock the boat. If Bruce didn't want to associate with Mitch, so be it.

"Have it your way," she said, trying for a nonchalant tone as she pushed away from the counter and turned back to the spaghetti sauce. "So should we forget about the farm for spring break?"

Tess held her breath while he mulled her question over in silence.

"I'll think about it," he finally said noncommittally as he snagged another cookie and headed toward his room.

Tess watched him disappear down the hall, her expression troubled. He hadn't said no outright. Which was a good sign, she told herself encouragingly.

What wasn't so good was his reaction to her relationship with Mitch. She'd felt him withdrawing as they discussed her "friendship" with the principal. And she couldn't let that happen. Bruce needed to think of her as an ally, not a traitor. So until he made peace with Mitch, she needed to keep her distance. Make that *if* he made peace with Mitch, she corrected herself.

Tess sighed. She'd known all along that her feelings for Mitch could get her into trouble. Especially since the attraction appeared to be mutual.

Then again, she could be wrong. She didn't have much experience in such things. And she hadn't heard from him once since their trip to the farm, though her heart had skipped a beat every time the phone rang.

Maybe he had been interested, but the attraction had waned during their weekend at the farm. Or more likely she'd just read more into his kindness than was intended. Chalk it up to the overreaction of a lonely woman starved for affection, she thought with a bitter-sweet pang.

Besides, if Mitch *was* attracted to her, things could get really complicated. It was better this way.

At least for Bruce.

Bruce wasn't sure what had awakened him, but suddenly he was staring wide-eyed at the ceiling above him. Or at least in the direction of the ceiling. It was too dark to see anything. He turned and squinted at the illuminated dial of the clock on his nightstand. Two o'clock in the morning. That was weird. He never woke up in the middle of the night. Unless he was sick or something. But he felt fine.

With a shrug he flopped onto his back and closed his eyes. Better get back to sleep or he'd never make it through the American lit class tomorrow. Mrs. Bederman's droning voice was a sure cure for insomnia, he thought with a sleepy grin, especially on Fridays. In fact, just last week Dan…

Suddenly his eyes flew open again. Now he knew what had awakened him. That low, moaning sound. From his mom's bedroom. Cold fear gripped him, and he swung his legs over the side of the bed and took off at a run.

He stopped in front of her door, which was unchar-acteristically shut, and knocked cautiously. "Mom?"

There was no response, but now he could hear the sound much more clearly. Something was really wrong. Without bothering to knock again, he pushed the door open. And that's when he got really scared.

Tess was lying on her side, doubled up, gasping for breath. Her face was gray, her eyes were tightly closed and beads of sweat dotted her forehead.

"Mom?" He dropped down beside her and touched her shoulder, his voice laced with panic. "Mom?"

Her eyelids flickered open, and for a moment she seemed to have trouble focusing.

"Mom, what's wrong?"

Even through a fog of pain Tess could hear the fear in his voice. And though his face was hazy, the terror in his eyes was clear.

"I got sick…a couple of hours ago," she gasped. "I didn't want to…bother you, so I shut the door, but…the pain just keeps…getting worse."

Bruce's face drained of color. "What's wrong?"

"I…don't know." She closed her eyes again and moaned.

"What should I do?"

No response. Bruce wasn't sure if she'd even heard him. And if she had, she was too sick to give him any instructions.

Bruce stood and stared down at his mom. He'd seen her sick before. She'd had the flu last winter, in fact. But he'd never seen her like this. Something was really wrong. She needed help—fast.

Bruce ran to the kitchen, snatched up the phone and punched in 911. The woman on the other end took some preliminary information and assured him that an ambulance was on the way.

He raced back to Tess's room, where he dropped down beside her and awkwardly laid his hand on her shoulder. His heart was hammering so hard he thought it would burst through his chest at any moment. "It will be okay, Mom," he said, his voice quivering.

And for the first time in a long time he prayed.

The policeman laid his hand on Bruce's shoulder. "Is there someone you can call? A family member?"

Bruce watched the paramedics carry his mom out on a stretcher. He'd never felt so alone in his life. "We don't have any family. It's just me and my mom."

"How about a friend, then?"

A friend. He thought of the guys at school, and just as quickly dismissed them. They weren't the kind of people you called in an emergency. He thought of Uncle Ray. But the older man was a long way away. He needed somebody *now*. Somebody who would know what to do in an emergency like this. Somebody you could count on to take care of things. Somebody you could trust.

His gaze suddenly fell on Mitch Jackson's card, still thumbtacked to the message board in the kitchen. That was the *last* person he wanted to call.

But he knew with absolute certainty that Mitch Jackson was the *right* person to call.

Mitch didn't like middle-of-the-night phone calls. Never had. They almost always spelled trouble.

So when the phone rang at twenty minutes past two in the morning, he was instantly awake.

"Yes." His voice was clipped, terse.

Silence on the other end. He frowned, impatient now. "Hello?"

"Mr. Jackson? It—it's Bruce Lockwood."

The voice was high and tight, teetering on the edge of hysteria. He swung his feet over the side of his bed and reached for his shirt as a wave of fear coursed through him.

"Okay, Bruce, I'm here. Tell me what's wrong." It took every ounce of his self-control to modulate his voice, keep his own terror from showing.

A strangled sob. "My m-mom's sick. I called 911 and the paramedics are taking her to the hospital."

Mitch felt as if someone had kicked him in the gut. "Which hospital?"

Muffled voices while Bruce asked the policeman, then relayed the information to Mitch.

"That's a fine hospital, Bruce. They'll take good care of her. You ride with the paramedics, and I'll meet you there. Okay?"

"Yeah."

The line went dead. For a moment Mitch just sat there, numb. Tess seriously sick? It was inconceivable. She'd been fine at the farm. More than fine, in fact. Beautiful. Vivacious. And very, very desirable. That's why he'd kept his distance since their return, though he'd lost track of the number of times he'd been tempted to reach for the phone and dial her number. And now she was in an ambulance on her way to the hospital.

Another surge of adrenaline shot through him, and he went into action. Pants. Wallet. Socks. Where were his socks? Forget the socks. Shoes. He was in the car in three minutes flat.

Bruce was in the waiting room when he arrived, a forlorn figure huddled in a straight chair, who looked as scared as he'd sounded. For the first time in their relationship the boy actually seemed happy to see him.

Mitch strode toward him and instinctively placed a hand on his thin, trembling shoulder.

"You okay?" His voice was gentle.

"Yeah."

"Has anyone talked to you yet?"

"Only to ask about insurance."

Mitch bit back a curse. There was something wrong with a health-care system that would ask a scared kid about insurance in the middle of the night. "Okay. Sit tight. I'll find out how your mom is doing."

In five minutes Mitch had his answer. Appendicitis. They were running some tests to verify the preliminary diagnosis, but given the symptoms, the doctors were 99 percent sure. Their biggest concern was removing it before it ruptured. Tess had already authorized surgery, and they were prepping her now. They'd do laparoscopy if possible, to minimize postoperative pain and recovery, but they wouldn't know for sure if that was feasible until they got a look at the appendix.

Mitch relayed all this to Bruce when he rejoined him in the waiting room. He didn't minimize the problem, but neither did he make it sound like life or death.

"So will she be okay?" Bruce asked anxiously when Mitch finished.

"I'm sure she will," he replied honestly. "But depending on which kind of surgery they do, she could be pretty sore for a while. She'll need some help with day-to-day things."

"I can help her."

"I know you can."

Mitch didn't add that she'd need more help than a fourteen-year-old boy could provide. There would be time for that later. First they needed to get past the surgery.

They didn't talk much while they waited. Mitch got them both a soda at one point, but Bruce refused food. Mitch could understand that. His own stomach was roiling. Hospitals always did that to him. They simply sat there, together. And that was enough.

Three hours later, it was over. Fortunately the more minor, less invasive surgery had been possible. The doctor, still dressed in his surgical garb, told this to Bruce and Mitch just as the morning light was beginning to touch the horizon through the window.

"She'll be just fine," he assured them. "But she'll be sore for a few days. And she'll need to take it easy for a couple of weeks."

"When can she come home?" Bruce asked, the relief in his voice almost palpable.

"Probably tomorrow, if things go well. And I have no reason to think they won't."

"Can I see her?"

"She's in recovery right now, but she should be

awake enough to talk to you in an hour or so." The doctor turned to Mitch, who had already identified himself as a friend. "I'll let the nurse know where to find you. And then I'd suggest you both go home and get some sleep," he added with a weary smile. "That's what I intend to do."

As the man departed, Bruce turned to Mitch. "What about school?"

"I'll call for both of us. After we see your mom, I think we better follow the doctor's advice. I don't know about you, but four hours of sleep doesn't cut it for me." Actually, Mitch had survived on far less. But Bruce couldn't. And he wasn't about to leave the boy alone after his traumatic night.

"I am pretty beat," Bruce admitted.

"So how about some bacon and eggs while we wait for your mom to wake up?"

Bruce's eyes lit up. "Yeah! I'm starved."

Tess felt strange. As if she was floating. And she was cold. Really cold. So cold her teeth were chattering. Then someone tucked a nice warm blanket around her. She smiled and snuggled deeper under it. That felt good.

"Is she okay?"

Tess heard the voice. It sounded like Bruce.

Now a woman was speaking. "She's fine. Most patients are cold after surgery. The operating room is pretty chilly."

Surgery? Operating room? Was someone sick?

"Is she awake?"

Tess knew that voice, too. It had filled her dreams for the past few weeks. So this must be a dream, too.

"Half and half. But she'll be coming out of it pretty rapidly now."

Who on earth were they talking about? Tess wondered, struggling to open eyelids that felt heavy as lead. She tried to reach up, but someone restrained her hand, engulfing it in a warm, tender clasp.

"It's Mitch, Tess. And Bruce. Just rest. Don't try to move around. We're here with you."

The gentle voice sounded so real. Not like a dream at all. This time her eyelids cooperated, and she stared up at the fuzzy world above her.

"Hi, Mom."

Bruce's voice. Her eyes sought out the source. She frowned, trying to focus. There were two faces above, and slowly the fuzzy images became clear.

"Bruce? Mitch?" Was that raspy voice hers?

"Welcome back."

She gazed up at Mitch. She'd never seen him look so—disheveled. He was sporting a day's growth of beard, his shirt was wrinkled, his hair was tousled and there were deep lines of worry and fatigue etched into his face. With a frown she turned to Bruce. He didn't look much better. His face was pale and his hair was sticking up in odd spikes. There was something very wrong here.

"Are you guys okay?" she rasped.

Mitch felt his throat tighten with tenderness. How like her to think first of them. He glanced at Bruce. "You've got quite a mom, you know that."

Bruce blinked rapidly and swiped at his eyes. "Yeah. I know."

Mitch bent down so that his eyes were only inches from Tess's. She stared into them, mesmerized by the glints of gold—and the tenderness—in their dark brown depths.

"We're fine, Tess. But you just had an emergency appendectomy."

The events of the night before suddenly came rushing back. The searing pain. The nausea. The disorienting ride in the ambulance.

"It was a relatively simple surgery," Mitch continued. "But not a moment too soon. If Bruce hadn't called the ambulance when he did, it could have been a very different story. The doctor said your appendix was on the verge of rupturing. Thanks to Bruce, they caught it in time."

Tess transferred her gaze to her son. She reached out to him, and he took her hand.

"Why am I not surprised?" she said softly. "I've always been able to count on him."

Bruce's face reddened. "Not so much lately," he amended, clearly struggling with the admission. "But I'll try to do better, Mom. I promise."

Tess's eyes filled with tears. If it had taken an evening in jail and appendicitis to make Bruce see the light, it was a small price to pay. "I believe you, Bruce. And I love you."

"I love you, too, Mom."

Mitch watched the exchange, encouraged that Bruce seemed to truly be on the road to a turnaround—and surprised by a sudden, sharp stab of jealousy. It took him all of two seconds to figure out his reaction. While they might look like a cozy little family group, the only family here was Tess and Bruce. Mitch was an outsider.

That hurt. A lot. And reminded him of what was missing from his life. It had been a long time since he'd thought about having a family. A long time since he'd *let* himself think about it. Because it just wasn't in the cards for him. He'd had his chance once. And blown it big time. Now he focused on helping kids. It was good work. Worthy work. Work that had made a difference in countless lives.

But it was also lonely work. Because when the families he worked with went home at night, they had each other. He had no one. Except Uncle Ray, of course. Thank God for Uncle Ray! But as kind and good as the older man was, he couldn't fill the empty place in Mitch's heart that was made for a wife and family.

"If these gentlemen will let go of your hands, I think it's time we got you settled in your room."

The teasing tone of the nurse jolted him back to reality, and he and Bruce simultaneously relinquished their hold on Tess. She missed their touch immediately.

The nurse smiled and gave her a wink. "Don't worry, it's only a temporary situation. I have a feeling these two handsome men aren't going to let you out of their sight for very long. They waited a long time for you to wake up."

Tess frowned. "What time is it?"

The nurse consulted her watch. "Seven o'clock."

"How long have you two been up?"

"Since about two o'clock," Bruce replied. "I called Mr. Jackson when the ambulance got there."

Tess looked at Mitch. "I want you both to go home and get some rest. And Mitch…I hate to ask, but could you call Caroline James at the newspaper for me? Let her know I won't be in?"

"No problem. And don't worry about Bruce. He can stay at my place till you're released."

The two Lockwoods stared at him, one in gratitude, the other in shock.

"Mom, I can stay by myself. Honest," Bruce spoke up quickly. "The doctor says you can probably come home tomorrow. I'll be fine till then."

Tess reached out to take his hand again. "I won't get any rest if I'm worrying about you all by yourself in the apartment. Stay with Mitch. For me."

Put that way, it was pretty hard to refuse. But Bruce was clearly not happy about the turn of events. "I guess it will be okay for one night," he acquiesced reluctantly.

Tess smiled and squeezed his hand. "Thank you." Then she turned to Mitch and, without even thinking about it, reached for his hand, as well. He laced his fingers with hers in a reassuring touch that communicated both caring and rock-solid strength. "And thank *you*."

Their gazes met briefly, but it was long enough for Tess to know one thing with absolute certainty.

The attraction *was* mutual.

Chapter Eight

Mitch reached down for Bruce's duffel bag, then paused as a half-hidden stack of canvases in the boy's bedroom caught his eye. He squatted down to examine the top one, a pastoral fall landscape vibrant with color and life. The room grew still, and Mitch sensed Bruce moving behind him.

Mitch studied the impressive canvas silently for a long moment, then turned slowly. "Did you paint this?"

A flush seeped onto the teenager's face and he shoved his hands into his pockets. "Yeah. It's not very good."

Mitch looked again at the canvas, then nodded to the stack. "May I?"

Bruce shrugged indifferently, but stayed close as Mitch carefully examined each painting. By the time Mitch reached the last one he was completely blown away by the boy's talent. Once more he turned and looked up at Bruce.

"These are incredible."

The boy's flush deepened at the straightforward, sincere compliment. "They're okay, I guess."

"What are you working on now?"

"I don't paint anymore."

Mitch's eyebrows arched in surprise. "Why not?"

"Artsy stuff is for geeks and wimps."

Mitch studied the boy for a moment, then carefully replaced the paintings as a plan slowly took shape in his mind. "I don't know," he said conversationally. "My cousin Jeff—Uncle Ray's son—was a fabulous artist. One of his sculptures won first prize in a contest sponsored by the art museum here in St. Louis."

"Yeah?" A gleam of interest sparked in the teenager's eyes. "I saw that ship in a bottle he did, the one in Uncle Ray's room."

"I forgot all about that," Mitch admitted. "Anyway, he was no nerd. He was a track star on the high school team, and he was voted most-likely-to-succeed by his classmates."

"Well, maybe *all* artsy people aren't geeks," Bruce conceded. "Just most of them."

Mitch was tempted to pursue the subject, but Bruce's sudden yawn made him realize that the boy was exhausted. Not a good time to try to make a point. Besides, he had another type of persuasion in mind. He lifted Bruce's duffel bag and smiled. "Let's go get some shut-eye."

This time there was no disagreement. And once Bruce was settled, Mitch intended to get a couple of hours rest himself before they headed back to the hospital. But first he had a call to make.

* * *

"Why are we stopping here?" Bruce stared at the YMCA building, then turned to Mitch.

"I thought we could both use a little exercise after being cooped up in the hospital all afternoon."

Tess had looked remarkably improved when they'd returned to the hospital around lunchtime with an oversize bouquet. But by four o'clock she was tiring, and Bruce was becoming restless after hours of inactivity. When Mitch suggested that they go get a bite to eat and then return for a brief visit later in the evening, neither Lockwood objected. And it played right into his plan.

"But I didn't bring any gym clothes," Bruce protested.

Mitch glanced at the boy as he set the brake. "That sweat suit is fine for the weight room. Ever done weights before?"

"No."

"I'll show you the ropes." He retrieved his gym bag from the trunk and headed for the front door, leaving Bruce no option but to follow. "Give me a couple of minutes to change," he said over his shoulder as he disappeared into the locker room.

When he returned, in sweatpants and a muscle shirt that revealed well-developed biceps, Bruce looked at him with new respect.

"Do you work out all the time?"

"Not every day. But I try to stay on a schedule. And farm chores definitely build muscles," he added with a grin. "Ready for the tour?"

Mitch led the way to the weight room, where a

couple of other men were already engrossed in their routines. One of them smiled and nodded.

"Hi, Mitch." The man carefully set down the barbells and stood. He was dressed in a sleeveless T-shirt that revealed bulging biceps, and the corded muscles in his legs were clearly visible below his gym shorts.

Mitch returned his greeting. "Joe, I'd like you to meet Bruce Lockwood. He's a student at Southfield High. Bruce, this is Joe Davis."

The man held out his hand, taking Bruce's in a powerful grip. "Nice to meet you, Bruce." Then he directed his gaze at Mitch. "A new recruit for the weight room?"

Mitch grinned. "Yet to be determined. This is his first visit." Mitch folded his arms across his chest consideringly. "You know, I should let *you* show him the ropes. You're the expert."

The man brushed the comment aside. "You know as much about weight lifting as I do."

"Don't listen to him," Mitch told Bruce. "I'm not even in his league. He's won national weight-lifting titles."

Bruce looked in awe at the man across from him. "No kidding?"

"A few," he admitted.

"So how about it? Can you spare a few minutes for an introductory lesson?" Mitch asked.

"Sure. Glad to."

"Thanks. I'll leave you to it, then."

Twenty minutes later, when Mitch was ready to leave, it was clear that Joe had made a friend. He and

Bruce were talking animatedly, and Bruce was listening attentively to the man's instructions as he tried out a few simple weight routines.

"I hate to break up the party, but I'm starving," Mitch interrupted, wiping his face on a towel as he joined them.

Joe smiled. "We were done, anyway." He laid his hand on Bruce's shoulder. "We may have a convert here."

Mitch grinned. "I knew you'd do a good sell job. How about joining us for dinner? We're just going to grab something quick."

The man glanced at his watch, then shook his head regretfully. "I'd like to, but I need to finish up here and then head back to the theater. We've got an opening in a week, so we're putting in some extra hours."

"Another time, then. And thanks."

"Yeah. Thanks," Bruce seconded.

"You bet."

Bruce was waiting when Mitch returned from the locker room after a quick shower, and he fell into step beside the older man as they left the Y.

"Is Joe an actor?"

Mitch chuckled. "Hardly. He did try it briefly, though. But as he once told me, it was a good thing the days of throwing rotten tomatoes were long gone by the time he set foot on stage."

"So what did he mean about the theater, then?"

"He's a set designer."

Bruce frowned. "You mean like scenery and stuff?"

"That's right." Mitch tossed his gym bag into the back seat and slid behind the wheel. "How does pizza sound?"

"Fine," Bruce replied distractedly, the frown still furrowing his brow. Several silent moments passed before he spoke again. "So what exactly does Joe do?"

"He paints some of the backdrops himself and oversees the other set painters," Mitch replied. "And he knows a lot about construction, because he designs the platforms and framework for the sets and supervises the carpenters who build them. He's a pretty versatile guy."

Silence again while Bruce pondered that new information. Not until they pulled into the restaurant parking lot did Mitch finally get the question he'd been hoping for. "Do you think maybe someday…if he had time, I mean…he might show me some of the stuff he works on at the theater?"

"I think he'd be happy to," Mitch replied. "How about if I give him a call and ask?"

"Yeah. That would be cool." For a moment the boy fiddled with the seat belt, and then he took a deep breath as he reached to open his door. "Thanks."

The word was said begrudgingly and without eye contact. But that single syllable meant a lot to Mitch. Because it marked a first in their relationship. And maybe a turning point, as well.

"Are you sure you'll be okay, Mom?"

Tess looked at her son with affection. In the two weeks since her surgery he'd been like a mother hen, waiting on her hand and foot. He'd done the laundry, gone to the grocery store, even laid out her breakfast before he left for school each day. She had been touched—and proud. Bruce was once again the boy she'd always known—helpful, kind, considerate, loving. It gave her new hope that he was beginning to turn a corner, that the clouds over these past difficult months were starting to lift.

She was glad she had *that* hope to cling to. Because the *other* hope, the one that had nothing to do with being a mom and everything to do with being a woman, was slowly slipping away. For a brief moment in time, foolish though it had been, she'd allowed herself to believe that maybe the years ahead might not be so lonely. That maybe she'd met a man who could someday come to love her and want to share her life. Of course, Bruce's relationship with Mitch had been a major hurdle. But in the past couple of weeks the tension between the two of them had eased. Unfortunately, *her* relationship with the handsome principal had taken the opposite turn.

"Mom?"

Tess realized she hadn't answered Bruce's question, heard the undertone of anxiety in his voice and smiled. She didn't want his time at the farm overshadowed by unnecessary worry.

"I'll be fine," she assured him firmly. "I feel almost back to normal."

The doorbell rang, and Tess started to rise from the couch.

"I'll get it, Mom," Bruce told her.

She didn't protest. His willingness to answer the door, as well as his eagerness to visit the farm, were a far cry from his hostile attitude before their first visit. In fact, in the past two weeks his whole attitude had undergone an amazing turnaround. And she had Mitch to thank for it. Not only had he brought Uncle Ray into their lives and watched over her son when she was in the hospital, he'd also found a way to reawaken Bruce's interest in art—something Tess had tried without success to do. Mitch and Bruce had made more than one visit to the local repertory theater to get a behind-the-scenes-look at scenic design, and much to Tess's surprise, Bruce had agreed to help paint sets for the spring play at school. That, in turn, had exposed him to an entirely different social group—and left him little time to hang around with his old gang. No question about it—Tess owed Mitch big time. Her early intuition that he could help Bruce straighten out his life had been right on target.

Unfortunately, her intuition about Mitch's interest in *her* had been way off base. It wasn't that he was uncaring. He'd called frequently to see how she was and stopped by several times with take-out dinners for them. But something…some subtle nuance in their relation-ship…had changed over the past two weeks. The day he'd stood by her hospital bed after the surgery she'd been sure that his interest went beyond friendship. But she'd finally been forced to acknowledge that the attrac-tion she had thought she'd glimpsed in his eyes must simply have been a side effect of the anesthesia. And that she'd also misread his earlier warmth and friend-liness for something more.

The important thing, however, was the change in Bruce, she reminded herself firmly. After all, she could deal with her own hurt. She hadn't been able to deal with Bruce. Thank heaven Mitch had. He'd gone way above and beyond the call of duty by getting personally involved in Bruce's problems. And if that personal involvement didn't extend to Bruce's mom—well, what had she expected, really? She was just an average-looking divorced mother struggling to make ends meet. Not exactly the type of person likely to attract a dynamic, accomplished man like Mitch.

And yet, as he stepped into the room she couldn't stop herself from searching his eyes, hoping yet again to see something that simply wasn't there. The familiar spasm of disappointment in her heart was as real as the pain she'd felt the night of her appendicitis attack.

"How's the patient today?"

With an effort, she summoned up a too-bright smile. "No longer a patient. In fact, I'll be back at work next week while you two gentlemen are enjoying country life."

Mitch frowned. "That seems a bit fast."

"I don't plan to overdo it," she assured him. "But I can sit at a keyboard and write copy just fine."

"I wish you could come with us, mom," Bruce added.

"So do I, hon. But duty calls. I've had two whole weeks to lie around and take it easy. And I'll be down next weekend, like I promised."

Actually, she wished she could back out of that commitment. But when Uncle Ray had called to formally invite Bruce, and then presented a convincing argument that a couple of days in the country would be just the thing to speed up her recuperation, she'd given in. Of course, that had been over a week ago, before she'd finally admitted to herself that Mitch's interest in her was strictly friendship. If her own feelings were stronger…well, that was her problem. And it wasn't fair to disappoint her son just because she was having a hard time coping with her feelings.

Those feelings had also made it difficult to think of a way to thank Mitch for his help during her recuperation. Few principals would take a student into their own home when a parent became ill, even for one night. Not to mention all of the take-out dinners he'd dropped off for them during the past couple of weeks. She owed him more than a simple thank-you note.

At first she'd planned to invite him over for a home-cooked meal. But now that seemed too personal somehow. She'd finally settled on inviting him to dinner at one of the nicer local restaurants. And she would make it very clear that it was just a friendly thank-you. Because the last thing she wanted to do was put him in the awkward position of having to deal with a woman whose feelings he didn't share.

When Bruce hefted his backpack into position, clearly eager to be on the road, Mitch grinned. "Looks like you're ready."

The ghost of an answering smile hovered around Bruce's lips. "Yeah."

"You may not be so eager once Uncle Ray puts you to work," Mitch teased. "He can be a hard taskmaster. I have a feeling he has a list of chores for us a mile long."

"That's okay. I don't mind."

"Is this the same person who complains about taking out the trash?" Tess kidded her son.

"That's different, Mom. This will be fun." He turned to Mitch. "Do you want me to load my stuff in the car?"

"Sure. I need to talk to your mother for a minute, anyway."

He'd given her the perfect opportunity to issue the dinner invitation, Tess realized as Bruce headed out the front door. She took a deep breath and tried to quiet the thumping of her heart as Mitch walked closer. He stopped a couple of feet away, frowned and shoved his hands into his pockets.

"Are you really sure you'll be okay alone for a few days?"

She nodded. "Absolutely." Her voice sounded a bit breathless, and she struggled for a more normal tone. "Besides, you guys will only be an hour away if I really need anything."

"You'll call if you do?"

"Of course."

He paused, as if trying to decide whether he believed her or not, then let it drop. "Okay. We'll check in every day. And I'll be back Thursday. I need to put in a couple days of work, even if it is spring break. I plan to head back down early on Saturday, so I'll pick you up about eight, if that's okay."

"Fine." It was now or never, she realized, forcing herself to take a deep, steadying breath. "Mitch, I—I can't thank you enough for all you've done for Bruce and me over the past couple of weeks. I know how busy you are, and I'm sorry we added to the demands on your time. But I honestly don't know how we'd have managed without you."

An odd light flickered in his eyes, so briefly that Tess wondered if she'd imagined it. "I was glad to help."

She was struck by the husky quality in his voice, but too distracted by what she was about to say to analyze it. "The thing is, I know I can never repay you for your kindness. But I'd like to at least say 'thank you' in some sort of concrete way. So I thought…that is, if you can spare a couple of hours…I'd like to treat you to dinner Friday night."

For a moment Mitch seemed taken aback by the invitation. "You don't have to do that, Tess."

"I know I don't. But I'd like to. You've been a good friend to us, Mitch, and I want you to know that we value that friendship."

Their gazes locked, but his eyes were shuttered, giving Tess no clue what was going through his mind. She tried desperately to follow his lead and keep her eyes from reflecting the feelings in her heart. But she had no idea if she succeeded.

He looked at her for a long moment, clearly engaged in a silent debate, while she held her breath. Part of her hoped he would accept. Part of her hoped he would decline. Logically speaking, the latter was certainly preferable. Why prolong one-on-one contact when the attraction was one-sided? That was only an exercise in frustration. But good manners had compelled her to issue the invitation, so she'd done her duty. Now the ball was in his court.

"Is it okay if I take some painting stuff to the farm? Just in case I have time?"

There was a momentary pause before Mitch broke eye contact with her to look at Bruce, who was already clutching his easel in his hands. "Sure. I don't think Uncle Ray expects you to work every minute."

"Great! Thanks!"

"I'll be right with you."

"Bye, Mom."

Before she could respond, Bruce disappeared out the door. She turned back to Mitch and forced her stiff lips into a smile. "I hope Uncle Ray doesn't regret this. Bruce could tire him out by the end of the week. He's got an unbelievably high energy level when he's interested in something."

"I'm not worried. Those two seem to understand each other. I think they'll set their own limits."

"Well, just give me a call if I need to talk to Bruce."

"I will." He paused, and the expression in his eyes shifted again. *Troubled* was the word that came to Tess's mind. "I appreciate the offer of dinner, Tess," he said slowly. "It's just that I don't want you to feel under any obligation. It was an emergency, and I was glad to help. You'd have done the same thing if the situation was reversed."

"That doesn't mean I appreciate it any less," she countered, then tried for a joking tone. "Besides, Caroline told me about a great restaurant, and this would give me an excuse to try it."

When she mentioned the name, his eyebrows rose. "It is a great restaurant. Also very pricey."

Did he think she couldn't afford dinner for two at a nice restaurant, she wondered? She sat up a little straighter, and her chin tilted up ever so slightly as her pride kicked in. "I can afford an occasional splurge, Mitch. Especially for a special occasion. Like thanking a friend for a very generous favor."

A muscle in his jaw twitched. "I didn't mean to imply you couldn't afford it, Tess." He paused and took a deep breath. "How about this? I'll check with you Thursday, and if you're feeling up to it, it's a date."

Hardly, she thought. But at least she had her answer. "That's fine." She hadn't meant to sound put out, but she couldn't prevent a slight touch of coolness from creeping into her voice.

Mitch raked his fingers through his hair, his expression contrite. "Look, Tess, I didn't mean to sound ungracious. I really do appreciate the invitation."

"It's okay."

"No, it's not. And I'm sorry."

It suddenly occurred to Tess that not once during her ten-year marriage to Peter had her husband ever apologized for anything. He seemed to feel that acknowledging a mistake somehow diminished him. But Tess viewed it in exactly the opposite way. To her, the ability to admit mistakes, to say "I'm sorry," increased a person's stature. Her expression softened and she smiled. "Accepted."

"I'll call you, then?"

"That would be fine. And Mitch…keep an eye on Bruce, okay?"

"Count on it. He'll be in good hands."

Of that she had no doubt.

* * *

"I'd say that was one tuckered-out youngster. I'd be willing to bet he was out cold the minute his head hit the pillow."

Mitch chuckled as he joined Uncle Ray on the porch swing, savoring a long, slow sip of coffee as they enjoyed the unseasonably warm spring evening. "I warned him you were a slave driver."

Uncle Ray smiled. "You should have seen me in my heyday."

Mitch gave an exaggerated groan. "I don't think my back would have survived."

Now it was Uncle Ray's turn to chuckle. "Hard work is good for the soul. And the body."

"You may have a hard time convincing Bruce of that tomorrow when he can barely move."

"That boy is a hard worker, I'll say that for him. Willing to tackle anything. And he put in a full day. Nice young man, too. Not too many boys his age would give up a Saturday, let alone a whole spring break, to work on a farm with an old man."

"He likes you."

Uncle Ray looked pleased. "I like him, too."

"I wish he felt the same about me."

"Maybe he does."

Mitch shook his head. "No way. I'm the authority figure who's been cramping his style."

"You're also the friend who helped him out when his mom was sick and who introduced him to Joe Davis. He mentions him every time he e-mails me. That was a brilliant move on your part."

Mitch shrugged. "I was lucky I knew someone who could tap into Bruce's talent. And I was lucky Joe was willing to cooperate."

"I take it that the episode at the Y wasn't a chance meeting."

Mitch hesitated, then shook his head. "No."

"Didn't think so. I could see your hand in it. It was a nice thing to do, son."

"I was just glad I finally hit on something that seemed to reach him. He was definitely heading for trouble, and Tess was at her wit's end."

"Mmm. Hard thing, raising a boy that age alone. I don't envy her."

"Single parenthood is never easy," Mitch concurred. "But from what she's told me, they're better off without Bruce's father. I have a feeling he did more harm than good—to both of them."

Uncle Ray shook his head. "Makes you wonder, doesn't it? Bruce is a great kid. And even though I don't know Tess all that well, she sure seems like a nice person. Conscientious and genuine and caring."

"She is."

"Can't imagine why any man would let someone like her slip away."

"Me, neither."

Silence fell as the two men swung gently, a comfortable stillness born of secrets shared, absolute trust and mutual respect. Several minutes passed before Uncle Ray spoke.

"I've got some news for you, son."

Something in the older man's voice put Mitch on

alert, momentarily driving thoughts of Tess out of his mind. "What is it?"

"I've sold the farm."

With an instinct honed long ago Mitch had braced himself for bad news. But his uncle's calm announcement stunned him. "What?"

"I've sold the farm," Uncle Ray repeated. "At least, most of it. I kept the five acres around the house and barn."

"But why?" Mitch couldn't even conceive of his uncle without the farm, or vice versa.

"Because it was time, son." The older man's voice was quiet but firm.

"But…but this is your life."

"It *was* my life," Uncle Ray corrected him. "And it was a good one. But also a hard one. I'm getting older, Mitch. I can't keep up with things anymore."

"But I'm more than happy to help."

"I know that. But I can't expect you to spend what little free time you have out here. You need to live your own life, not help me keep memories of my old one alive. The Lord and I had a long talk about this, and I know it's the right thing to do."

Mitch felt as if someone had kicked him in the gut. "You mean you did this for me?"

"Partly. But only partly," he clarified. "Mostly I did it for me. And that's the truth, Mitch. The fact is, time brings changes. People change. Circumstances change. And sometimes you just have to realize that it's time to move on."

Time to move on. The words echoed in Mitch's heart, and he stared down into his coffee.

"It's not an easy thing, letting go, is it, son?" His uncle's voice was gentle, and Mitch suddenly knew they weren't talking about the farm anymore. He turned, and though the light was dim, the kindness and understanding in the older man's eyes were clear.

"Not everyone has your courage, Uncle Ray," he replied quietly.

"You do."

Mitch shook his head. "I'm not so sure."

"I am. And I'm sure about something else, too. You shouldn't spend the rest of your life alone. And lonely."

For once Mitch didn't deny his loneliness. He'd dealt with it successfully for years, but lately the emptiness of his personal life had become oppressive, leaving him keenly aware of the hollow echo in his heart.

Mitch rose and walked restlessly to the edge of the porch, planting his hands on the railing as he stared out into the darkness. "So what are you saying, Uncle Ray?"

"You know."

Yeah, he knew. Mitch drew a deep breath and let it out slowly. "I said I'd never get involved with anyone again."

"That was years ago, son. And Tess seems like a real special woman. The kind that doesn't come around very often."

He knew that, too. "She asked me to dinner."

There was a moment of silence. "Are you going?"

"I don't know."

"Why not?"

Mitch drew in a deep breath, let it out slowly. As

usual, his uncle had honed right to the heart of the matter. "Because I'm afraid."

"Of what?"

"Messing things up. Making the same mistakes. Hurting the people I love. Just like before."

"That was a long time ago, son."

"I'm the same man."

"Are you?"

Mitch thought about that. Was he? Hadn't he learned a great deal—about selflessness and sensitivity and listening—during the intervening years? Hadn't he learned to recognize what was precious and cherish it? Or was he just kidding himself that he'd grown and changed and become a better person?

"I don't know," he said at last with a sigh.

"Well, I do. And the answer is no. You're not the same person you were six years ago. No one is. That's why I'm selling the farm. Because it's time to move on. Maybe it's time for you to do the same."

Mitch didn't respond. But in his heart he acknowledged the truth of Uncle Ray's words. Though he'd always vowed never again to get involved with anyone, Tess had made him rethink that pledge. Because Uncle Ray was also right about her. She was special. Very special.

Mitch knew all that. Knew that he needed to revisit the decision he'd made six years ago, when his life was an emotional hell. Knew that if he didn't pursue his interest in Tess, he could very well lose the chance to build a new life. Knew, also, that he might very well let this opportunity pass him by, even if it meant spending the rest of his life alone.

Because the bottom line was, he was just plain scared..

Chapter Nine

Tess checked her watch and frowned. Mitch was fifteen minutes late. It seemed highly unlikely that he'd forgotten their dinner date, considering that he'd called to confirm the time yesterday. He'd even offered to pick her up, but she'd figured it was safer simply to meet him at the restaurant. Since he wasn't the type to stand someone up, something must have detained him at the office.

Tess looked around the lounge of the upscale restaurant, where the maître d' had suggested she wait, and shifted uncomfortably in her seat. She felt out of her element amid the cozy twosomes and intimate laughter coming from the small, candlelit tables. A more casual place would have been far more appropriate for a thank-you dinner than this romantic dining establishment, with its dim light, elegant rose-colored decor and mellow background music, she realized. Had Caroline purposely set her up? Her boss had hinted more than once that Tess should consider the handsome principal in more than a professional light, but Tess had always sidestepped the suggestion. Maybe this was Caroline's not-so-subtle way of giving her a little push in what she considered the right direction, Tess mused wryly.

She just hoped Mitch didn't interpret it that way. His voice had still sounded a bit cautious on the phone when he'd called to confirm their dinner, and she'd been tempted once again to offer him an out. But something had held her back. So here she was, meeting a friend to repay a debt in what was clearly a place designed to foster romance.

Tess glanced yet again at her watch. Mitch was now twenty minutes late. They'd agreed on an early dinner, since she still tired easily, and he'd said he would come straight from his office. It was time to call, she decided.

Tess reached for her purse and stood. But she'd walked no more than two steps toward the foyer when she suddenly froze. Though she hadn't seen him in years, and his once-ebony hair now contained glints of silver, there was no question about the identity of the man who stood on the threshold of the lounge, coolly surveying the occupants.

It was Peter, her ex-husband.

"I'm glad you stopped by, Tony." Mitch laid his hand on the boy's shoulder as they walked toward the office reception area.

"Yeah. Me, too."

"My door's always open, you know."

"Yeah. But it's easier to stop by when school's out."

"The guys give you a hard time about talking to me, I take it."

The fourteen-year-old shrugged. "You know how it is."

"Unfortunately, I do." He paused on the threshold and looked at Tony. "Hang in there, okay? I know things aren't great at home, but there are a lot of people who care about you. Including me. Don't forget that. And I'm here if you need me, anytime, day or night. You've got my home number, right?"

"Yeah."

"Will you stop in and see me again next week?"

"I'll try."

"We can meet somewhere away from here if that's easier, okay?"

"Yeah. Thanks, Mr. Jackson."

"You bet. Just remember that I'm here for you."

"I will. See ya."

Mitch watched the teenager cross the small reception room, then glanced toward Karen's desk, a troubled expression on his face. "I worry about him."

"You worry about all of them," she countered as she pushed her keyboard under the desk.

"Some more than others."

"Are things still bad at home?"

"Yeah."

She raised one eyebrow knowingly. "I'm not surprised. I heard his mother just got a big promotion. She'll probably be around even less now. Which means his dad will drink more than ever."

Mitch looked at her and shook his head incredulously. "How do you know so much about everything?"

"Certainly no thanks to you," she retorted. "You never tell me anything."

"If I want the kids to trust me, I have to keep their confidences."

She grinned. "I know. I'm just giving you a hard time. I know something else, too."

"What?"

"You're late for your six-o'clock appointment."

Mitch glanced at his watch, muttered something under his breath, then turned and strode toward his desk. He stuffed a handful of papers into his briefcase, sparing only a brief glance for Karen, who had followed in a more leisurely fashion. She surveyed him from the doorway, one shoulder propped against the door frame, arms folded over her chest.

Mitch looked at her again as he snapped his brief-case shut, noting her amused expression. "What?" he asked.

"Considering it's Friday night, and considering that classy suit and tie you're wearing, I have a feeling that *appointment* may be too businesslike a term for whatever you have planned for tonight."

He flashed her a grin as he shrugged into a gray pin-stripe jacket. "Fishing?"

"Maybe."

"They're not biting tonight."

"Maybe not here. But this isn't the only fishing hole in town."

Mitch chuckled. "I told you before, Karen. You missed your calling. Are you sure you don't want me to put you in touch with my FBI contacts? They could use more good agents."

"Ha, ha. Very funny. So are you going to fess up, or

do I have to keep fishing?" When Mitch silently picked up his briefcase and headed for the door, Karen sighed and stepped aside. "Okay, have it your way. But the truth will come out."

As he passed his secretary, Mitch winked. "Good luck."

She grinned. "You, too. And by the way—it's about time."

Please, God, don't let him see me! Tess prayed silently but fervently. Peter was the last person she wanted to see, especially tonight. Not when she was already nervous about her dinner plans with Mitch. Not when she was so unprepared for a verbal sparring match with her ex-husband. Not when she needed every ounce of the confidence she had so painstakingly rebuilt after Peter's masterful job of destroying it. Just being in his presence made her feel insecure and shaky.

She glanced around desperately, hoping there was an alcove, a ladies' room, anything that would offer her an escape so she could mentally regroup.

"Tess?"

Too late. With dread she turned slowly to face the man who had once been her husband. He strolled over, and his gaze blatantly raked over her—cold, assessing, critical. He hadn't changed a bit, she thought bitterly. "It *is* you. I wasn't sure. You look more gaunt than I remember."

Not "How are you?" or "Nice to see you." Just a derogatory comment. She should have been used to it by now. Should have developed a skin tough enough to deflect his barbs. Yet they still had the power to sting. And intimidate.

"Hello, Peter." She tried for a cool, aloof tone, but couldn't quite pull it off. "What are you doing here?"

He knew exactly what she meant, but chose to play games, as he always had. "Meeting a couple of colleagues for a drink."

"I mean in St. Louis."

"Why didn't you say so? I'm in town for a convention. Just for a couple of days. I'm leaving tomorrow."

It suddenly occurred to Tess that Peter hadn't even let his son know he would be in town. Had made no attempt to see or even call him while he was here. A deep, seething anger swept over her, and this time the coolness in her tone was real.

"I'm surprised you didn't call."

He gave her a smirk. "Don't tell me you've been missing me."

"Don't flatter yourself. I wasn't thinking of me."

For a moment his face went blank, and then, for one brief moment, he had the decency to look embarrassed. "Oh, yeah. How is the kid?"

Her knuckles whitened on her purse. "His name is Bruce," she said tersely. "Or have you forgotten that, too?"

"Same smart mouth, I see," he sneered. "You always were a master at dishing out guilt." He glanced pointedly at the bare fingers of her left hand. "I'm not surprised you never remarried. No man wants to have someone constantly lecturing to him. Believe me, there are plenty of women out there a lot better looking than you who know how to make a man feel good about himself."

Tess's temples began to throb, and her legs suddenly felt shaky. The memories of her unhappy, bitter years with this man who was now little more than a stranger came rushing back, leaving a sick feeling in the pit of her stomach. Dear God, how had she managed to put up with his vitriolic verbal abuse for ten long years?

Tess had never been very good at hiding her feelings, and she knew from the smirk on Peter's face that he'd correctly deduced that his barbs had hit home. "So what are you doing in a classy place like this, anyway? Reporters must be getting paid more than they used to."

"Tess! Sorry I'm late. I got held up at the office."

Tess felt the comfort of a protective arm around her shoulders, and she turned, her throat tightening with emotion. He might not be wearing a suit of shining armor, but as far as she was concerned Mitch was every bit the knight rescuing the damsel in distress.

Mitch looked down into her eyes, and his gut clenched. He had hesitated on the sidelines when he'd discovered Tess talking with Peter, thinking that perhaps she'd run into an old friend. But her tense body posture quickly put that theory to rest. The man was no friend. Mitch had moved closer, and though he'd picked up only part of the conversation, it had been enough for him to identify the man—and for a white-hot anger to erupt inside him. Tess had implied that her ex-husband was insensitive and uncaring. But what Mitch had witnessed went beyond that. The man was arrogant. Conceited. Self-centered. And abusive. He had hurt Tess before. Deeply. Now he was doing it again. And Mitch had no intention of letting him get away with it. Without even

stopping to consider his actions, he leaned down and
brushed his lips across hers. He didn't wait to assess her
reaction, but instead smoothly transferred his gaze to
Peter.

As Mitch had anticipated, the gesture wasn't lost on
Tess's ex-husband. The other man's eyes narrowed appraisingly, and there was a glimmer of admiration in
them when he spoke again to Tess. As if Mitch's interest
in Tess somehow made her more worthy of his respect,
Mitch thought with disgust.

"Are you going to introduce your…friend?" Peter
prompted.

Tess was still trying to recover from Mitch's unexpected kiss and the brief but breathtaking sensation of
his lips on hers that had, for just a second, made her
completely forget that Peter was standing only inches
away. She turned back to her ex-husband, taking
comfort in the shelter of Mitch's arm, and quickly made
the introductions.

When Peter extended his hand, Mitch hesitated.
Finally, with obvious reluctance, he withdrew his arm
from around her shoulders. As soon as the brief hand-
shake was completed, however, he reached over and
entwined his fingers with hers, noting the coldness of
her hand and the tremors that ran through it.

"Nice to meet you, Mitch. Can I buy you both a
drink?"

Tess looked at Peter in disgust. He hadn't changed
one bit. Jovial and considerate in public, an ogre in
private. Would Mitch be fooled, as so many others had
been? she wondered.

"Sorry, we're already late for our dinner reservations."

"Another time, maybe."

Mitch ignored that comment and turned to Tess. The smile he gave her was warm and intimate. "You look fabulous tonight. New dress?"

She looked at him in surprise. Actually, it was. She hadn't intended to buy anything new for tonight. But she'd seen a dress in the window of a small shop and hadn't been able to resist. The simple, elegant lines of the black cocktail dress were suited to her slender curves, and the moment she'd slipped it over her head she'd felt young and attractive and more woman than mom. It had been a foolish extravagance, of course, but it had done wonders for her self-esteem. Until Peter's opening comment about her gauntness, which had quickly deflated her ego. But Mitch's appreciative gaze helped restore her shaky self-confidence, even if it was only a gallant act for Peter's benefit.

"Yes."

He gave her a lazy smile, then reached up and gently brushed a wayward strand of hair back from her face. "I like it."

"So,, you two seem like old friends."

Mitch frowned, as if he'd completely forgotten the other man was there and was annoyed at being interrupted. He spared him only a quick glance, and once again ignored his remark as he turned back to Tess. "Ready for dinner?"

"Yes."

"I think our table is ready."

His hand still linked with hers, he deliberately turned away from Peter and led the way toward the dining room. Tess followed his lead, turning for a brief parting look at Peter. Her ex's face was slightly ruddy, and his eyes glinted with anger. The picture of a man clearly not accustomed to having his charm rebuffed. As Tess turned away, she couldn't help but feel vindicated. Mitch hadn't been fooled. He had seen right through Peter and had very clearly put him in his place.

As they took their seats at the linen-covered table, the waiter smiled in greeting. "Can I get either of you something from the bar while you look over the menu?"

Mitch glanced at Tess questioningly.

"Just water, please," she said.

"How about some wine?" Mitch suggested.

Tess didn't drink much. But if ever there was a night for it, this was it. "That would be nice."

"I'll bring a wine menu, sir," the waiter offered.

When he left, Tess drew a shaky breath and gave Mitch an apologetic look. "Sorry about that. I had no idea he was even in town."

"So I gathered. And I'm the one who's sorry. I heard enough to get a very clear picture of your ex's character. I'm sorry he upset you."

Tess tried for a smile, but barely pulled it off. "It was that obvious, huh?"

"To me."

"And to him. Which was exactly what he intended." She combed her fingers through her hair distractedly, then clasped her hands tightly together on the table in front of her. "More than anything, though, I'm angry at myself that I still let him do that to me, after all these years."

"Some scars run deep."

"Yes, they do. Thank you for stepping in, Mitch. I was sinking fast."

"You would have been fine."

"I don't know," she said doubtfully. "I can't believe he can still make me feel so…unworthy, somehow. Of respect. Of consideration. Of love. It wasn't until you came along that he looked at me with anything but contempt."

"You didn't need me to validate your worth."

"I agree with you, in theory. And in my heart. But you're right—some scars do run deep." She closed her eyes and gave a little shudder. "I had forgotten just how bad he could make me feel with only a word or a look." She took a deep breath, and when she opened her eyes, she could see the concern in his. Again she tried for a smile. "I really am sorry, Mitch. I wanted to give you a pleasant evening, not force you to deal with ghosts from my past."

Instinctively he reached over and laid his hand over hers. His eyes grew warm and his smile was genuine. "The evening is young, Tess. And ghosts don't scare me." For a moment his own eyes clouded, but they cleared so quickly she wondered if it had just been a play of light from the flickering candle on their table. "Now, how about that wine?" he suggested as he gave her clasped hands a gentle squeeze, then released them to open the menu.

After that, the evening seemed to fly. The food was

good. The pianist excellent. The atmosphere relaxing. Her tension gradually melted away, leaving her feeling peaceful and happy. Or had her mellow state of mind been induced by the wine? Tess wasn't sure. All she knew was that she was having one of the most pleasant evenings of her life. Mitch was warm and witty, and their conversation ranged from politics to music to favorite vacations. They talked about Uncle Ray and Bruce. About their own childhoods. About philosophy and history and art. About the importance of faith in their lives. And they discovered they had amazingly similar tastes and values. It was one of those evenings she wished would never end.

Mitch seemed to feel the same way. Only after they'd lingered over their coffee and dessert did he finally, reluctantly, look at his watch.

Tess savored the last bite of her dessert, feeling completely at ease and relaxed. "What time is it?"

"Ten o'clock."

Her eyes widened. "You're kidding!"

"I wish I was."

Carefully she laid her fork down, trying to hide her disappointment. "Well, we do have an early day tomorrow. I guess we should go."

"I guess so."

But neither made a move to rise. Tess risked a look at Mitch, and their gazes locked. Oddly enough, she saw conflict in his eyes. As if he was wrestling with a difficult problem. What was he thinking? she wondered. And what did he see in her eyes? Liking? Yearning? Attraction? Heaven help her, she hoped not!

But since all of those things were in her heart, they might well be reflected in her eyes.

As Mitch gazed at the woman across from him, he struggled to reconcile his conflicting desires. Earlier she'd seemed vulnerable, and he'd wanted to protect her. During dinner her unaffected charm and spontaneity made him want to learn everything about her. Now, as the evening waned and her eyes grew luminous in the candlelight, he just plain wanted. He wanted to feel her soft hair against his cheek. He wanted to run his hands over her silky skin. He wanted to hold her so close that they would forget the past, the present and the future. He wanted no barriers between them.

And there lay the problem. Physical barriers could be dispensed with. But the secrets and the ghosts would remain, making true intimacy impossible. Mitch sighed. It was definitely time to say good-night.

But Tess spoke first, in a voice that was hesitant and uncertain. "I know we drove separately, but I—I have some Irish Cream liqueur at home if you'd like to stop by for a nightcap before calling it a night."

Mitch took a deep breath. Dear Lord, how much willpower was a man supposed to have? he pleaded silently. How could he refuse the very invitation his heart yearned for? But he had to be firm, he told himself resolutely. He had to stay the course he'd set six years before. *He had to!*

Yet when he spoke, his heart betrayed him. "That sounds great."

The words stunned both of them. Tess clearly hadn't

been expecting him to accept her invitation, and Mitch couldn't believe he had.

"I'll just follow you home in my car," he added.

And so he did, Tess noted, her gaze moving back and forth between the rearview mirror and the road in front of her. And with every block she drove, her panic grew. What was she getting herself into? She had asked Mitch to her apartment for one simple reason—a desire to extend one of the most perfect evenings of her life. Her motives were straightforward. The real question was, why had he accepted? And what did he expect? She wished she knew!

So did Mitch. As he drove through the darkness behind her, he asked himself those same questions. He liked Tess. A lot. He enjoyed her company. He admired her spunk and courage. She made him feel happy and somehow whole.

But the real reason he'd accepted her invitation was because he was powerfully attracted to her. To pretend otherwise would be foolish. She made him feel things he hadn't felt in a very long time, fueled the flames of longing he'd so carefully banked. But Tess didn't fit into his plans. So it would be better to keep his distance before the flames she was fanning to life erupted into a white-hot blaze. And yet here he was putting himself in a position that could very easily get out of hand.

Mitch sighed. For six years he'd put his life in the Lord's hands and resolved to devote himself to helping teens find the right path—to the exclusion of pretty much everything and everyone else, other than Uncle Ray. And he'd stuck to it resolutely. Yet tonight he'd accepted Tess's invitation for a nightcap. Which was clearly a mistake. One of the lessons he'd learned as a cop was that the best way to avoid danger was to stay away from dangerous situations if at all possible and to proceed with extreme caution when danger couldn't be avoided. It was a cardinal rule.

And it was a rule he'd just broken.

Chapter Ten

By the time Tess set the parking brake and took a couple of deep breaths, Mitch had pulled in beside her. A moment later he opened her door.

"I won't stay long," he said, his voice huskier than it had been at the restaurant. "You need your rest."

She looked up at him, but in the dim light it was impossible to discern the expression in his eyes. Nevertheless, she felt reassured that he hadn't interpreted her invitation for a drink as an invitation for something more.

He accompanied her to the door, his hand resting lightly and protectively in the small of her back, and Tess thought again about how he had come to her rescue earlier in the evening. And how right and good this man's touch felt.

Until she'd met Mitch, she'd successfully stifled her needs, had put all her energies into raising her son and creating a stable home life for them. Then had come her problems with Bruce. Problems that stemmed not from lack of trying or insufficient commitment on her part, but from long-ago hurts inflicted on her son by the man Mitch had so accurately assessed and dispensed with tonight. Without the man beside her, Tess wasn't sure where Bruce would be right now. Mitch had brought Uncle Ray into their lives and found the key to unlock Bruce's artistic talents—two great blessings for which she would be forever grateful.

Tess knew how she felt about what Mitch had done for Bruce. She wasn't as sure how to feel about what he'd done for her. To her. Because of Mitch, she'd lain awake for too many nights, tense, lonely, wanting. Because of Mitch, she'd begun to realize just what a difference the right man might have made in her life. Because of Mitch, she'd begun to believe once again in the possibility of fairy-tale endings. Because of Mitch, she felt more like a woman than a mother for the first time in years.

None of those were bad things, she supposed. But Mitch and Bruce still had issues to work out between them, and she wasn't at all sure about Mitch's feelings for her. Early on, she'd thought she'd detected interest in his eyes. Attraction, possibly. But since her surgery, he'd grown more distant, despite his act tonight in front of Peter. He'd obviously heard enough of the conversation to realize how little Peter thought of her, had most likely heard the man's remark about her still-single state—and the reason for it. Mitch had meant to neutralize the biting words of her ex-husband, to throw them back in his face and show him how wrong he was, and he'd succeeded. It was a noble gesture, handled with taste and tenderness, and it had touched her deeply.

She just wished it had been motivated by more than nobility.

They paused at the threshold of the apartment while Tess fitted her key in the lock, then Mitch followed her inside.

"Make yourself comfortable," she said over her shoulder. "I'll get the drinks."

By the time she reappeared with two glasses, Mitch had removed his jacket and was checking out her meager supply of CDs. He extracted one and held it up as he turned to her.

"You didn't tell me you were a fan of Satchmo."

She smiled. "Didn't I? I'm surprised. We talked about everything else tonight."

"Do you mind if I put this on?"

"Not at all. I like a little Louis Armstrong late at night."

A moment later the gravelly voice of the singer, backed by mellow jazz, filled the room, and Mitch joined her on the couch.

"I ditched the jacket. I hope you don't mind."

"You can do the same with the tie if you'd be more comfortable."

He grinned. "A woman after my own heart." He reached up and loosened the tie, but left it in place. "*Much* better."

She swirled her drink, glanced down and took a deep breath. "Mitch…thank you again for tonight."

He tilted his head and looked at her quizzically. "I think that's my line. *You* treated *me*."

"I mean about Peter. For pretending that we

were…that you were my…" She flushed and grasped her drink with both hands to steady them. "You know what I mean. Anyway, it…it made me feel sort of…vindicated, I guess…to have him think that maybe he wasn't the only one who was attractive to the opposite sex."

Mitch studied her, a slight frown marring his brow. "There are no maybes about it, Tess. You're a beautiful woman. Frankly, I think your ex-husband was an idiot to let you walk away."

Tess's flush deepened and she took a sip of her drink. When she spoke, her voice was slightly unsteady. "I was just a tool to Peter. Someone who could help him make the right connections for his work." She paused, then took a deep breath to muster her courage. "He…he never loved me, Mitch. Not even in the beginning." There. She'd finally put into words the painful truth that she'd hidden in her heart for years.

Mitch sensed that Tess had just shared something with him that few, if any, had been privy to. Without even stopping to think, he reached over and took her hand, enfolding it in a warm, protective clasp. "I'm sorry, Tess." The simple statement, spoken from the heart, communicated all that needed to be said.

Tess looked down at their entwined hands, and her throat tightened. Gentle, supportive touches like these had never been part of her marriage. Nor had such simple but heartfelt expressions of caring. She swallowed, struggling to hold in check the tears that suddenly welled in her eyes. Tears for all she had missed, and tears of tenderness for this special man.

"Even after all these years, it hurts to say those

words," she admitted in a choked voice. "But I don't really think Peter knows how to love. He's always been too absorbed in his career, assessing and evaluating everything in terms of how it might enhance his advancement opportunities. Bruce and I were just props. There was nothing between us in the end. No love. No warmth. No respect."

"So why did you stay so long, Tess?"

The question was gentle. Curious, not accusatory, though surely Mitch must think she was a fool to have endured such a loveless marriage. But she'd had her reasons, and she looked at him directly. "Because I'd taken a vow before God that said for better or worse, till death do us part. And because I believe in keeping my promises, Mitch." She drew a shaky breath and once more looked down at her drink. "I just never realized how bad the 'worse' part could get." Her voice caught and she closed her eyes, struggling again to control the tears that threatened to spill down her cheeks.

Mitch saw the raw anguish in her face, and his gut clenched painfully even as his grip on her hand tightened. Tess had never told him any details about her relationship with her ex-husband, only that it had been bad. And it was clear that Peter had hurt Tess and Bruce psychologically. But for the first time he wondered if there was a component of physical abuse, as well. The very thought that anyone might lay a hand on this gentle woman filled him with a cold fury that he had to struggle mightily to control.

"Tess, I know what you told me at the school

carnival, and I got a firsthand look at your ex tonight," he said as calmly as possible. "Tell me to mind my own business if this question is out of line, but…did he ever physically hurt you or Bruce?"

Tess opened her eyes and looked over at him. There was a fierceness in his expression, a coldness that was at odds with the warmth of his tender touch. As if the thought of any harm coming to her or Bruce mattered to him personally, far beyond his role as a caring principal. Slowly she shook her head, deeply touched by his concern. "No. He never laid a hand on us. I would have walked out sooner if he had. But the scars are still there, Mitch. You just can't see them."

He was quiet for a moment, as if debating whether to ask his next question, but at last he spoke. "Can I ask what finally made you decide to leave?"

She looked at him, into the eyes of this man whom she trusted implicitly. Their deep brown depths radiated strength and integrity. He was the kind of man you could count on. In the three months she'd known him, never once had he been anything but supportive and understanding in his dealings with her. And from what she heard, he was that way with everyone.

Tess gazed down at her drink. Should she trust this special man with her final humiliation or allow it to remain hidden, just as the intricate design on the bottom of her mother's antique glasses was hidden by the opaque liquid? Caution advised her to play it safe and leave the question unanswered. But her heart told her otherwise. And suddenly she knew that it was time to listen to her heart—and to place her trust in the Lord. She took a deep breath and then forced herself to meet his eyes.

"Are you sure you want to know? It's not pretty."

He stroked the back of her hand with his thumb, never relinquishing his hold. "Life isn't sometimes. And I've seen my share of the sordid side. More than my share, in fact. I'm willing to listen, if you're willing to share."

Carefully she set her glass on the coffee table, and with a final squeeze of his hand, she extricated hers and rose to walk over to the window. She pulled the drape aside to stare out into the darkness while Mitch waited quietly on the couch behind her. Though they weren't touching, she could feel his support. It was an almost tangible thing, reaching across the distance that separated them, enveloping her with warmth and caring, giving her the courage she needed to begin.

"Bruce was eight at the time," she said, striving with only limited success to control the tremor that ran through her voice. "We'd gone to my parents' house for the weekend to celebrate Bruce's birthday. As usual, Peter said he was too busy to make it. Even though my parents and I did our best to make it a happy weekend, and even though Bruce pretended he didn't care about Peter's absence, I could tell that he was upset by it. So on Sunday I told Bruce we'd head home early and surprise his dad, and that maybe the three of us could go out for a birthday dinner."

Tess let the drape fall back into place, but still she didn't turn to face Mitch. "When we got home, there was a strange car parked in the driveway. It didn't really surprise me. Peter worked at all hours of the day and night, seven days a week, so even though it was a Sunday afternoon, I just figured a colleague had stopped by. And that's exactly what had happened." Her mouth twisted wryly at the memory. "His twenty-year-old summer intern, in fact. Only, they weren't working."

She paused and drew a deep breath. "Fortunately, Peter heard the car and met us in the upstairs hall. He'd barely had time to throw on a robe, and I could see her through the crack in the bedroom door, which wasn't quite closed. She was…in my bed." Tess closed her eyes and wrapped her arms around her body. When she spoke again, her voice was barely a whisper, and Mitch had to lean closer to hear her. "Peter was furious. At *me!* As if I should apologize for catching him in a compromising position." She gave a brief, bitter laugh. "Believe it or not, I almost felt as if I should. But I didn't. I just hustled Bruce out of there, and except for returning to get our things, I never set foot in that house again."

There was a long moment of silence, and then Tess finally found the courage to face Mitch. His mouth was set in a thin, unsmiling line, and she could see the tension in his jaw. "I don't know how many there were before her, Mitch. Probably quite a few. I was completely oblivious. It just never occurred to me that Peter would be unfaithful. I always knew his work came first, that it was his mistress and his first love. I figured no woman could compete with that. But I was wrong. I just wasn't the right woman."

She turned away again to hide the hurt and embarrassment in her eyes, struggling to maintain an even tone. "Needless to say, I was devastated. And humiliated. How could this kind of behavior have been going on—in my own house and in my own *bed*—without my knowledge? I felt like a fool. And I knew then that I had to get out. For my sake and for Bruce's. Peter was just plain bad news. So we left. And we built a new life. And now you have my life s-story." Despite her best efforts, her voice broke on the last word.

Mitch was on his feet and beside her in three long strides. Silently he gathered her into his arms and held her close, one hand tangled in her hair, the other wrapped around her slender waist. She was trembling, and for several long moments he simply held her, pressing her cheek against his solid chest as he silently cursed the man who had hurt her so badly.

Tess struggled to control her tears, but finally lost the battle. A ragged sob escaped her lips, and she felt Mitch tighten his grip. She clung to him, drawing comfort from his strong arms and the steady beating of his heart against her ear. Though she'd spent many a lonely night berating Peter in her heart and silently lashing out at him for the devastation he'd wreaked on his family, she'd never let herself cry. She'd told herself that he wasn't worth tears. But now she let them flow. Not for what had been. But for what might have been, with the right man beside her. Like the one now holding her so tenderly in his arms.

Mitch gazed down at the bowed head resting against his chest, and a surge of emotion swept over him. It was almost like…love, he realized with a frown. But how could that be? He and Tess were little more than acquaintances, really. And yet, he couldn't deny the feeling of connection between them at some deep, intrinsic level. As if they were soul mates. This strong woman, who had faced adversity head-on and moved ahead with courage and determination, had made him reexamine his priorities for the first time in six years. Her tenderness had touched his heart, awakening emotions that he'd long ago suppressed. And her touch left him aching with need, igniting a deep, powerful desire that had kept him awake for far too many nights.

Tess moved in his arms then, nestling even closer to him, and warning bells began to flash in his mind. Mitch knew he was on dangerous ground. Knew the self-control he'd always prided himself on was slipping. Knew he had to get out of there. Fast.

But just as he prepared to release his hold on her, Tess tilted her head back and looked up at him. Her tearstained eyes were so trusting, so soft, so filled with love that Mitch was simply left with no option.

He had to kiss her.

Even as Mitch leaned down to her, his brain kicked into overdrive. He told himself to stop. Told himself that he might regret this later. Told himself it was too soon.

And then his lips touched hers, and his brain stopped working. He couldn't have come up with a rational thought if he'd wanted to. Not with the hammering of her heart thudding against his chest. Not with the silky strands of her hair tangled in his hand. Not with her soft sounds of pleasure filling his ears.

No, there was no way he could think, rationally or otherwise. And so he finally admitted defeat and simply gave himself up to the moment.

Tess wasn't sure exactly how they had gone from confession to clinch. All she knew was that when she looked up at Mitch, the hunger in his gaze had crumbled her defenses. The need reflected in his eyes matched that in her own heart, and she simply couldn't fight the attraction any longer. From the beginning, she'd felt drawn to this man. She'd told herself that a relationship with him simply wasn't possible, given her need to put Bruce's interests first. But lately, Bruce's attitude seemed to be softening and she'd begun to hope that maybe something could develop. Now, it seemed, her hopes were being realized far beyond her wildest dreams.

Tess hadn't been kissed in more years than she could count. Peter had stopped kissing her long before their marriage disintegrated, and she'd dated no one since. She'd almost been afraid that she'd forgotten *how* to kiss. But Mitch quickly put those fears to rest. His lips were hungry yet gentle. Tess had never been kissed with such intensity, such focus, and she surprised even herself by her response. A heart-thudding, breathless excitement swept over her as his strong hands pressed her close. The power of her response made her feel euphoric—and suddenly very scared.

The scared part was what finally made her brain turn back on. And fear was what made her tense—ever so slightly, but enough for Mitch to sense the subtle change.

Slowly, reluctantly, he released her lips. With their

gazes only inches apart, he studied her eyes. They were hazy with longing, but he couldn't ignore the glimmer of uncertainty in their depths—much as he wanted to. Tess wasn't the kind of woman to share her heart lightly. She'd opened up to him emotionally tonight in ways that had surprised them both, clearly taking more risk than she'd planned. But he could sense that she was now moving beyond her comfort level.

And much as he hated to admit it, she was right. Neither of them needed to rush into anything. In fact, he'd probably taken advantage of her when she was most vulnerable and in need of a caring touch. With a frown, he reached over to trace a gentle finger along the curve of her cheek.

"I didn't plan for this to happen, Tess," he said softly, his gaze locked on hers.

"Me, neither."

"Should I apologize?"

"Are you sorry?"

He studied her for a moment, then slowly shook his head. "No."

"Me, neither."

His frown disappeared then, and he somehow managed to dredge up a shaky smile. "In case you haven't figured it out, I wasn't pretending tonight when I implied to your ex that I was attracted to you."

Her face grew warm, and a feeling of elation and hope surged through her. "I just hope you're not disappointed. I haven't done this for a long time," she said tentatively.

Mitch chuckled, and Tess loved the intimate sound

of the laughter rumbling deep in his chest. "Let's just say that I'm glad you're out of practice, because I'm not sure I could be responsible for my actions if you were any more responsive."

His tone was teasing, but Tess had a feeling he was more than half-serious. "I guess if…if we believe everything we read, at this point you should swing me up into your arms and…and…" She tried to tease, too, but her voice trailed off.

His eyes darkened and his intense gaze probed hers. His voice no longer held even a pretense of teasing. "Would you like that, Tess?"

Tess looked at him steadily, her heart banging against her rib cage. "Yes," she whispered, the ardent light in her eyes confirming the honesty of her answer. "But I don't believe in casual intimacy. I think it cheapens what can otherwise be a beautiful emotional and spiritual experience."

His gaze never left hers, and after a beat of silence he spoke, his voice husky. "I feel the same way." He stroked her cheek tenderly with a whisper touch. "Besides, there's a lot we don't know about each other, Tess. And rushing into intimacy is never wise. Both of us still have issues we're dealing with. Time is on our side."

She looked at him wonderingly. "You continue to amaze me, Mr. Jackson."

"Why is that?"

"Patience isn't a virtue I've seen very often in men."

He grinned. "Well, I must admit it goes against all my instincts in this situation."

"Then I admire your self-control even more."

He chuckled and touched the tip of her nose with his index finger. "Then let me tell you, pretty lady, that you are one serious test of a man's self-control. So I'd better say good-night. Right now. Besides, you need your sleep." He looped his hands around her waist and pulled her close once again. "But how about one more good-night kiss first?"

Tess put her arms around his neck and tilted her head back to gaze up at him. "I want you to know that this has been the best night I've had in years, Mitch," she said softly. "Thank you."

His lazy smile was warm and very, very appealing. "Trust me, Tess. It's been my pleasure."

And as his lips closed over hers, making it clear that it was, indeed, his pleasure, Tess felt her heart sing. And for the first time in a very long while, she let herself believe, for just a moment, in happy endings.

"Are you going to tell Bruce that you ran into your ex?"

Tess glanced at Mitch. They were almost at the farm, and he looked as tired as she felt. Clearly, neither had slept well after their emotional encounter the evening before. Even now, the very thought of their kisses made Tess's nerve endings tingle. Her gaze drifted to Mitch's hands on the wheel, and as she recalled his touch a shudder of delight ran through her. But she needed to get her mind on something else, and Mitch had given her the perfect opening.

"I don't see any reason to. He made it pretty clear

that he didn't have any intention of seeing Bruce while he was in town, and by now he's probably gone. I'm not sure it would serve any purpose, except to hurt Bruce. What do you think?"

Mitch nodded. "I agree. When did Bruce last see his father?"

Tess frowned thoughtfully. "Let's see…he moved to Washington right after the divorce. He did stop in once or twice when he was in Jeff City on business, but it's probably been…two or three years ago, I guess."

"And he never calls?"

"Sometimes on Christmas."

A muscle in Mitch's jaw twitched. "How does Bruce feel about him?"

Tess frowned. "He doesn't talk about him at all anymore. I've tried to broach the subject a few times, thinking maybe it would be better if we did talk through his feelings, but he never responds. I know the hurt is still there, though. And it's had a big effect on his self-image. That feeling of being unwanted, of being unworthy, can have a lasting impact on an impression-able child."

He sent another quick glance her way. "And on a sensitive woman."

"Yes," she said quietly, turning to look at the passing countryside. "But at least an adult is a bit better equipped to cope. And I had my faith to sustain me. Adolescents often don't."

Mitch took one hand off the wheel and reached over to enfold her cold fingers in his warm clasp. "I know that Peter did a number on you both, Tess," he said gently. "But I hope by now you realize that the problem in your marriage was due to a lack on his part, not yours. No man in his right mind would do anything to jeopardize a relationship with a woman like you."

Warm color suffused her face. "Thank you for saying that."

"I'm saying it because it's true. You are a kind, intelligent, courageous, beautiful, appealing woman, Tess. I think I made that pretty clear last night."

Her color deepened. "You did. I just wish we could find a way to get through to Bruce, make him feel better about himself. I try, but it's hard to erase Peter's influence."

Mitch frowned. "I'm not sure that's even possible. None of us can escape the past. But maybe, in time, with enough love and understanding, Bruce will come to recognize Peter for what he is—a selfish, self-centered man who never deserved to have a wife and son. And to recognize that no one man can validate his worth, even if that man happens to be his biological father."

Tess sighed. "I hope so, Mitch. I do feel good about the progress he's made in the last few weeks—thanks to you."

"Now, if only he could stop seeing me as the enemy," Mitch said ruefully.

"I think it's coming."

"Maybe. In any case, I agree with you about the changes in him. He seems like a different kid now. He's enthusiastic about working on the sets for the school play, and he seems to be hanging out with a safer crowd. His teachers tell me his schoolwork is improving, too."

"Let's just hope it continues."

Mitch glanced over at her and flashed a smile. "I think it will. Especially if we work on it together."

As he turned back to the road, Tess studied his profile. *Together* was a beautiful word, she realized. It spoke of sharing and caring and mutual support. Of partnership and companionship. Things that had long been absent from her life.

Tess didn't really know where she and Mitch were headed. Last night had left her filled with hope for the future. But life rarely kept its promises, at least in her experience. Great expectations often led to great disappointments.

She would be wise to consider *caution* her operative word, Tess told herself firmly. She needed to move carefully and thoughtfully and make no decisions without weighing all the pros and cons. That rational approach would be her life vest, keeping her afloat while she assessed her options.

There was only one little problem with that scenario, Tess realized with a sigh as she glanced at Mitch's strong profile, his capable and sensitive hands, the firm lines of his well-toned body.

When it came to Mitch, she was sinking fast.

Chapter Eleven

"Hey, Uncle Ray, who's this?"

Bruce held up a dusty, framed photograph retrieved from a box of memorabilia that the older man was sorting through in his bedroom.

Uncle Ray peered at the faded color print, a studio portrait of a youngster with an impish grin and a sprinkling of freckles across his nose. "Land," he said softly. "I haven't seen that in years."

He reached out, and the teenager handed him the photo. "Was that your son?" Bruce asked cautiously.

Uncle Ray slowly shook his head. "No." He sat down wearily on the edge of the bed, still studying the photo. "But he was a special boy, too."

Bruce joined him. "Who was he?"

"So here's where you two are hiding! Tess and I are starving. Isn't it about time for—" Mitch's voice stopped abruptly and he froze in the doorway, his gaze riveted on the framed picture in Uncle Ray's hands. The color drained from his face and a bolt of white-hot pain zigzagged across his eyes.

Uncle Ray gave him a worried look. "We found this in my closet, Mitch," he said gently. "It must have been there for a long time. What with selling the land and all, it kind of got me in the mood to clean things out. Bruce has been helping me. We just came across this a minute ago."

Mitch drew in a harsh, ragged breath, then slowly walked over to the bed and held out an unsteady hand. Uncle Ray silently passed the framed picture to him, and for a long moment Mitch simply stared down at it, his lips a grim, unsmiling line. Finally, as if he couldn't bear to look at it any longer, he thrust the photograph back toward Uncle Ray. "Why did you keep it?" he asked harshly.

"I thought you might want it someday, son." The older man's voice was still gentle.

"Why? It only reminds me of…" His voice broke, and he sucked in a deep breath. When he spoke again, his voice was cold. "I never want to see it again, Uncle Ray. And I'd appreciate it if you'd get rid of it. Lunch will be ready in a few minutes."

With that, he turned stiffly and strode out of the room.

After a few beats of silence Bruce looked at the older man in disgust. "Boy, he sure can be a jerk sometimes. He was really mean to you, and all because of some dumb picture."

Uncle Ray turned to him. For the first time in their acquaintance, Bruce detected disapproval in the older man's gaze. "Sometimes people have reasons for the way they act," he said tersely. "You'll find that out as you get older." Then he stood and moved to his bureau, where he carefully stowed the picture that had caused such contention. "Let's go eat," Uncle Ray said shortly, leaving Bruce to follow at his own pace.

Bruce stared after him. Adults could be so weird sometimes! All that fuss about some old picture. And now he was more curious than ever about the identity of the mystery boy.

But he was pretty sure he wasn't going to find out today.

Though Tess had sensed Mitch's distraction for much of the afternoon, he'd certainly been single-minded in his determination to get her alone before they all retired for the night. And after a lingering good-night kiss, stolen surreptitiously out of sight and sound of Bruce and Uncle Ray, it had taken her a long time to get to sleep. But eventually she had fallen into a deep, sound slumber that was filled with the kinds of pleasant dreams she wished would go on and on forever.

Which was why she fought so hard to block the odd, unidentifiable noise that kept intruding on her subconscious, nudging her awake. It was a valiant but ultimately unsuccessful effort. With an irritated frown she opened her eyes and stared sleepily at the darkened ceiling of Uncle Ray's guest room.

Now, of course, all was silent. Only the distant whinny of a horse broke the stillness. But something had awakened her, she thought, her frown deepening.

And then she heard it. A muffled cry. Hoarse with pain, laced with anguish. A cry of such raw desolation and suffering that she became instantly and fully awake. It took her only a moment to pinpoint the location—the other side of the wall. The den. Where Mitch was sleeping.

Without even stopping to don a robe or slippers, she threw back the covers and swung her feet to the floor, panic rising within her. The sounds she was hearing were barely human, and they clawed at her insides. Something was very, very wrong.

Tess paused for only a brief moment at the den door. Now she could hear thrashing, and the guttural sounds of pain were louder. When her knock produced no response, she took a deep breath and opened the door.

In the dim moonlight filtering through the open window, Tess realized immediately that Mitch was having a nightmare. The bed linens were in disarray, his arms were flailing about, his face was contorted with pain and every muscle was tense. A sheen of sweat covered his torso, and his chest heaved with labored breathing.

Without hesitating, Tess moved toward him and dropped to one knee on the bed. She leaned over and took his shoulders in a firm grip, shaking gently at first, then harder when her initial efforts produced no results.

"Mitch. Mitch! Wake up!" she said urgently.

Neither her words nor her touch seemed to penetrate his consciousness. In fact, his thrashing intensified, and Tess found it difficult to maintain her hold on him. She'd always been aware of Mitch's strength, but now she had a firsthand demonstration of the dangerous power in his coiled muscles. She suddenly realized that in his frenzied state he could hurt not only her, but himself.

She also realized that she was in over her head. Mitch was too strong for her to restrain, and she couldn't rouse him short of shouting, which would only frighten Uncle Ray and Bruce. As she wrestled with the dilemma, Mitch suddenly reached out and grabbed her, his grip like a steel vise as his fingers bit into the tender flesh of her upper arms. She gasped in pain, and this time when she spoke, there was fear in her voice. And it was the fear that finally seemed to penetrate his cloud of horror. His eyelids fluttered open and he stared at her, disoriented and confused.

"It's okay, Mitch," Tess reassured him shakily, speaking deliberately and clearly. "You were just having a nightmare. You're all right."

Slowly the lines of strain in his face eased, and gradually his grip on her arms loosened. He closed his eyes and sucked in a deep breath, then reached out and pulled her close, holding her fiercely against his chest. She could feel the tremors running through him, and she murmured soothingly as she would to a frightened child.

"It's all right, Mitch. It's over. I'm here. Just relax. It was only a bad dream. It's not real."

Slowly she began to feel the tension in his coiled muscles ease. She gently stroked his face until the wild thudding of his heart gradually subsided. When at last he drew a shuddering breath and made a move to sit up, Tess started to stand.

"Stay. Please. Just for a few minutes," he said hoarsely, reaching out a hand to restrain her.

His plea was filled with raw need, and as she stared

into his haggard face a wave of tenderness washed over her. She inched closer until she was sitting beside him, then reached over to lay her hand on his cheek. He covered it with his own. "Of course I'll stay," she said, her voice choked with emotion. "For as long as you need me."

Mitch took her hand and pressed it to his lips, his intense gaze riveted on hers. "That could be a very long time," he said, his voice still hoarse.

Tess stared at him, and her mouth went dry. He seemed to be talking about far more than recovering from a nightmare. And she'd meant far more than that with her statement as well, she realized. But now was not the time to go into that. Not when Mitch was still reeling from a visit to some private hell. "I'm glad I was here for you tonight," she said huskily.

"So am I. Usually I have to deal with that nightmare alone."

She frowned. "You've had it before?"

"Many times."

"Oh, Mitch!" Her voice was laced with compassion. "I'm sorry. It seemed horrible."

He grimaced. "Not as horrible as the reality."

The furrows in her brow deepened. "What do you mean?"

Mitch looked at her in the dim light. He was fast falling in love with Tess. To deny it would be foolish. And unless he had completely misread the situation, she felt the same way about him.

And now they were at a crossroads. If they were going to move forward, they had to be honest with each other.

There could be no secrets between them, no fears. She'd taken a great risk yesterday by trusting him with a painful episode from her past, something she'd shared with no one. She'd bared her soul by revealing her humiliation and pain at Peter's infidelity. Turnabout was only fair play—even if there was a good chance she might want nothing more to do with him when she heard what he had done. Yet it was a risk he had to take eventually. And putting it off was the coward's way out. *Lord, please be with me,* he prayed silently. *Give me the courage to share this terrible secret. And please give Tess the strength to bear it without turning away from me.*

At last Mitch drew a deep breath and laced his fingers with hers, his gaze once more locked on hers. "I mean the nightmare really happened, Tess. Six years ago."

She looked into his eyes, still shadowed with horror, and a cold knot of fear formed in her stomach. An experience that had the power to completely unnerve a strong, capable man like Mitch, to haunt his dreams for years, to leave him physically and mentally shaken was an experience she wasn't sure she wanted to hear about. And yet Mitch seemed to be encouraging her to ask about it.

"Do…do you want to tell me about it?" she asked hesitantly.

His gaze held hers prisoner, and though she couldn't clearly read the expression in his eyes in the dim light, she could sense he was assessing her question and debating his response. Several long seconds ticked by before he slowly spoke. "I've only talked about this to one person, Tess."

"Uncle Ray." It was more statement than question. The bond between the two men was almost tangible.

He nodded. "We've shared a lot. And I *owe* him a lot. In fact, he saved my life six years ago." Again he hesitated, and when he spoke it was clear he was carefully choosing his words. "You remember last night, when you said that what you had to tell me wasn't pretty? Well, this is even less pretty."

Tess swallowed. "I've seen ugly, Mitch."

"Not like this."

She gripped his hand more tightly. "I can handle it," she replied with more assurance than she felt.

He angled his body toward hers and took her free hand in his, studying her eyes once again, his gaze compelling and touched with fear. "I don't want to lose you over this, Tess."

The knot in her stomach tightened at the raw honesty of his statement. He was warning her that she was about to hear something bad. Very bad. So bad that he was afraid she would walk away afterward. But Tess couldn't imagine Mitch doing something terrible enough to change her feelings for him. Yet his fear was very real. And Mitch wasn't a man who frightened easily. Which only made *her* afraid. And uncertain.

Tess realized he was waiting for a response, and so she also spoke honestly, from her heart. "I don't want to lose you, either, Mitch," she whispered, her voice catching.

He almost lost his courage then. She hadn't said, "I'll stick by you, no matter what." But then, what did he expect? Their relationship was still too new, too tenuous, to breed promises. He probably should have waited to bring this up, until they were on more solid footing. But it was too late now for second thoughts. He'd gone too far to back out.

Several long moments of silence passed, and then Mitch took a deep, steadying breath. Telling his story to Uncle Ray had been hard. Yet he'd known the older man would offer support, even if he didn't approve of Mitch's behavior. But this was even harder. Because there was no such guarantee with Tess. He could only hope and trust that she would find it in her heart to still care for him despite what he had done.

"I told you once that when I was a cop, my job always came first," he said slowly, his voice not quite steady. "And because of that, I wasn't always the best husband. What I didn't tell you was that I also wasn't the best…father."

He stopped, giving Tess a moment to digest this revelation. He watched the rapid succession of emotions flash across her face as she processed this new information. Confusion. Shock. Uncertainty.

"You have a child?" She said it wonderingly, as if her ears were playing tricks on her.

"No. I *had* a child," he corrected her.

She frowned and gave a slight shake of her head. "Had?"

"I had a son, Tess. His name was…" He paused and tried to swallow past the lump in his throat. "David. He died when he was thirteen."

A mask of shock slipped over her face. "Oh, Mitch!" she breathed. "I'm so sorry."

"That's not the worst of it."

Tess couldn't even *imagine* anything worse than losing a child. "What do you mean?"

"He didn't have to die."

They were coming to the nightmare part of the story. Tess could sense it. She squeezed his hand, but remained silent, waiting for him to continue.

"Do you remember you asked me once how I know so much about kids?" he asked.

She nodded.

"Well, I learned the hard way. And too late to save my own son." He drew an unsteady breath, then let it out slowly. "When Dana died, I was beside myself with grief. And guilt. I realized how unfair I'd been to her by always putting my job first. I gave what I thought was enough to her and David, and I loved them both in my own way, but it was a love that was secondary to my commitment to my job. And I can't even claim that it was a noble commitment. Sure, I liked seeing justice done. But what I enjoyed most was the thrill of the chase and the excitement.

"When Dana died, I couldn't think straight. Even though I dealt with life-and-death situations every day, it had never even occurred to me that my own life could be affected by an untimely death. I just figured that the three of us had plenty of time to be a family, and that I'd get around to it eventually. Then reality hit me in the face."

He paused, and a flash of pain seared across his eyes. "You'd think that an experience like that would make me step back and take stock of my priorities. To back off the job and spend more time with the people I loved—particularly my son. Instead, I immersed myself even more deeply in my work. Not because of the excitement anymore. At least I'd gotten past that. But because it was an escape. I simply couldn't deal with my loss, and I figured if I kept myself busy enough I wouldn't have time to think about it.

"And that was a huge mistake. Because David needed me during those months. Desperately. He'd lost his mother, and he needed my emotional support. But I was so caught up in my own grief, I was oblivious to his. For all intents and purposes, I was lost to him, too. My mother, who was a widow, moved in with us and she tried her best to help David, but he needed me. She told me that, many times, but I simply didn't get the message.

"That's when David started slipping away, finding his own way to deal with his grief. Namely, drugs. I had no clue what was happening—that's how out of touch I was with my own son." He paused and gave a brief, bitter laugh, his mouth twisting in irony. "Me, the hotshot cop who dealt with dealers and addicts every day, didn't even recognize the signs in my own son. Until the night of…of the nightmare."

Mitch closed his eyes, and a spasm of pain crossed his face. When he spoke again, his voice was raw, his words choppy. "One night my partner and I were sent to check out a deserted warehouse. It was reportedly being used for drug deals. The minute I walked inside I sensed something was wrong. You develop that sixth sense after a while working as a cop. You have to, or you don't survive. My partner and I split up to check the place out. It was absolutely quiet inside. And dark. All I had was a flashlight. The place was littered with debris. There was so much trash that I almost missed…the shoe."

Mitch's grip had tightened painfully on her hand, but Tess remained silent, her gaze riveted on his face.

"I was sweeping the flashlight back and forth, and I went right over it. But something…something made me turn the light back on it. It was a sneaker. Next to some crates. And it was…attached to a leg."

Tess drew in a sharp breath, and her heart began to beat rapidly. Mitch continued to speak, but it was almost as if he didn't realize she was there anymore. He was staring past her, his gaze focused not on this safe, cozy room, but on a dark warehouse that held unspeakable horror.

"I had this…this awful feeling of dread," he said in a choked voice. "I moved the light up the body. Slowly. Everything suddenly seemed to be happening in slow motion. But finally I got to the face, and it was…it was…" His voice broke on a sob and his head dropped forward. "Dear God! I can never forget that moment! He was my only s-son and I f-failed him. He d-died because of m-me."

The knot in Tess's stomach tightened convulsively, and for a moment her lungs seemed to stop working. The horror of it was almost too great to imagine. How could a parent survive such a cruel twist of fate? No wonder Mitch was still having nightmares about it six years after the fact. Especially since he held himself responsible for his son's death.

Tess looked at Mitch's bowed head. His shoulders

were heaving, and though his tears were silent, they were no less wrenching. Tess knew intuitively that Mitch rarely, if ever, cried. And that when and if he did, it was in solitude. He was the kind of man people leaned on, the kind of man people looked to for strength. And he knew that. And lived up to those expectations. But once in a very great while that burden was too great to bear, too heavy for even the strongest shoulders. And this was one of those moments.

Tess didn't have to reassess her feelings for Mitch. If anything, his confession made her care for him more, not less. Yes, he had made mistakes. Bad ones. But he had learned from them. Had transformed his life because of them. And while he couldn't bring back his son, he had given the youngster's death some meaning by subsequently devoting his own life to helping other troubled teens avoid that same tragic end.

Tess's heart contracted with tenderness for this special man who had suffered such loss. She'd always sensed that his character had been forged in fire, and now her intuition had been verified. Despite his own self-deprecating remarks, Tess knew in her heart that Mitch had always been a good man. But it was the trials he'd gone through that had made him a *great* one. A man worthy of admiration. Of respect. And of love.

Love. Tess replayed that word in her mind, savoring the sound of it. Until Mitch came along, she had believed that love wasn't in the cards for her. But he had changed all that. He'd made her feel young and beautiful and desirable. And he'd made her believe in happy endings again. He'd given her hope that her tomorrows need not be as lonely as her yesterdays. He'd opened the door to a whole new world of possibilities. And along the way, she'd fallen in love with him.

Hot tears rose to her eyes as her heart overflowed with love and compassion for this wonderful man who gave and gave without asking anything in return. Who was capable of dealing with pain alone. But who didn't need to anymore.

Tess reached out to him then, scooting closer until she could wrap her arms around his broad shoulders. His arms went around her involuntarily, and he buried his face in her neck, clinging to her with a desperation that said more eloquently than words how much he needed her, how much he cared for her, how much he trusted her.

For several long moments they held each other, until Mitch at last backed off slightly to stare down at her. He touched her face gently, reverently, as if to reassure himself that she really was there. "You didn't bolt."

"Did you think I would?"

"I wouldn't have blamed you if you had."

"You're harder on yourself than anyone else would be."

"I'm honest. If I'd been there for David in his grief, he might still be alive."

"You were dealing with your own grief, Mitch. You weren't thinking clearly."

"That's no excuse," he said harshly. "I neglected David. And he died. Period."

"A lot of kids get involved with drugs even when they have attentive parents."

"Yeah. But I was never an attentive parent even

before Dana's death. I was always too busy with my job. And both she and David suffered."

"Would you do the same thing today?"

He frowned and gave her a startled look. "Of course not."

"Because you learned and you grew and you moved on. You devoted yourself to helping kids, and you're making a difference in a lot of lives. Like Bruce's. And you do it with absolute dedication and selflessness. I suspect you're a different man today than you were six years ago, Mitch."

He stared at her. "That's what Uncle Ray said."

"He's a very wise man. You should listen to him."

"He also said I shouldn't spend the rest of my life alone. And lonely."

Tess stared at him silently in the dim light, suddenly finding it difficult to breathe. "And what did you say?"

He drew a deep breath. "That I was scared. Of messing things up. Making the same mistakes. Hurting the people I love. Just like before. But he didn't buy it. He said I'd changed, and that it was time to move on." Mitch gently caressed her face, and she quivered under his touch. "I think maybe he's right," he whispered hoarsely.

Tess felt as if her heart was going to burst, it was so filled with joy and elation and hope. "Oh, Mitch!" she said in a choked voice.

"I love you, Tess."

"I love you, too."

"I didn't plan for this to happen, you know."

"Neither did I."

"Are you sorry?"

She smiled up at him, and though the light was dim, there was no mistaking the happiness in her eyes. "Do I look sorry?"

One corner of his mouth rose in amusement. "Hardly."

"Are you…sorry?"

His smile disappeared. "No. But I *am* scared."

"Join the crowd."

He ran his hand around the back of her neck, under her hair, and caressed her nape. "Maybe cautious is a better word," he said softly. "Because when I'm with you, I'm not scared at all. It's only when we're apart that I have doubts."

"I feel the same way," she breathed.

"Then there's only one solution. We have to spend as much time together as possible."

"I like the sound of that. Except…" Her eyes grew troubled, and though her instinct was to throw caution to the wind and simply go with the flow, her maternal instinct was too strong to allow her that luxury.

"Except what?" he prompted gently, caressing her nape with his thumb.

She swallowed, trying to hold on to rational thought for at least another few seconds. "Except I have to think of Bruce, too. And what's best for him."

"And?"

"And you two haven't exactly…I mean, I'd want anyone I was going to—" She cut herself off. She'd almost said "marry," but she suddenly realized that Mitch hadn't used that word. "Anyone I was going to be involved with to have a good relationship with him."

"I understand that, Tess. He's your first responsibility. Trust me, I respect that. And I like Bruce. He's a great kid with great potential. And he and I are making progress. How about if we just put this in the Lord's hands, give it a little time and see how things go?"

Her eyes misted. "You're willing to do that?"

He smiled gently. "If that's what it takes to put your mind at ease."

She shook her head unbelievingly. "How did I ever find you?"

"I've been asking myself that same question about you for quite a while now."

She searched his eyes, and the love she saw made her throat tighten with emotion. She reached up and touched his face, and suddenly he pulled her even closer, until she was again pressed tightly against him. She clung to him for a long moment, then drew a shuddering breath and gazed up at him.

"I should leave," she whispered tremulously.

His eyes deepened in color, and he swallowed convulsively. "In a minute," he replied hoarsely.

And then his lips came down on hers, as greedy, hungry and demanding as her own. It was a kiss filled with urgency and need and long-suppressed desires, a kiss that ignited, that consumed, that possessed, that promised. And though they both knew that there were still challenges ahead, for just this moment they forgot the world. As his hands pressed her closer, Tess was lost to everything but his touch. Just as he was lost to everything but the feel of her soft curves and her sweet lips on his.

In fact, they were so lost that neither saw the shadow of the lanky teenager slide across the hall wall and disappear into the darkness.

Chapter Twelve

"**B**ruce! What on earth happened?"

Tess crossed the kitchen in two swift strides and took Bruce's chin in her hand, tilting his head toward the light coming from the window to examine a brand-new black eye that was discoloring rapidly.

"Nothing," he replied, trying to pull away.

"This is not nothing," she said sharply, leading him toward a kitchen chair. "Sit here while I get some ice."

"I don't need any ice."

"Sit," she repeated sternly.

He complied without further argument, and she turned away to prepare a makeshift ice bag out of a dish towel. Her heart was pounding, and she had to force herself to take several long, slow breaths as anger, concern and disappointment all clamored for top billing. Anger because Bruce appeared to once again be in trouble. Concern about his physical condition. And disappointment because things had been going so well. But when she turned back to her son and looked again at the angry purple and red of his injured eye, her heart contracted and concern won hands down.

She walked over to him and placed the bag carefully against his bruised skin, touching his shoulder comfortingly when he flinched. "I'm sorry," she said gently. "I know it hurts. But this will keep the swelling down. Hold it in place, okay?"

"Yeah."

She sank into the chair next to him and reached out to cover his free hand with her own, noting with a jolt that his knuckles were bruised and scraped. "Oh, Bruce!" she said in dismay, rising as she spoke. "I'll get some antiseptic."

"It's okay, Mom."

She ignored him and headed for the medicine cabinet in the bathroom, suddenly wondering as she rummaged among the first-aid items if he might have other, less visible injuries. She hurried back, and though she tried to remain calm, there was a note of panic in her voice when she spoke. "Are you hurt anywhere else?"

"No."

"Bruce."

For the first time, he met her gaze. "No, Mom," he said firmly. "This is it."

She searched his eyes, but saw only honesty. With a sigh, she nodded and set to work with the antiseptic. "Okay. Do you want to tell me what happened?"

"I got in a fight."

"I figured that. What about?"

Her question was met with silence, and she looked over at him. "Well?"

He shifted uncomfortably, and his gaze slid away. "Nothing."

She expelled a long, frustrated sigh. "Come on, Bruce. Fights don't happen because of nothing. Does Mr. Jackson know about this?"

He gave her a defiant look. "No. If he did, don't you think he'd have called you by now?"

She frowned. "What do you mean?"

"You guys tell each other everything."

Her frown deepened. "Why do you say that?"

He shrugged. "You hang around together a lot."

"We're friends."

"Yeah, well…the guys say you're more than that."

She looked startled. "What?"

His gaze skittered away. "They say you're sleeping together."

Bright spots of anger began to burn in her cheeks. "What guys are these?"

"The guys I used to hang around with."

The gang. It figured. "And what did *you* say?"

"I told them they were full of cr…that they were wrong."

Suddenly the light began to dawn. "Is that how you got the black eye?" she asked slowly.

"Yeah. I was just going to ignore them and walk away, but they started shoving me around."

Tess's stomach clenched. "How many of them were there?"

"Three. But only two of them hit me."

Anger bubbled to the surface again—and with it, fear. If they'd beaten up on Bruce once, they could do it again. And next time he might not escape with only a black eye. Abruptly she rose and headed for the phone.

"What are you doing?" Bruce asked in alarm.

"Calling Mitch. Those hoodlums need to be reported."

"Mom! Don't do that! This didn't happen at school. Besides, they won't bother me again."

She paused in midstride and turned to him. "Why not?"

"Because they look worse than I do."

She stared at him, then slowly walked back to the table and sank into her chair. She knew he'd been going to the gym for the past few weeks, knew that he'd filled out and was developing muscles. But she hadn't realized he was so capable of taking care of himself.

"Joe's been helping me with my workouts. And he showed me some tricks," Bruce added, confirming her conclusion.

There was a touch of pride in his voice, and Tess couldn't blame him. She didn't condone fighting, but she was relieved to know he could defend himself if necessary. And the ability to deal with a situation like today's was obviously a boost to his self-esteem. Besides, he'd done nothing wrong. He hadn't started the fight. He'd just taken care of himself when things started getting rough.

"I think you handled this in exactly the right way, Bruce," she said slowly. "I'm proud of you. I'm just sorry they said those things to you about me."

He shifted uncomfortably, and when he spoke he sounded suddenly like a little boy, uncertain and afraid and desperately in need of reassurance. "They aren't true, are they, Mom?" he asked in a small voice.

She stared at him. "Of course not!"

He flushed and looked away. "Sorry. I didn't think so, but…well, you and Mr. Jackson seem pretty… close. Even the guys noticed."

Tess took a deep breath and then reached out to hold his bruised hand, forcing him to look at her again. She needed to be honest, and to say this just the right way, so she chose her words carefully. "We are, Bruce. We're very close. In fact, we've fallen in love. Mitch is a very special man, and I feel blessed that he's part of our life. But just because we're in love doesn't mean we're sleeping together. That would go against everything I believe, everything our faith teaches. Sleeping together, making love, only means something when it's done in the context of a long-term commitment. Of marriage. Knowing that your partner will be with you for always, through the good times and the bad times, is what gives lovemaking its deepest meaning. Mitch feels the same way."

"So are you going to marry him, then?"

She took a deep breath and once again struggled to find the right words. "First of all, he hasn't asked me to yet. And second, a lot depends on you. You are my first and most important commitment," she said fervently, her gaze locked on his. "I would never do anything that wasn't in your best interest. I happen to think that having Mitch in your life *is* in your best interest, and I hope you will feel the same way in time. Because I have room in my life—and my heart—for both of you. Loving Mitch takes nothing away from the special relationship that we have. Do you understand that?"

There was silence for a moment, and then he slowly nodded. "Yeah."

He sounded sincere, and relief surged through Tess. "So tell me how you feel about Mitch."

Bruce shrugged. "He's okay, I guess. He's not as bad as I thought at first."

Tess considered extolling Mitch's virtues, pointing out all the wonderful things he'd done for Bruce and for her. The evidence was pretty compelling. But she refrained. Bruce needed to come to those conclusions himself. And he would, she was sure, given time.

Mitch was willing to wait, so that wasn't a problem.

The problem was her. Because after years of being alone, she was suddenly tired of waiting.

"Tess? Jenny Stevenson."

Tess frowned at the phone. Why in the world would Peter's sister be calling her?

"Tess? Are you there?"

"Yes. Hello, Jenny. Sorry. I was just surprised."

"I'm sure you were. We haven't talked in years. And I wouldn't have bothered you now, except I thought you might want to know, for Bruce's sake." The woman's voice broke on the last word, and Tess heard her take a deep breath as she struggled to regain her composure. "Peter had a massive heart attack yesterday. He died this morning."

Tess stared at the phone. Peter dead at age forty-two? Of a heart attack? He'd never been sick a day in his life!

"Tess?"

"Yes. I—I'm here. I'm just so…shocked."

"We all feel the same way. The funeral will be in Washington on Saturday, and I thought maybe Bruce might like to come."

"Thanks for letting me know. I'll…I'll talk with him about it."

"Let me give you the information. Do you have a piece of paper handy?"

She reached for a notepad. "Yes. Go ahead."

As Tess jotted down the details, her mind was reeling. Even after she'd expressed her polite condolences and said goodbye, she was still too stunned to fully absorb the news. She sat there unmoving as the minutes ticked by, thinking about the man who had been her husband, and about the sham of their marriage. About his selfishness and unfaithfulness. About the way he'd hurt his only son. His legacy to both of them had been only pain and tattered self-esteem.

Tess supposed she should feel some hint of sadness at his death. Some remorse.

But, God forgive her, all she felt was relief. Because now he could never hurt them again.

"Hey, Mom, I'm home!"

Tess's heart began to pound and she carefully set the paring knife on the counter. She didn't know how Bruce was going to react to the news about Peter. He'd talked so little about his father through the years, guarded his feelings so closely, that she had no idea how he felt about him now. For that reason, she had decided to leave the decision to him about whether to attend the funeral. If he needed to go, for closure, she would see that he got there. But she would also fully support him if he decided to stay in St. Louis.

She turned as he came into the kitchen and threw his books onto the table, noting with relief that the black and blue of his eye had faded dramatically in the week since the fight.

"What's for dinner?" he asked.

"Stir-fry. How was school?"

"Okay."

"And the play?"

"Scenery's almost done. But I'll probably have to stay late again tomorrow to help finish up." He reached over and snatched a piece of raw carrot from the pile of crisp vegetables. "I'm gonna check my e-mail before dinner. Uncle Ray's supposed to send me some stuff about putting up fences before I go out there Saturday."

He started to turn away, but Tess reached out a hand to restrain him. "Bruce, before you go I need to talk with you for a minute."

At the serious tone of her voice he turned back to her with a worried look. "What's wrong?"

"Let's sit down for a minute, okay?"

"You aren't sick again, are you?"

He followed her to the table but stood hovering over her anxiously, his face tense.

"No, honey, I'm fine. Come on, sit down."

"Is something wrong with Uncle Ray?" A note of panic crept into his voice.

"As far as I know, he's fine, too. It's your…your dad, Bruce."

Bruce frowned and slowly sat down. "What about him?" he asked cautiously.

"He had a heart attack yesterday. He died this morning."

Bruce's face grew a shade paler, and his eyes shuttered. Tess couldn't even begin to gauge his reaction. But his hand was ice-cold when she reached for it. She waited for several moments, but when he made no comment, she continued.

"Peter's sister, your aunt Jenny, called about half an hour ago. She gave me all the information on the funeral. It's going to be on Saturday, in Washington. You can go if you'd like to, Bruce."

He frowned. "Do I have to?"

"No. It's completely up to you. I just want you to know that you *can* go if that's what you want to do."

"You aren't going, are you?"

"Not to the funeral. But I'll go to Washington with you and make sure you get to the service if you decide to go."

Bruce stared down at the table. "Do you think I *should* go, Mom?"

Tess leaned closer and put her arm around his shoulders. "You don't owe your father anything, Bruce," she said quietly. "Don't go because you think you're supposed to. Only go if you want to. And either way is fine with me."

He was silent for a moment. "Can I think about it tonight?"

"Of course."

Bruce sighed. "He wasn't much of a father."

Tess felt her throat constrict. That was the closest Bruce had ever come to revealing his feelings about the man who had been a father in name only. "No, honey. He wasn't. It just wasn't a role he was cut out to play."

"Yeah." He leaned over and gave her a quick bear hug. "But you're a great mom." When he drew back, his eyes were suspiciously moist, and he swiped at them with the back of his hand as he stood. "I think I'll check my e-mail now."

Before Tess could respond, he grabbed his books and headed for his room. She watched him disappear down the hall, too choked up to speak. Peter might not have been much of a father. But he had certainly fathered a wonderful son.

"Well now, I think it's about time for lunch." Uncle Ray mopped his brow and squinted at his watch, shading it from the sun. "Putting up fences sure can build up an appetite. You boys hungry yet?"

"I could use some food," Mitch replied. "How about you, Bruce?"

"Yeah. I guess so," the teenager concurred. "Do you need some help, Uncle Ray?"

"Nope. Got all the sandwich fixings in the refrigerator. Only take me a few minutes to whip everything up. I'll ring the bell when it's ready."

For a moment they watched the older man make his

way back toward the house, and then Bruce reached for the posthole digger and went back to work.

Mitch did the same, keeping a surreptitious eye on the teenager. Bruce had been unusually subdued this morning—which wasn't surprising, considering his father was being buried even as they worked. The funeral was clearly on his mind, though he hadn't mentioned it. Tess had warned Mitch about Bruce's reticence. Other than telling her he'd decided not to go to the funeral, he hadn't spoken about the subject. He was making a valiant effort to ignore the whole thing, pretend it didn't matter. But Mitch could sense the tension in the boy. His movements were stiff, and there was an unnatural tautness to his face. Mitch had tried to raise the subject of the funeral during the drive to the farm, only to have his efforts rebuffed. But the boy was clearly hurting, so Mitch decided to make another attempt using a different approach.

"I wonder if Uncle Ray will miss having the farm," he said, keeping his tone conversational. "He hasn't said much about it."

At first Mitch thought Bruce was going to ignore the comment. But after a few moments he spoke. "He has to me."

"Is that right? So what do you think?"

Bruce kept digging. "I don't think he'll miss the work. And he kept some land, so he can still have a garden. I think he's happy. At least, he seems like he is whenever we talk about it."

"You two seem to talk a lot."

"Yeah. We e-mail almost every day. He's a great guy. It must be neat to have an uncle like that."

"It is. He's been almost like a father to me since my own dad died ten years ago," Mitch said evenly, keeping his tone casual.

There was silence for a few moments, and again Mitch thought Bruce was going to shut down. But the boy surprised him. "Did you have a good dad?"

"Yes. He worked too hard. And he wasn't around as much as I would have liked. But he loved me. And he let me know it. In the end, that's all that matters."

"You were lucky." Bruce thrust the posthole digger into the ground and clamped it shut on the dark earth.

"Yes, I was."

Bruce withdrew the dirt and deposited it in a pile beside the hole, kicking a few wayward clumps back into place. "I guess Mom told you a lot about my dad."

"Some."

Bruce looked at him skeptically. "More than that, I bet."

"Enough," Mitch amended. "He didn't sound like the best dad—or husband."

"He wasn't," Bruce said tersely, his voice edged with anger. He thrust the digger into the ground again. "He hurt Mom real bad."

"I figured that. What about you?"

Bruce shrugged as he withdrew another digger of dirt. "He never wanted me around. That's pretty hard for a little kid."

Or a teenager, Mitch thought silently. "Even adults have a hard time dealing with rejection," he replied quietly.

"Yeah. I guess so." Bruce paused and wiped his forehead on his sleeve.

"How about some lemonade?" Mitch suggested.

"Sure."

Mitch filled two paper cups from the cooler Uncle Ray had provided, then nodded toward a large rock a few yards away in the shade. "What do you say we take a break?"

"We'll be stopping for lunch in a few minutes."

Mitch smiled. "I don't think Uncle Ray will fire us if we cut out a few minutes early."

Mitch headed for the rock and settled down. Bruce followed more slowly and perched on the edge, his body tense, his eyes fixed on the distant field. It was quiet at the farm, the stillness broken only by the faint hum of a tractor and the birds twittering in the trees. There was silence between them for a minute or two, but finally Bruce sighed.

"I wish my dad had been more like Uncle Ray," he said, his tone subdued but intense. "I only met him a couple of months ago, but already I know I'd miss him real bad if…if anything happened to him. I never felt that way about my dad. He was never very nice to me. Or to Mom. It's real hard to…to love somebody like that, you know? Even though you're supposed to."

Mitch took a sip of his lemonade. *Lord, let me say the right thing,* he prayed silently, forming his words carefully. "You don't have to love him just because he was your biological dad, Bruce. That kind of love isn't something that's owed. It's something that's earned. And from what I know about your dad, he didn't earn your love. Or your mom's. And you know something? That was his loss. Because he could have had the love of two very special people if he'd just made an effort."

Bruce turned to look at him, and Mitch met his gaze directly. After a moment Bruce blinked and turned away. "He didn't think I was special," he said in a small voice. "He never wanted me."

"Then he was a fool. I would give anything to…to have a son like you." Mitch's own voice broke, and he suddenly found it difficult to swallow past the lump in his throat.

Bruce turned back to him, remembering the photo that Uncle Ray had so carefully placed in his dresser drawer, recalling the scene he'd witnessed—and the confession he'd overheard—the night of Mitch's nightmare. "That picture in Uncle Ray's room…the day you came in to call us for lunch. That boy was your son, wasn't he?" Bruce said slowly.

Mitch nodded.

"I'm sorry he died. He looked like a nice kid."

Mitch sucked in a deep breath, struggling to control his own emotions. "He was."

"You still miss him, don't you?"

"Yes."

"The same way Uncle Ray misses his son."

Again Mitch nodded.

"I know that they both died when they were pretty young, but they were kind of lucky in a way," Bruce said, his eyes suddenly old beyond his years.

Mitch frowned. "What do you mean?"

He shrugged. "They had fathers who cared. And who loved them. And who still think about them a long time after they're gone. If something had happened to me, my dad would never have even given it a second thought. He would have forgotten all about me by the next day."

Mitch's heart contracted, and he once more silently cursed the man who had come very close to ruining a young boy's life. But he couldn't deny what was obviously a true statement. So he didn't even try. "Maybe you should follow his lead, then."

Bruce sent him a puzzled look. "What do you mean?"

"Now that he's gone, forget about him. Recognize him for what he was—and what he wasn't—and move on with your life. You don't need your dad to validate your worth, Bruce. You never did. You're a smart, caring, talented young man. And if your dad failed to recognize how special you are, that's his fault, not yours."

Bruce's face grew slightly pink at Mitch's compliment, and he looked away. "It's not easy to forget," he said quietly.

A flash of pain flared in Mitch's eyes. "No, it's not. That's why it's important to have people around who love us and believe in us and stand by us when we have doubts."

"Like Mom."

"And your friends, too. Like Uncle Ray. And me."

Bruce looked at him, and for a moment their gazes connected and held. The boy's Adam's apple bobbed convulsively, and he took a deep breath. "I haven't been very friendly to you."

"Principals are used to that."

"I thought you were picking on me when I first came to the school."

"How about now?"

Bruce met his gaze steadily. "I guess I was wrong."

The clanging of the dinner bell suddenly broke the stillness, and after a moment Mitch forced his lips into a smile. "Sounds like Uncle Ray's ready for us."

"Yeah. He's worse than Mom when you're late for a meal."

This time Mitch's grin was genuine. "Then we'd better hurry."

They stood, and Bruce shoved his hands into his pockets. But when he held back, Mitch turned to him questioningly.

"I don't think I ever said thanks for everything you've done for Mom and me," the boy said quietly.

Mitch put his hand on Bruce's shoulder. "You just did. And it was my pleasure."

He slung his arm around Bruce's shoulders, and as they made their way to the house, Mitch felt more at peace than he had in a very long while. Because for the first time he and Bruce had finally found some common ground. And in the process they'd forged a new bond.

Chapter Thirteen

"I take it the news was good."

Mitch paused at Karen's desk and grinned. "Did you have a spy planted in the boardroom?"

"Didn't need one. Your face tells the story. Let me give you one word of advice—don't ever play poker."

"Don't worry. It's not my game."

"Good. So…the assistant-principal position was approved and you will now have some time to call your own. You should go out and celebrate."

Mitch reached into his pocket and fingered the square velvet case, anticipating his dinner with Tess. "I intend to."

"Not alone, I hope."

"Hardly."

"I didn't think so. Give Ms. Lockwood my best," Karen said breezily, turning back to her word processor.

Mitch stared at her. "How did you know?"

Karen sent him a smug look over her shoulder. "I have my ways."

Mitch shook his head. "I told you you missed your calling. Would you care to let me know how you found out I was seeing her?"

"Well, I usually don't reveal my sources," Karen said, pretending to give his request serious consideration before relenting. "But just this once I guess it couldn't hurt. My neighbor, a nice older woman, Mrs. Brown, was at the grocery store and ran into Ted Randall—you remember Ted, he used to do some of the groundskeeping work here—and he told her that he'd seen you going into a very nice restaurant the night you left here in the suit. He couldn't remember the name of it, but Mrs. Brown did, and I happen to know one of the hostesses there. Strangely enough, I crossed paths with her a couple of days later, and I asked if by chance she'd seen you at the restaurant. She knew what you looked like from that article in the paper when you won the award, because I'd called it to her attention and she thought you were a hunk. Well, turns out she did see you. And oddly enough, she recognized Tess Lockwood from some meeting she attended that Tess was covering for the paper. So she told me who you were with. Small world, isn't it?"

Mitch gave her a dazed look. "I think I'm sorry I asked."

Karen chuckled. "That's what my husband always says. So why don't you get out of here? For once in your life, leave before seven o'clock. The world won't end. And remember—thanks to the board, help is on the way."

"Not until next year," he reminded her.

She waved his caveat aside. "Be here before you know it. And school's almost out for this year, anyway. There's more to life than work, you know."

He thought of Tess, and his lips slowly curved upward. "Yeah. I know."

"Well, it's about time," she declared with a satisfied smile.

Mitch chuckled and shook his head. "Karen, you are priceless."

She sniffed. "Remember that when it comes time for raises."

Mitch was still chuckling as he entered his office and headed for his desk. All he had to do was put a few papers in his briefcase and he could be on his way.

Out of habit, he glanced at the phone, noting that the message light was on. Nothing new there. It always seemed to be on. He hesitated and glanced at his watch. The board meeting had run long, and Tess was expecting him in less than fifteen minutes. There was no way he'd be on time if he began checking his messages. And tonight was one night he did *not* want to be late, he reminded himself, reaching into his pocket again to finger the velvet box.

His expression grew tender and a smile stole over his face. He'd hinted to Tess that big things were up at school and he might have some news after the board meeting. So she was expecting a celebration dinner. But although the addition of an assistant principal was definitely worth celebrating, he had an entirely different kind of celebration in mind.

* * *

"*That* was a fabulous dinner," Tess declared, leaning back with a sigh in the upholstered chair. "And so is this restaurant," she added, glancing around admiringly at the discreetly elegant decor.

"And how about the company?" Mitch teased with a smile.

Her gaze returned to his, and her own lips curved up. "Even better than the food and the setting," she assured him softly.

He reached for her hand and leaned closer. "I was hoping you'd say that."

Tess studied him for a moment in the candlelight. It still astounded her that this amazing man had come into her life. He was handsome, yes. But even more, he had integrity and character and compassion and honor—all the qualities that really mattered, but which were so lacking in her first husband. Those were the qualities that had made her fall in love with him.

Best of all, he loved her, too. He'd told her so. But he'd also made it clear that he was scared. And that he'd never planned to marry again. He'd been very up front about that. But she sensed that, like her, he'd undergone a change of heart in recent weeks.

Because more and more, she had come to believe that having Mitch in her life—in *their* lives—was in both Bruce's and her best interests. Mitch had graciously offered her time to think things through, but she didn't need any more time to make up her mind. She wanted him in her life. For always. And maybe it was time to tell him that.

Tess took a deep breath and opened her mouth to speak, only to be interrupted by the waiter.

"Could I offer you two some coffee or dessert?"

It took Tess a moment to switch gears, and Mitch seemed to be having the same problem. At last they reluctantly broke eye contact and looked up at the waiter.

"Coffee for both of us," Mitch said, then transferred his gaze to Tess. "How about dessert?" He winked at her wickedly. "I will if you will."

She smiled and reached for her purse, glad now for the interruption. She needed to escape for a moment, compose her thoughts, decide exactly what she wanted to say to Mitch so she didn't sound pushy, just receptive. "Anything chocolate will be fine. Surprise me," she said as she stood. "Will you excuse me for a moment?"

Mitch stood as well, and the warmth in his smile made her tingle. "Hurry back."

He watched her disappear before he took his seat again and turned back to the waiter. "You heard the lady. Bring us two of your best chocolate desserts."

The waiter bowed slightly. "Of course."

Mitch reached for his wineglass and leaned back, willing his pulse to slow down. In a few minutes he was going to ask Tess to be his wife. And he wasn't at all sure of her answer. Yes, they'd acknowledged their love. But they'd also acknowledged their reservations. He'd admitted his fear. What he hadn't yet told her was that now he was more afraid of living without her than of taking another chance on love. On her side, she'd told him of her concerns about Bruce, and he'd promised to give it a little time and see how things worked out.

Maybe he was rushing it. But frankly, his patience was wearing thin. He wanted her with him every day, wanted to wake up beside her in the morning and hold her in his arms through the night. He wanted their lives to merge. He wanted to create a new, shared life together. And he didn't want to wait any longer to tell her that. He reached in again and touched the velvet case. In just a few minutes he would…

His pager began to vibrate, and he automatically reached to his belt and shut it off. He probably should have left it in the car, he realized with a frown. That would have eliminated the possibility of distractions. Since he used the pager only for emergencies, the vibrating warning always signaled a crisis of some kind. Karen had the number, as did the president of the school board. And the police, in case there was an off-hours emergency at the school. So a vibrating pager was *not* a good omen.

Mitch debated for a moment, fighting against the urge to check the message. Tonight was supposed to be about him and Tess, alone, and he resented the intrusion. But it simply wasn't in his nature to ignore an emergency—much as he might want to.

He checked his pager. The message was cryptic, and it was from the police. "Please call ASAP."

Mitch felt his stomach clench. He'd never been paged by the police. Something must be very wrong.

"Mitch, what is it?"

He looked over at Tess, who had already taken her seat, and frowned. "I don't know. The police just paged me."

Her face grew concerned. "You'd better call right away."

"Yeah." He hesitated for one more moment, then laid his napkin on the table and stood. "I'll be right back," he promised. "And I'm sorry about the interruption."

She waved his apology aside. "Emergencies come up. Take your time."

He sent her a grateful look and his eyes grew tender. "Thanks for understanding."

It took Mitch only a moment to locate a phone, and a few seconds after that he was talking to the sergeant on duty, whom he knew.

"Thanks for calling so quickly, Mitch."

"Sure, Jack. What's up?"

"Steve just called in. They've got an OD situation, and they found your name and phone number in the kid's pocket. No other ID. Could be one of your students. We need you to do a positive ID."

Mitch's grip tightened on the phone. "Is he…still alive?"

"No."

He closed his eyes and sucked in his breath, feeling the color drain from his face. "Where is he?"

The sound of papers being rustled came over the wire, and then the sergeant gave Mitch the location—a small, largely unused park in Southfield.

"I can be there in fifteen minutes."

"You don't need to do that, Mitch. Might be easier just to stop by the morgue in an hour or so."

"No. I'll go. Thanks, Jack."

"Sure. I'll let Steve know you're on the way."

The line went dead, and Mitch slowly replaced the receiver. His hands were shaking, and he jammed them into the pockets of his slacks, fists clenched. Dear God, it was like being plunged back into his own nightmare! It wasn't *his* son this time. But it was *someone's* son. And deep in his gut he had a feeling he knew who it was. Very few of his students were likely to carry his phone number. Except Tony Watson, who had come to him on more than one occasion to talk through his problems. Who had thought of Mitch as his friend, as someone he could count on. The knot in his stomach twisted more tightly.

He hadn't even reached the table before Tess was on her feet and reaching for her purse. "What's wrong?" she asked, panic edging her voice. "Is it Bruce?"

He shook his head. "No. But the police think they've found one of my students. He overdosed. My name was in his pocket, and there was no other ID. They need me to come and identify him."

"Oh, dear God!" Tess breathed, her face a mask of shock. "Is he…is he alive?"

Mitch shook his head.

She swallowed, and he could see the sheen of tears in her eyes. "Do you want me to come with you?"

Though he hadn't expected that offer, he was tempted to take it. Maybe it would be easier to face if Tess was beside him. But that was selfish. He couldn't subject her to the scene in the park. He'd been there before, and he knew it would give her nightmares for months. Slowly he shook his head. "You don't need to see this. I'll have the restaurant call you a cab."

She studied his face for a moment, then nodded. "Okay."

He reached out to her then, laced his fingers with hers. "I'm sorry about this, Tess."

Her earnest gaze connected with his. "Don't be. I understand." And then she moved closer and wrapped her arms around him, as if she sensed his need for some concrete sign of reassurance and support. Despite the curious, if discreet, glances of diners at nearby tables, he held her fiercely, letting her love envelop him and insulate him for just a moment from the horror ahead, drawing from her the courage to face what was to come.

"Be careful," she whispered close to his ear.

"I will."

"Call me later?"

"It could be late."

"I'll be up."

"Okay."

Reluctantly he released her and stepped away, hesitating long enough to reach over and touch her face. She covered his hand with hers, and for a moment their hearts touched. Then he turned away.

He looked back once, when he reached the door. Tess was still standing by the table, her beautiful features bathed in the golden glow of candlelight. And suddenly he had the oddest feeling. It was almost as if his time with Tess had been merely a dream, a brief respite from his true reality—a destiny of nightmares and loneliness. And as he stepped out into the night, a frightening sense of foreboding swept over him that the dream was about to come to an end.

* * *

It was a scene right out of his nightmare. The harsh glare of spotlights. The static buzz of walkie-talkies. The flashing lights on police cars. Reporters jockeying for position behind the police barricade. It was sur-realistic—and all too familiar.

Mitch hesitated on the sidelines until Steve noticed him and came forward.

"Sorry to interrupt your evening, Mitch," the officer said.

Mitch tried to speak, but nothing came out. He cleared his throat and tried again. "No problem."

Steve lifted the police tape and Mitch ducked under. "He's over there." The man pointed to a heavily wooded section of the park, then led the way.

Mitch followed. His legs felt wooden, and he had to concentrate on simply putting one foot in front of the other. Steve held aside the brush as they made their way about ten yards into the woods, to a small clearing where a draped body lay. For a moment Mitch thought he was going to lose his dinner, and he forced himself to take several slow, deep breaths.

"I guess you've been here before, in your police days," the officer said sympathetically.

The man's comment jolted Mitch, until he reminded himself that no one on the force knew about David. The man was simply talking in generic terms. "Yeah."

"You never get used to it, though, do you?"

Mitch's throat tightened. "No."

Steve reached down to lift the drape, and Mitch steeled himself. A moment later, when the boy's face was revealed in the glare of a flashlight, his fears were confirmed.

"Do you know him?" Steve asked.

Mitch nodded jerkily. "Tony Watson. He…he was one of my students."

The man gently lowered the shroud and stood, taking down the information Mitch provided on the boy's parents. Then he closed his notebook and gazed down at the draped form, shaking his head. "What a waste." Steve sighed and turned back to Mitch, holding out his hand. "Listen, thanks for coming over. Sorry to interrupt your plans for the evening."

As Mitch made his way back to his car, Steve's words echoed ominously in his mind. For in his gut he had the disquieting premonition that the man had interrupted not only his plans for the evening, but his plans for his life.

Why hadn't Tony called?

The question echoed in Mitch's mind as he drove home. He'd tried so hard to get through to the boy, to let him know that he had a friend, anytime, day or night.

Why hadn't he called?

Mitch went over and over the situation in his mind as he drove. Where had he failed? He'd talked to the boy's parents, though their lack of interest had been evident. He'd set up counseling for Tony, but the boy had gone to only one session. He'd tried to get Tony involved in any number of school activities, introduce him to new people, but always the boy returned to the gang. What else could he have done? he asked himself helplessly.

Mitch pulled into his driveway and for a long moment simply sat behind the wheel, too weary to move. Right about now he had hoped to be planning a future with the woman he loved. Instead, a boy was dead, with no future to look forward to. And somehow he felt at fault. There was something he was missing, some connection he wasn't making, that would point the finger of guilt at him. He knew that instinctively, and his instincts had rarely failed him.

With a tired sigh Mitch eased himself out of the car and let himself into the silent, dark house. The message light was blinking on the phone as he passed, and he remembered his promise to call Tess. It was getting late, but she was probably still…

He stopped abruptly, and suddenly the missing connection fell into place. Tony had had Mitch's phone number in his pocket. Which meant he hadn't forgotten about Mitch's offer of help. But Mitch had left the office without checking his voice mail. Nor had he checked his home voice mail since early this afternoon.

A sick feeling of dread enveloped him as he stared at the blinking light on his answering machine. He didn't want to play back his voice mail—here or at work. But he couldn't hide from the truth. With his heart hammering in his chest, he reached for the phone and forced himself to dial his voice mail at work.

The first few messages were innocuous. The sixth one was like a punch in the gut.

"Mr. Jackson, this is Tony. Tony Watson. Listen, things are kind of…kind of rough right now, you know? I just wanted to talk to somebody, and you said to call anytime so…well, I'm calling. I need to do something to feel better soon, you know? Listen, I'll, uh, I'll try your home number. Yeah. Thanks."

The time on the message was a little after five.

Mitch felt as if his lungs were in a vise, as if the air was being squeezed out of them. Tony *had* tried to call him. He *had* reached out. Except Mitch hadn't been there.

A muscle in his jaw clenched, and he punched the button on his home machine, which showed two messages. Both were from Tony, and had clearly been made from a cell phone.

"Hey, Mr. Jackson, if you're there maybe you could pick up? It's me, Tony Watson…" There was a pause, and Mitch heard the desperate note in his voice. "Okay, I guess not. Look, life's pretty bad, you know? My mom's gone to Europe or someplace for work, and Dad's pretty out of it on the booze. He's not real nice when he's drunk, so I've been trying to stay out of his way. Only, there's nowhere to go. And school stinks, too. All the kids are creeps—except the guys. I know you don't like me to hang around with them, but a guy's gotta have somebody, you know? And they gave me some stuff to try…. They said it would help me feel better. I don't know, though…"

The line went dead. Mitch steeled himself and punched the button for the last message, his heart hammering painfully.

"It's Tony. Hey, listen, forget those other messages, okay? I feel real good now." He erupted into a peal of high-pitched laughter. "Yeah, I'm okay. Man, this stuff is cool! The guys were right. See ya later."

The line went dead.

Mitch closed his eyes, and his fingers clenched around the receiver. If only he'd played his answering machine back earlier! He might have gotten to Tony in time to dissuade him from using whatever stuff his "friends" had given him. He replaced the phone in the holder, his chest tight with emotion. Once again he had failed to recognize when someone needed him desperately. Just as he'd failed David.

And suddenly he realized that he'd been fooling himself all along. Six years ago he'd learned a very painful lesson—that he was apt to get so caught up in his job that his personal life, and those he loved, suffered. Today the reverse had been demonstrated. He'd put his personal life first, and a boy had died. The message was obvious—he simply couldn't manage both.

He thought of what Uncle Ray had said. That he wasn't the same man he'd been six years ago. Maybe that was true in some ways. But one thing hadn't changed, as he'd tragically learned tonight. He still wasn't able to discern an urgent need for help. He'd missed it with Tony, just as he'd missed it with his own son. And how could someone so out of touch with those who needed him most possibly be a good husband or father?

The sudden ringing of the phone startled him, and he reached for it automatically. "Hello."

"Mitch? It's Tess. I know you said you'd call, but I've been so worried…did you just get in?"

He propped one shoulder against the wall and wearily wiped a hand down his face. "Yeah. A few minutes ago. I was just going to call you."

"Was it…one of your students?"

"Yes. Tony Watson."

Tess frowned. The name sounded familiar. "The boy who was having problems at home? From Bruce's class?"

"That's right."

"Oh, Mitch! What happened?"

He couldn't tell her about the phone calls. Not yet. The pain was too raw. "He couldn't handle life. He thought drugs could help. The classic story."

There was silence for a moment, and he knew that she was thinking how close Bruce had come to going down this same path. "I'm so sorry," she finally said softly.

"Me, too."

"You sound exhausted."

"Yeah."

"Do you want me to come over?"

He closed his eyes and sucked in a breath. Oh, yes! He needed Tess now, desperately. Needed to feel her arms around him, to touch her softness, to inhale her goodness. He needed to hold her until the nightmares receded and he recaptured the dream of their future together. But that could never be. It wouldn't be fair to her. Because he would fail her. Maybe not next week. Or next year. But someday. And he couldn't do that again to someone he loved.

"No. It's late. We both need to get some sleep."

There was a moment's hesitation before she spoke. "All right. We'll talk tomorrow."

"Right."

Again she hesitated. He knew she wanted him to say more. But he couldn't.

"Good night, then."

"Good night," he replied.

He replaced the receiver, then reached into his jacket pocket and removed the velvet box, cradling it gently in his hand. His time with Tess had been a lovely interlude, giving him a tantalizing taste of joy. Making him believe once again in the magic of love and happily-ever-afters. In the end, though, it had been but a burst of sweetness that quickly dissolved, like cotton candy on the tongue. Though difficult at the time and made only after heartfelt prayers for guidance, his decision six years before appeared to have been the right one after all. He wasn't husband or father material. He'd failed his first wife. He'd failed his son. And now he'd failed Tony.

As a cop, he'd dealt with evidence every day. Sometimes it was difficult to reach a conclusion. But there was no question at all in this instance.

It was an open-and-shut case.

Chapter Fourteen

"I sure don't understand grown-ups, Uncle Ray."

The older man studied the chessboard for a moment before replying. "Why is that?"

"They do stuff that doesn't make sense."

Uncle Ray picked up a knight and made his move. "Anything in particular?"

"Well, like Mr. Jackson. He quit calling Mom. I mean, he was hanging around all the time, then all of a sudden he just disappeared. Mom's been moping around ever since, jumping every time the phone rings like she's hoping it's him. I told her she should call him, but she just got this real sad look and didn't say anything."

Uncle Ray nodded understandingly. "It's hard to lose someone you love, Bruce."

The teenager looked at him in surprise. "How did you know she loved him?"

Uncle Ray tilted his head and his lips turned up in a melancholy smile. "I was in love once. I recognize the signs. And I'll tell you something else. Mitch loves her, too."

Bruce frowned in confusion. "Then why doesn't he call?"

The older man sighed and leaned back in his chair. "Life can be pretty complicated when you're grown up, Bruce. People do things for lots of reasons. Some of them wrong, even when the intentions are good."

Bruce's frown deepened. "Mom said Mr. Jackson stopped coming around because he feels responsible for Tony's death. But what did that have to do with us?"

Uncle Ray regarded the teenager for a moment. "Did Mitch ever tell you about his son?"

Bruce hesitated. "He told me he still misses him."

"Did he tell you what happened to him?"

Bruce looked down and fiddled with a chess piece. "Not exactly. But I…I know."

Now it was Uncle Ray's turn to frown. "How?"

"When we stayed here one night, I heard a noise in the den. By the time I got there, Mom was talking to Mr. Jackson. I think he'd been having a nightmare or something, and Mom heard him, too. Anyway, he told her about his son, and the drugs, and how he…how he found him in that warehouse. I felt real bad for him."

Uncle Ray nodded. "We all did. But no one felt worse than Mitch. He believed he'd failed his son. And the fact is, he had. But he was grieving, too, because his wife had just died. So he wasn't entirely to blame, even though he felt he was. For a long time after that I wasn't sure he was going to make it. But when he did, he decided to spend the rest of his life helping other kids get their act together."

"Kids like me?"

"Yes. And like Tony. But his plans didn't quite work out, because he met your mom and fell in love."

"Was that bad?"

"Not at all. I personally think it was the best thing that could have happened. But I'm sure he feels that if he hadn't been with your mom the night Tony died, if he'd picked up his messages, maybe he could have saved him."

Bruce propped his chin in his hand, his face grave. "Man. That's heavy."

"Yes, it is. And Mitch might be right. But he'll never be able to save the whole world, no matter how hard he tries. All he can do is his best. And that's plenty good enough, if you ask me. He's done a lot of fine work in the past six years."

Bruce grinned. "Yeah. Look at me."

Uncle Ray chuckled. "Good point."

Once more Bruce's face grew serious. "So he thinks that Mom and I would get in the way of him doing his job."

"Partly," Uncle Ray conceded. "But I think he's even more afraid that his job will get in the way of him being a good husband and father. That eventually he would let you and your mom down."

Bruce frowned. "He'd never do that. He always tries his best to do what's right. And you can't let somebody down if you're trying your best."

Uncle Ray leaned forward and once more examined the chessboard. "That's true, son. Trouble is, I'm not sure how we can convince Mitch that his best would be good enough."

* * *

"There's someone here to see you, Mitch."

Mitch looked at Karen distractedly, then glanced at his watch. "Why are you still here?"

"I was keeping your visitor company."

Mitch frowned and transferred his gaze to his calendar. "I don't have anything scheduled."

"He doesn't have an appointment."

"Who is it?"

"Bruce Lockwood. He's been waiting for three hours."

Mitch felt his heart stop, then race on. He was on his feet instantly. "Three hours! What's wrong?"

"Nothing that I can determine," Karen said calmly. "Relax. He said it wasn't an emergency. I asked that first thing. But he insisted on waiting, even though I told him you were busy all afternoon. I tried to break in and let you know he was here, but you went right from the committee meeting to three conference calls back-to-back and I couldn't get a word in edgewise. Which is a record for me. I suggested he try another day, when you weren't so busy, but he refused to leave."

Mitch frowned. "Then it must be important." He flexed the muscles in his shoulders and sighed wearily. "Send him in, okay?"

She tilted her head and regarded him disapprovingly. "I thought these long days were over. I think you're regressing."

Instead of responding, he nodded toward the door. "Go home, Dr. Freud. And send in Bruce." She gave him an exasperated look and started to leave, but paused when he spoke again. "Thanks for waiting, Karen. And for caring."

She looked back and smiled. "No problem."

By the time Bruce entered a moment later, looking slightly ill at ease, Mitch had moved out from behind his desk. "Hello, Bruce. Come in. I'm sorry you waited so long. I had no idea you were out there."

"It's okay. I know you're busy."

"Not that busy. Sit down." He motioned toward the chairs off to the side. "Does your mom know where you are?"

"Yeah. I said I had a meeting after school. She's gonna pick me up when I'm finished," the boy replied, perching tensely on the edge of a chair.

"So what can I do for you?" Mitch asked, trying hard to maintain simple professional friendliness when what he really wanted to do was put his arm around the boy's hunched shoulders.

Bruce fidgeted and broke eye contact. "Since it's the last week of school I guess I won't see you for a while, so I just wanted to stop in and see…see how you were. I guess I got used to you being around the apartment, and it's kind of weird now that it's just Mom and me."

Mitch's gut clenched, and he took a deep breath. The boy hadn't come right out and said he missed Mitch, but the implication was clear. Mitch tried to swallow past the lump that suddenly appeared in his throat. "I'm fine," he lied, striving for a conversational tone. "How about you and your mom?"

Bruce shrugged. "We're okay, I guess. But Mom… well…she misses you. A lot."

The knot in Mitch's stomach tightened, and the

sudden pressure in his chest squeezed the air out of his lungs. "I miss her, too," he said, his voice not quite steady. "And you."

Bruce studied him, as if trying to discern his sincerity. "Yeah?"

"Yeah."

There was silence for a moment before Bruce spoke again. "I've been thinking about Tony a lot."

A spasm of pain tightened Mitch's features. "I have, too."

"He was an okay kid, you know? He just didn't have much of a life. Things were pretty bad at home."

"I know. He told me about some of it."

"Yeah, he said he talked to you once in a while. He said you helped him a lot."

Another twist of the knife. "Not enough, though."

Bruce gazed at him steadily. "You did your best, Mr. Jackson. Tony told me that you were the only one who ever really cared about him. His own mom and dad only cared about their own stuff. She was gone all the time, and his dad always criticized him, telling him he would never amount to anything." Bruce paused and took a deep breath, his own voice suddenly none too steady. "That's real tough, you know? My dad was like that, too. Nothing I ever did was good enough for him. But at least I had my mom. I knew she loved me no matter what, and that made a really big difference. But Tony didn't have that. He didn't have anyone who cared about him, except you."

Bruce leaned closer, his voice urgent—and earnest. "He told me once that he wished he'd had a dad like you. That maybe things would have been different. But see, you weren't his dad, Mr. Jackson. You couldn't do all the things a dad is supposed to do. Tony needed a real, full-time dad. And a mom. They were the ones who let him down, not you."

Bruce stood then, and a flush slowly crept up his neck. "I gotta get home, but…but there's something else I wanted to say." He hesitated, and the flush moved to his face. "I just wanted you to know that I think Tony was right about one thing. You really would make a great dad."

Mitch felt the sudden sting of tears behind his eyes, and his throat constricted with emotion. For months the boy had considered him an enemy. But somewhere along the way he'd earned Bruce's respect and affection—to the point that the boy would welcome him as a father. It was the most flattering, most moving thing anyone had ever said to him.

Except, that is, when Tess had said, "I love you." Even after he'd revealed his greatest flaws, when he'd told her about his failures as a husband and father, she had still found it in her heart to love him. Surely there could be no greater compliment—or miracle—than that. She believed that his past failures, rather than diminishing him, had forged his character. Like Uncle Ray, she believed that he had changed over the past six years. And as Bruce had pointed out, with insight beyond his years, Mitch *had* done his best with Tony. It was just that he simply couldn't be the father Tony— and so many other boys—desperately needed. There just wasn't enough of him to go around. And that would be true whether he had his own family or remained single, he realized.

Suddenly he recalled Uncle Ray's words when the older man had talked about selling the farm. *Time brings changes,* he'd said. *People change. Circumstances change. And sometimes you just have to realize that it's time to move on.*

Bruce shifted uncomfortably and jammed his hands into his pockets as the silence lengthened. "Anyway, that's what I wanted to tell you," he said self-consciously, transferring his gaze to the toe of his shoe.

Slowly Mitch rose and reached over to put his arm around the boy's tense shoulders. "Thank you, Bruce," he said huskily. "I wasn't the best father before, so it's nice to know someone thinks I'm up to the job now." He drew a deep breath, and in that moment made a decision that he knew would affect the rest of his life. "How about I give you a ride home?"

Bruce stared at him, his face guarded but hopeful. "You don't have to do that."

"I want to," he said gently. "You and I have done a lot of fence-mending with Uncle Ray lately. Maybe it's time for me to mend another kind of fence with your mom. What do you think?"

The caution in Bruce's eyes gave way to joy, and he grinned broadly at Mitch. "Awesome!"

Tess heard the front door open, and with a frown she tossed the dish towel on the counter and headed for the living room. "Bruce, is that you? I thought you were going to…" Her voice died as she stepped across the threshold.

"Hi, Mom. Mr. Jackson gave me a ride home."

With an effort, Tess transferred her gaze from Mitch's intense eyes to her son. She drew a deep breath, struggling to cope with this unexpected turn of events. "Y-your dinner's in the oven," she said distractedly.

"Cool. See you guys later."

With that he breezed by, pausing only to bestow a quick kiss on Tess's forehead. She stared after him, thrown off balance by his uncharacteristically affectionate behavior, which had largely disappeared with the onset of adolescence.

"Can I interest you in a cup of coffee?"

Tess's gaze swiveled back to Mitch. He looked as if he'd been through hell in the two weeks since she'd seen him. His face was haggard, and there were dark circles under his eyes, as if he hadn't slept in days. Her heart overflowed with love for this extraordinary man, who cared so deeply about others that he took on their burdens as if they were his own. She wanted to go to him, pull him close and hold him fiercely to her heart until he understood that their love wasn't a liability to his work, but an asset. Just as his work was an asset to their love, for it was what had made him the man he was today—compassionate, caring, committed. She wanted to hold him until he believed what Uncle Ray had said, that he *was* a different man from the one who'd lost his son six years before. That the incident with Tony, while tragic, didn't mean he had failed. It just meant he was human. That he could have missed Tony's call for any number of reasons, not necessarily personal ones. That he was the man who had earned her eternal gratitude for saving her son. That he was the man she loved with all her heart and wanted to spend the rest of her life with.

Tess wanted to say all those things. But her voice had deserted her. All she could do was stare at Mitch, as if trying to reassure herself that he wasn't a mirage.

Meanwhile, Mitch took his own inventory. The fine lines at the corners of Tess's eyes were new, and her face seemed taut and strained. Clearly, his unexpected arrival had only added to her distress. Her shallow breathing was reflected in the rapid rise and fall of her chest, and her hand was white-knuckled on the door frame. Above the V of her soft sweater he could see the wild beating of her pulse, and her hand was trembling when she raised it to her throat.

A surge of remorse swept over Mitch, leaving a bitter taste in his mouth. Tess had offered him her love, and he'd pulled back for reasons he'd felt at the time were noble and selfless, putting her through hell in the process. But he'd been wrong, and he intended to do everything in his power to make amends.

"Coffee w-would be nice," Tess said breathlessly when she finally found her voice. "I'll just let Bruce know and—"

"I'll be fine, Mom," her son called out, clearly tuned in to the conversation in the living room. "Take your time."

She flushed, and Mitch gave her a crooked grin. "So much for privacy," she muttered as she walked past him toward the door.

He followed her out, then nodded toward a bench tucked beneath a flowering crab apple tree in a tiny park across the street. "I'm not retracting my offer of coffee, but do you mind if we just sit for a few minutes first? I have a few things I'd like to say privately."

Tess nodded, gathering her courage. "So do I."

He held out his hand, in a gesture of…friendship? Apology? Empathy? She had no idea, but she would happily accept any of the three. Because his reaching out told her more eloquently than words that he still cared, that the dialogue was still open. And that gave her new hope that maybe, just maybe, he'd had a change of heart. She looked down at his long, lean fingers, then slipped her hand into his, closing her eyes for a moment to savor the feel of his strong yet gentle touch.

When their gazes reconnected, she read much in his—gratitude, repentance, tenderness…and yes, love. It was what she had dreamed of seeing every night for the past two weeks, when she had at last managed to fall into a restless sleep. But now she began to hope that maybe, just maybe, her dream might really come true.

He gave her fingers a gentle squeeze, and the warmth in his eyes was like the caress of the sun on a spring day, holding the promise of new life after a long, dark winter. There was a sense of unreality about the scene, an almost too-good-to-be-true quality, but their linked hands dispelled any notion of make-believe. Mitch was here, every wonderful, handsome inch of him, and Tess knew with absolute certainty that this was where they belonged— together, for always. She prayed that Mitch had reached the same conclusion. But if he hadn't, she was prepared to fight for what she knew was their destiny.

Mitch led her to the bench, angling his body toward hers as they sat, never relinquishing his hold on her hand. "First of all, as inadequate as the words are, I want you to know how sorry I am for what I put you through these past two weeks," he said huskily. "And all because of some misguided notion that I could be all things to all people. But the fact is, I realize I can't be a father to every boy who needs one. I can be a support system, I can help, but I can't take the place of a father and a mother, of parents who are in their life every day and every night. To think otherwise is not only unrealistic, it's arrogant."

Impulsively Tess reached over and laid her hand tenderly on his cheek. He immediately covered it with his own as their gazes locked. "Not arrogant, Mitch. Never arrogant," she said fervently. "Your only fault, if it can even be called that, is that you care *too* much. You want to help everyone who is in pain. And you go out of your way to avoid inflicting pain on others. You may not always succeed, but you do a far better job of it than most people. You don't need to apologize for doing what you think is right."

The deep, unconditional love in Tess's clear green eyes told Mitch all he needed to know. She still loved him. And she was willing to give him another chance to prove he loved her.

This time Mitch didn't hesitate. He pulled her into his arms, buried his face in her soft hair, and in her loving embrace found solace for the anguish and regret in his heart, forgiveness for the pain he'd inflicted on her. He held her tightly, his hands on her back, in her hair, pressing her close, as if he never wanted to let her go.

"I love you, Tess," he whispered fiercely, his voice ragged with emotion. "You've brought sunshine back to my soul, filled my days with a joy I never hoped to find again, given me hope for a brighter tomorrow than I ever dared dream of. I can't promise you a perfect life, but I can promise that I'll try my best to be the kind of husband and father you and Bruce deserve."

He pulled back and looked down at her shimmering eyes, and his own face softened with love as he traced the path of one tear down her cheek with a gentle finger. "I never wanted to make you cry, Tess," he said softly. "That's what held me back—I was so afraid I would end up hurting you and Bruce."

"*I'm* not afraid, Mitch. Because I love you, and I know that together we can make this work."

The absolute trust in her eyes and the conviction in her voice made his throat tighten with emotion, and he shook his head wonderingly. "What did I ever do to deserve you?" he said in awe, cupping her face with his hands.

"I've been asking myself that same question. I never thought I'd find a man like you."

"Believe me, I'm getting the better end of this deal, Tess. I'm far from perfect."

"You're perfect for me."

He shook his head and gave her a crooked smile. "You have all the right answers."

She shook her head firmly. "No. I've had a lot of wrong answers. And made a lot of bad decisions. But I'm willing to trust my heart on this one."

"So am I. It just took me longer to realize something you seemed to know all along...that love doesn't *get* in the way—it *lights* the way."

The smile she gave him was luminous. "What a beautiful thought."

"No more beautiful than you." Then he took her hands in his, and with his gaze locked on hers, spoke in a voice that was steady and sure. "I planned to ask you this question two weeks ago. I'd like to try again now. Tess Lockwood, would you do me the great honor of becoming my wife?"

Tess's eyes once more brimmed with tears. "Yes," she breathed, her own voice choked with emotion. "Oh, yes!"

Mitch's heart soared with joy. He framed her face with his hands, giving himself one brief moment to glory in her radiance before he lowered his lips to hers in a kiss that was gratitude, hunger, passion and tenderness all in one. As his lips moved over hers, at times giving, at times demanding, she met him every step of the way. It was a kiss filled with need, with hope and with the urgency of long-restrained passion suddenly released. Mitch tangled his fingers in her soft hair, cupping her head as his other hand splayed across her back, molding her body even closer to his. He felt her trembling, but he also felt her sweet surrender to fate...destiny...divine Providence...whatever force had brought them together. And with her in his arms, he had the courage to surrender as well, to recognize that the gift of Tess's love had at last freed him from the legacy of loneliness that had shadowed his life for the past six years. As he held her close, he knew that this woman was, above all things, a miracle, for she had given him back his life. And he sent a silent, heartfelt prayer of thanks heavenward.

Tess felt as if she was drowning in a sea of emotion, overwhelmed by a joy like none she had ever before experienced and by a passion intensified and enriched by the promise of a lifelong commitment. Here, in this man's strong, sure arms, she felt loved and cherished and protected. If for years she had considered herself more mom than romantic interest, tonight she felt all woman. Mitch had awakened in her a hunger that had long lain dormant, had brought to life a passion that she thought had long ago been extinguished. And his kiss tonight, which sealed their engagement, held the promise of so much more, filling her with excitement, eagerness—and gratitude to the Lord for sending this very special man into her life and for giving her the courage to take another chance on love.

When Mitch at last reluctantly eased away, his lips warm and lingering, Tess felt as if every nerve in her body was vibrating. And when their gazes connected, she was able to utter but one simple word.

"Wow!"

He grinned crookedly and leaned over to nuzzle her neck. "My sentiments exactly," he agreed, his warm lips leaving a trail of fire against her skin. "I hope you aren't planning on a long engagement."

"H-how does a couple of weeks sound?" she said faintly.

He groaned. "Too long." His lips claimed hers once again in a lingering, spell-weaving kiss that sent her world spinning out of orbit.

At last, with great reluctance, she pulled back. "We'll never make it two weeks if we keep this up," she said with a shaky grin. "And we need to set a good example for Bruce."

Mitch's gaze momentarily flickered to the apartment behind Tess, and suddenly his mouth twitched in amusement. "Speaking of Bruce…I think he just got a great preview of romance 101."

Her eyes widened and her cheeks grew red. "Tell me he isn't watching."

Mitch grinned. "I can't do that without lying."

Tess frowned and bit her lip. "I wanted to sort of prepare him. I mean, I'm not sure he's ready for us to get married."

Mitch chuckled. "Oh, he's ready, all right."

Tess looked at him, puzzled. "How do you know?"

"Because he came to see me this afternoon. Waited three hours, in fact. He was a man with a mission. And then he gave it to me straight, laid it on the line about Tony. He also told me that he thought I'd make a great father." Mitch's voice caught on the last word.

Tess stared at him. "He said all that?"

"Mmm-hmm. And he was very happy when I told him I was going to talk to you tonight. So I think you can be sure that he'll be pleased at the outcome."

Tess shifted her position so she, too, could see the window of the apartment. Sure enough, Bruce was standing there, a huge grin plastered on his face. Mitch raised his hand, and Bruce gave them a very clear thumbs-up sign.

"See what I mean?" Mitch said with a smile.

Tess turned back to him, and once more her eyes glistened with unshed tears. "I think this is what they call a happy ending."

"I think it is," he replied with a grin. "So what do you say the three of us go out and celebrate?"

A euphoric joy radiated through Tess, filling her with absolute happiness and contentment, and she smiled radiantly. "I think that would be awesome!"

* * * * *

Dear Reader,

As I write this letter, the school year is ending—and I find myself envying the students who have a carefree summer ahead, with no worries over tasks yet to be completed or issues to be resolved. For someone who has spent many years in the corporate world, that kind of closure seems very, very appealing. As does the opportunity to make a fresh beginning each fall.

Life is filled with such endings and beginnings, many of them externally imposed and out of our control. Like moving from one grade to the next. But sometimes we have to take the initiative and recognize that it's up to us to make the decision to move on.

In *Crossroads,* Mitch and Tess face that challenge. So do Bruce and Uncle Ray. Though their challenges differ, they must each choose to end one way of life before they can start another.

Such choices are not usually easy. They require us to take a long, hard look at our priorities, our fears and hopes. They also require trust—in ourselves, in others and in God. As you face such turning points in your life, may you take comfort in knowing that you are never alone. For as the Lord promised, "I am with you always, even to the end of time."

Irene Hannon

REQUEST YOUR FREE BOOKS!

2 FREE INSPIRATIONAL NOVELS
PLUS 2
FREE
MYSTERY GIFTS

Love Inspired®

YES! Please send me 2 FREE Love Inspired® novels and my 2 FREE mystery gifts. After receiving them, if I don't wish to receive any more books, I can return the shipping statement marked "cancel." If I don't cancel, I will receive 4 brand-new novels every month and be billed just $3.99 per book in the U.S., or $4.74 per book in Canada, plus 25¢ shipping and handling per book and applicable taxes, if any*. That's a savings of 20% off the cover price! I understand that accepting the 2 free books and gifts places me under no obligation to buy anything. I can always return a shipment and cancel at any time. Even if I never buy another book from Steeple Hill, the two free books and gifts are mine to keep forever.

113 IDN EF26   313 IDN EF27

Name	(PLEASE PRINT)

Address	Apt. #

City	State/Prov.	Zip/Postal Code

Signature (if under 18, a parent or guardian must sign)

Order online at www.LoveInspiredBooks.com

Or mail to Steeple Hill Reader Service™:

IN U.S.A.: P.O. Box 1867, Buffalo, NY 14240-1867
IN CANADA: P.O. Box 609, Fort Erie, Ontario L2A 5X3

Not valid to current Love Inspired subscribers.

Want to try two free books from another series?
Call 1-800-873-8635 or visit www.morefreebooks.com

* Terms and prices subject to change without notice. NY residents add applicable sales tax. Canadian residents will be charged applicable provincial taxes and GST. This offer is limited to one order per household. All orders subject to approval. Credit or debit balances in a customer's account(s) may be offset by any other outstanding balance owed by or to the customer. Please allow 4 to 6 weeks for delivery.

Your Privacy: Steeple Hill is committed to protecting your privacy. Our Privacy Policy is available online at www.eHarlequin.com or upon request from the Reader Service. From time to time we make our lists of customers available to reputable firms who may have a product or service of interest to you. If you would prefer we not share your name and address, please check here. ☐

LIREG07

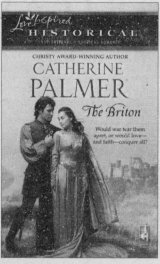

INTRODUCING

Love Inspired

H I S T O R I C A L

A NEW TWO-BOOK SERIES.

Every month, acclaimed
inspirational authors
will bring you engaging stories
rich with romance, adventure
and faith set in a variety
of vivid historical times.

History begins on **February 12**
wherever you buy books.

Steeple
Hill®

www.SteepleHill.com